Ex Libris

M. E. Anderson
Oct. 1977.

The DORÉ Illustrated
BALZAC DROLL STORIES

The DORÉ Illustrated

BALZAC DROLL STORIES

COLLECTED FROM

THE ABBEYS OF TOURAINE.

TRANSLATED INTO ENGLISH, COMPLETE AND UNABRIDGED.

ILLUSTRATED WITH 425 DESIGNS

By GUSTAVE DORÉ.

BELL PUBLISHING COMPANY
NEW YORK

INTRODUCTION

Some years ago a rare book dealer listed this book among the most valuable of his collection. "Suppressed and scarce" is the way the dealer described it. "This book is a fund of amusement, and the designs are the most singular ever attempted by an artist. So crammed is it with pictures, that even the contents are adorned with thirty-three illustrations. Now the reader is jade to smile at the mishaps of some fat monks; then a battle scene, with fighting men jammed in inexplicable confusion, occupies his attention; next, some portraits of fellows who would pass for Plato's firemen, all sacred, as though they had been for a thousand years stirring molten lava; then knights making love and kissing through their visors; then the dreamy old German cities, with diablerie or astanella going on right and left—but all so quaint, so wonderful, that the beholder confesses he never looked upon the like before. Although very witty, some are rather free in style."

It has been said that after God and Shakespeare there has been no greater creator of human beings than Honore de Balzac (1799-1850), the author of *Eugenie Grandet, Pere Goriot, Cousin Pons, The Cure of Tours* and *Cousin Betty,* some in the long series of successful novels under the title "The Human Comedy."

Gustave Dore (1832-1883) was enormously popular in England and America, as well as in France. His output was prodigious. Among the books he illustrated were the Bible, Dante's *Inferno* and Cervantes' *Don Quixote.*

DROLL STORIES.

TRANSLATOR'S PREFACE.

WHEN, in March, 1832, the first volume of the now famous *Contes Drolatiques* was published by Gosselin of Paris, Balzac, in a short preface, written in the publisher's name, replied to those attacks which he anticipated certain critics would make upon his hardy experiment. He claimed for his book the protection of all those to whom literature was dear, because it was a work of art—and a work of art, in the highest sense of the word, it undoubtedly is. Like Boccaccio, Rabelais, the Queen of Navarre, Ariosto, and Verville, the great author of *The Human Comedy* has painted an epoch. In the fresh and wonderful language of the Merry Vicar of Meudon, he has given us a marvellous picture of French life and manners in the sixteenth century. The gallant knights and merry dames of that eventful period of French history stand out in bold relief upon his canvas. The background to these life-like figures is, as it were, "sketched upon the spot." After reading the *Contes Drolatiques*, one could almost find one's way about the towns and villages of Touraine, unassisted by map or guide. Not only is this book a work of art from its historical information and topographical accuracy ; its claims to that distinction rest upon a broader foundation. Written in the nineteenth century in imitation of the style of the sixteenth, it is a triumph of literary archæology. It is a model of that which it professes to imitate; the production of a writer who, to accomplish it, must have been at once historian, linguist, philosopher, archæologist, and anatomist, and each in no ordinary degree. In France his work has long been regarded as a classic— as a faithful picture of the last days of the *moyen âge*, when kings and princesses, brave gentlemen and haughty ladies, laughed openly at stories and jokes which are considered disgraceful by their more fastidious descendants. In England the difficulties of the language employed, and the quaintness and peculiarity of its style, have placed it beyond the reach of all but those thoroughly acquainted with the French of the sixteenth century. Taking into consideration the vast amount of historical information enshrined in its pages, the archæological value which it must always possess for the student, and the dramatic interest of its stories, the translator has thought that an English edition of Balzac's chef-d'œuvre would be acceptable to many. It has, of course, been impossible to reproduce in all its vigour and freshness the language of the original. Many of the quips and cranks and puns have been lost in the process of Anglicizing. These unavoidable blemishes apart, the writer ventures to hope that he has treated this great masterpiece in a reverent spirit, touched it with no sacrilegious hand, but, on the contrary, given as close a translation as the dissimilarities of the two languages permit. With this idea, no attempt has been made to polish or round many of the awkwardly constructed sentences which are characteristic of this volume. Rough, and occasionally obscure, they are far more in keeping with the spirit of the original than the polished periods of modern romance. Taking into consideration the many difficulties which he has had to overcome, and which those best acquainted with the French edition will best appreciate, the translator claims the indulgence of the critical reader for any shortcomings he may discover. The best plea that can be offered for such indulgence is the fact that, although *Les Cent Contes Drolatiques* were completed and published in 1837, the present is the first English version ever brought before the public.

LONDON, *January*, 1874.

LIST OF ENGRAVINGS.

THE FIRST TEN TALES.

THE FAIR IMPERIA.

The rendezvous.

LIST OF ENGRAVINGS.

THE VENIAL SIN.

Those cursed pages.

THE KING'S SWEETHEART.

The sedan chair.

LIST OF ENGRAVINGS.

THE DEVIL'S HEIR.

The decapitation.

THE MERRY JESTS OF KING LOUIS THE ELEVENTH.

Indiscretion.

THE HIGH CONSTABLE'S WIFE.

The ambuscade.

THE MAID OF THILOUSE.

The stumble.

LIST OF ENGRAVINGS.

THE BROTHER-IN-ARMS.

A declaration of love.

THE VICAR OF AZAY-LE-RIDEAU.

The road to the Vicarage.

LIST OF ENGRAVINGS.

THE REPROACH.

The misery of being an hunchback.

THE SECOND TEN TALES.

THE THREE CLERKS OF ST. NICHOLAS.

The three clerks.

THE CONTINENCE OF KING FRANCIS THE FIRST.

The prisoner.

THE MERRY TATTLE OF THE NUNS OF POISSY.

The round ring.

HOW THE CHATEAU D'AZAY CAME TO BE BUILT.

The consultation.

THE FALSE COURTESAN.

The impregnable fortress.

THE DANGER OF BEING TOO INNOCENT.

The school of love.

THE DEAR NIGHT OF LOVE.

The jealous husband.

THE SERMON OF THE MERRY VICAR OF MEUDON.

LIST OF ENGRAVINGS.

The arms of Rabelais.

THE SUCCUBUS.

The succubus, or female demon.

LIST OF ENGRAVINGS.

DESPAIR IN LOVE.

The violent man.

THE THIRD TEN TALES.

PERSEVERANCE IN LOVE.

Joy of Master Anseau.

CONCERNING A PROVOST WHO DID NOT RECOGNISE THINGS.

The last hour.

CONCERNING THE MONK AMADOR, WHO WAS A GLORIOUS ABBOT OF TURPENAY.

The danger of death.

BERTHA THE PENITENT.

The last sigh.

HOW THE FAIR MAID OF PORTILLON CONVINCED HER JUDGE.

The Lord of the Manor

IN WHICH IT IS DEMONSTRATED THAT FORTUNE IS ALWAYS FEMININE.

The men in the wood.

CONCERNING A BEGGAR WHO WAS CALLED LE VIEUX PAR-CHEMINS.

The thinker.

STRANGE SAYINGS OF THREE PILGRIMS.

The three pilgrims.

INNOCENCE.

Dangerous playthings.

THE FAIR IMPERIA MARRIED.

Love in the fields.

LIST OF ENGRAVINGS.

TABLE OF CONTENTS.

TABLE OF CONTENTS.

THE SECOND TEN TALES.

THE THIRD TEN TALES.

TABLE OF CONTENTS.

The DORÉ Illustrated

BALZAC DROLL STORIES

The First Ten.

THE FIRST TEN.

PROLOGUE

THIS is a book of the highest flavour, full of right hearty merriment, spiced to the palate of the illustrious and very precious tosspots and drinkers, to whom our worthy compatriot, François Rabelais, the eternal honour of Touraine, addressed himself. Be it nevertheless understood, the author has no other desire than to be a good Tourainian, and joyfully to chronicle the merry doings of the famous people of this sweet and productive land, more fertile in cuckolds, dandies, and witty wags than any other, and which has furnished a good share of men of renown to France, as witness the departed Courier of piquant memory; Verville, author of the *Moyen de parvenir*, and others equally

well known, among whom we will specially mention the
Sieur Descartes, because he was a melancholy genius, and
devoted himself more to brown studies than to drinks and
dainties, a man of whom all the cooks and confectioners of
Tours have a wise horror, whom they despise, and will not
hear spoken of, and say, "Where does he live?" if his
name is mentioned. Now this work is the production of the
joyous leisure of the good old monks, of whom there are
many vestiges scattered about the country, at Grenadière-
les-Saint-Cyr, in the village of Sacché-les-Azay-le-Rideau, at
Marmoutièrs, Veretz, Roche-Corbon, and in certain storehouses of good stories, which storehouses are the upper
stories of old canons and wise dames, who remember the
good old days when you could enjoy a hearty laugh without
looking to see if your hilarity disturbed the sit of your ruffle,
as do the young women of the present day, who wish to
take their pleasure gravely—a custom which suits our gay
France as much as a water-jug would the head of a queen.
Since laughter is a privilege granted to man alone, and
he has sufficient causes for tears within his reach, without
adding to them by books, I have considered it a thing
most patriotic to publish a drachm of merriment for these
times, when weariness falls like a fine rain, wetting us,
soaking into us, and dissolving those ancient customs which
made the people to *reap public* amusement from the
Republic. But of those old pantagruelists who allowed
God and the king to conduct their own affairs without
putting of their finger in the pie oftener than they could help,
being content to look on and laugh, there are very few left.
They are dying out day by day in such manner that I fear

Youth and Folly.

greatly to see these illustrious fragments of the ancient breviary spat upon, staled upon, set at naught, dishonoured, and blamed, the which I should be loth to see, since I have and bear great respect for the refuse of our Gallic antiquities.

Bear in mind also, ye wild critics, ye scrapers-up of words harpies who mangle the intentions and inventions of every one, that as children only do we laugh, and as we travel onward laughter sinks down and dies out, like the light of the oil-lit lamp. This signifies, that to laugh you must be innocent, and pure of heart, lacking which qualities you purse your lips, drop your jaws, and knit your brow, after the manner of men hiding vices and impurities. Take, then, this work as you would a group or statue, certain features of which an artist cannot omit, and he would be the biggest of all big fools if he put leaves upon them, seeing that these said works are not, any more than is this book, intended for nunneries. Nevertheless, I have taken care, much to my vexation, to weed from the manuscripts the old words, which, in spite of their age, were still strong, and which would have shocked the ears, astonished the eyes, reddened the cheeks, and sullied the lips of trousered maidens, and Madame Virtue with three lovers; for certain things must be done to suit the vices of the age, and a periphrase is much more agreeable than the word. Indeed, we are old, and find long trifles better than the short follies of our youth, because at that time our taste was better. Then spare me your slanders, and read this rather at night than in the daytime, and give it not to young maidens, if there be any, because this book is inflammable. I will now rid you of myself. But I fear nothing for this book, since it is extracted from a high and splendid source, from which all that has issued has had a great success, as is amply proved by the royal orders of the Golden Fleece, of the Holy Ghost, of the Garter, of the Bath, and by many notable things which have been taken therefrom, under shelter of which I place myself.

Now make ye merry, my hearties, and gaily read with ease of body and rest of reins, and may a cancer carry you off if you disown me after having read me. These words are those of our good Master Rabelais, before whom we must all stand, hat in hand, in token of reverence and honour to him, prince of all wisdom, and king of comedy.

The beauty of Constance.

THE FAIR IMPERIA.

THE Archbishop of Bordeaux had added to his suite when going to the Council at Constance quite a good-looking little priest of Touraine whose ways and manner of speech were so charming that he passed for a son of La Soldée and the Governor. The Archbishop of Tours had willingly given him to his confrère for his journey to that town, because it was usual for archbishops to make each other presents, they well knowing how sharp are the itchings of theological palms. Thus this young priest came to the Council and was lodged in the establishment of his prelate, a man of good morals and great science.

Philippe de Mala, as he was called, resolved to behave well and worthily to serve his protector, but he saw in this mysterious Council many men leading a dissolute life and yet not making less, nay—gaining more indulgences, gold crowns and benefices than all the other virtuous and well-behaved ones. Now during one night—dangerous to his virtue—the devil whispered into his ear that he should live

more luxuriously, since every one sucked the breasts of our Holy Mother Church and yet they were not drained, a miracle which proved beyond doubt the existence of God. And the little priest of Touraine did not disappoint the devil. He promised to feast himself, to eat his bellyful of roast meats and other German delicacies, when he could do so without paying for them as he was poor. As he remained quite continent, (in which he followed the example of the poor old archbishop, who sinned no longer because he was unable to, and passed for a saint,) he had to suffer from intolerable desires followed by fits of melancholy, since there were so many sweet courtezans, well developed, but cold to the poor people, who inhabited Constance, to enlighten the understanding of the Fathers of the Council. He was savage

that he did not know how to make up to these gallant sirens, who snubbed cardinals, abbots, councillors, legates, bishops, princes, and margraves, just as if they had been penniless clerks. And in the evening, after prayers, he would practise speaking to them, teaching himself the breviary of love.

He taught himself to answer all possible questions, but on the morrow if by chance he met one of the aforesaid princesses dressed out, seated in a litter and escorted by her proud and well-armed pages, he remained open - mouthed, like a dog in the act of catching flies, at the sight of the sweet countenance that so much inflamed him. The secretary of Monseigneur, a gentleman of Perigord, having clearly explained to him that the Fathers, procureurs, and auditors of the Rota bought by certain presents, not relics or indulgences, but jewels and gold, the favour of being familiar with the best of these pampered cats who lived under the protection of the lords of the Council; the poor Tourainian, all simpleton and innocent as he was, treasured up under his mattress the money given him by the good archbishop for writings and copying—hoping one day to have enough just to see a cardinal's lady-love, and trusting in God for the rest. He was hairless from top to toe and re-sembled a man about as much as a goat with a night-dress on resembles a young lady, but prompted by his desires he wandered in the evenings through the streets of Constance, careless of his life, and, at the risk of having his body halberded by the soldiers, he peeped at the cardinals entering the houses of their sweethearts. Then he saw the wax-candles lighted in the houses and suddenly the doors and the windows closed. Then he heard the blessed abbots or others jumping about, drinking, enjoying themselves, love-making, singing *Alleluia* and applauding the music with which they were being regaled. The kitchen performed miracles, the Offices said were fine rich pots-full, the Matins sweet little hams, the Vespers luscious mouthfuls, and the Laudes delicate sweetmeats, and after their little carouses, these brave priests were silent, their pages diced upon the stairs, their mules stamped restively in the streets; every-thing went well—but faith and religion were there. That is how it came to pass the good man Huss was burned. And the reason? He put his finger in the pie without being asked. Then why was he a huguenot before the others? To return, however, to our sweet little Philippe, not unfrequently did he receive many a thump and hard blow, but the devil sustained him, inciting him to believe that sooner or later it would come to his turn to play the cardinal to some lovely dame. This ardent desire gave him the boldness of a stag in autumn, so much so that one evening he quietly tripped up the steps and into one of the first houses in Constance where often he had seen officers, seneschals, valets, and pages waiting with torches for their masters, dukes, kings, cardinals, and archbishops.

" Ah !" said he, " she must be very beautiful and amiable, this one."

A soldier well armed allowed him to pass, believing him to belong to the suite of the Elector of Bavaria, who had just left, and that he was going to deliver a message on behalf of the above-mentioned nobleman. Philippe de Mala mounted the stairs as lightly as a greyhound in love, and was guided by a delectable odour of perfume to a certain chamber where, surrounded by her handmaidens, the lady of the house was divesting herself of her attire. He stood quite dumbfoundered like a thief surprised by sergeants. The lady was without petticoat or head-dress. The chambermaids and the servants, busy taking off her stockings and undressing her, so quickly and dexterously had her stripped, that the priest, overcome, gave vent to a long *Ah !* which had a flavour of love about it.

" What want you, little one ?" said the lady to him.

" To yield my soul to you," said he, flashing his eyes upon her.

He stood quite dumbfoundered like a thief surprised by sergeants.

" You can come again to-morrow," said she, in order to be rid of him.

To which Philippe replied, blushing, " I will not fail."

Then she burst out laughing. Philippe, struck motionless, stood quite at his ease, letting wander over her his eyes that glowed and sparkled with the flame of love. What lovely thick hair hung over her ivory white back, showing sweet white places, fair and shining between the many tresses ! She had upon her snow-white brow a ruby circlet, less fertile in rays of fire than her black eyes, still moist with tears from her hearty laugh. She even threw her slipper at a statue gilded like a shrine, twisting herself about from very ribaldry, and allowed her bare foot, smaller than a swan's bill, to be seen. This evening she was in a good humour, otherwise she would have had the little shaven-crown put out by the window without more ado than her first bishop.

" He has fine eyes, Madame," said one of the handmaids.

" Where does he come from ?" asked another.

" Poor child !" cried Madame, "his mother must be looking for him. Show him his way home."

The Tourainian, still sensible, gave a movement of delight at the sight of the brocaded bed where the sweet form was about to repose. This glance, full of amorous intelligence, awoke the lady's fantasy, who, half laughing and half smitten, repeated " To-morrow," and dismissed him with a gesture which the pope Jehan himself would have obeyed, especially as he was like a snail without a shell, since the Council had just deprived him of the holy keys.

"Ah ! Madame, there is another vow of chastity changed into an amorous desire," said one of her women ; and the chuckles commenced again thick as hail.

Philippe went his way, bumping his head against the wall like a hooded rook as he was. So giddy had he become at the sight of this creature, even more enticing than a siren rising from the water. He noticed the animals carved over the door and returned to the house of the archbishop with his head full of diabolical longings and his entrails sophisticated. Once in his little room he counted his coins all night long, but could make no more than four of them; and as that was all his treasure, he counted upon satisfying the fair one by giving her all he had in the world.

"What is it ails you?" said the good archbishop, uneasy at the groans and "oh! oh's!" of his clerk.

"Ah! my lord," answered the poor priest, "I am wondering how it is that so light and sweet a woman can weigh so heavily upon my heart."

"Which one?" said the archbishop, putting down his breviary which he was reading for others—the good man.

"Oh! Mother of God! you will scold me, I know, my good master, my protector, because I have seen the lady of a cardinal at the least, and I am weeping because I lack more than one little crown to enable me to convert her.

The archbishop, knitting the circumflex accent that he had above his nose, said not a word. Then the very humble priest trembled in his skin to have confessed so much to his superior. But the holy man directly said to him, "She must be very dear then——"

"Ah!" said he, "she has swallowed many a mitre and stolen many a cross.."

"Well, Philippe, if thou wilt renounce her, I will present thee with thirty angels from the poor-box."

"Ah! my lord, I should be losing too much," replied the lad, emboldened by the treat he promised himself.

"Ah! Philippe," said the good prelate, "thou wilt then go to the devil and displease God, like all our cardinals," and the master, with sorrow, began to pray St. Gatien, the patron saint of Innocents, to save his servant. He made him kneel down beside him, telling him to recommend himself also to St. Philippe, but the wretched priest implored the saint beneath his breath to prevent him from failing if on the morrow the lady should receive him kindly and mercifully ; and the good archbishop, observing the fervour of his servant, cried out to him, "Courage, little one, and Heaven will exorcise thee."

On the morrow, while Monsieur was declaiming at the Council against the shameless behaviour of the apostles of Christianity, Philippe de Mala spent his angels—acquired with

so much labour—in perfumes, baths, fomentations, and other
fooleries. He played the fop so well, one would have
thought him the fancy cavalier of a gay lady. He wandered

about the town in order to find the residence of his heart's
queen ; and when he asked the passers-by to whom belonged
the aforesaid house, they laughed in his face, saying—

"Whence comes this precious fellow that has not heard
of La Belle Imperia ?"

He was very much afraid that he and his angels were
gone to the devil when he heard the name, and knew into
what a nice mess he had voluntarily fallen.

Imperia was the most precious, the most fantastic girl in
the world, although she passed for the most dazzlingly
beautiful, and the one who best understood the art of
bamboozling cardinals and softening the hardest soldiers and
oppressors of the people. She had brave captains, archers,
and nobles, ready to serve her at every turn. She had only
to breathe a word, and the business of any one who had
offended her was settled. A free fight only brought a smile

A free fight only brought a smile to her lips.

to her lips, and often the Sire de Baudricourt—one of the
King's Captains—would ask her if there was any one he
could kill for her that day—a little joke at the expense of
the abbots. With the exception of the potentates among
the high clergy with whom Madame Imperia managed to
accommodate her little tempers, she ruled every one with a
high hand in virtue of her pretty babble and enchanting
ways, which enthralled the most virtuous and the most un-
impressionable. Thus she lived beloved and respected,
quite as much as the real ladies and princesses, and was
called Madame, concerning which the good Emperor
Sigismund replied to a lady who complained of it to him,
" That they, the good ladies, might keep to their own proper
way and holy virtues, and Madame Imperia to the sweet
naughtiness of the goddess Venus"—Christian words which
shocked the good ladies, to their credit be it said.

Philippe, then thinking over in his mind that which on
the preceding evening he had seen with his eyes, doubted
if more did not remain behind. Then was he sad, and
without taking bite or sup, strolled about the town waiting
the appointed hour, although he was well-favoured and
gallant enough to find others less difficult to overcome than
was Madame Imperia.

The night came ; the little Touranian, exalted with pride,
caparisoned with desire, and spurred by his " alacks" and
" alases" which nearly choked him, glided like an eel into the
domicile of the veritable Queen of the Council—for before
her bowed humbly all the authority, science, and wisdom of
Christianity. The *major domo* did not know him, and was
going to bundle him out again, when one of the chamber-
women called out from the top of the stairs—" Eh, M.
Imbert, it is Madame's young fellow," and poor Philippe,
blushing like a wedding night, ran up the stairs, shaking
with happiness and delight. The servant took him by the
hand and led him into the chamber where sat Madame,
lightly attired, like a brave woman who awaits her conqueror.

The dazzling Imperia was seated near a table covered
with a shaggy cloth ornamented with gold, and with all the
requisites for a dainty carouse. Flagons of wine, various

drinking glasses, bottles of hippocras, flasks full of the good wine of Cyprus, pretty boxes full of spices, roast peacocks, green sauces, little salt hams—all that would gladden the eyes of the gallant if he had not so madly loved Madame Imperia. She saw well that the eyes of the young priest were all for her. Although accustomed to the curl-paper devotion of the churchmen, she was well satisfied that she had made a conquest of the young priest who all day long had been in her head.

The windows had been closed ; Madame was decked out

and in a manner fit to do the honours to a prince of the Empire. Then the rogue, beatified by the holy beauty of

Imperia, knew that emperor, burgraf, nay, even a cardinal about to be elected pope, would willingly for that night have changed places with him, a little priest who, beneath his gown, had only the devil and love.

He put on a lordly air, and saluted her with a courtesy by no means ungraceful ; and then the sweet lady said to him, regaling him with a piercing glance—

" Come and sit close to me, that I may see if you have altered since yesterday."

" Oh yes," said he.

" And how ?" said she.

" Yesterday," replied the artful fellow, " I loved you : to-day, we love each other, and from a poor sinner I have become richer than a king."

" Oh, little one, little one !" cried she, merrily ; " yes, you are indeed changed, for from a young priest I see well you have turned into an old devil." And side by side they sat down before a large fire, which helped to spread their ecstacy around. They remained always ready to begin eating, seeing that they only thought of gazing into each other's eyes, and never touched a dish. Just as they were beginning to feel comfortable and at their ease, there came a great noise at Madame's door, as if people were beating against it, and crying out.

" Madame," cried the little servant, hastily, " here's another of them."

" Who is it ?" cried she in a haughty manner, like a tyrant, savage at being interrupted.

" The Bishop of Coire wishes to speak with you."

" May the devil take him !" said she, looking at Philippe gently.

" Madame, he has seen the lights through the chinks, and is making a great noise."

" Tell him I have the fever, and you will be telling him no lie, for I am ill of this little priest who is torturing my brain."

But just as she had finished speaking, and was pressing with devotion the hand of Philippe who trembled in his skin, appeared the fat Bishop of Coire, indignant and angry. The officers followed him, bearing a trout canonically dressed, fresh drawn from the Rhine, and shining in a golden platter, and spices contained in little ornamented boxes, and a thousand dainties, such as liqueurs and jams, made by the holy nuns at his Abbey.

"Ah, ah," said he, with his deep voice, "I haven't time to go to the devil, but you must give me a touch of him in advance, eh ! my little one."

"Your belly will one day make a nice sheath for a sword," replies she, knitting her brows above her eyes, which from being soft and gentle had become mischievous enough to make one tremble.

"And this little chorus singer is here to offer that ?" said the bishop, insolently turning his great rubicund face towards Philippe.

"Monseigneur, I am here to confess Madame."

"Oh, oh, do you not know the canons ? To confess the ladies at this time of night is a right reserved to bishops, so take yourself off; go and herd with simple monks, and never come back here again under pain of excommunication."

"Do not move," cried the blushing Imperia, more lovely with passion than she was with love, because now she was possessed both with passion and love. "Stop, my friend. Here you are in your own house." Then he knew that he was really loved by her.

"Is it not in the breviary, and an evangelical regulation, that you shall be equal before God in the valley of Jehoshaphat ?" asked she of the bishop.

"'Tis an invention of the devil, who has adulterated the holy book," replied the great numskull of a bishop in a hurry to fall to.

"Well then be equal now before me, who am here below your goddess," replied Imperia, " otherwise one of these days I will have you delicately strangled between the head and shoulders ; I swear it by the power of my tonsure, which is as good as the pope's." And wishing that the trout

should be added to the feast as well as the sweets and
other dainties, she added, cunningly, "Sit you down and
drink with us." But the artful minx, being up to a trick or
two, gave the little one a wink which told him plainly not to
mind the German, whom she would soon find a means to be
rid of.

The servant-maid seated the bishop at the table and
tucked him up, while Philippe, wild with a rage that closed his
mouth, because he saw his plans ending in smoke, gave the
archbishop to more devils than there ever were monks
alive. Thus they got half way through the repast, which
the young priest had not yet touched, hungering only for
Imperia, near whom he was already seated, but speaking
that sweet language which the ladies so well understand,

that has neither stops, commas, accents, letters, figures,
characters, notes, nor images. The fat bishop, sensual and
careful enough of the sleek ecclesiastical garment of skin
for which he was indebted to his late mother, allowed himself to be plentifully served with hippocras by the delicate
hand of Madame, and it was just at his first hiccough that
the sound of an approaching cavalcade was heard in the

street. The number of horses, the "Ho, ho!" of the pages, showed plainly that some great prince hot with love was about to arrive. In fact, a moment afterwards the Cardinal of Ragusa, against whom the servants of Imperia had not dared to bar the door, entered the room. At this terrible sight the poor courtezan and her young lover be- came ashamed and em- barrassed, like fresh cured lepers; for it would be tempting the devil to try and oust the cardinal, the more so as at that time it was not known who would be pope, three as- pirants having resigned their hoods for the benefit of Christianity. The car- dinal, who was a cunning Italian, long bearded, a great sophist, and the life and soul of the Council, guessed, by the feeblest exercise of the faculties of his understanding, the alpha and omega of the adventure. He only had to weigh in his mind one little thought before he knew how to pro- ceed in order to be able to hypothecate his manly vigour. He arrived with the appetite of a hungry monk, and to obtain its satisfaction he was just the man to stab two monks and sell his bit of the true cross, which was wrong.

"Holloa! friend," said he to Philippe, calling him towards him.

The poor Tourainian, more dead than alive, and expecting the devil was about to interfere seriously with his arrange- ments, rose and said, "What is it?" to the redoubtable cardinal.

He taking him by the arm led him on to the staircase,

looked him in the white of the eye and said, without any nonsense—

"Ventredieu ! you are a nice little fellow, and I should not like to have to let your master know the weight of your carcase. My revenge might cause me certain pious expenses in my old age, so choose to espouse an abbey for the remainder of your days, or to marry Madame to-night and die to-morrow."

The poor little Tourainian in despair murmured, " May I come back when your passion is over ?"

The cardinal could scarcely keep his countenance, but he said sternly, " Choose the gallows or a mitre."

" Ah !" said the priest, maliciously ; " a good fat abbey."

Thereupon the cardinal went back into the room, opened an escritoire, and scribbled upon a piece of parchment an order to the envoy of France.

" Monseigneur," said the Tourainian to him while he was spelling out the order, " you will not get rid of the Bishop of Coire so easily as you have got rid of me, for he has as many abbeys as the soldiers have drinking shops in the town ; besides, he is in the favour of his lord. Now I fancy to show you my gratitude for this so fine abbey I owe you a good piece of advice. You know how fatal has been and how rapidly spread this terrible pestilence which has cruelly harassed Paris. Tell him that you have just left the bedside of your old friend the Archbishop of Bordeaux ; thus you will make him scutter away like straw before a whirlwind."

" Oh, oh," cried the cardinal, " thou meritest more than an abbey. Ah, Ventredieu ! my young friend, here are 100 golden crowns for thy journey to the abbey of Turpenay, which I won yesterday at cards, and of which I make you a free gift."

Hearing these words, and seeing Philippe de Mala disappear without giving her the amorous glances she expected, the beautiful Imperia, puffing like a dolphin, denounced all the cowardice of the priest. She was not then a sufficiently good Catholic to pardon her lover deceiving her, by not knowing how to die for her pleasure. Thus the death of Philippe was foreshadowed in the viper's glance she cast at him to insult him, which glance pleased the cardinal much, for the wily Italian saw he would soon get his abbey back again. The Tourainian, heeding not the brewing storm, avoided it by walking out silently and with his ears down, like a wet dog being kicked out of church. Madame drew a sigh from her heart. She must have had her own ideas of humanity for the little value she held it in. The fire which possessed her had mounted to her head, and scintillated in rays about her, and there was good reason for it, for this was the first time that she had been humbugged by a priest. Then the cardinal smiled, believing it was all to his advantage : was not he a cunning fellow ? Yes, he was the possessor of a red hat.

"Ah ! ah ! my friend," said he to the bishop, "I con gratulate myself on being in your company, and I am glad to have been able to get rid of that little wretch unworthy of Madame, the more so as if you had gone near him, my lovely and amiable creature, you would have perished miserably, through the deed of a simple priest."

"Ah ! How ?"

"He is the secretary of the Archbishop of Bordeau. The good man was seized this morning with the pestilence.

The bishop opened his mouth wide enough to swallow a dutch cheese.

"How do you know that ?" asked he.

"Ah !" said the cardinal, taking the good German's hand. "I have just administered to him, and consoled him ; at this moment the holy man has a fair wind to waft him to paradise."

The Bishop of Coire demonstrated immediately how light fat men are ; for when men are big-bellied, a merciful providence, in the consideration of their works, often makes their internal tubes as elastic as balloons." The aforesaid bishop sprang backwards with one bound, burst into a perspiration, and coughed like a cow who finds feathers mixed with her hay. Then becoming suddenly pale, he rushed down the stairs without even bidding Madame adieu. When the door had closed upon the bishop, and he was fairly in the street, the Cardinal of Ragusa began laughing fit to split his sides.

"Ah, my fair one, am I not worthy to be pope, and better than that, thy lover this evening?"

But seeing Imperia thoughtful, he approached her to take her in his arms, and pet her after the usual fashion of cardinals, men who embrace better than all others, even the soldiers, because they are lazy, and do not spare their essential properties.

"Ha!" said she, drawing back, "you wish to cause my death, you ecclesiastical idiot. The principal thing for you is to enjoy yourself; my sweet carcase, a thing accessory Your pleasure will be my death, and then you'll canonize me perhaps? Ah, you have the plague, and you would give it to me. Go somewhere else, you brainless priest. "Ah! touch me not," said she, seeing him about to advance, " or I will stab you with this dagger."

And the clever hussy drew from her armoire a little dagger, which she knew how to use with great skill when necessary.

"But my little paradise, my sweet one," said the other, laughing, " don't you see the trick? Wasn't it necessary to get rid of that old bullock of Coire?"

"Well then, if you love me, show it," replied she. " I desire that you leave me instantly. If you are touched with the disease, my death will not worry you. I know you well enough to know at what price you will put a moment of pleasure at your last hour. You would drown the earth. Ah! ah! you have boasted of it when drunk. I love only myself, my treasures, and my health. Go, and if to-morrow your veins are not frozen by the disease, you can come again. To-day, I hate you, my good cardinal," said she, smiling.

"Imperia!" cried the cardinal, on his knees, " my blessed Imperia, do not play with me thus."

"No," said she, "I never play with blessed and sacred things."

"Ah! ribald woman, I will excommunicate thee to-morrow."

"And now you are out of your cardinal sense."

"Imperia, cursed daughter of Satan! Oh, my little beauty—my love—"

"Respect yourself more. Don't kneel to me, fie for shame!"

"Wilt thou have a dispensation *in articulo mortis?* Wilt thou have my fortune—or better still, a bit of the veritable true cross?—Wilt thou?"

"This evening, all the wealth of heaven above and earth beneath would not buy my heart," said she, laughing. "I should be the blackest of sinners, unworthy to receive the Blessed Sacrament if I had not my little caprices."

"I'll burn the house down. Sorceress, you have bewitched me. You shall perish at the stake. Listen to me, my love—my gentle dove—I promise you the best place in heaven. Eh? No. Death to you then—death to the sorceress."

"Oh! oh! I will kill you, Monseigneur."

And the cardinal foamed with rage.

"You are making a fool of yourself," said she. "Go away, you'll tire yourself."

"I shall be pope, and you shall pay for this!"

"Then you are no longer disposed to obey me?"

"What can I do this evening to please you?"

"Get out."

And she sprang lightly like a wagtail into her room, and locked herself in, leaving the cardinal to storm that he was obliged to go. When the fair Imperia found herself alone, seated before the fire, and without her little priest. she exclaimed, snapping angrily the gold links of her chain, "By the double triple horn of the devil, if the little one has made me have this row with the cardinal, and ex-posed me to the danger of being poisoned to-morrow, unless I pay him over to my heart's content, I will not die till I have seen him burnt alive before my eyes. Ah!" said she, weeping, this time real tears, " I lead a most unhappy life, and the little pleasure I have costs me the life of a dog, let alone my salvation."

As she finished this jeremiad, wailing like a calf that is being slaughtered, she beheld the blushing face of the young priest, who had hidden himself, peeping at her from behind her large Venetian mirror.

" Ah !" said she, "thou art the most perfect monk that ever dwelt in this blessed and amorous town of Constance. Ah! ah! come my gentle cavalier, my dear boy, my little charm, my paradise of delectation, let me drink thine eyes, eat thee, kill thee with love. Oh! my ever-flourishing, ever green, sempiternal god ; from a little monk I would make thee a king, emperor, pope, and happier than either. There, thou canst put anything to fire and sword, I am thine, and thou shalt see it well ; for thou shalt be all a cardinal, even when to redden thy hood I shed all my heart's blood." And with her trembling hands all joyously she filled with Greek wine the golden cup, brought by the Bishop of Coire, and presented it to her sweetheart, whom she served upon her knee, she whose slipper princes found more to their taste than that of the pope.

But he gazed at her in silence, with his eye so lustrous with love, that she said to him, trembling with joy, " Ah, be quiet, little one. Let us have supper."

THE VENIAL SIN.

HOW THE GOODMAN BRUYN TOOK A WIFE.

MESSIRE BRUYN, he who completed the Castle of Roche-Corbon-les-Vouvray, on the banks of the Loire, was a boisterous fellow in his youth. When quite little, he squeezed the young maidens, turned the house out of windows, and played the devil with everything, when he was called upon to put his sire the Baron of Roche-Corbon

some few feet under the turf. Then he was his own master, free to lead a life of wild dissipation, and indeed he worked very hard to get a surfeit of enjoyment. Now by making his crowns sweat and his goods scarce, draining his land, and bleeding his hogsheads, and regaling frail beauties, he found himself excommunicated from decent

The castle of the goodman Bruyn.

society, and had for his friends only the plunderers of
towns and the Lombardians. But the usurers turned rough
and bitter as chestnut husks, when he had no other security
to give them than his said estate of Roche-Corbon, since
the *Rupes Carbonis* was held from our lord the king. Then
Bruyn found himself just in the humour to give a blow here

and there, to break a collar-
bone or two, and quarrel
with every one about trifles.
Seeing which the Abbot of
Marmoustiers, his neigh-
bour, and a man liberal
with his advice, told him
that it was an evident sign
of lordly perfection, that
he was walking in the right
road, but if he would go
and slaughter, to the great

glory of God, the Mahommedans who defiled the Holy
Land, it would be better still, and that he would un-
doubtedly return full of wealth and indulgences into
Touraine, or into Paradise, whence all barons formerly came.

The said Bruyn, admiring the great sense of the prelate, left
the country equipped by the monastery, and blessed by the
abbot, to the great delight of his friends and neighbours.
Then he put to the sack many towns of Asia and Africa,

and fell upon the infidels without giving them warning,
burning the Saracens, the Greeks, the English and others,

He put to the sack many towns of Asia and Africa, and fell upon the
infidels without giving them warning.

caring little whether they were friends or enemies, or where
they came from, since among his merits he had that of being

in no way curious, and he never questioned them until after
he had killed them. At this business, agreeable to God, to
the King, and to himself, Bruyn gained renown as a good
Christian and loyal knight, and enjoyed himself thoroughly
in these lands beyond the seas, since he more willingly gave
a crown to the girls than to the poor, although he met more
poor people than perfect maids; but like a good Tourai-

nian he made soup of anything. At length, when he was
satiated with Turks, relics, and other blessings of the Holy

Land, Bruyn, to the
great astonishment of
the people of Vouvril-
lons, returned from the
Crusades laden with
crowns and precious
stones; rather diffe-
rently from some who,
rich when they set out,
came back heavy with leprosy, but light with gold. On his
return from Tunis, our Lord, King Philippe, made him a
Count, and appointed him his seneschal in our country

and in that of Poitou. There
he was greatly beloved and
properly thought well of, since
over and above his good qualities he founded the Church
of the Carmes-Deschaulx, in
the parish of Egrignolles, as
a peace-offering to Heaven
for the follies of his youth.
Thus was he cardinally consigned to the good graces of
the Church and of God. From
a wicked youth and reckless
man, he became a good, wise
man, and discreetly bald from

losing his hair; rarely was in anger, unless some one
blasphemed God before him, the which he would not
tolerate because he had blasphemed enough for every one
in his wild youth. In short, he never quarrelled, because,
being seneschal, people gave up to him instantly. It
is true that he at that time beheld all his desires accomplished, the which would render even an imp of Satan
calm and tranquil from his horns to his heels. And
beside this he possessed a castle all jagged at the corners,
and shaped and pointed like a Spanish doublet, situated

upon a bank from which it was reflected in the Loire.
In the rooms were royal tapestries, furniture, Saracen pomps,

vanities, and inventions which were much admired by the
people of Tours, and even by the archbishop and clerks of
St. Martin, to whom he sent
as a free gift a banner fringed
with fine gold. In the neighbourhood of the said castle
abounded fair domains, wind-
mills, and forests, yielding a harvest of rents of all kinds, so that
he was one of the strongest
knights-banneret of the province, and could easily have led
to battle for our lord the king
a thousand men. In his old
days, if by chance his bailiff, a

diligent man at hanging, brought before him a poor peasant
suspected of some offence, he would say, smiling—

"Let this one go, Breddiff, he will count against those I inconsiderately slaughtered across the seas;" ofttimes, however, he would let them bravely hang on a chestnut tree, or swing on his gallows, but this was solely that justice might be done, and that the custom should not lapse in his domain. Thus the people on his lands were good and orderly, like fresh veiled nuns, and peaceful since he protected them from robbers and vagabonds whom he never

spared, knowing by experience how much mischief is caused by these cursed beasts of prey. For the rest, most devout, finishing everything quickly, his prayers as well as good wine, he managed the processes after the Turkish fashion, having a thousand little jokes ready for the losers, and dining with them to console them. He had all the people who had been hanged buried in consecrated ground like godly ones, some people thinking they had been sufficiently punished by having their breath stopped. He only persecuted the Jews now and then, and when they were glutted with usury and wealth. He let them gather their spoil as the bees do honey, saying that they were the best of tax-gatherers. And never did he despoil them save for the profit and use of the churchmen, the king, the province, or himself.

This jovial way gained for him the affection and esteem of every one, great and small. If he came back smiling from his judicial throne, the Abbot of Marmoustiers, an old man like himself, would say, "Ha! ha! messire, there is some hanging on since you laugh thus!" And when coming from Roche-Corbon to Tours he passed on horse-back along the Faubourg St. Symphorien, the little girls would say, "Ah, this is the justice day, here is the good man Bruyn," and without being afraid they would look at him astride on a big white hack, that he had brought back

with him from the Levant. On the bridge the little boys would stop playing with the ball, and would call out, "Good day, Mr. Seneschal," and he would reply, jokingly, "Enjoy yourselves, my children, until you get whipped." "Yes, Mr. Seneschal."

Also he made the country so contented and so free from robbers that during the year of the great overflowing of the Loire there were only twenty-two malefactors hanged that winter, not counting a Jew burned in the Commune of Chateau-Neuf for having stolen a consecrated wafer, or bought it, some said, for he was very rich.

One day in the following year about harvest time, or mowing time, as we say in Touraine, there came Egyptians, Bohemians, and other wandering troupes who stole the holy

things from the Church of St. Martin, and in the place and exact siuation of Madame the Virgin, left by way of insult and mockery to our Holy Faith, an abandoned pretty little girl, about the age of an old dog, stark naked,

an acrobat, and of Moorish descent like themselves. For
this almost nameless crime it was equally decided by the
king, people, and the churchmen that the Mooress, to pay
for all, should be burned and cooked alive in the square
near the fountain where the herb market is. Then the
good man Bruyn clearly and dexterously demonstrated to
the others that it would be a thing most profitable and
pleasant to God to gain over this African soul to the true
religion, and if the devil were lodged in this feminine body
the faggots would be useless to burn him, as said the said
order. The which the archbishop sagely thought most
canonical and conformable to Christian charity and the
gospel. The ladies of the town and other persons of authority
said loudly that they were cheated of a fine ceremony,
since the Mooress was crying her eyes out in the gaol and
would certainly be converted to God in order to live as long
as a crow, if she were allowed to do so, to which the seneschal replied that if the foreigner would holily commit herself
to the Christian religion there would be a gallant ceremony
of another kind, and that he would undertake that it should
be royally magnificent, because he would be her sponsor at
the baptismal font, and that a virgin should be his partner
in the affair in order the better to please the Almighty, while
himself was reputed never to have lost the bloom of
innocence, in fact to be a *coquebin*. In our country of Touraine thus are called the young virgin men, unmarried or so
esteemed, to distinguish them from the husbands and the
widowers, but the girls always pick them out without the
name, because they are more lighthearted and merry than
those seasoned in marriage.

The young Mooress did not hesitate between the flaming
faggots and the baptismal water. She much preferred to be
a Christian and live than be an Egyptian and be burnt; thus
to escape a moment's baking, her heart would burn un-
quenched through all her life, since for the greater surety of
her religion she was placed in the convent of nuns near
Chardonneret, where she took the vow of sanctity. The said
ceremony was concluded at the residence of the archbishop,
where on this occasion, in honour of the Saviour of men, the

lords and ladies of Touraine hopped, skipped, and danced,
for in this country the people dance, skip, eat, flirt, have
more feasts and make merrier than any in the whole world.
The good old seneschal had taken for his associate the
daughter of the lord of Azay-le-Ridel, which afterwards became Azay-le-Bruslé, the which lord being a Crusader was
left before Acre, a far distant town, in the hands of a Saracen
who demanded a royal ransom for him because the said lord
was of high position.

The lady of Azay having given his estate as security to
the Lombards and extortioners in order to raise the sum, remained, without a penny in the world, awaiting her lord in a
poor lodging in the town, without a carpet to sit upon, but
proud as the Queen of Sheba and brave as a mastiff who
defends the property of his master. Seeing this great distress the seneschal went delicately to request this lady's
daughter to be the godmother of the said Egyptian, in order
that he might have the right of assisting the Lady of Azay.
And, in fact, he kept a heavy chain of gold which he had
preserved since the commencement of the taking of Cyprus,
and the which he determined to clasp about the neck of
his pretty associate, but he hung there at the same time
his domain, and his white hairs, his money and his horses ; in
short, he placed there everything he possessed, directly he had
seen Blanche of Azay dancing a pavan among the ladies of
Tours. Although the Moorish girl, making the most of her
last day, had astonished the assembly by her twists, jumps,
steps, springs, elevations and artistic efforts, Blanche had
the advantage of her, as every one agreed, so virginally and
delicately did she dance.

Now Bruyn, admiring this gentle maiden whose toes
seemed to fear the boards, and who amused herself so
innocently for her seventeen years—like a grasshopper trying
her first note—was seized with an old man's desire ; a desire
apoplectic and vigorous from weakness, which heated him
from the sole of his foot to the nape of his neck—for his
head had too much snow on the top of it to let love lodge
there. Then the good man perceived that he needed a wife
in his manor, and it appeared more lonely to him than it

Now Bruyn, admiring this gentle maiden, whose toes seemed to fear the boards, and who amused herself so innocently for her seventeen years—like a grasshopper trying her first note—was seized with an old man's desire; a desire apoplectic, and vigorous from weakness.

was. And what then was a castle without a chatelaine? As well have a clapper without its bell. In short, a wife was the only thing that he had to desire, so he wished to have one promptly, seeing that if the Lady of Azay made him wait, he had just time to pass out of this world into the other. But during the baptismal entertainment, he thought little of his severe wounds, and still less of the eighty years that had stripped his head; he found his eyes clear enough to see distinctly his young companion, who, following the injunctions of the Lady of Azay, regaled him well with glance and gesture, believing there could be no danger near so old a fellow, in such wise that Blanche—naïve and nice as she was in contradistinction to the girls of Touraine, who are as wide-awake as a spring morning—permitted the good man first to kiss her hand, and afterwards her neck, rather low down; at least so said the archbishop who married them the week after; and that was a beautiful bridal, and a still more beautiful bride.

The said Blanche was slender and graceful as no other girl, and still better than that, more maidenly than ever maiden was; a maiden all ignorant of love, who knew not why or what it was; a maiden who wondered why certain people lingered in their beds; a maiden who believed that children were found in parsley beds. Her mother had thus reared her in innocence, without even allowing her to consider, trifle as it was, how she sucked in her soup between her teeth. Thus was she a sweet flower, and intact, joyous, and innocent; an angel, who needed but the wings to fly away to Paradise. When she left the poor lodging of her weeping mother to consummate her betrothal at the cathedral of St. Gatien and St. Maurice, the country people came to feast their eyes upon the bride, and on the carpets which were laid down all along the Rue de la Scellerie, and all said that never had tinier feet pressed the ground of Touraine, prettier eyes gazed up to heaven, or a more splendid festival adorned the streets with carpets and with flowers. The young girls of St. Martin and of the borough of Chateau-Neuf, all envied the long brown tresses with which doubtless Blanche had fished for a count, but much

The country people came to feast their eyes upon the bride.

more did they desire the gold embroidered dress, the foreign stones, the white diamonds, and the chains with which the little darling played, and which bound her for ever to the said seneschal. The old soldier was so merry by her side, that his happiness showed itself in his wrinkles, his looks, and his movements. Although he was hardly as straight as a billhook, he held himself so by the side of Blanche, that one would have taken him for a soldier on parade receiving his officer, and he placed his hand on his diaphragm like a man whose pleasure stifles and troubles him. Delighted with the sound of the swinging bells, the procession, the pomps and vanities of this said marriage, which was talked of long after the episcopal rejoicings, the women desired a harvest of Moorish girls, a deluge of old seneschals, and baskets full of Egyptian baptisms. But this was the only one that ever happened in Touraine, seeing that the country is far from Egypt and from Bohemia. The Lady of Azay received a large sum of money after the ceremony, which enabled her to start immediately for Acre to go to her spouse, accompanied by the lieutenant and soldiers of the Count of Roche-Corbon, who furnished them with everything necessary. She set out on the day of the wedding, after having placed her daughter in the hands of the seneschal, enjoining him to treat her well ; and later on she returned with the Sire d'Azay, who was leprous, and she cured him, tending him herself, running the risk of being contaminated, the which was greatly admired.

The marriage ceremony finished and at an end—for it lasted three days, to the great contentment of the people— Messire Bruyn with great pomp led the little one to his castle, and, according to the custom of husbands, had her put solemnly to bed in his couch, which was blessed by the Abbot of Marmoustiers ; then came and placed himself beside her in the great feudal chamber of Roche-Corbon, which had been hung with green brocade and ribbon of golden wire. When old Bruyn, perfumed all over, found himself side by side with his pretty wife, he kissed her first upon the forehead and then upon the little round, white breast, on the same spot where she had allowed him to clasp the fastenings of the chain, but that was all. The old fellow had too great confidence in himself in fancying himself able to accomplish more; so then he abstained from love in spite of the merry nuptial songs, the epithalamiums and jokes which were going on in the rooms beneath where the dancing was still kept up. He refreshed himself with a drink of the marriage beverage, which, according to custom, had been blessed and placed near them in a golden cup. The spices warmed his stomach well enough, but not the heart of his dead ardour. Blanche was not at all astonished at the demeanour of her spouse, because she was a virgin in mind, and in marriage she only saw that which is visible to the eyes of young girls—namely, dresses, banquets, horses, to be a lady and mistress, to have a country seat, to amuse oneself and give orders; so, like the child that she was, she played with the gold tassels of the bed, and marvelled at the richness of the shrine in which her innocence should be interred. Feeling, a little later in the day, his culpability, and relying on the future, which, however, would spoil a little every day that with which he pretended to regale his wife, the seneschal tried to substitute the word for the deed. So he entertained his wife in various ways, promised her the keys of his sideboards his granaries and chests, the perfect government of his houses and domains without any control, hanging round her neck " the other half of the loaf," which is the popular saying in Touraine. She being like a young charger full of hay, found her good man the most gallant fellow in the world, and raising herself upon her pillow began to smile, and beheld with greater joy this beautiful green brocaded bed, where henceforward she would be permitted, without any sin, to sleep every night. Seeing she was getting playful, the cunning lord, who had not been used to maidens, but knew from experience the little tricks that women will practise, seeing that he had much associated with ladies of the town, feared those handy tricks, little kisses, and minor amusements of love which formerly he did not object to, but which at the present time would have found him cold as the obit of a pope. Then he drew back towards the edge of the bed, afraid of his happiness, and said to his too delectable spouse, " Well, darling, you are a seneschal's wife now, and very well seneschaled as well."

" Oh no !" said she.

" How no !" replied he, in great fear; " are you not a wife ?"

" No," said she. " Nor shall I be till I have a child."

" Did you while coming here see the meadows ?" began again the old fellow.

" Yes," said she.

" Well, they are yours."

" Oh ! oh !" replied she laughing, " I shall amuse myself much there catching butterflies."

" That's a good girl," said her lord. " And the woods ?"

" Ah ! I should not like to be there alone, you will take me there. But," said she, " give me a little of that liquor which La Ponneuse has taken such pains to prepare for us."

" And why, my darling ? It would put fire into your body."

" Oh ! that's what I should like," said she, biting her lips with vexation, " because I desire to give you a child as soon as possible ; and I am sure that liquor is good for the purpose."

" Ah, my little one," said the seneschal, knowing by this that Blanche was a virgin from head to foot, " the goodwill of God is necessary for this business, and women must be in a state of harvest."

" And when shall I be in a state of harvest ?" asked she, smiling.

" When nature so wills it," said he, trying to laugh.

" What is it necessary to do for this ?" replied she.

" Bah ! a cabalistical and alchemical operation which is very dangerous."

" Ah !" said she, with a dreamy look, " that's the reason why my mother cried when thinking of the said metamorphosis ; but Bertha de Breuilly, who is so thankful for being made a wife, told me it was the easiest thing in the world."

" That's according to the age," replied the old lord.

"But did you see at the stable the beautiful white mare so much spoken of in Touraine?"

"Yes, she is very gentle and nice."

"Well, I give her to you, and you can ride her as often as the fancy takes you."

"Oh, you are very kind, and they did not lie when they told me so."

"Here," continued he, "sweetheart : the butler, the chaplain, the treasurer, the equerry, the farrier, the bailiff, even the Sire de Montsoreau, the young varlet whose name is Gauttier and bears my banner, with his men at arms, captains, followers, and beasts—all are yours, and will instantly obey your orders under pain of being incommoded with a hempen collar."

"But," replied she, "this mysterious operation—cannot it be performed immediately ?"

"Oh no !" replied the seneschal. "Because it is necessary above all things that both the one and the other of us should be in a state of grace before God ; otherwise we should have a bad child, full of sins ; which is forbidden by the canons of the Church. This is the reason there are so many incorrigible scapegraces in the world. Their parents have not wisely waited to have their souls pure, and have given wicked souls to their children. The beautiful and the virtuous come of immaculate fathers ; that is why we cause our beds to be blessed, as the Abbot of Marmoustiers has done this one. Have you not transgressed the ordinances of the Church ?"

"Oh no," said she, quickly, "I received before Mass absolution for all my faults and have remained since without committing the slightest sin."

"You are very perfect," cried the cunning lord, "and I am delighted to have you for a wife ; but I have sworn like an infidel."

"Oh ! and why ?"

"Because the dancing did not finish, and I could not have you to myself to bring you here and kiss you."

Thereupon he gallantly took her hands and covered them with kisses, whispering to her little endearments and superficial words of affection which made her quite pleased and contented.

Then, fatigued with the dance and all the ceremonies, she settled down to her slumbers, saying to the seneschal—

"I will take care to-morrow that you shall not sin," and she left the old man quite smitten with her white beauty, amorous of her delicate nature, and as embarrassed to know how he should be able to keep her in her innocence as to explain why oxen chew their food twice over. Although he did not augur to himself any good therefrom, it inflamed him so much to see the exquisite perfections of Blanche during her innocent and gentle sleep, that he resolved to preserve and defend this pretty jewel of love. With tears in his eyes he kissed her sweet golden tresses, her beautiful eyelids, and her ripe red mouth, and he did it softly for fear of waking her. That was all his fruition, the dumb delight which still inflamed his heart without in the least affecting Blanche. Then he deplored the snows of his leafless old age, the poor old man, and he saw clearly that God had amused himself by giving him nuts when his teeth were gone.

HOW THE SENESCHAL STRUGGLED WITH HIS WIFE'S MODESTY.

During the first days of his marriage the seneschal invented many fibs to tell his wife, whose so estimable innocence he abused. Firstly, he found in his judicial functions good excuses for leaving her at times alone; then he occupied himself with the peasants of the neighbourhood, and took them to dress the vines on his lands at Vouvray, and at length pampered her up with a thousand absurd tales.

At one time he would say that lords did not behave like common people, that the children were only planted at certain celestial conjunctions ascertained by learned astrologers; at another that one should abstain from begetting children on feast days because it was a great undertaking; and he observed the feasts like a man who wished to enter into Paradise without contest. Sometimes he would pretend that if by chance the parents were not in a state of grace, the children commenced on the day of St. Claire were blind, of St. Gatien had the gout, of St. Agnes were scaldheaded, of St. Roch had the plague; sometimes that

those begotten in February were chilly ; in March, too turbu-
lent ; in April, were worth nothing at all; and that handsome
boys were conceived in May. In short, he wished his to be
perfect, to have his hair of two colours ; and for this it was
necessary that all the required conditions should be observed. At other times he would say to Blanche that the
right of a man was to bestow a child upon his wife according to his sole and unique will, and that if she pretended to
be a virtuous woman she should conform to the wishes of
her husband ; in fact, it was necessary to await the return of
the Lady of Azay in order that she should assist at the confinement ; from all of which Blanche concluded that the
seneschal was annoyed by her requests, and was perhaps
right, since he was old and full of experience ; so she submitted herself and thought no more, except to herself, of
this so much-desired child, that is to say, she was always
thinking of it, like a woman who has a desire in her head,
without suspecting that she was behaving like a gay lady or a
town-walker running after her enjoyment. One evening by
accident Bruyn spoke of children, a discourse that he
avoided as cats avoid water, but he was complaining of
a boy condemned by him that morning for great misdeeds,
saying for certain he was the offspring of people laden with
mortal sins.

"Alas," said Blanche, "if you will give me one, although
you have not got absolution, I will correct him so well that
you will be pleased with him."

Then the count saw that his wife was bitten by a warm
desire, and that it was time to dissipate her innocence in
order to make himself master of it, to conquer it, to beat it,
or to appease and extinguish it.

"What, my dear, you wish to be a mother ?" said he ; "you
do not yet know the business of a wife, you are not accustomed to being mistress of the house."

"Oh ! oh !" said she, " to be a perfect countess, and have
in my loins a little count, must I play the great lady ? I will
do it, and thoroughly."

Then Blanche, in order to obtain issue, began to hunt the
fawns and the stags, leaping the ditches, galloping upon

her mare over valley and mountain, through the woods and
the fields, taking great delight in watching the falcons fly, in
unhooding them and while hunting always carried them

gracefully upon her little wrist, which was what the seneschal
had desired. But in this pursuit, Blanche gained an appetite
of nun and prelate, that is to say, wished to procreate, had her
desires whetted, and could scarcely restrain her hunger, when
on her return she gave play to her teeth. Now by reason of
reading the legends written by the way, and of separating by
death the embraces of birds and wild beasts, she discovered a
mystery of natural alchemy, while colouring her complexion,
and superagitating her feeble imagination, which did little to
pacify her warlike nature, and strongly tickled her desire
which laughed, played, and frisked unmistakably. The
seneschal thought to disarm the rebellious virtue of his wife

by making her scour the country ; but his fraud turned out badly, for the unknown lust that circulated in the veins of Blanche emerged from these assaults more hardy than before, inviting jousts and tourneys as a herald the armed knight.

The good lord saw then that he had grossly erred and that he was now upon the horns of a dilemma ; also he no longer knew what course to adopt; the longer he left it the more it would resist. From this combat, there must result one conquered and one contused—a diabolical contusion which he wished to keep distant from his physiognomy by God's help until after his death. The poor seneschal had already great trouble to follow his lady to the chase, without being dismounted; he sweated under the weight of his trappings, and almost expired in that pursuit wherein his frisky wife cheered her life and took great pleasure. Many times in the evening she wished to dance. Now the good man, swathed in his heavy clothing, found himself quite worn out with these exercises, in which he was constrained to participate either in giving her his hand, when she performed the vaults of the Moorish girl, or in holding the lighted faggot for her, when she had a fancy to do the torchlight dance ; and in spite of his sciaticas, accretions, and rheumatisms, he was obliged to smile and say to her some gentle words and gallantries after all the evolutions, mummeries, and comic pantomimes which she indulged in to divert herself ; for he loved her so madly that if she had asked him for an impossibility he would have sought one for her immediately.

Nevertheless one fine day he recognised the fact that his frame was in a state of too great debility to struggle with the vigorous nature of his wife, and humiliating himself before his wife's virtue, he resolved to let things take their course, relying a little upon the modesty, religion, and bashfulness of Blanche, but he always slept with one eye open, for he suspected that God had made virginities to be taken like partridges, to be spitted and roasted. One wet morning, when the weather was that in which the snails make their tracks, a melancholy time, and suitable to reverie, Blanche was in the house sitting in her chair in deep thought, because nothing produces more lively coctions of the substantive essences, and no receipt, specific or philtre is more penetrating, transpiercing, or doubly transpiercing and titillating than the subtle warmth which simmers between the nap of a chair and a maiden sitting during certain weather.

Now without knowing it, the countess was incommoded by her innocence, which gave more trouble than it was worth to her brain and gnawed her all over. Then the good man, seriously grieved to see her languishing, wished to drive away the thoughts which were ultra-conjugal principles of love.

" Whence comes your sadness, sweetheart ?" said he.

" From shame."

" What then affronts you ?"

" The not being a good woman ; because I am without a child, and you without lineage ! Is one a lady without progeny ? Nay ! look ! . . . all my neighbours have it, and I was married to have it, as you to give it me ; the nobles of Touraine are all amply furnished with children, and their

wives give them lapfuls you alone have none, they laugh at you there. What will become of your name and your fiefs and your seigniories. A child is our natural company ; it is a delight to us to make a fright of it, to fondle it, to swaddle it, to dress and undress it, to cuddle it, to sing it lullabies, to cradle it, to get it up, to put it to bed, and to nourish it, and I feel that if I had only the half of one, I would kiss it, swaddle it and unharness it, and I would make it jump and crow all day long, as the other ladies do."

"Were it not that in giving them birth women die, and that for this you are still too delicate and too close in the bud, you would be already a mother," replied the seneschal, made giddy with the flow of words. "But will you buy one ready made—that will cost you neither pain nor labour."

"But," said she, "I want the pain and labour, without which it will not be ours. I know very well it should be the fruit of my body, because at church they say that Jesus was the fruit of the Virgin's womb."

"Very well, then pray God that it may be so," cried the seneschal, "and intercede with the Virgin of Egrignolles. Many a lady has conceived after the neuvaine; you must not fail to do one."

Then the same day Blanche set out towards Notre-Dame de l'Egrignolles, decked out like a queen, riding her beautiful mare, having on her a robe of green velvet, laced down with fine gold lace, open at the breast, having sleeves of scarlet, little shoes, and a high hat ornamented with precious stones, and a gold waistband that showed off her little waist, as slim as a pole. She wished to give her dress to Madame the Virgin, and in fact promised it her, for the day of her churching. The Sire de Montsoreau galloped before her, his eye bright as that of a hawk, keeping the people back and guarding with his knights the security of the journey. Near Marmoustiers the seneschal, rendered sleepy by the heat, seeing it was the month of August, waggled about in his saddle, like a diadem upon the head of a cow, and seeing so frolicsome and so pretty a lady by the side of so old a fellow, a peasant girl, who was squatting near the trunk of a tree and drinking water out of her stone jug, inquired of a toothless old hag, who picked up a trifle by gleaning. if this princess was going to bury her dead.

"Nay," said the old woman, "it is our lady of Roche-

Then the same day Blanche set out towards Notre-Dame de l'Egrignolles.

Corbon, wife of the seneschal of Poictou and Touraine, in quest of a child."

" Ah ! ah !" said the young girl, laughing like a fly just satisfied ; then pointing to the handsome knight who was at the head of the procession—" he who marches at the head would manage that ; she would save the wax-candles and the vow."

" Ha ! my little one," replied the hag, " I am rather surprised that she should go to Notre-Dame de l'Egrignolles, seeing that there are no handsome priests there. She might very well stop for a short time beneath the shadow of the belfry of Marmoustiers ; she would soon be fertile, these good fathers are so lively."

" By a nun's oath !" said a tramp walking up, "look ; the Sire de Montsoreau is lively and delicate enough to open the ladies' heart, the more so as he is well formed to do so."

And all commenced to laugh. The Sire de Montsoreau wished to go to them and hang them to a lime-tree by the road as a punishment for their bad words, but Blanche cried out quickly—

" Oh, sir, do not hang them yet. They have not said all they mean ; and we shall see them on our return."

She blushed, and the Sire de Montsoreau looked at her eagerly, as though to shoot into her the mystic comprehensions of love, but the clearing out of her intelligence had already been commenced by the sayings of the peasants, which were fructifying in her understanding—her innocence was like touchwood, there was only need for a word to inflame it.

Thus Blanche perceived now the notable and physical differences between the qualities of her old husband and the perfections of the said Gauttier, a gentleman who was not over affected with his twenty-three years, but held himself upright as a ninepin in the saddle, and as wide-awake as the matin chimes, while in contrast to him, slept the seneschal ; he had courage and dexterity there where his master failed. He was one of those smart fellows whom the jades would sooner wear at night than a leathern garment, because they then no longer fear the fleas ; there are some who vituperate them, but no one should be blamed, because every one should sleep as he likes.

So much did the seneschal's lady think, and so imperially well, that by the time she arrived at the bridge of Tours, she loved Gauttier secretly, as a maiden loves, without suspecting that it is love. From that she became a proper woman, that is to say, she desired the good of others, the best that men have, she fell into a fit of love-sickness, going at the first jump to the depth of her misery, seeing that all is flame between the first coveting and the last desire, and she knew not how she then learnt that by the eyes can flow in a subtle essence, causing such powerful corrosions in all the veins of the body, recesses of the heart, nerves of the members, roots of the hair, perspiration of the substance, limbo of the brain, orifices of the epidermis, windings of the pluck, tubes of the hypochondriac and other channels, which in her were suddenly dilated, heated, tickled, envenomed, clawed, harrowed and disturbed, as if she had a basketful of needles in her inside. This was a maiden's desire, a well-conditioned desire, which troubled her sight to such a degree that she no longer saw her old spouse, but clearly the young Gauttier, whose nature was as ample as the glorious chin of an abbot. When the good man entered Tours, the *Ah! Ah!* of the crowd woke him up, and he came with great pomp with his suite to the church of Notre-Dame de l'Egrignolles, formerly called *la greigneur,* as if you said that which has the most merit. Blanche went into the chapel where children are asked of God and of the Virgin, and went there alone, as was the custom, always however in presence of the seneschal, of his varlets and the loiterers who remained outside the grill. When the countess saw the priest come who had charge of the masses said for children, and who received the said vows, she asked him if there were many barren women. To which the good priest replied, that he must not complain, and that the children were good revenue to the Church.

" And do you often see," said Blanche, " young women with such old husbands as my lord?"

" Rarely," said he.

" But have those obtained offspring ?"

'' Always," replied the priest, smiling.

" And the others whose companions are not so old ?"

" Sometimes."

" Oh ! oh !" said she, " there is more certainty than with one like the seneschal ?"

" To be sure," said the priest.

" Why ?" said she.

" Madame," gravely replied the priest, " before that age God alone interferes with the affair, after, it is the men."

At this time it was a true thing that all the wisdom had gone to the clergy. Blanche made her vow, which was a very profitable one, seeing that her decorations were worth quite two thousand gold crowns.

" You are very joyful !" said the old seneschal to her when on the home journey she made her mare prance, jump, and frisk.

" Yes, yes !" said she. " There is no longer any doubt about my having a child, because any one can help me, the priest said ; I shall take Gauttier."

The seneschal wished to go and slay the monk, but he thought that was a crime which would cost him too much, and he resolved cunningly to arrange his vengeance with the help of the archbishop ; and before the housetops of Roche-Corbon came in sight he had ordered the Sire de Montsoreau to seek a little retirement in his own country, which the young Gauttier did, knowing the ways of his lord. The seneschal put in the place of the said Gauttier the son of the Sire de Jallanges, whose fief was

held from Roche-Corbon. He was a young boy named René, approaching fourteen years, and he made him a page, awaiting the time when he should be old enough to be equerry, and gave the command of his men to an old cripple, with whom he had knocked about a great deal in Palestine and other places. Thus the good man believed he would avoid the horned trappings of cuckoldom, and would still be able to girth, bridle, and curb the factious innocence of his wife, which struggled like a mule held by a rope.

And gave the command of his men to an old cripple, with whom he had knocked about a great deal in Palestine and other places.

THAT WHICH IS ONLY A VENIAL SIN.

The Sunday following the arrival of René at the manor of Roche-Corbon, Blanche went out hunting without her goodman, and when she was in the forest near Les Carneaux, saw a monk who appeared to be pushing a girl about more than was necessary, and spurred on her horse, saying to her people, " Ho there ! don't let him kill her." But when the seneschal's lady arrived close to them, she turned her horse's head quickly and the sight she beheld prevented her from hunting. She came back pensive, and then the lantern of her intelligence opened, and received a bright light, which made a thousand things clear, such as church and other pictures, fables, and lays of the troubadours, or the domestic arrangements of birds : suddenly she discovered the sweet mystery of love written in all languages, even in that of the carps'. Is it not silly thus to seal this science from maidens? Soon went Blanche to bed, and soon said she to the seneschal—

" Bruyn, you have deceived me, you ought to behave as the monk of the Carneaux behaved with the girl."

Old Bruyn suspected the adventure, and saw well that his evil hour was at hand. He regarded Blanche with too much fire in his eyes for the same ardour to be lower down, and answered her softly—

" Alas ! sweetheart, in taking you for my wife I had more love than strength, and I have taken advantage of your clemency and virtue. The great sorrow of my life is to feel all my capability in my heart only. This sorrow hastens my death little by little, so that you will soon be free. Wait for my departure from this world. That is the sole request that he makes of you, he who is your master, and who could command you, but who wishes only to be your prime minister and slave. Do not betray the honour of my white hairs ! Under these circumstances there have been lords who have slain their wives."

" Alas ! you will not kill me ?" said she.

" No," replied the old man, " I love thee too much, little one ; why, thou art the flower of my old age, the joy of my soul. Thou art my well-beloved daughter ; the sight of thee does good to mine eyes, and from thee I could endure anything, be it a sorrow or a joy ; I give thee full licence in everything, provided that thou dost not curse too much the poor Bruyn who has made thee a great lady, rich and honoured. Wilt thou not be a lovely widow ? And thy happiness will soften the pangs of death."

And he found in his dried-up eyes still one tear which trickled quite warm down his fir-cone coloured face, and fell upon the hand of Blanche who, grieved to behold this great love of her old spouse who would put himself under the ground to please her, said laughing—

" There ! there ! don't cry, I will wait !"

Thereupon the seneschal kissed her hands and regaled her with little endearments, saying with a voice quivering with emotion—

" If you knew, Blanche my darling, how I devour thee in thy sleep with caresses, now here, now there !" And the old ape patted her with his two hands, which were nothing but bones. And he continued, "I dared not awaken the cat that would have strangled my happiness, since at this occupation of love I only embraced with my heart."

" Ah !" replied she, " you can fondle me thus even when my eyes are open ; that has not the least effect upon me."

At these words the poor seneschal, taking the little

dagger which was on the table by the bed, gave it to her, saying with passion—

"My darling, kill me, or let me believe that you love me a little !"

"Yes, yes," said she, quite frightened, "I will try to love you much."

Behold how this young maidenhood made itself master of this old man and subdued him, for in the name of the sweet face of Venus, Blanche, endowed with the natural art-fulness of women, made her old Bruyn come and go like a miller's mule.

"My good Bruyn, I want this ! Bruyn, I want that—go on Bruyn !" Bruyn ! Bruyn ! and always Bruyn in such a

way that Bruyn was more worn out by the clemency of his wife than he would have been by her unkindness. She turned his brain, wishing that everything should be in scarlet, making him turn everything topsy-turvy at the least move-ment of her eyebrow, and when she was sad the seneschal, distracted, would say to everything from his judicial seat, "Hang him !" Another would have died like a fly at this conflict with the maid's innocence, but Bruyn was of such an iron nature that it was difficult to finish him off. One evening that Blanche had turned the house upside-down, upset the men and the beasts, and would by her aggravating humour have made the eternal father desperate—he who has

such an infinite treasure of patience since he endures us—she
said to the seneschal while getting into bed, "My good Bruyn,
I have low down fancies, that bite and prick me ; thence
they rise into my heart, inflame my brain, incite me therein
to evil deeds, and in the night I dream of the monk of the
Carneaux."

"My dear," replied the seneschal, "these are devilries
and temptations against which the monks and the nuns know
how to defend themselves. If you will gain salvation, go and
confess to the worthy Abbot of Marmoustiers, our neighbour ;

he will advise you well and will holily direct you in the good
way."

"To-morrow I will go," said she.

And indeed directly it was day, she trotted off to the monastery of the good brethren, who marvelled to see among them so pretty a lady ; committed more than one sin through her in the evening, and for the present led her with great ceremony to their reverend abbot.

Blanche found the said good man in a private garden near the high rock under a flowery arcade, and remained stricken with respect at the countenance of the holy man, although she was accustomed not to think much of grey hairs.

"God preserve you, Madame ; what come you to seek of one so near death, you so young?"

"Your precious advice," said she, saluting him with a courtesy ; "and if it will please you to guide so undutiful a sheep, I shall be well content to have so wise a confessor."

"My daughter," answered the monk, with whom old Bruyn had arranged this hypocrisy and the part to play, "if I had not the chills of a hundred winters upon this un-thatched head, I should not dare to listen to your sins, but say on ; if you enter paradise, it will be through me."

Then the seneschal's wife set forth the small fry of

her stock in hand, and when she was purged of her little iniquities, she came to the postscript of her confession.

"Ah, my father !" said she, "I must confess to you that I am daily exercised by the desire to have a child. Is it wrong?"

"No," said the abbot.

But she went on, "It is by nature commanded to my husband not to draw from his wealth to bring about his poverty, as the old women say by the way."

"Then," replied the priest, "you must live virtuously and abstain from all thoughts of this kind."

"But I have heard it professed by the Lady of Jallanges,

that it was not a sin when from it one derived neither profit nor pleasure."

"There always is pleasure," said the abbot, "but don't count upon the child as a profit. Now fix this in your understanding, that it will always be a mortal sin before God and a crime before men to bring forth a child through the embraces of a man to whom one is not ecclesiastically married. Thus those women who offend against the holy laws of marriage, suffer great penalties in the other world, are in the power of horrible monsters with sharp and tearing claws,

who thrust them into flaming furnaces in remembrance of the fact that here below they have warmed their hearts a little more than was lawful."

Thereupon Blanche scratched her ear, and having thought to herself for a little while, she said to the priest, "How then did the Virgin Mary?"

"Ah!" replied the abbot, "that is a mystery."

"And what is a mystery?"

"A thing that cannot be explained, and which one ought to believe without inquiring into it."

"Well then," said she, "cannot I perform a mystery."

"This one," said the abbot, "only happened once, because it was the Son of God."

"Alas! my father, is it then the will of God that I should die, or that from wise and sound comprehension my brain

should be turned? Of this there is great danger. Now in
me something moves and excites me, and I am no longer
in my senses. I care for nothing, and to find a man I
would leap the walls, dash over the fields without shame and
tear my things into tatters, only to see that which so much
excited the monk of the Carneaux; and during these passions
which work and prick my mind and body, there is neither
God, devil, nor husband. I spring, I run, I smash up the
wash-tubs, the pots, the farm implements, the fowl-house,
the household things, and everything, in a way that I cannot
describe. But I dare not confess to you all my misdeeds,
because speaking of them makes my mouth water, and the
thing with which God curses me makes me itch dreadfully. If
this folly bites and pricks me, and slays my virtue, will God,
who has placed this great love in my body, condemn me to
perdition?"

At this question it was the priest who scratched his ear,
quite dumbfoundered by the lamentations, profound wisdom, controversies and intelligence that this virginity
secreted.

" My daughter," said he, " God has distinguished us from
the beasts and made us a paradise to gain, and for this
given us reason, which is a rudder to steer us against
tempests and our ambitious desires, and there is a means
of easing the imaginations in one's brain by fasting, excessive
labours and other virtues; and instead of frisking and fretting
like a child let loose from school, you should pray to the
Virgin, sleep on a hard board, attend to your household
duties, and never be idle."

" Ah ! my father, when I am at church in my seat, I see
neither the priest nor the altar, only the infant Jesus, who
brings the thing into my head. But to finish, if my head is
turned and my mind wanders, I am in the lime-twigs of
love."

" If thus you were," said the abbot, imprudently, " you
would be in the position of Saint Lidoire, who in a deep
sleep one day, one leg here and one leg there, through the
great heat and scantily attired, was approached by a young
man full of mischief, who dexterously seduced her, and as

of this trick the saint was thoroughly ignorant, and much-
surprised at being brought to bed, thinking that her unusual
size was a serious malady, she did
penance for it as a venial sin, as
she had no pleasure in this wicked
business, according to the statement
of the wicked man, who said upon
the scaffold where he was exe-
cuted, that the saint had in nowise
stirred."

"Oh, my father," said she, "be sure that I should not
stir more than she did !"

With this statement she went away prettily and gracefully,
smiling and thinking how she could commit a venial sin.
On her return from the great monastery, she saw in the
courtyard of her castle the little Jallanges, who under the
superintendence of an old groom was turning and wheeling
about on a fine horse, bending with the movements of the
animal, dismounting, and mounting again by vaults and
leaps most gracefully, and with lissome thighs, so pretty, so
dexterous, so upright, as to be indescribable, so much so,
that he would have made the Queen Lucrece long for him,
she who killed herself from being contaminated against her
will.

"Ah !" said Blanche, "if only this page were fifteen, I
would go to sleep comfortably very near to him."

Then, in spite of the too great youth of this charming
 servitor, during the collation and supper,
she eyed frequently the black hair, the
white skin, the grace of René, above all
his eyes, where was an abundance of limpid
warmth and a great fire of life, which he was
afraid to shoot out—child that he was.

Now in the evening, as the seneschal's
wife sat thoughtfully in her chair in the corner of the fireplace, old Bruyn interrogated her as to her trouble.

"I am thinking," said she, "that you must have fought
the battles of love very early, to be thus completely broken
up."

"Oh !" replied he, smiling like all old men questioned upon their amorous remembrances, "at the age of thirteen and a half I had overcome the scruples of my mother's waiting woman."

Blanche wished to hear nothing more, but believed the page René should be equally advanced, and she was quite joyous, and practised little allurements on the good man, and wallowed silently in her desire, like a cake which is being floured.

HOW AND BY WHOM THE SAID CHILD WAS PROCURED.

The seneschal's wife did not think long over the best way quickly to awaken the love of the page, and had soon discovered the natural ambuscade in the which the most wary are taken. This is how : at the warmest hour of the day the good man took his siesta after the Saracen fashion, a habit in which he had never failed, since his return from the Holy Land. During this time Blanche was alone in the grounds, where the women work at their minor occupations, such as broidering and stitching, and often remained in the rooms looking after the washing, putting the clothes tidy, or running about at will. Then she appointed this quiet hour to complete the education of the page, making him read books and say his prayers. Now on the morrow, when at the midday hour the seneschal slept, succumbing to the sun which warms with its most luminous rays the slopes of Roche-Corbon, so much so that one is obliged to sleep, unless annoyed, upset, and continually roused by a devil of a young woman. Blanche then gracefully perched herself in the great seignorial chair of her good man, which she did not find any too high, since she counted upon the chances of perspective. The cunning jade settled herself dexterously therein, like a swallow in its nest, and leant her head maliciously upon her arm like a child that sleeps ; but in making her preparations, she opened fond eyes, that smiled and winked in advance of the little secret thrills, sneezes, squints, and trances of the page who was about to lie at her feet, separated from her by the jump of an old flea ; and in fact she advanced so much and so near the square of velvet where the poor child should kneel, whose life and soul she trifled with, that had he been a saint of stone, his glance would have been constrained to follow the flexuosities of the dress in order to admire and readmire the perfections and beauties of the shapely leg, which moulded the white stocking of the seneschal's lady. Thus it was certain that a weak varlet would be taken in a snare, wherein the most vigorous knight would willingly have succumbed. When she had turned, returned, placed, and displaced her body, and found the situation in which the page would be most comfortable, she cried, gently, " René !" René, whom she well knew was in the guard-room, did not fail to run in and quickly thrust his brown head between the tapestries of the door.

"What do you please to wish ?" said the page. And he held with great respect in his hand his shaggy scarlet cap, less red than his fresh dimpled cheeks.

"Come hither," replied she, under her breath, for the child attracted her so strongly that she was quite overcome.

And forsooth there were no jewels so sparkling as the eyes of René, no vellum whiter than his skin, no woman more exquisite in shape—and so near to her desire, she found him still more sweetly formed—and was certain that the merry frolics of love would radiate well from all this youth, the warm sun, the silence, *et cetera*.

" Read me the litanies of Madame the Virgin," said she to him, pushing an open book to him on her prie-dieu. " Let me see if you are well taught by your master."

" Do you not think the Virgin beautiful ?" asked she of him, smiling when he held the illuminated prayer book in glowed the silver and the gold.

" It is a painting," replied he, timidly, and casting a little glance upon his so gracious mistress.

" Read ! read !"

Then René began to recite the so sweet and so mystic litanies ; but you may imagine that the " *Ora pro nobis*" of Blanche became still fainter and fainter, like the sound of the horn in the woodlands, and when the page went on, " Oh, Rose of mystery," the lady, who certainly heard distinctly, replied by a gentle sigh. Thereupon René suspected that his mistress slept. Then he commenced to cover her with his regard, admiring her at his leisure, and had then no wish to utter any anthem save the anthem of love. His happiness made his heart leap and bound into his throat ; thus, as was but natural, these two innocences burned one against the other, but if they could have foreseen never would have intermingled. René feasted his eyes, planning in his mind a thousand fruitions of love that brought the water into his mouth. In his ecstacy he let his book fall, which made him feel as sheepish as a monk surprised at a child's tricks ; but also from that he knew that Blanche was sound asleep, for she did not stir, and the wily jade would not have opened her eyes even at the greatest dangers, and reckoned on something else falling as well as the book of prayer.

There is no worse longing than the longing of woman in a certain condition. Now, the page noticed his lady's foot, which was delicately slippered in a little laced shoe of a delicate blue colour. She had angularly placed it on a footstool, since she was too high in the seneschal's chair. This foot was of narrow proportions, delicately curved, as broad as two fingers, and as long as a sparrow, tail included, small at the top—a true foot of delight, a virginal foot that merited a kiss as a robber does the gallows ; a roguish foot ; a foot wanton enough to damn an archangel ; an ominous foot ; a devilishly enticing foot, which gave one a desire to make two new ones just like it to perpetuate in this

lower world the glorious works of God. The page was
tempted to take the shoe from this persuasive foot. To
accomplish this his eyes, glowing with the fire of his age,
went swiftly, like the clapper of a bell, from this said foot of
delectation to the sleeping countenance of his lady and
mistress, listening to her slumber, drinking in her respiration again and again, and did not know where it would be
sweetest to plant a kiss—whether on the ripe red lips of the
seneschal's wife or on this speaking foot. At length, from
respect or fear, or perhaps from great love, he chose the
foot, and kissed it hastily, like a maiden who dares not.
Then immediately he took up his book, feeling his red
cheeks redder still, and exercised with his pleasure, he cried
like a blind man—" *Janua cœli*, gate of Heaven." But
Blanche did not move, making sure that the page would go
from foot to knee, and thence to " Janua cœli, the gate of
Heaven." She was greatly disappointed when the litanies
finished without any other mischief, and René, believing he
had had enough happiness for one day, ran out of the room
quite lively, richer from this hardy kiss than a robber who
has robbed the poor-box.

When the seneschal's lady was alone, she thought to
herself that the page would be rather a long time at his
task if he amused himself with singing of the *Magnificat* at
matins. Thus she determined on the morrow to raise her
foot a little, and then bring to light those hidden beauties
that are called perfect in Touraine, because they take no hurt
in the open air, and are always fresh. You can imagine that
the page, burned by his desire and his imagination, heated
by the day before, awaited impatiently the hour to read in
this breviary of gallantry, and was called ; and the conspiracy
of the litanies commenced again, and Blanche did not fail
to fall asleep. This time the said René fondled with his
hand the pretty limb, and even ventured so far as to verify
if the polished knee and its surroundings were satin. At
this sight the poor child, armed against his desire, so great
was his fear, dared only make brief devotion and curt
caresses, and although he kissed softly this fair surface, he
remained bashful, the which, feeling by the senses of her

soul and the intelligence of her body, the seneschal's lady who took great care not to move, called out to him—" Ah, René, I am asleep."

Hearing what he believed to be a stern reproach, the page frightened ran away, leaving the books, the task, and all. Thereupon, the seneschal's better half added this prayer to the litany—" Holy Virgin, how difficult children are to make."

At dinner her page perspired all down his back while waiting on his lady and her lord ; but he was very much surprised when he received from Blanche the most shameless of all glances that ever woman cast, and very pleasant and powerful it was, seeing that it changed this child into a man of courage. Now, the same evening Bruyn staying a little longer than was his custom in his own apartment, the page went in search of Blanche, and found her asleep, and made her dream a beautiful dream.

He knocked off the chains that weighed so heavily upon her, and so plentifully bestowed upon her the sweets of love, that the surplus would have sufficed to render two others blessed with the joys of maternity.

So then the minx, seizing the page by the head and squeezing him to her, cried out—" Oh, René ! thou hast awakened me !"

And in fact, there was no sleep could stand against it, and it is certain that saints must sleep very soundly. From this business, without other mystery, and by a benign faculty which is the assisting principle of spouses, the sweet and graceful plumage, suitable to cuckolds, was placed upon the head of the good husband without his experiencing the slightest shock.

After this sweet repast, the seneschal's lady took kindly to her siesta after the French fashion, while Bruyn took his

according to the Saracen. But by the said siesta she learned
how the good youth of the page had a better taste than that
of the old seneschal, and at night she buried herself in the
sheets far away from her husband, whom she found strong
and stale. And from sleeping and waking up in the day,
from taking siestas and saying litanies, the seneschal's wife
felt growing within her that treasure for which she had so
often and so ardently sighed ; but now she liked more the
commencement than the fructifying of it.

You may be sure that René knew how to read, not only
in books, but in the eyes of his sweet lady, for whom he
would have leapt into a flaming pile, had it been her wish
he should do so. When well and amply, more than a
hundred times, the train had been laid by them, the little
lady became anxious about her soul and the future of her
friend the page. Now one rainy day, as they were playing
at touch-tag, like two children, innocent from head to foot,
Blanche, who was always caught, said to him—

" Come here, René ; do you know that while I have
committed only venial sins because I was asleep, you have
committed mortal ones ?"

" Ah, Madame !" said he, " where then will God stow
away all the damned if that is to sin ?"

Blanche burst out laughing, and kissed his forehead.

" Be quiet, you naughty boy ; it is a question of paradise,
and we must live there together if you wish always to be
with me."

" Oh, my paradise is here."

" Leave off," said she. " You are a little wretch—a
scapegrace who does not think of that which I love—yourself ! You do not know that I am with child, and that in a
little while I shall be no more able to conceal it than my
nose. Now, what will the abbot say ? What will my lord
say ? He will kill you if he puts himself in a passion. My
advice is, little one, that you go to the Abbot of Marmoustiers,
confess your sins to him, asking him to see what had better
be done concerning my seneschal."

" Alas," said the artful page, " if I tell the secret of our
joys, he will put his interdict upon our love."

" Very likely," said she ; " but thy happiness in the other world is a thing so precious to me."

" Do you wish it, my darling ?"

" Yes," replied she, rather faintly.

" Well, I will go, but sleep again that I may bid thee adieu."

And the couple recited the litany of Farewells as if they had both foreseen that their love must finish in its April. And on the morrow, more to save his dear lady than to save himself, and also to obey her, René de Jallanges set out towards the great monastery.

And on the morrow, more to save his dear lady than to save himself, and also to obey her, René de Jallanges set out towards the great monastery.

HOW THE SAID LOVE-SIN WAS REPENTED OF AND LED TO GREAT MOURNING.

"Good God!" cried the abbot, when the page had chanted the Kyrie eleison of his sweet sins, "thou art the accomplice of a great felony, and thou hast betrayed thy lord. Dost thou know, page of darkness, that for this thou wilt burn through all eternity? and dost thou know what it is to lose for ever the heaven above for a perishable and change- ful moment here below? Unhappy wretch! I see thee precipitated for ever in the gulfs of hell unless thou payest to God in this world that which thou owest him for such offence."

Thereupon, the good old abbot, who was of that flesh of which saints are made, and who had great authority in the country of Touraine, terrified the young man by a heap of representations, Christian discourses, remembrances of the commandments of the Church, and a thousand eloquent things—as many as a devil could say in six weeks to seduce a maiden—but so many that René, who was in the loyal fervour of innocence, made his submission to the good abbot. The said abbot, wishing to make for ever a good and virtuous man of this child, now in a fair way to be a wicked one, commanded him first to go and prostrate himself before his lord, to confess his conduct to him, and then if he escaped from this confession, to depart instantly for the Crusades, and go straight to the Holy Land, where he should remain fifteen years of the time appointed to give battle to the Infidels.

"Alas, my reverend father," said he, quite unmoved, "will fifteen years be enough to acquit me of so much pleasure? Ah! if you but knew, I have had joy enough for a thousand years."

"God will be generous. Go," replied the old abbot, "and sin no more. On this account *ego te absolvo*."

Poor René returned thereupon with great contrition to the castle of Roche-Corbon, and the first person he met was the seneschal, who was polishing up his arms, helmets, gauntlets, and other things. He was sitting on a great marble bench in the open air, and was amusing himself by making shine again the splendid trappings which brought back to him the merry pranks in the Holy Land, the good jokes, and the wenches, *et cetera*. When René fell upon his knees before him, the good lord was much astonished.

"What is it?" said he.

"My lord," replied René, "order these people to retire."

Which the servants having done, the page confessed his fault, recounting how he had assailed his lady in her sleep, and that for certain he had made her a mother in imitation of the man and the saint, and came by order of the confessor to put himself at the disposition of the offended person. Having said which, René de Jallanges cast down his lovely eyes, which had produced all the mischief, and remained abashed, prostrate without fear, his arms hanging down, his head bare, awaiting his punishment, and humbling himself to God. The seneschal was not so white that he could not become whiter, and now he blanched like linen newly dried, remaining dumb with passion. And this old man, who had not in his veins the vital force to procreate a child, found in this moment of fury more vigour than was necessary to undo a man. He seized with his hairy right hand his heavy club, lifted it, brandished it and adjusted it so easily that you could have thought it a bowl at a game of skittles, to bring it down upon the pale forehead of the said René, who, knowing that he was greatly in fault towards his lord, remained placid, and stretching his neck, thought that he was about to expiate his sin for his sweetheart in this world and in the other.

But his fair youth, and all the natural seductions of this sweet crime, found grace before the tribunal of the heart of this old man, although Bruyn was still severe, and throwing his club away on to a dog who was catching beetles, he cried out, " May a thousand million claws, tear during all eternity, all the entrails of him, who made him, who planted the oak, that made the chair, on which thou hast antlered me—and the same to those who engendered thee, cursed page of misfortune ! Get thee to the devil, whence thou camest— go out from before me, from the castle, from the country, and stay not here one moment more than is necessary, otherwise I will surely prepare for thee a death by slow fire that shall make thee curse twenty times an hour thy villanous and ribald partner !"

Hearing the commencement of these little speeches of the seneschal, whose youth came back in his oaths, the page ran away, escaping the rest : and he did well. Bruyn, burning with a fierce rage, gained the gardens speedily, reviling everything by the way, striking and swearing ; he even knocked over three large pans held by one of his servants, who was carrying the mess to the dogs, and he was so beside himself that he would have killed a labourer for a " thank you." He soon perceived his unmaidenly maiden, who was looking towards the road to the monastery, waiting for the page, and unaware that she would never see him again.

" Ah, my lady ! by the devil's red three-pronged fork, am I a swallower of tarrididdles and a child, to believe that you are so fashioned that a page can behave in this manner and you not know it ? By the death ! By the head ! By the blood !"

" Hold !" she replied, seeing that the mine was sprung, " I knew it well enough, but as you had not instructed me in these matters I thought that I was dreaming !"

The great ire of the seneschal melted like snow in the sun, for the direst anger of God himself would have vanished at a smile from Blanche.

" May a thousand millions of devils carry off this alien child ! I swear that——"

" There ! there ! do not swear," said she. " If it is not yours, it is mine ; and the other night did you not tell me you loved everything that came from me ?"

Thereupon she ran on with such a lot of arguments, hard words, complaints, quarrels, tears, and other paternosters of women ; such as—firstly, the estates would not have to be returned to the king ; that never had a child been brought more innocently into the world, that this, that that, a thousand things; until the good cuckold relented, and Blanche, seizing a propitious interruption, said—

" And where is the page ?"

" Gone to the devil !"

" What, have you killed him?" said she. She turned pale and tottered.

Bruyn did not know what would become of him when he saw thus fall all the happiness of his old age, and he would to save her have shewn her this page. He ordered him to be sought, but René had run off at full speed, fearing he should be killed; and departed for the lands beyond the seas, in order to accomplish his vow of religion. When Blanche had learned from the above-mentioned abbot the penitence imposed upon her well beloved, she fell into a state of great melancholy, saying at times, " Where is he, the poor unfortunate, who is in the middle of great dangers for love of me ?"

And always kept on asking, like a child who gives its mother no rest until its request be granted it. At these lamentations the poor seneschal, feeling himself to blame, endeavoured to do a thousand things, putting one out of the question, in order to make Blanche happy ; but nothing was equal to the sweet caresses of the page. However, she

She fell into a state of great melancholy, saying at times, " Where is the
poor unfortunate who is in the middle of great dangers for love of me ?"

had one day the child so much desired.   You may be sure
that was a fine festival for the good cuckold, for the

resemblance to the father was distinctly engraved upon the
face of this sweet fruit of love.   Blanche consoled herself
greatly, and picked up again a little of her old gaiety and
flower of innocence, which rejoiced the aged hours of the
seneschal.   From constantly seeing the little one run about,
watching its laughs answer those of the countess, he
finished by loving it, and would have been in a great rage
with any one who had not believed him its father.

Now as the adventure of Blanche and her page had not
been carried beyond the castle, it was related throughout
Touraine that Messire Bruyn had still found himself
sufficiently in funds to afford a child.   Intact remained the
virtue of Blanche, and by the quintessence of instruction
drawn by her from the natural reservoir of women, she
recognised how necessary it was to be silent concerning the
venial sin with which her child was covered.   So she
became modest and good, and was cited as a virtuous
person.   And then to make use of him she experimented on
the goodness of her good man, and without giving him
leave to go farther than her chin, since she looked upon

herself as belonging to René, Blanche, in return for the
flowers of age which Bruyn offered her, coddled him, smiled
upon him, kept him merry, and fondled him with pretty
ways and tricks, which good wives bestow upon the
husbands they deceive; and all so well, that the seneschal
did not wish to die, squatted comfortably in his chair, and
the more he lived the more he became partial to life. But
to be brief, one night he died without knowing where he
was going, for he said to Blanche, " Ho ! ho ! my dear, I
see thee no longer ! Is it night ?"

It was the death of the just, and he had well merited it as
a reward for his labours in the Holy Land.

Blanche held for this death a great and true mourning,

weeping for him as one weeps for one's father. She remained
melancholy, without wishing to lend her ear to the music of
a second wedding, for which she was praised by all good
people, who knew not that she had a husband in her heart,
a life in hope; but she was the greater part of her time
widow in fact and widow in heart, because hearing no news
of her lover at the Crusades, the poor countess reputed him

dead, and during certain nights seeing him wounded and lying at full length, she would wake up in tears. She lived thus for fourteen years in the remembrance of one day of happiness. Finally, one day when she had with her certain ladies of Touraine, and they were talking together after dinner, behold her little boy, who was at that time about thirteen and a half, and resembled René more than it is allowable for a child to resemble his father, and had nothing of the Sire Bruyn about him but his name—behold the little one, a madcap and pretty like his mother, who came in from the garden, running, perspiring, panting, jumping, scattering all things in his way, after the uses and customs of infancy, and who ran straight to his well-beloved mother, jumped into her lap, and interrupting the conversation, cried out—

"Oh, mother, I want to speak to you, I have seen in the courtyard a pilgrim, who squeezed me very tight."

"Ah!" cried the chatelaine, hurrying towards one of the servants who had charge of the young count and watched over his precious days, "I have forbidden you ever to leave my son in the hands of strangers, not even in those of the holiest man in the world. You quit my service."

"Alas! my lady," replied the old equerry, quite overcome, "this one wished him no harm for he wept while kissing him passionately."

"He wept?" said she; "ah! it's the father."

Having said which, she leaned her head upon the chair

in which she was sitting, and which you may be sure was the chair in which she had sinned.

Hearing these strange words, the ladies were so surprised that at first they did not perceive that the seneschal's widow was dead, without its ever being known if her sudden death was caused by her sorrow at the departure of her lover, who, faithful to his vow, did not wish to see her, or from great joy at his return and the hope of getting the interdict removed which the Abbot of Marmoustiers had placed upon their loves. And there was great mourning for her, for the Sire de Jallanges lost his spirits when he saw his lady laid in the ground, and became a monk of Marmoustiers, which at that time was called by some Maimoustier, as much as to say *Maius Monasterium*, the largest monastery, and it was indeed the finest in all France.

The King's Sweetheart.

THE KING'S SWEETHEART.

THERE lived at this time at the forges of the Pont-au-Change, a goldsmith whose daughter was talked about in Paris on account of her great beauty, and renowned above all things for her exceeding gracefulness. There were those who sought her favours by the usual tricks of love, but others offered large sums of money to the father to give them his daughter in lawful wedlock, the which pleased him not a little.

One of his neighbours, a parliamentary advocate, who by selling his cunning devices to the public had acquired as many lands as a dog has fleas, took it into his head to offer the said father a domain in consideration of his consent to this marriage, which he ardently desired to undertake. To this arrangement our goldsmith was nothing loth. He bargained away his daughter, without taking into consideration the fact that her patched-up old suitor had the features of an ape and had scarcely a tooth in his jaws. The smell which emanated from his mouth did not however disturb his own nostrils, although he was filthy and high flavoured, as are all those who pass their lives amid the smoke of chimneys, yellow parchment, and other black proceedings. Immediately the sweet girl saw him she exclaimed, "Great Heaven! I would rather not have him."

"That concerns me not," said the father, who had taken a violent fancy to the proffered domain. "I give him to you for a husband. You must get on as well as you can together. That is his business now, and his duty is to make himself agreeable to you."

"Is it so?" said she. "Well then, before I obey your orders I'll let him know what he may expect."

And the same evening, after supper, when the love-sick man of law was pleading his cause, telling her he was mad for her, and promising her a life of ease and luxury, she taking him up, quickly remarked—

"My father has sold me to you, but if you take me, you will make a bad bargain, seeing that I would rather offer myself to the passers-by than to you. I promise you a disloyalty that shall only finish with death—yours or mine."

Then she began to weep, like all young maidens will before they become experienced, for afterwards they never cry with their eyes. The good advocate took this strange behaviour for one of those artifices by which the women seek to fan the flames of love and turn the devotion of their admirers into the more tender caress and more daring osculation that speak a husband's right. So that the knave took little notice of it, but laughing at the complaints of the charming creature, asked her to fix the day.

"To-morrow," replied she, "for the sooner this odious marriage takes place, the sooner I shall be free to have gallants and to lead the gay life of those who love where it pleases them."

Thereupon this foolish fellow—as firmly fixed as a fly in a glue pot—went away, made his preparations, spoke at the Palace, ran to the High Court, bought dispensations, and conducted his purchase more quickly than he had ever done one before, thinking only of the lovely girl. Meanwhile the king, who had just returned from a journey, heard nothing spoken of at court but the marvellous beauty of the jeweller's daughter who had refused a thousand crowns from this one, snubbed that one ; in fact, would yield to no one, but turned up her nose at the finest young men of the city, gentlemen who would have forfeited their seat in paradise only to possess one day, this little dragon of virtue.

The good king, who was a judge of such game, strolled into the town, passed the forges, and entered the goldsmith's shop, for the purpose of buying jewels for the lady of his heart, but at the same time to bargain for the most precious jewel in the shop. The king not taking a fancy to the jewels, or they not being to his taste, the good man looked in a secret drawer for a big white diamond.

"Sweetheart," said he, to the daughter, while her father's

nose was buried in the drawer, "sweetheart, you were not made to sell precious stones, but to receive them, and if you were to give me all the little rings in the place to choose from, I know one that many here are mad for; that pleases me; to which I should ever be subject and servant; and whose price the whole kingdom of France could never pay."

"Ah, sire!" replied the maid, "I shall be married to-morrow, but if you will lend me the dagger that is in your belt, I will defend my honour, and you shall take it, that the gospel may be observed wherein it says, 'Render unto Cæsar the things which be Cæsar's.'"

Immediately the king gave her the little dagger, and her brave reply rendered him so amorous that he lost his appetite. He had an apartment prepared, intending to lodge

"Sweetheart," said he, to the daughter, while the father's nose
was buried in the drawer, "you were not made to sell precious
stones, but to receive them."

his new lady-love in the Rue à l'Hirundelle, in one of his
palaces.

And now behold my advocate, in a great hurry to get
married, to the disgust of his rivals, leading his bride to the
altar to the clang of bells and the sound of music, so timed as
to provoke the qualms of diarrhœa. In the evening, after the
ball, comes he into the nuptial chamber, where should be
reposing his lovely bride. No longer is she a lovely bride—
but a fury—a wild she-devil, who, seated in an arm-chair,
refuses her share of her lord's couch, and sits defiantly before
the fire warming at the same time her ire and her calves.

The good husband, quite astonished, kneels down gently
before her, inviting her to the first passage of arms in
that charming battle which heralds a first night of love ;
but she utters not a word, and when he tries to raise her
garment, only just to glance at the charms that have cost
him so dear, she gives him a slap that makes his bones rattle,
and refuses to utter a syllable.

This amusement, however, by no means displeased our
friend the advocate, who saw at the end of his troubles
that which you can as well imagine as did he ; so played he

his share of the game manfully, taking cheerfully the punishment bestowed upon him. By so much hustling about, scuffling, and struggling he managed at last to tear away a sleeve, to slit a petticoat, until he was able to place his hand upon his own property. This bold endeavour brought Madame to her feet, and drawing the king's dagger, "What would you with me?" she cried.

"Everything," answered he.

"Ha! I should be a great fool to give myself against my inclination! If you fancied you would find my virtue unarmed you made a great error. Behold the poniard of the king, with which I will kill you if you make the semblance of a step toward me."

So saying, she took a cinder, and having still her eye upon her lord she drew a circle on the floor, adding, "These are the confines of the king's domain. Beware how you pass them."

The advocate, with whose ideas of love-making the dagger sadly interfered, stood quite discomfited, but at the same time he heard the cruel speech of his tormentor he caught sight through the slits and tears in her robe of a sweet sample of a plump white thigh, and such voluptuous specimens of hidden mysteries, et cetera, that death seemed sweet to him if he could only taste of them a little. So that he rushed within the domain of the king, saying, " I mind not death." In fact he came with such force that his charmer fell backwards on to the bed, but keeping her presence of mind she defended herself so gallantly that the advocate enjoyed no further advantage than a knock at the door that would not admit him, and he gained as well a little stab from the poniard which did not wound him deeply, so that it did not cost him very dearly, his attack upon the realm of his sovereign. But maddened with this slight advantage, he cried, "I cannot live without the possession of that lovely body, and those marvels of love. Kill me then!"

And again he attacked the royal preserves. The young beauty, whose head was full of the king, was not even touched by this great love, said gravely, " If you menace me further, it is not you but myself I will kill." She glared at him so savagely that the poor man was quite terrified, and commenced to deplore the evil hour in which he had taken her to wife, and thus the night which should have been so joyous, was passed in tears, lamentations, prayers, and ejaculations. In vain he tempted her with promises ; she should eat out of gold, she should be a great lady, he would buy houses and lands for her. Oh! if she would only let him break one lance with her in the sweet conflict of love, he would leave her for ever and pass the remainder of his life according to her fantasy. But she, still unyielding, said she would permit him to die, and that was the only thing he could do to please her.

"I have not deceived you," said she. "Agreeable to my promise, I shall give myself to the king, making you a present of the pedlars, chance passers, and street loungers with whom I threatened you."

When the day broke she put on her wedding garments and waited patiently till the poor husband had to depart to his offices on clients' business, and then ran out into the

town to seek the king. But she had not gone a bow-shot from the house before one of the king's servants who had watched the house from dawn, stopped her with the question---

His friends and neighbours edified his ears with as many taunts and jeers
as Saint Jacques had the honour of receiving in Compostella.

" Do you not seek the king?"

" Yes," said she.

" Good ; then allow me to be your good friend," said the subtle courtier. " I ask your aid and protection, as now I give you mine."

With that he told her what sort of man the king was, which was his weak side, that he was passionate one day and silent the next, that she would be luxuriously lodged and well kept, but that she must keep the king well in hand ; in short, he chatted so pleasantly that the time passed quickly until she found herself in the Hôtel de l'Hirundelle where afterwards lived Madame d'Estampes. The poor husband shed scalding tears, when he found his little bird had flown, and became melancholy and pensive. His friends and neighbours edified his ears with as many taunts and jeers as Saint Jacques had the honour of receiving in Compostella, but the poor fellow took it so to heart, that at last they tried rather to assuage his grief. These artful compeers by a species of legal chicanery, decreed that the good man was not a cuckold, seeing that his wife had refused a con-summation, and if the planter of horns had been any one but the king, the said marriage might have been dissolved ;

but the amorous spouse was wretched unto death at my lady's trick. However, he left her to the king, determining one day

to have her to himself, and thinking that a life-long shame
would not be too dear a payment for a night with her.
One must love well to love like that, eh? and there are
many worldly ones, who mock at such affection. But he,
still thinking of her, neglected his cases and his clients, his
robberies and everything. He went to the palace like a
miser searching for a lost sixpence, bowed down, melancholy,
and absent-minded, so much so, that one day he relieved
himself against the robe of a counsellor, believing all the
while he stood against a wall. Meanwhile, the beautiful
girl was loved night and day by the king, who could not
tear himself from her embraces, because in amorous play
she was so excellent, knowing as well how to fan the flame
of love as to extinguish it—to-day snubbing him, to-
morrow petting him, never the same, and with it a thousand
little tricks to charm an ardent lover.

A lord of Bridoré killed himself through her, because she
would not receive his embraces, although he offered her his

land, Bridoré in Touraine.
Of these gallants of Tou-
raine, who gave an estate
for one tilt with love's
lance, there are none left.
This death made the fair
one sad, and since her confessor laid the blame of it
upon her, she determined
for the future to accept all
domains and secretly ease their owners' amorous pains
for the better saving of their souls from perdition. 'Twas
thus she commenced to build up that great fortune which
made her a person of consideration in the town. By
this means she prevented many gallant gentlemen from
perishing, playing her game so well, and inventing such
fine stories, that his Majesty little guessed how much
she aided him in securing the happiness of his subjects.
The fact is, she had such a hold over him that she
could have made him believe the floor was the ceiling,
which was perhaps easier for him to think than any one

The advocate Féron.

else seeing that at the Rue d'Hirundelle my lord king passed the greater portion of his time embracing her always as though he would see if such a lovely article would wear away : but he wore himself out first, poor man, seeing that he eventually died from excess of love. Although she took care to grant her favours only to the best and noblest in the court, and that such occasions were rare as miracles, there were not wanting those among her enemies and rivals who declared that for 10,000 crowns a simple gentleman might taste the pleasures of his sovereign, which was false above all falseness, for when her lord taxed her with it, did she not reply, " Abominable wretches ! curse the devils who put this idea in your head ! I never yet did have man who spent less than 30,000 crowns upon me."

The king, although vexed, could not repress a smile, and kept her on a month to silence scandal. At last, la demoiselle de Pisseleu, anxious to obtain her place, brought about her ruin. Many would have liked to be ruined in the same way, seeing she was taken by a young lord who was happy with her, the fires of love in her being still un-quenched. But to take up my thread again. One day that the king's sweetheart was passing through the town in her litter to buy laces, furs, velvets, broideries, and other ammunition, and so charmingly attired, and looking so lovely, that any one, especially the clerks, would have believed the heavens were open above them, behold, her good man, who comes upon her near the old cross. She, at that time lazily swinging her charming little foot over the side of the litter, drew in her head as though she had seen an adder. She was a good wife, for I know some who would have proudly passed their husbands, to their shame and to the great disrespect of conjugal rights.

" What is the matter ?" asked one M. de Lannoy, who humbly accompanied her.

" Nothing," she whispered ; " but that person is my husband. Poor man, how changed he looks. Formerly he was the picture of a monkey ; to-day he is the very image of Job."

The poor advocate stood open-mouthed. His heart

beat rapidly at the sight of that little foot—of that wife so wildly loved.

Observing which, the Sire de Lannoy said to him, with courtly insolence—

" If you are her husband, is that any reason you should stop her passage ?"

At this she burst out laughing, and the good husband, instead of killing her bravely, shed scalding tears at that laugh which pierced his heart, his soul, his everything, so much that he nearly tumbled over an old citizen whom the sight of the king's sweetheart had driven against the wall. The aspect of this sweet flower, which had been his in the bud, but far from him had spread its lovely leaves ; of the fairy figure, the voluptuous bust—all this made the poor advocate more wretched and more mad for her than it is possible to express in words. You must have been madly in love with a woman who refused your advances thoroughly to understand the agony of this unhappy man. Rare indeed is it to be so infatuated as was he. He swore that life, fortune, honour—all might go, but that for once at least he would be flesh to flesh with her, and make so grand a repast off her dainty body as would suffice him all his life. He passed the night saying, " Oh yes ; ah ! I'll have her !" and " Curses, am I not her husband ?" and " Devil take me," striking himself on the forehead and tossing about. There are chances and occasions which occur so opportunely in this world that little-minded men refuse them credence, saying they are supernatural, but men of high intellect know them to be true because they could not be invented. One of the chances came to the poor advocate, even the day after that terrible one which had been so sore a trial to him. One of his clients, a man of good renown, who had his audiences with the king, came one morning to the advocate, saying that he required immediately a large sum of money, about 12,000 crowns. To which the artful fellow replied, 12,000 crowns were not so often met at the corner of a street as that which often is

seen at the corner of a street ; that besides the sureties and
guarantees of interest, it was necessary to find a man who
had about him 12,000 crowns, and that those gentlemen
were not numerous in Paris, big city as it was, and various
other things of a like character the man of cunning remarked.

" Is it true, my lord, that you have a hungry and relentless
creditor ?" said he.

" Yes, yes," replied the other, " it concerns the mistress
of the king.   Don't breathe a syllable ; but this evening, in
consideration of 20,000 crowns, and my domain of Brie, I
shall take her measure."

Upon this the advocate blanched, and the courtier perceived he touched a tender point.   As he had only lately
returned from the wars, he did not know that the lovely
woman adored by the king had a husband.

" You appear ill," he said.

" I have a fever," replied the knave.

" But is it to her that you give the contract and the
money ?"

" Yes."

" Who then manages the bargain   is it she also?"

" No," said the noble ; " her little arrangements are concluded through a servant of hers, the cleverest little ladies'-
maid that ever was.   She's sharper than mustard, and these
nights stolen from the king have lined her pockets well."

" I know a Lombard who could accommodate you.   But
nothing can be done ; of the 12,000 crowns you shall not
have a brass farthing if this same ladies'-maid does not come
here to take the price of the article that is so great an
alchemist, that turns blood into gold, by Heaven !"

" It will be a good trick to make her sign the receipt,"
replied the lord, laughing.

The servant came faithfully to the rendezvous with the
advocate, who had begged the lord to bring her.   The
ducats looked bright and beautiful.   There they lay, all in
a row, like nuns going to vespers.   Spread out upon the
table they would have made a donkey smile, even if he were
being gutted alive ; so lovely, so splendid, were those brave

noble young piles. The good advocate, however, had prepared this view for no ass, for the little handmaiden looked
longing at the golden heap, and muttered a prayer at the
sight of them. Seeing which, the
husband whispered in her ear these
golden words, "These are for you."

" Ah !" said she ; " I have never
been so well paid."

" My dear," replied the dea
man, " you shall have them without being troubled with me ; and,
turning her round, " Your client
has not told you who I am, eh ? No ? Learn then, I am
the husband of the lady whom the king has debauched,
and whom you serve. Carry her these crowns, and come
back here. I will hand over yours to you on a condition
which will be to your taste."

The servant did as she was bidden, and being very curious
to know how she could get 12,000 crowns without sleeping
with the advocate, was very soon back again.

" Now, my little one," said he, "here are 12,000
crowns. With that sum I could buy lands, men, women,
and the conscience of three priests at least ; so that I
believe if I give it you I can have you, body, soul, and
toe nails. And I shall have faith in you like an advocate.
I expect that you will go to the lord who expects to pass the
night with my wife, and you will deceive him, by telling him
that the king is coming to supper with her, and that to-night
he must seek his little amusements elsewhere. By so doing
I shall be able to take his place and the king's."

" But how ?" said she.

" Oh !" replied he ; " I have bought you, you and your
tricks. You wont have to look at these crowns twice without
finding me a way to have my wife. In bringing this conjunction about you commit no sin. It is a work of piety to
bring together two people whose hands only have been put
one into the other, and that by the priest."

" By my faith, come," said she ; " after supper the lights

will be put out, and you can enjoy Madame if you remain silent. Luckily, on these joyful occasions she cries more than she speaks, and asks questions with her hands alone, for she is very modest, and does not like loose jokes, like the ladies of the Court."

" Oh," cried the advocate, " look, take the 12,000 crowns, and I promise you twice as much more if I get by fraud that which belongs to me by right."

Then he arranged the hour, the door, the signal, and all; and the servant went away, bearing with her on the back of the mules the golden treasure wrung by fraud and trickery from the widow and the orphan, and they were all going to that place where everything goes—save our lives, which come from it. Now behold my advocate, who shaves himself, scents himself, goes without onions for dinner that his breath may be sweet, and does everything to make himself as presentable as a gallant signor. He gives himself the airs of a young dandy, tries to be lithe and frisky and to disguise his ugly face ; he might try all he knew, he always smelt of the musty lawyer. He was not so clever as the pretty washerwoman of Portillon who one day wishing to appear at her best before one of her lovers, got rid of a disagreeable odour in a manner well known to young women of an inventive turn of mind. But our crafty fellow fancied himself the nicest man in the world, although in spite of his drugs and perfumes he was really the nastiest. He dressed himself in his thinnest clothes although the cold pinched him like a rope collar, and sallied forth, quickly gaining the Rue d'Hirundelle. There he had to wait some time. But just as he was beginning to think he had been made a fool of, and just as it was quite dark, the maid came down and opened the door to him and the good husband slipped gleefully into the king's apartment. The girl locked him carefully in a cupboard that was close to his wife's bed, and through a crack he feasted his eyes upon her beauty, for she undressed herself before the fire, and put on a thin night-gown, through which her charms were plainly visible. Believing herself alone with her maid she made those little jokes that women will when undressing. "Am I not worth 20,000 crowns to-night? Is that overpaid with a castle in Brie?"

And saying this she gently raised two white supports, firm as rocks, which had well sustained many assaults, seeing they had been furiously attacked and had not softened. "My shoulders alone are worth a kingdom; no king could make their equal. But I am tired of this life. That which is hard work is no plea- sure." The little maid smiled, and her lovely mistress said to her, " I should like to see you in my place." Then the maid laughed outright, saying—

" Be quiet, Madame, he is there."

" Who?"

" Your husband."

" Which?"

" The real one."

" Chut!" said Madame.

And her maid told her the whole story, wishing to keep her favour and the 12,000 crowns as well.

" Oh well, he shall have his money's worth. I'll give his desires time to cool. If he tastes me may I lose my beauty and become as ugly as a monkey's baby! You get into bed in my place and thus gain the 12,000 crowns. Go and tell him that he must take himself off early in the morning in order that I may not find out your trick upon me, and just before dawn I will get in by his side."

The poor husband was freezing and his teeth were chattering, and the chambermaid coming to the cupboard on pretence of getting some linen, said to him, " Your hour of bliss approaches. Madame to-night has made grand pre-parations and you will be well served. But work without whistling, otherwise I shall be lost."

At last, when the good husband was on the point of

perishing with cold, the lights were put out. The maid cried softly in the curtains to the king's sweetheart, that his lordship was there, and jumped into the bed, while her mistress went out as if she had been the chambermaid. The advocate, released from his cold hiding-place, rolled rapturously into the warm sheets, thinking to himself, "Oh! this is good!" To tell the truth, the maid gave him his money's worth—and the good man thought of the difference between the profusion of royal houses and the niggardly ways of the citizens' wives. The servant laughing, played her part marvellously well, regaling the knave with gentle cries, shiverings, convulsions and tossings about, like a new-caught fish on the grass, giving little Ah! ah's! in default of other words; and as often as the request was made by her, so often was it complied with by the advocate, who dropped off to sleep at last, like an empty pocket. But before finishing, the lover, who wished to preserve a souvenir of this sweet night of love, by a dexterous turn, plucked out one of his wife's hairs, where from I know not, seeing I was not there, and kept in

his hand this precious gage of the warm virtue of that lovely creature. Towards the morning, when the cock crew, the wife slipped in beside her husband, and pretended to sleep. Then the maid tapped gently on the happy man's forehead, whispering in his ear, "It is time, get into your clothes and off you go—it's daylight." The good man grieved to lose his treasure, and wished to see the source of his vanished happiness."

"Oh! oh!" said he, proceeding to compare certain things, "I've got light hair, and this is dark."

"What have you done?" said the servant; "Madame will see she has been duped."

"But, look."

"Ah!" said she, with an air of disdain, "do you not know, you who know everything, that that which is plucked dies and discolours?" and thereupon roaring with laughter at the good joke, she pushed him out of doors. This became known. The poor advocate, named Féron, died of shame, seeing that he was the only one who had not his own wife ; while she, who from this was called La belle Féronière, married, after leaving the king, a young lord, Count of Buzançois. And in her old days she would relate the story, laughingly adding, that she had never scented the knave's flavour.

This teaches us not to attach ourselves more than we can help to wives who refuse to support our yoke.

Mau-cinge and Pasquerette.

THE DEVIL'S HEIR.

THERE once was a good old Canon of Notre Dame
de Paris, who lived in a fine house of his own, near
St. Pierre-aux-Bœufs, in the Parvis. This canon had come
a simple priest to Paris, naked as a dagger without its sheath.
But since he was found to be a handsome man, well furnished with everything, and so well constituted, that if
necessary he was able to do the work of many without
doing himself much harm, he gave himself up earnestly to
the confessing of ladies, giving to the melancholy a gentle absolution, to the sick a drachm of his balm, to all some little
dainty. He was so well known for his discretion, his
benevolence, and other ecclesiastical qualities, that he had
customers at Court. Then in order not to awaken the
jealousy of the officials, that of the husbands and others, in
short, to endow with sanctity these good and profitable practices, the Lady Desquerdes gave him a bone of St. Victor
by virtue of which all the miracles were performed. And to
the curious it was said, " He has a bone which will cure everything ;" and to this, no one found anything to reply, because
it was not seemly to suspect relics. Beneath the shade of

his cassock, the good priest had the best of reputations, that of a man valiant under arms. So lived he like a king. He made money with holy water; sprinkled and transmitted the holy water into good wine. More than that, his name

lay snugly in all the et ceteras of the notaries, in wills or in caudicils, which certain people have falsely written CODICIL, seeing that the word is derived from *cauda*, as if to say the tail of the legacy. In fact, the good old Long Skirts would have been made an archbishop if he had only said in joke, " I should like to put on a mitre for a head-kerchief in order to have my head warmer." Of all the benefices offered to him, he chose only a simple canon's stall, to keep the good profits of the confessional. But one day the courageous canon found himself weak in the back, seeing that he was all sixty-eight years old, and had held many confessionals. Then thinking over all his good works, he thought it about time to cease his apostolic labours, the more so, as he possessed about one hundred thousand crowns earned by the sweat of his body. From that day he only confessed ladies of high lineage, and did it very well. So that it was said at Court that in spite of the efforts of the best young clerks there was still no one but the Canon o St. Pierre-aux-Bœufs to properly bleach the soul of a lady of condition. Then at length the canon became by force of

nature a fine nonagenarian, snowy about the head, with
trembling hands, but square as a tower having spat so much
without coughing, that he coughed now without being able
to spit; no longer rising from his chair, he who had so often
risen for humanity ; but drinking dry, eating heartily, saying
nothing, but having all the appearance of a living Canon of
Notre Dame. Seeing the immobility of the aforesaid canon ;
seeing the stories of his evil life which for some time had circulated among the common people, always ignorant ; seeing his
dumb seclusion, his flourishing health, his young old age
and other things too numerous to mention—there were
certain people who to do the marvellous and injure our holy
religion, went about saying that the true canon was long
since dead, and that for more than fifty years the devil had
taken possession of the old priest's body. In fact, it seemed
to his former customers that the devil only could by his
great heat have furnished those hermetic distillations, that
they remembered to have obtained on demand from this
good confessor, who always had *le diable au corps*. But as this
devil had been undoubtedly cooked and ruined by them, and
that for a queen of twenty years he would not have moved,
well-disposed people and those not wanting in sense, or the
citizens who argued about everything, people who found lice
in bald heads, demanded why the devil rested under the form
of a canon, went to the church of Notre Dame at the hours
when the canons usually go, and ventured so far as to sniff
the perfume of the incense, taste the holy water, and a
thousand other things. To these heretical propositions some
said that doubtless the devil wished to convert himself, and
others that he remained in the shape of the canon to mock
at the three nephews and heirs of this said brave confessor
and make them wait until the day of their own death for the
ample succession of this uncle, to whom they paid great
attention every day, going to look if the good man had his
eyes open, and in fact found him always with his eye clear,
bright, and piercing as the eye of a basilisk, which pleased
them greatly, since they loved their uncle very much—in words.
On this subject an old woman related that for certain the
canon was the devil, because his two nephews, the procureur

and the captain, conducting their uncle at night, without lamp or lantern, returning from a supper at the penitentiary's, had caused him by accident to tumble over a heap of stones gathered together to raise the statue of St. Christopher. At first the old man had struck fire in falling, but was, amid the cries of his dear nephews and by the light of the torches they came to seek at her house, found standing up as straight

as a skittle and as gay as a weaving whirl, exclaiming that the good wine of the penitentiary had given him the courage to sustain this shock and that his bones were exceedingly hard and had sustained rude assaults. The good nephews believing him dead, were much astonished, and perceived that the day that was to despatch their uncle was a long way off, seeing that at the business stones were of no use. So that they did not falsely call him their good uncle, seeing that he was of good quality. Certain scandal-mongers said that the canon found so many stones in his path that he stayed

at home not to be ill with the stone, and the fear of worse
was the cause of his seclusion.

Of all these sayings and rumours, it remains that the old
canon, devil or not, kept his house, refused to die, and
had three heirs with whom he lived as with his sciaticas,
lumbagos, and other appendage of human life. Of the
said three heirs, one was the wickedest soldier ever born
of a woman, and he must have considerably hurt her
in breaking his egg, since he was born with teeth and
bristles. So that he ate twofold, for the present and the
future, keeping wenches whose cost he paid; inheriting
from his uncle the continuance, strength, and good use of
that which is often of service. In great battles, he
endeavoured always to give blows without receiving them,

which is, and always will be, the only problem to solve in
war, but he never spared himself there, and, in fact, as he
had no other virtue except his bravery, he was captain of a
company of lancers, and much esteemed by the Duke of
Bourgoyne, who never troubled what his soldiers did elsewhere. This nephew of the devil was named Captain
Cochegrue; and his creditors, the blockheads, citizens, and
others, whose pockets he slit, called him the Mau-cinge,
since he was as mischievous as strong; but he had moreover his back spoilt by the natural·infirmity of a hump, and
it would have been unwise to attempt to mount thereon to
get a good view, for he would incontestably have run you
through.

The second had studied the laws, and through the favour

of his uncle had become a procureur, and practised at the

palace, where he did the business of the ladies, whom formerly the canon had the best confessed. This one was called *Pille-grue*, to banter him upon his real name, which was Cochegrue, like that of his brother the captain. Pille-grue had a lean body, seemed to throw off very cold water, was pale of face, and possessed a physiognomy like a pole-cat.

This notwithstanding, he was worth many a penny more than the captain, and had for his uncle a little affection, but since about two years his heart had cracked a little, and drop by drop his gratitude had run out, in such a way that,

from time to time, when the air was damp, he liked to put his feet into his uncle's hose, and press in advance the juice of this good inheritance. He and his brother, the soldier, found their share very small, since loyally, in law, in fact, in justice, in nature, and in reality, it was necessary to give the third part of every-thing to a poor cousin, son of another sister of the canon, the which heir, but little loved by the good man, remained in the

country, where he was a shepherd, near Nanterre.

This guardian of beasts, an ordinary peasant, came to

This guardian of beasts, an ordinary peasant, came to town.

town by the advice of his two cousins, who placed him in their uncle's house, in the hope that, as much by his silly tricks as his clumsiness, his want of brain, and his ignorance, he would be displeasing to the canon, who would kick him out of his will.   Now this poor Chiquon, as

the shepherd was named, had lived about a month alone with his old uncle, and finding more profit or more amusement in minding an abbot than looking after sheep, made himself the canon's dog, his servant, the staff of his old age, saying, " God keep you," when he passed wind, "God save you," when he sneezed, and " God guard you," when he belched ; going to see if it rained, where the cat was, remaining silent, listening, speaking, receiving the coughs of the old man in his face, admiring him as the finest canon there ever was in the world, all heartily and in good faith, knowing that he was licking him after the manner of animals who clean their young ones ; and the uncle, who stood in no need of learning which side the bread was buttered, repulsed poor Chiquon, making him turn about like a die, always calling Chiquon, and always saying to his other nephews that this Chiquon was helping to kill him, such a numskull was he.   Thereupon, hearing this, Chiquon determined to do well by his uncle, and puzzled his understanding to appear better; but as he had a behind shaped like a pair of pumpkins, was broad shouldered, large limbed, and far from sharp, he more resembled old Silenus than a gentle Zephyr.   In fact, the poor shepherd, a simple man, could not reform himself, so he remained big and fat, awaiting his inheritance to make himself thin.

One evening the canon began discoursing concerning the devil and the grave agonies, penances, tortures, &c., which God will get warm for the accursed, and the good Chiquon, hearing it, began to open his eyes as wide as the door of an oven, at this statement, without believing a word of it.

"What," said the canon, "are you not a Christian?"

"In that, yes," answered Chiquon.

"Well, there is a paradise for the good; is it not necessary to have a hell for the wicked?"

"Yes, Mr. Canon; but the devil's of no use. If you had here a wicked man who turned everything upside down, would you not kick him out of doors?"

"Yes, Chiquon."

"Oh, well, mine uncle; God would be very stupid to leave in this world, which he has so curiously constructed, an abominable devil whose special business it is to spoil everything for him. Pish! I recognise no devil if there be a good God; you may depend upon that. I should very much like to see the devil. Ha! ha! I am not afraid of his claws!"

"And if I were of your opinon I should have no care of my very youthful years in which I held confessions at least ten times a day."

"Confess again, Mr. Canon. I assure you that will be a precious merit on high."

"There, there! do you mean it?"

"Yes, Mr. Canon."

"Thou dost not tremble, Chiquon, to deny the devil?"

"I trouble no more about it than a sheaf of corn."

"The doctrine will bring misfortune upon you."

"By no means. God will defend me from the devil because I believe him more learned and less stupid than the *savans* make him out."

Thereupon the other two nephews entered, and perceived from the voice of the canon that he did not dislike Chiquon very much, and that the jeremiads which he made concerning him were simply tricks to disguise the affection which he bore him, looked at each other in great astonishment.

Then, seeing their uncle laughing. they said to him—

"If you make a will, to whom will you leave the house?"

"To Chiquon."

"And the quit rent of the Rue St. Denys?"

"To Chiquon."

"And the fief of Ville Parisis?"

"To Chiquon?"

"But," said the captain, with his big voice, "everything then will be Chiquon's."

"No," replied the canon, smiling, "because I shall have made my will in proper form, the inheritance will be to the sharpest of you three; I am so near to the future, that I can therein see clearly your destinies."

And the wily canon cast upon Chiquon a glance full of malice, like a decoy bird would have thrown upon a little one to draw him into her net. The fire of this flaming eye enlightened the shepherd, who from that moment had his understanding and his ears all unfogged, and his brain open, like that of a maiden the day after her marriage. The procureur and the captain, taking these sayings for gospel prophecies, made their bow and went out from the house, quite perplexed at the absurd designs of the canon.

"What do you think of Chiquon?" said Pille-grue to Mau-cinge.

"I think, I think," said the soldier, growling, "that I think of hiding myself in the Rue d'Hiérusalem, to put his head below his feet; he can pick it up again if he likes."

"Oh! oh!" said the procureur, "you have a way of wounding that is easily recognised, and people would say, 'It's Cochegrue.' As for me, I thought to invite him to dinner, after which, we would play at putting ourselves in a sack, in order to see, as they do at Court, who could walk best thus attired. Then, having sewn him up, we could throw him into the Seine, at the same time begging him to swim."

"This must be well matured," replied the soldier.

"Oh! it's quite ripe," said the advocate. "The cousin gone to the devil, the heritage would then be between us two."

"I'm quite agreeable," said the fighter, "but we must stick as close together as the two legs of the same body, for if you are fine as silk, I am strong as steel, and daggers are always as good as traps—you hear that, my good brother."

"Yes," said the advocate, "the cause is heard—now shall it be the thread or the iron?"

"Eh? ventre de Dieu! is it then a king that we are going to settle? For a simple numskull of a shepherd are so many words necessary? Come! 20,000 francs out of the heritage to the one of us who shall first cut him off: I'll say to him in good faith, 'Pick up your head.'"

"And I, 'Swim, my friend,'" cried the advocate, laughing like the gap of a pourpoint.

And then they went to supper, the captain to his wench, and the advocate to the house of a jeweller's wife, of whom he was the lover.

Who was astonished? Chiquon! The poor shepherd heard the planning of his death, although his two cousins had walked in the parvis, and talked to each other as every one speaks at church when praying to God. So that Chiquon was much troubled to know if the words had come up or if his ears had gone down.

"Do you hear, Mister Canon?"

"Yes," said he, "I hear the wood crackling in the fire."

"Ho! ho!" replied Chiquon, "if I don't believe in the devil, I believe in St. Michael, my guardian angel; I go there where he calls me."

"Go, my child," said the canon, "and take care not to wet yourself, nor to get your head knocked off, for I think I hear more rain, and the beggars in the street are not always the most dangerous beggars."

At these words Chiquon was much astonished, and stared at the canon; found his manner gay, his eye sharp, and his feet crooked; but as he had to arrange matters concerning the death which menaced him, he thought to himself that he would always have leisure to admire the canon, or to cut his nails; and he trotted off quickly through the town, as a little woman trots towards her pleasure.

His two cousins, having no presumption of the divinatory science, of which shepherds have had many passing attacks, had often talked before him of their secret goings on, counting him as nothing.

Now one evening to amuse the canon, Pille-grue had re-

counted to him how had fallen in love with him the wife of
a jeweller on whose head he had adjusted certain carved,

burnished, sculptured, historical
horns, fit for the brow of a prince.
The good lady was to hear him,
a right merry wench, quick at
opportunities, giving an embrace while her husband was
mounting the stairs, devouring
the commodity as if she were
swallowing a strawberry, only
thinking of love-making, always
trifling and frisky, gay as an
honest woman who lacks nothing, contenting her husband,
who cherished her as much as
he loved his own gullet; subtle as a perfume, so much
so, that for five years she managed so well his household
affairs, and her own love affairs, that she had the reputation of
a prudent woman, the confidence of her husband, the keys
of the house, the purse, and all.

"And when do you play upon this gentle flute?" said
the canon.

"Every evening, and sometimes I stay all the night."

"But how?" said the canon, astonished.

"This is how. There is in a room close to, a chest into
which I get. When the good husband returns from his friend
the draper's, where he goes to supper every evening, because
often he helps the draper's wife in her work, my mistress
pleads a slight illness, lets him go to bed alone, and comes
to doctor her malady in the room where the chest is.
On the morrow, when my jeweller is at his forge, I depart,
and as the house has one exit on to the bridge, and
another into the street, I always come to the door where
the husband is not, on the pretext of speaking to him of his
suits, which commence joyfully and heartily, and I never let
them come to an end. It is an income from cuckoldom,
seeing that in the minor expenses and loyal costs of the
proceedings, he spends as much as on the horses in his

stable. He loves me well, as all good cuckolds should love the man who aids them, to plant, cultivate, water, and dig the natural garden of Venus, and he does nothing without me.

Now these practices came back again to the memory of the shepherd, who was illuminated by the light issuing from his danger, and counselled by the intelligence of those measures of self-preservation, of which every animal possesses a sufficient dose to go to the end of his ball of life. So Chiquon gained with hasty feet the Rue de la Calandre, where the jeweller should then be supping with his companion, and after having knocked at the door, replied to the question put to him through the little grill, that he was a messenger on state secrets, and was admitted to the draper's house. Now coming straight to the fact, he made the happy jeweller get up from the table, led him into a corner, and said to him, "If one of your neighbours had planted a horn on your forehead, and he were delivered to you, bound hand and foot, would you throw him into the river?"

"Rather," said the jeweller, "but if you are mocking me I'll give you a good drubbing."

"There, there!" replied Chiquon, "I am one of your friends, and come to warn you that as many times as you have conversed with the draper's wife here, as often has your good wife been served the same way by the advocate Pille-grue, and if you will come back to your forge, you'll find a good fire there. On your arrival, he who looks after your you-know-what, to keep it in good order, gets into the big clothes chest. Now make a pretence that I have bought the said chest of you, and I will be upon the bridge with a cart, waiting your orders.

The said jeweller took his cloak and his hat, and parted company with his crony without saying a word, and ran to his hole like a poisoned rat. He arrives and knocks, the door is opened, he runs hastily up the stairs, finds two covers laid, sees his wife coming out of the chamber of love, and then says to her, "My dear, here are two covers laid."

"Well, my darling, are we not two?"

"No," said he, "we are three."

"Is your friend coming?" said she, looking towards the stairs with perfect innocence.

"No, I speak of the friend who is in the chest."

"What chest?" said she. "Are you in your sound senses? where do you see a chest? is it usual to put friends in chests? am I a woman to keep chests full of friends? How long have friends been kept in chests? are you come home mad to mix up your friends with your chests? I know no other friend than Master Cornille the draper, and no other chest than the one with our clothes in."

"Oh!" said the jeweller, "my good woman, there is a bad young man, who has come to warn me that you allow yourself to be embraced by our advocate, and that he is in the chest."

"I!" said she, "I would not put up with his knavery, he does everything the wrong way."

"There, there, my dear," replied the jeweller, "I know you to be a good woman, and wont have a squabble with you about this paltry chest. The giver of the warning is a box-maker, to whom I am about to sell this cursed chest that I wish never again to see in my house, and for this one he will sell me two pretty little ones, in which there will not be space enough even for a child; thus the scandal and the babble of those envious of thy virtue, will be extinguished for want of nourishment."

"You give me great pleasure," said she; "I don't attach any value to my chest, and by chance there is nothing in it. Our linen is at the wash. It will be easy to have the mischievous chest taken away to-morrow morning. Will you sup?"

"Not at all," said he, "I shall sup with a better appetite without this chest."

"I see," said she, "that you wont easily get the chest out of your head."

" Halloa there !" said the jeweller to his smiths and apprentices ; " come down !"

In the twinkling of an eye his people were before him. Then he, their master, having briefly ordered the handling of the said chest, this piece of furniture dedicated to love was suddenly tumbled across the room, but in passing, the advocate, finding his feet in the air to the which he was not accustomed, tumbled over a little.

" Go on," said the wife, " go on, it's the lid shaking."

" No, my dear, it's the bolt."

And without any other opposition the chest slid gently down the stairs.

" Ho there, carrier !" said the jeweller, and Chiquon came whistling his mules, and the good apprentices lifted the litigious chest into the cart.

" Hi ! hi !" said the advocate.

" Master, the chest is speaking," said an apprentice.

" In what language ?" said the jeweller, giving him a good kick between two features that luckily were not made of glass. The apprentice tumbled over on to a stair in a way that induced him to discontinue his studies in the language of chests. The shepherd, accompanied by the good jeweller, carried all the baggage to the water-side without listening to the high eloquence of the speaking wood, and having tied several stones to it, the jeweller threw it into the Seine.

" *Swim, my friend,*" cried the shepherd, in a voice sufficiently jeering at the moment when the chest turned over, giving a pretty little plunge like a duck.

Then Chiquon continued to proceed along the quay, as far as the Rue-du-port, St. Laudry, near the cloisters of Notre Dame. There he noticed a house, recognised the door, and knocked loudly.

" Open," said he, " open by order of the king."

Hearing this, an old man who was no other than the famous Lombard, Versoris, ran to the door.

"What is it?" said he.

"I am sent by the provost to warn you to keep good watch to-night," replied Chiquon, "as for his own part he will keep his archers ready. The hunchback who has robbed you has come back again. Keep under arms, for he is quite capable of easing you of the rest."

Having said this, the good shepherd took to his heels and ran to the Rue des Marmouzets, to the house where Captain Cochegrue was feasting with La Pasquerette, the prettiest of town-girls, and the most charming in perversity that ever was ; according to all the gay ladies, her glance was sharp and piercing as the stab of a dagger. Her appearance was so tickling to the sight, that it would have put all paradise to rout. Besides which she was as bold as a woman who has no other virtue than her insolence. Poor Chiquon was greatly embarrassed while going to the quarter of the Marmouzets. He was greatly afraid that he would be unable to find the house of La Pasquerette, or find the two pigeons gone to roost, but a good angel arranged things speedily to his satisfaction. This is how. On entering the Rue des Marmouzets, he saw several lights at the windows, and night-capped heads thrust out, and good wenches, gay girls, housewives, husbands, and young ladies, all of them just out of bed, looking at each other as if a robber were being led to execution by torchlight.

"What's the matter?" said the shepherd to a citizen who in great haste had rushed to the door with a chamber utensil in his hand.

"Oh! it's nothing," replied the good man. "We thought it was the Armagnacs descending upon the town, but it's only Mau-cinge beating La Pasquerette."

"Where?" asked the shepherd.

"Below there, at that fine house where the pillars have the mouths of flying frogs delicately engraved upon them. Do you hear the varlets and the serving maids?"

And in fact there were nothing but cries of "Murder! Help! Come some one !" and in the house blows were rain-

ing down and the Mau-cinge said with his gruff voice, " Death
to the wench ! Ah, you sing out now, do you ? Ah, you want
money now, do you ? Take that——"

And La Pasquerette was groaning, " Oh ! oh ! I die !
Help ! help ! Oh ! oh !" Then came the blow of a sword,
then the heavy fall of the light body of the fair girl sounded,

and was followed by a great silence, after which the lights
were put out, servants, waiting women, roysterers, and
others went in again, and the shepherd who had come
opportunely mounted the stairs in company with them, but
on beholding in the room above broken glasses, slit carpets,
and the cloth on the floor with the dishes, every one remained at a distance.

The shepherd, bold as a man with but one end in view,
opened the door of the handsome chamber where slept
La Pasquerette, and found her quite exhausted, her hair
dishevelled, and her neck twisted, lying upon a bloody carpet,
and Mau-cinge frightened, with his tone considerably lower,
and not knowing upon what note to sing the remainder of
his anthem.

" Come, my little Pasquerette, don't pretend to be dead.
Come, let me put you tidy. Ah ! little minx, dead or alive,
you look so pretty in your blood I'm going to kiss you."
Having said which the cunning soldier took her and threw

her upon the bed, but she fell there all of a heap, and stiff
as the body of a man that had been hanged.   Seeing which

her companion found it was time
for his hump to retire from the
game ; however, the artful fellow
before slinking away said, "Poor
Pasquerette, how could I murder
so good a girl, and one I loved so
much ? But, yes, I have killed her,
the thing is clear, for in her life
never did her sweet breast hang
down like that.   Good God, one
would say it was a crown at the
bottom of a wallet." Thereupon
La Pasquerette opened her eyes
and bent her head slightly to look at
her flesh, which was white and firm, and she brought herself
to life again by a box on the ears, administered to the captain.

"That will teach you to beware of the dead," said she,
smiling.

"And why did he kill you, my cousin ?" asked the shepherd.

"Why ? to-morrow the bailiffs seize everything that's here,
and he who has no more money than virtue, reproached me
because I wished to be agreeable to a handsome gentleman,
who would save me from the hands of justice."

"Pasquerette, I'll break every bone in your skin."

"There ! there !" said Chiquon, whom the Mau-cinge had
just recognised, "is that all? Oh well, my good friend, I
bring you a large sum."

"Where from ?" asked the captain, astonished.

"Come here, and let me whisper in your ear—if 30,000
crowns were walking about at night under the shadow of a
pear-tree, would you not stoop down to pluck them, to
prevent them spoiling ?"

"Chiquon, I'll kill you like a dog if you are making game
of me, or I will kiss you there where you like it, if you will
put me opposite 30,000 crowns, even when it shall be
necessary to kill three citizens at the corner of the Quay."

"You will not even kill one. This is how the matter

stands. I have for a sweetheart in all loyalty, the servant of the Lombard who is in the city near the house of our good uncle. Now I have just learned on sound information that this dear man has departed this morning into the country, after having hidden under a pear-tree in his garden a good bushel of gold, believing himself to be seen only by the angels. But the girl who had by chance a bad toothache, and was taking the air at her garret window, spied the old crookshanks, without wishing to do so, and chattered of it to me in fondness. If you will swear to give me a good share I will lend you my shoulders in order that you may climb on to the top of the wall, and from there throw yourself into the pear-tree, which is against the wall. There, now do you say that I am a blockhead, an animal?"

"No, you are a right loyal cousin, an honest man, and if you have ever to put an enemy out of the way, I am there, ready to kill even one of my own friends for you. I am no longer your cousin, but your brother. Ho there, sweetheart," cried Mau-cinge to La Pasquerette, "put the tables straight, wipe up your blood, it belongs to me, and I'll pay you for it, by giving you a hundred times as much of mine as I have taken of thine. Make the best of it, shake the black dog off your back, adjust your petticoats, laugh, I wish it, look to the stew, and let us recommence our evening prayer where we left it off. To-morrow I will make thee braver than a queen. This is my cousin whom I wish to entertain, even when to do so it were necessary to turn the house out of windows. We shall get back everything to-morrow in the cellars. Come, fall to."

Thus, and in less time than it takes a priest to say his

They went along, disputing about a thousand theological subjects,
which got very much mixed up.

Dominus vobiscum, the whole rookery passed from tears to laughter as it had previously passed from laughter to tears. It is only in these houses of ill-fame that love is made with the blow of a dagger, and where tempests of joy rage between four walls. But these are things ladies of the high-necked dress do not understand.

The said Captain Cochegrue was gay as a hundred school-boys at the breaking up of class, and made his good cousin drink deeply, who swilled everything country fashion, and pretended to be drunk, spluttering out a hundred stupidities, as, that " to-morrow he would buy Paris, would lend a hundred thousand crowns to the king, that he would be able to roll in gold ;" in fact, talked so much nonsense that the captain, fearing some compromising avowal and thinking his brain quite muddled enough, led him outside with the good intention, instead of sharing with him, of ripping Chiquon open to see if he had not a sponge in his stomach, because he had just soaked in a big quart of the good wine of Suresne. They went along, disputing about a thousand theological subjects, which got very much mixed up, and finished by rolling quietly up against the garden where were the crowns of the Lombard. Then Cochegrue, making a ladder of Chiquon's broad shoulders, jumped on to the pear-tree like a man expert in attacks upon towns, but Versoris, who was watching him, made a blow at his neck, and repeated it so vigorously that with three blows fell the upper portion of the said Cochegrue, but not until he had heard the clear voice of the shepherd, who cried to him, " *Pick up your head, my friend.*" Thereupon the generous Chiquon, in whom virtue received its recompense, thought it would be wise to return to the house of the good canon, whose heritage was by the grace of God considerably simplified. Thus he gained the Rue St. Pierre-aux-Bœufs with all speed, and soon slept like a new-born

Pick up your head, my friend !

baby, no longer knowing the meaning of the word " cousin-
german." Now on the morrow he rose according to the
habit of shepherds, with the sun, and came into his uncle's
room to inquire if he spat white, if he coughed, if he had
slept well ; but the old servant told him that the canon,
hearing the bells of St. Maurice, the first patron of Notre
Dame, ring for matins, he had gone out of reverence to the
cathedral, where all the Chapter were to breakfast with the
Bishop of Paris ; upon which Chiquon replied, " Is his
reverence the canon out of his senses thus to disport himself, to catch a cold, to get rheumatism ? does he wish to
die ? I'll light a big fire to warm him when he returns ;"
and the good shepherd ran into the room where the canon
generally sat, and to his great astonishment beheld him
seated in his chair.

" Ah ! ah ! What did she mean, that fool of a Buyrette ?
I knew you were too well advised to be shivering at this
hour in your stall."

The canon said not a word. The shepherd, who was
like all thinkers, a man of hidden sense, was quite aware
that sometimes old men have strange crotchets, converse
with the essence of occult things, and mumble to themselves discourses concerning matters not under consideration : so that, from reverence and great respect for the
secret meditations of the canon, he went and sat down at a
distance, and waited the termination of these dreams ;
noticing silently the length of the good man's nails, which
looked like cobblers' awls, and looking attentively at the
feet of his uncle, he was astonished to see the flesh of
his legs so crimson, that it reddened his breeches and
seemed all on fire through his hose.

He is dead, thought Chiquon. At this moment the door
of the room opened, and he still saw the canon, who, his
nose frozen, came back from church.

" Ho ! ho !" said Chiquon, " my dear uncle, are you out
of your senses ? Kindly take notice that you ought not to
be at the door, because you are already seated in your chair
in the chimney corner, and that it is impossible for there to
be two canons like you in the world."

"Ah! Chiquon, there was a time when I could have wished to be in two places at once, but such is not the fate of man, he would be too happy. Are you getting dim-sighted? I am alone here."

Then Chiquon turned his head towards the chair, and found it empty; and much astonished, as you will easily believe, he approached it, and found on the seat a little pat of cinders, from which ascended a strong odour of sulphur.

"Ah!" said he merrily, "I perceive that the devil has behaved well towards me—I will pray God for him."

And thereupon he related naïvely to the canon how the devil had amused himself by playing at providence, and had loyally aided him to get rid of his wicked cousins, the which the canon admired much, and thought very good, seeing that he had plenty of good sense left, and often had observed things which were to the devil's advantage. So the good old priest remarked that as much good was always

 met with in evil as evil in good, and that therefore one should not trouble too much after the other world, the which was a grave heresy, which many councils have put right.

And this was how the Chiquons became rich, and were able in these times, by the fortunes of their ancestors, to help to build the bridge of St. Michael, where the devil cuts a very good figure under the angel, in memory of this adventure now consigned to these veracious histories.

THE MERRIE JESTS

KING LOUIS THE ELEVENTH.

KING LOUIS THE ELEVENTH was a merry fellow, loving a good joke, and—the interests of his position as king, and those of the church on one side—he lived jovially, giving chase to soiled doves as often as to hares, and other royal game. Therefore the sorry scribblers who have made him out a hypocrite, show plainly that they knew him not, since he was a good friend, good at repartee, and a jollier fellow than any of them.

It was he who said when he was in a merry mood, that four things are excellent and opportune in life—to keep warm, to drink cool, to stand up hard, and to swallow soft. Certain persons have accused him of taking up with dirty trollops; this is a notorious falsehood, since all his mistresses, of whom one was legitimatized, came of good houses and had notable establishments. He did not go in for waste and extravagance, always put his hand upon the solid, and because certain devourers of the people found no crumbs at his table, they have all maligned him. But the real collectors of facts know that the said king was a capital

Nicole de Beaupertuys.

fellow in private life, and even very agreeable; and before
cutting off the heads of his friends, or punishing them—for
he did not spare them—it was necessary that they should
have greatly offended him, and his vengeance was always
justice; I have only seen in our friend Verville that this
worthy sovereign ever made a mistake; but
once does not make a habit, and even for this
his boon companion Tristan was more to
blame than he, the king. This is the circumstance related by the said Verville, and I suspect he was cracking a joke. I reproduce it
because certain people are not familiar with the exquisite
work of my perfect compatriot. I abridge it and only give
the substance, the details being more ample, of which fact
the savans are not ignorant.

Louis XI. had given the Abbey of Turpenay (mentioned in *Imperia*) to a gentleman who, enjoying the
revenue, had called himself Monsieur de Turpenay. It
happened that the king being at Plessis-les-Tours, the
real abbot, who was a monk, came and presented himself
before the king, and presented also a petition, remonstrating with him that, canonically and monastically, he
was entitled to the abbey, and that the usurping gentleman
wronged him of his right, and therefore he called upon his
majesty to have justice done to him. Nodding his
peruke, the king promised to render him contented.
This monk, importunate as are all hooded animals, came
often at the end of the king's meals, who, bored with the
holy water of the convent, called friend Tristan and said
to him, "Old fellow, there is here a Turpenay who angers
me, rid the world of him for me." Tristan, taking a frock
for a monk, or a monk for a frock, came to this gentleman,
whom all the Court called Monsieur de Turpenay, and
having accosted him, managed to lead him on one side,
then taking him by the button-hole gave him to understand
that the king desired he should die. He tried to resist,
supplicating and supplicating to escape, but in no way could
he obtain a hearing. He was delicately strangled between
the head and the shoulders, so that he expired; and, three

hours afterwards, Tristan told the king that he was discharged. It happened five days afterwards, which is the space in which souls come back again, that the monk came into the room where the king was, and when he saw him he was much astonished. Tristan was present; the king called him, and whispered into his ear—

"You have not done that which I told you to."

"Saving your Grace, I have done it. Turpenay is dead."

"Eh? I meant this monk."

"I understood the gentleman."

"What, it is done then?"

"Yes, sire."

"Very well then"—turning towards the monk—"come here, monk." The monk approached. The king said to him, "Kneel down." The poor monk began to shiver in his shoes. But the king said to him, "Thank God that he has not willed that you should be killed as I had ordered,

He who took your estates has been instead. God has done you justice. Go and pray God for me, and don't stir out of your convent."

This proves the good-heartedness of Louis XI. He might very well have hanged the monk, the cause of the error. As for the said gentleman, he died in the king's service.

In the early days of his sojourn at Plessis-les-Tours King Louis, not wishing to hold his drinking-bouts and give vent to his rakish propensities in his chateau, out of respect to her Majesty (a kingly delicacy which his successors have not possessed) became enamoured of a lady named Nicole Beaupertuys, who was, to tell the truth, wife of a citizen of the town. The husband he sent into Ponent, and put the said Nicole in a house near Chardonneret, in that part where is the Rue Quincangrogne, because it was a lonely place, far from other habitations. The husband and the wife were thus both in his service, and he had by La Beaupertuys, a daughter, who died a nun. This Nicole had a tongue as sharp as a popinjay's, was of stately proportions, furnished with large beautiful cushions of nature, firm to the touch, white as the wings of an angel, and known for the rest to be fertile in peripatetic ways, which brought it to pass that never with her was the same thing encountered twice in love, so deeply had she studied the sweet solutions of the science, the manners of accommodating the olives of Poissy, the expansions of the nerves, and hidden doctrines of the breviary, the which much delighted the king. She was as gay as a lark, always laughing and singing, and never made any one miserable, which is the characteristic of women of this open and free nature, who have always an occupation—an equivocal one if you like. The king often went with the hail-fellows his friends to the lady's house, and in order not to be seen always went at night-time and without his suite. But being always distrustful, and fearing some snare, he gave to Nicole all the most savage dogs he had in his kennels, beggars that would eat a man without saying "By your leave," the which royal dogs knew only Nicole and the king. When the

Sire came Nicole let them loose in the garden, and the
door of the house being sufficiently barred and closely

shut, the king put the keys
in his pocket, and in perfect
security gave himself up, with
his satellites, to every kind of
pleasure, fearing no betrayal,
jumping about at will, playing
tricks, and getting up good games. Upon these occasions
friend Tristan watched the neighbourhood, and any one
who had taken a walk on the Mall of Chardonneret would
have been rather quickly placed in a position in which it
would have been easy to give the passers-by a benediction
with his feet, unless he had the king's pass, since
often would Louis send out in search of lasses for his
friends, or people to entertain him with the amusements suggested by Nicole or the guests. People
of Tours were there for these little amusements,
to whom he gently recommended silence, so that
no one knew of these pastimes until after his death.
The farce of "Baiser mon cul" was, it is said, invented by the said Sire. I will relate it, although it is not
the subject of this tale, because it shows the natural
comicality and humour of this merry monarch. There
were at Tours three well-known misers : the first was
Master Cornelius, who is sufficiently well known ; the

second was called Peccard, and sold
the gilt-work, coloured papers, and
jewels used in churches ; the third was
hight Marchandeau, and was a very
wealthy wine-grower. These two men
of Touraine were the founders of good
families, notwithstanding their sordidness. One evening
that the king was with Beaupertuys, in a good humour,
having drunk heartily, joked heartily, and offered early in
the evening his prayer in Madame's oratory, he said to
Le Daim, his crony, to the Cardinal, La Balue, and to old
Dunois, who were still soaking, "Let us have a good

laugh ! I think it will be a good joke to see misers before a bag of gold without their being able to touch it. Hi, there !"

Hearing which, appeared one of his varlets.

"Go," said he, "seek my treasurer, and let him bring hither six thousand gold crowns—and at once ! And you will go and seize the bodies of my friend Cornelius, of the jeweller of the Rue de Cygnes, and of old Marchandeau, and bring them here, by order of the king."

Then he began to drink again, and to judiciously wrangle as to which was the better, a woman with a gamy odour or a woman who soaped herself well all over ; a thin one or a stout one; and as the company comprised the flower of wisdom it was decided that the best was the one a man had all to himself like a plate of warm mussels, at that precise moment when God sent him a good idea to communicate to her. The cardinal asked which was the most precious thing to a lady ; the first or the last kiss ? To which La Beaupertuys replied, " that it was the last, seeing that she knew then what she was losing, while at the first she did not know what she would gain." During these sayings, and others which have most unfortunately been lost, came the six thousand gold crowns, which were worth all three hundred thousand francs of to-day, so much do we go on decreasing in value every day. The king ordered the crowns to be arranged upon a table, and well lighted up, so that they shone like the eyes of the company which lit up involuntarily, and made them laugh in spite of themselves. They did not wait long for the three misers, whom the varlet led in, pale and panting, except Cornelius, who knew the king's strange freaks.

"Now then, my friends," said Louis to them, "have a good look at the crowns on the table."

And the three townsmen nibbled at them with their eyes. You may reckon that the diamond of La Beaupertuys sparkled less than their little minnow eyes.

"These are yours," added the king.

Thereupon they ceased to admire the crowns to look at each other. and the guests knew well that old knaves are more expert in grimaces than any others, because their physiognomies become tolerably curious, like those of cats lapping up milk, or girls titillated with marriage.

"There," said the king, "all that shall be his who shall say three times to the two others, ' Baiser mon cul,' thrusting his hand into the gold ; but if he be not as serious as a fly who has violated his lady-love, if he smile while repeating the jest, he will pay ten crowns to Madame. Nevertheless he can essay three times."

"That will be soon earned," said Cornelius, who, being a Dutchman, had his lips as often compressed and serious as Madame's mouth was often open and laughing. Then he bravely put his hand upon the crowns to see if they were good, and clutched them gravely, but as he looked at the others to say civilly to them, "Baiser mon cul," the two misers, distrustful of his Dutch gravity, replied, "Certainly, sir," as if he had sneezed. The which caused all the company to laugh, and even Cornelius himself. When the vine-grower went to take the crowns he felt such a commotion in his cheeks that his old scummer face let little laughs exude from all its pores like smoke pouring out of a chimney, and he could say nothing. Then it was the turn of the jeweller, who was a little bit of a bantering fellow, and whose lips were as tightly squeezed as the neck of a hanged man. He seized a handful of the crowns, looked at the others, even the king, and said, with a jeering air, "Baiser mon cul."

" Is it dirty ?" asked the vine-dresser.

" Look and see," replied the jeweller, gravely.

Thereupon the king began to tremble for his crowns, since the said Peccard began again, without laughing, and for the third time was about to utter the sacramental word, when La Beaupertuys made a sign of consent to his modest request, which caused him to lose his countenance, and his mouth broke up into dimples.

" How did you do ?" asked Dunois, " to keep a grave face before six thousand crowns ?"

" Oh, my lord, I thought first of one of my cases which is

tried to-morrow, and, secondly, of my wife, who is a sorry plague."

The desire to gain this good round sum made them try again, and the king amused himself for about an hour at the expression of these faces, the preparations, jokes, grimaces, and other monkeys' paternosters that they performed; but they were baling their boats with a sieve, and for men who preferred closing their fists to opening them it was a bitter sorrow to have to count out, each one, a hundred crowns to Madame.

When they were gone, Nicole said boldly to the king, " Sire, will you let me try ?"

" Holy Virgin !" replied Louis ; " no ! I can kiss you for less money."

That was said like a thrifty man, which indeed he always was.

One evening the fat Cardinal La Balue carried on gallantly with words and actions, a little farther than the canons of the Church per- mitted him, with this Beauper-tuys, who, luckily for herself, was a clever hussy, not to be asked with impunity how many holes there were in her mo- ther's chemise.

"Look you here, Sir Car-dinal !" said she; " the thing which the king likes is not to receive the holy oils."

Then came Olivier le Daim, whom she would not listen to either, and to whose nonsense she replied, that she would ask the king if he wished her to be shaved.

Now as the said shaver did not supplicate her to keep his proposals secret, she suspected that these little plots were ruses practised by the king, whose suspicions had perhaps been aroused by her friends. Now, not being able to revenge herself upon Louis, she at least deter-mined to pay out the said lords, to make fools of them,

and amuse the king with the tricks she would play upon
them.   One evening that they had come to supper,
she had a lady of the city with her, who wished to speak
with the king.   This lady was a lady of position, who
wished to ask of the king pardon for her husband, the
which, in consequence of this adventure, she obtained.
Nicole Beaupertuys having led the king aside for a mo-

ment into an antechamber, told him to
make their guests drink hard and eat to
repletion ; that he was to make merry,
and joke with them ; but when the cloth
was removed, he was to pick quarrels
with them about trifles, dispute their
words, and be sharp with them ; and that
then she would divert him by turning
them inside out before him.   But above
all things, he was to be friendly to the said lady, and it
was to appear genuine, as if she enjoyed the perfume of
his favour, because she had gallantly lent herself to this
good joke.

    " Well, gentlemen," said the king, re-entering the room,
" let us fall-to ; we have had a good day's sport."

    And the surgeon, the cardinal, a fat bishop, the captain
of the Scotch guard, a parliamentary envoy, and a judge
loved of the king, followed the two ladies into the room
where one rubs the rust off one's jawbones.   And there
they lined the mould of their doublets.   What is that?
It is to pave the stomach, to practise the chemistry of
nature, to register the various dishes, to regale your tripes,
to dig your grave with your teeth, play with the sword of
Cain, to inter sauces, to support a cuckold. But more philosophically it is to make ordure with one's teeth.   Now do
you understand ?   How many words does it require to burst
open the lid of your understanding ?

    The king did not fail to distil into his guests this splendid
and first-class supper.   He stuffed them with green peas,
returning to the hotch-potch, praising the plums, commend-
ing the fish, saying to one, " Why do you not eat ?" to
another, " Drink to Madame ;" to all of them, " Gentlemen,

taste these lobsters ; put this bottle to death ! You do not know the flavour of this forcemeat. And these lampreys— ah ! what do you say to them ? And, by the Lord ! the finest barbel ever drawn from the Loire ! Just stick your teeth into this pasty. This game is my own hunting ; he who takes it not offends me." And again, "Drink, the king's eyes are the other way. Just give me your opinion of these preserves, they are Madame's own. Have some of these grapes, they are my own growing. Have some med- lars." And while inducing them to swell out their abdominal protuberances, the good monarch laughed with them, and they joked, and disputed, and spat, and blew their noses, and kicked up just as though the king had not been with them. Then so much victuals had been taken on board, so many flagons drained and stews spoilt, that the faces of the guests were the colour of cardinals' gowns, and their doublets appeared ready to burst, since they were crammed with meat like Troyes sausages from the top to the bottom of their paunches. Going into the saloon again, they broke into a profuse sweat, began to blow, and to curse their glut- tony. The king sat quietly apart ; each of them was the more willing to be silent because all their forces were re- quired for the intestinal digestion of the huge platefuls con- fined in their stomachs, which began to wabble and rumble violently. One said to himself, " I was stupid to eat of that sauce." Another scolded himself for having indulged in a plate of eels cooked with capers. Another thought to himself, " Oh ! oh ! the forcemeat is serving me out." The cardinal, who was the biggest bellied man of the lot, snorted through his nostrils like a frightened horse. It was he who was first compelled to give vent to a loud sounding belch, and then he soon wished himself in Germany, where this is a form of salutation, for the king hearing this gastric language looked at the cardinal with knitted brows.

" What does this mean ?" said he, " am I a simple clerk ?"

This was heard with terror, because usually the king made much of a good belch well off the stomach. The other guests determined to get rid in another way of the

vapours which were dodging about in their pancreatic
retorts; and at first they endeavoured to hold them for a
little while in the pleats of their mesenteries. It was then
that some of them puffed and swelled like taxgatherers.
Beaupertuys took the good king aside and said to him—

"Know now that I have had made by the Church
jeweller, Peccard, two large dolls, exactly resembling this
lady and myself. Now when hard pressed by the drugs
which I have put in their goblets, they desire to mount the
throne to which we are now about to pretend to go, they
will always find the place taken; by this means you will
enjoy their writhings."

Thus having said, La Beaupertuys disappeared with the
lady to go and turn the wheel, after the custom of women,
and of which I will tell you the origin in another place.
And after an honest lapse of water, Beaupertuys came back
alone, leaving it to be believed that she had left the lady at
the little laboratory of natural alchemy. Thereupon the king,
singling out the cardinal, made him get up, and talked with

him seriously of his affairs,
holding him by the tassel
of his amice. To all that
the king said, La Balue
replied, "Yes, sir," to be
delivered from this favour,
and to slip out of the room,
since the water was in his
cellars, and he was about

to lose the key of his back-door. All the guests were in a
state of not knowing how to arrest the progress of the fæcal
matter to which nature has given, even more than to water,
the property of finding a certain level. Their substances
modified themselves and glided working downward, like
those insects who demand to be let out of their cocoons
raging, tormenting, and ungrateful to the higher powers;
for nothing is so ignorant, so insolent as those cursed
objects, and they are importunate like all things detained to
whom one owes liberty. So they slipped at every turn like
eels out of a net, and each one had need of great efforts

and science not to disgrace himself before the king. Louis took great pleasure in interrogating his guests, and was much amused with the vicissitudes of their physiognomies, on which were reflected the dirty grimaces of their writhings. The counsellor of justice said to Olivier, " I would give my office to be behind a hedge for half a dozen seconds."

"Oh, there is no enjoyment to equal a good stool; and now I am no longer astonished at the sempiternal droppings of a fly," replied the surgeon.

The cardinal believing that the lady had obtained her receipt from the bank of deposit, left the tassels of his girdle in the king's hand, making a start as if he had forgotten to say his prayers, and made his way towards the door.

"What is the matter with you, Monsieur le Cardinal?" said the king.

"By my halidame, what is the matter with me? It appears that all your affairs are very extensive, sire !"

The cardinal slipped out, leaving the others astonished at his cunning. He proceeded gloriously towards the lower room, loosing a little the strings of his purse ; but when he opened the blessed little door he found the lady at her functions upon the throne, like a pope about to be consecrated. Then restraining his impatience, he descended the stairs to go into the garden. However, on the last steps the barking of the dogs put him in great fear of being bitten in one of his precious hemispheres ; and not knowing where to deliver himself of his chemical produce he came back into the room, shivering like a man who has been in the open air ! The others, seeing the cardinal return, imagined that he had emptied his natural reservoirs, unburdened his ecclesiastical bowels, and believed him happy. Then the surgeon rose quickly, as if to take note of the tapestries and count the rafters, but gained the door before any one else, and relaxing his sphincter in advance, he hummed a tune on his way to the retreat; arrived there he was compelled, like La Balue, to murmur words of excuse to this student of perpetual motion, shutting the door with as much promptitude as he had opened it; and he came back burdened with an accumulation which seriously impeded his private channels. And in the same way went the guests one after the other, without being able to unburden themselves of their sauces, and soon

again found themselves all in the presence of Louis the Eleventh, as much distressed as before, looking at each other slyly, understanding each other better with their tails than they ever understood with their mouths, for there is never any equivoque in the transactions of the parts of nature, and everything therein is rational and of easy comprehension, seeing that it is a science which we learn at our birth.

" I believe," said the cardinal to the surgeon, " that lady will go on until to-morrow. What was La Beaupertuys about to ask such a case of diarrhœa here ?"

" She's been an hour working at what I would get done in a minute. May the fever seize her !" cried Olivier le Daim.

All the courtiers seized with colic were walking up and down to make their importunate matters patient, when the said lady reappeared in the room. You can believe they found her beautiful and graceful, and would willingly have kissed her, there where they so longed to go ; and never did they salute the day with more favour than this lady, the liberator of their poor unfortunate bodies. La Balue rose ; the others, from honour, esteem, and reverence of the church, gave way to the clergy, and, biding their time, they continued to make grimaces, at which the king laughed to himself with Nicole, who aided him to stop the respiration of these loose-bowelled gentlemen. The good Scotch captain, who had more than all the others eaten of a dish in which the cook had put an aperient powder, became the victim of misplaced confidence. He went ashamed into a corner, hoping that before the king, his mistake might escape detection. At this moment the cardinal returned horribly upset, because he had found La Beaupertuys on the episcopal seat. Now, in his torments, not knowing if she were in the room, he came back and gave vent to a diabolical " *Oh !*" on beholding her near his master.

"What do you mean?" exclaimed the king, looking at the priest in a way to give him the fever.

"Sire," said La Balue, insolently, "the affairs of pur-gatory are in my ministry, and I am bound to inform you that there is sorcery going on in this house."

"Ah! little priest, you wish to make game of me !" said the king.

At these words the company were in a terrible state.

"So, you treat me with disrespect?" said the king, which made them turn pale. "Ho, there ! Tristan, my friend !" cried Louis XI. from the window, which he threw up suddenly, "come up here !"

The grand provost of the hotel was not long before he appeared ; and as these gentlemen were all nobodies, raised to their present position by the favour of the king, Louis, in a moment of anger, could crush them at will ; so that with the exception of the cardinal, who relied upon his cassock, Tristan found them all rigid and aghast.

"Conduct these gentlemen to the Pretorium, on the Mall, my friend, they have disgraced themselves through over-eating."

"Am I not good at jokes ?" said Nicole to him.

"The farce is good, but it is fetid," replied he, laughing.

This royal answer showed the courtiers that this time the king did not intend to play with their heads, for which they thanked heaven. This monarch was partial to these dirty tricks. He was not at all a bad fellow, as the guests re-

marked while relieving themselves against the side of the
Mall with Tristan, who, like a good Frenchman, kept
them company, and escorted them to their homes. This is
why since that time the citizens of Tours have never failed
to defile the Mall of Chardonneret, because the gentlemen
if the court had been there.

I will not leave this great king without committing to
writing the good joke which he played upon La Godegrand,
who was an old maid, much disgusted that she had not,
during the forty years she had lived, been able to find a lid
to her saucepan, enraged, in her yellow skin, that she was
still as virgin as a mule. This old maid had her apart-

ments on the other side of the house which belonged to
La Beaupertuys, at the corner of Rue de Hiérusalem, in
such a position that, standing on the balcony joining the
wall, it was easy to see what she was doing, and hear what
she was saying in the lower room where she lived; and
often the king derived much amusement from the antics of
the old girl, who did not know that she was so much within
the range of his majesty's culverin. Now one market day
it happened that the king had caused to be hanged a
young citizen of Tours, who had violated a noble lady of a
certain age, believing that she was a young maiden. There
would have been no harm in this, and it would have been

He was not at all a bad fellow, as the guests remarked while relieving themselves against the side of the Mall, with Tristan, who,
like a good Frenchman, kept them company and escorted them to
their homes.

a thing greatly to the credit of the said lady to have been
taken for a virgin; but on finding out his mistake, he had
abominably insulted her, and suspecting her of trickery,
had taken it into his head to rob her of a splendid silver
goblet, in payment of the present he had just made her.
This young man had long hair, and was so handsome
that the whole town wished to see him hanged, both from
regret and out of curiosity. You may be sure that at this
hanging there were more caps than hats. Indeed, the said
young man swung very well; and, after the fashion and
custom of persons hanged, he died gallantly with his lance
couched, which fact made a great noise in the town.
Many ladies said on this subject that it was a murder not
to have preserved so fine a fellow from the scaffold.

"Suppose we were to put this handsome corpse in the
bed of La Godegrand," said La Beaupertuys to the king.

"We should terrify her,'" replied Louis.

"Not at all, sire. Be sure that she will welcome even a
dead man, so madly does she long for a living one. Yesterday I saw her making love to a young man's cap placed on
the top of a chair, and you would have laughed heartily at
her words and gestures."

Now while this forty-year-old virgin was at vespers, the
king sent to have the young townsman, who had just finished
the last scene of his tragic farce, taken down, and having
dressed him in a white shirt, two officers got over the walls
of La Godegrand's garden, and put the corpse into her
bed, on the side nearest the street. Having done this they
went away, and the king remained in the room with the balcony to it, playing with Beaupertuys, and awaiting the hour
at which the old maid should go to bed. La Godegrand
soon came back with a hop, skip, and jump, as the Toura-
nians say, from the church of St. Martin, from which she
was not far, since the Rue d'Hiérusalem touches the walls of
the cloister. She entered her house, laid down her prayer-
book, chaplet, and rosary, and other ammunition which these
old girls carry, then poked the fire, blew it, warmed herself
at it, settled herself in her chair, and played with her cat for
want of something better; then she went to the larder, sup-

ping and sighing, and sighing and supping, eating alone, with
her eyes cast down upon the carpet ; and after having drunk,
behaved in a manner forbidden in court society.

"Ah !" if the corpse said to her, 'God bless you !'"

At this joke of La Beaupertuys, both laughed heartily in
their sleeves. And with great attention this very Christian
king watched the undressing of the old maid, who admired
herself while removing her things—pulling out a hair, or
scratching a pimple which had maliciously come upon her
nose ; picking her teeth, and doing a thousand little things
which, alas ! all ladies, virgins or not, are obliged to do, much
to their annoyance ; but without these little faults of nature,
they would be too proud, and one would not be able to
enjoy their society. Having achieved her aquatic and
musical discourse, the old maid got in between the sheets,
and yelled forth a fine, great, ample, and curious cry, when
she saw, when she smelt the fresh vigour of this hanged
man and the sweet perfume of his manly youth; then sprang
away from him out of coquetry. But as she did not know
he was really dead, she came back again, believing he was
mocking her, and counterfeiting death.

"Go away, you bad young man !" said she.

But you can imagine that she preferred this request in a most
humble and gracious tone of voice. Then seeing that he did
not move, she examined him more closely, and was much
astonished at this so fine human nature when she recognised
the young fellow, upon whom the fancy took her to perform
some purely scientific experiments in the interests of hanged
persons.

"What is she doing ?" said La Beaupertuys to the king.

"She is trying to reanimate him. It is a work of Christian humanity."

And the old girl rubbed and warmed this fine young man,
supplicating holy Mary the Egyptian to aid her to renew the
life of this husband who had for her fallen so amorously
from heaven, when, suddenly looking at the dead body she
was so charitably rubbing, she thought she saw a slight
movement in the eyes ; then she put her hand upon the
man's heart, and felt it beat feebly. At length, from the

warmth of the bed and of affection, and by the temperature of old maids, which is by far more burning than the warm blasts of African deserts, she had the delight of bringing to life that fine handsome young fellow who by a lucky chance had been very badly hanged.

"See how my executioners serve me!" said Louis, laughing.

"Ah!" said La Beaupertuys, "you will not have him hanged again? he is too handsome."

"The decree does not say that he shall be hanged twice, but he shall marry the old woman."

Indeed, the good lady went in a great hurry to seek a master leech, a good bleeder, who lived in the Abbey, and brought him back directly. He immediately took his lancet, and bled the young man. And as no blood came out: "Ah!" said he, "it is too late, the transhipment of blood in the lungs has taken place."

But suddenly this good young blood oozed out a little, and then came in abundance, and the hempen apoplexy, which had only just begun, was arrested in its course. The young man moved and came more to life; then he fell, from natural causes, into a state of great weakness and profound sadness, prostration of flesh and general flabbiness. Now the old maid, who was all eyes, and followed the great and notable changes which were taking place in the person of this badly hanged man, pulled the surgeon by the sleeve, and pointing out to him, by a curious glance of the eye, the piteous case, said to him—

"Will he for the future be always like that?"

"Often," replied the veracious surgeon.

"Oh! he was much nicer hanged!"

At this speech the king burst out laughing. Seeing him at the window, the woman and the surgeon were much frightened, for this laugh seemed to them a second sentence of death for their poor victim. But the king kept his word, and married them. And in order to do justice he gave the husband the name of the Sieur de Mortsauf in the place of the one he had lost upon the scaffold. As La Godegrand had a very big basket full of crowns, they founded a good family in Touraine, which still exists and is much respected, since M. de Mortsauf faithfully served Louis the Eleventh on different occasions. Only he never liked to come across gibbets or old women, and never again made amorous assignations in the night.

This teaches us to thoroughly verify and recognise women, and not to deceive ourselves in the local difference which exists between the old and the young, for if we are not hanged for our errors of love, there are always great risks to run.

The High Constable's Wife.

THE HIGH CONSTABLE'S WIFE.

THE high constable of Armagnac espoused from the desire of a great fortune, the Countess Bonne, who was already considerably enamoured of little Savoisy, son of the chamberlain to his majesty King Charles the Sixth.

The constable was a rough warrior, miserable in appearance, tough in skin, thickly bearded, always uttering angry words, always busy hanging people, always in the sweat of battles, or thinking of other stratagems than those of love. Thus this good soldier, caring little to flavour the marriage stew, used his charming wife after the fashion of a man with more lofty ideas ; of the which the ladies have a great horror, since they like not the joists of the bed to be the sole judges of their fondling and vigorous conduct.

Now the lovely countess, as soon as she was grafted on the constable, only nibbled more eagerly at the love with which her heart was laden for the aforesaid Savoisy, which that gentleman clearly perceived.

Wishing both to study the same music, they would soon harmonize their fancies, or decipher the hieroglyphic ; and this was a thing clearly demonstrated to the Queen Isabella, that Savoisy's horses were oftener stabled at the house of her cousin of Armagnac than in the Hôtel St. Pol, where the chamberlain lived, since the destruction of his residence, ordered by the university, as every one knows.

This discreet and wise princess, fearing in advance some unfortunate adventure for Bonne—the more so as the constable was as ready to brandish his broadsword as a priest to bestow benedictions—the said queen, as sharp as a dirk, said one day, while coming out from vespers, to her cousin, who was taking the holy water with Savoisy—

" My dear, don't you see some blood in that water ?"

" Bah !" said Savoisy to the queen.   " Love likes blood, Madame."

This the queen considered a good reply, and put it into writing, and, later on, into action, when her lord the king wounded one of her lovers, whose business you will see settled in this narrative.

You know by constant experience, that in the early time of love each of two lovers is always in great fear of exposing the mystery of the heart, and as much from the flower of prudence as from the amusement yielded by the sweet tricks of gallantry they play at who can best conceal their thoughts. But one day of forgetfulness suffices to inter the whole vir-

The sword of a husband is a pleasant death for a gallant, if there be pleasant deaths.

tuous past. The poor woman is taken in her joy as in a lasso ; her sweetheart proclaims his presence, or sometimes his departure, by some article of clothing—a scarf, a spur, left by some fatal chance, and there comes a stroke of the dagger that severs the web so gallantly woven by their golden delights. But when one is full of days, he should not make a wry face at death, and the sword of a husband

is a pleasant death for a gallant, if there be pleasant deaths. So may be will finish the merry amours of the constable's wife.

One morning Monsieur d'Armagnac having lots of leisure time in consequence of the flight of the Duke of Burgundy, who was quitting Lagny, thought he would go and wish his lady good day, and attempted to wake her up in a pleasant enough fashion, so that she should not be angry ; but she, sunk in the heavy slumbers of the morning, replied to the action—

" Leave me alone, Charles !"

" Oh, oh," said the constable, hearing the name of a saint who was not one of his patrons, "I have a Charles on my head !"

Then, without touching his wife, he jumped out of the bed, and ran upstairs with his face flaming and his sword drawn, to the place where slept the countess's maid-servant, convinced that the said servant had a finger in the pie.

" Ah, ah, wench of hell !" cried he, to commence the discharge of his passion, " say thy prayers, for I intend to kill thee instantly, because of the secret practices of Charles who comes here."

" Ah, Monseigneur," replied the woman, " who told you that ?"

" Stand steady, that I may rip thee at one blow, if you do not confess to me every assignation given, and in what

The constable having taken this excellent reply amiss, ran her through on the spot, so mad was he with rage.

manner they have been arranged. If thy tongue gets entangled, if thou falterest, I will pierce thee with my dagger !"

"Pierce me through !" replied the girl ; "you will learn nothing."

The constable, having taken this excellent reply amiss, ran her through on the spot, so mad was he with rage ; and came back into his wife's chamber and said to his groom, whom, awakened by the shrieks of the girl, he met upon the stairs, "Go upstairs ; I've corrected Billette rather severely."

Before he reappeared in the presence of Bonne he went to fetch his son, who was sleeping like a child, and led him roughly into her room. The mother opened her eyes pretty widely, you may imagine—at the cries of her little one ; and was greatly terrified at seeing him in the hands of her husband, who had his right hand all bloody, and cast a fierce glance on the mother and son.

"What is the matter ?" said she.

" Madame," asked the man of quick execution, "this child, is he the fruit of my loins, or those of Savoisy, your lover ?"

At this question Bonne turned pale, and sprang upon her son like a frightened frog leaping into the water.

" Ah, he is really ours," said she.

' If you do not wish to see his head roll at your feet confess yourself to me, and no prevarication. You have given me a lieutenant."

" Indeed !"

" Who is he ?"

" It is not Savoisy, and I will never say the name of a man that I don't know."

Thereupon the constable rose, took his wife by the arm to cut her speech with a blow of the sword, but she, casting upon him an imperial glance, cried—

" Kill me if you will, but touch me not."

" You shall live," replied the husband, "because I reserve you for a chastisement more ample than death."

And doubting the inventions, snares, arguments, and artifices familiar to women in these desperate situations, of which they study night and day the variations, by themselves, or between themselves, he departed with this rude and bitter speech. He went instantly to interrogate his servants, presenting to them a face divinely terrible; so all of them replied to him as they would to God the Father on the Judgment Day, when each of us will be called to his account.

None of them knew the serious mischief which was at the bottom of these summary interrogations and crafty interlocutions; but from all that they said, the constable came to the conclusion that no male in his house was in the business,

except one of his dogs, whom he found dumb, and to whom he had given the post of watching the gardens; so taking him in his hands, he strangled him with rage. This fact incited him by induction to suppose that the other constable came into his house by the garden, of which the only entrance was a postern opening on to the water side.

It is necessary here to explain to those who are ignorant of it, the locality of the Hôtel d'Armagnac, which had a notable situation near to the royal houses of St. Pol. On this site has since been built the Hôtel of Longueville. Then, as at the present time, the residence of d'Armagnac had a porch of fine stone in the Rue St. Antoine, was

fortified at all points, and the high walls by the river side,
in face of the Ile du Vaches, in the part where now
stands the port of La Grêve, were furnished with little
towers.   The design of this has for a long time been shown
at the house of Cardinal Duprat, the king's chancellor.
The constable ransacked his brains, and at the bottom,
from his finest stratagems, drew the best, and fitted it so
well to the present case, that the gallant would be certain
to be taken like a hare in the trap.   " 'Sdeath," said he,
" my planter of horns is taken, and I have the time now to
think how I shall finish him off."

Now this is the order of battle which this grand hairy
captain who waged such glorious war against Duke Jean-
sans-Peur commanded for the assault of his secret enemy.
He took a goodly number of his most loyal and adroit
archers. and placed them in the quay tower, ordering them

under the heaviest penalties to draw without distinction
of persons, except his wife, on those of his household
who should attempt to leave the gardens, and to admit

therein, either by night or by day, the favoured gentleman.
The same was done on the porch side, in the Rue St.
Antoine.

The retainers, even the chaplain, were ordered not to
leave the house under pain of death. Then the guard of
the two sides of the hotel having been committed to the
soldiers of a company of ordnance, who were ordered to
keep a sharp look out in the side streets, it was certain that
the unknown lover, to whom the constable was indebted for
his pair of horns, would be taken warm, when, knowing
nothing, he should come at the accustomed hour of love to
insolently plant his standard in the heart of the legitimate
appurtenances of the said lord count.

It was a trap into which the most expert man would fall
unless he were seriously protected by the fates, as was the
good St. Peter by the Saviour when he prevented him going to
the bottom of the sea the day when they had a fancy to try
if the sea were as solid as *terra firma.*

The constable had business with the inhabitants of Poissy,
and was obliged to be in the saddle after dinner, so that,
knowing his intention, the poor Countess Bonne determined
at night to invite her young gallant to that charming duel
in which she was always the stronger.

While the constable was making round his hotel a girdle
of spies and of death, and hiding his people near the postern
to seize the gallant as he came out, not knowing where he
would spring from, his wife was not amusing herself by
threading peas or seeing black cows in the embers. First,
the maid-servant who had been stuck, unstuck herself and
dragged herself to her mistress ; she told her that her
outraged lord knew nothing, and that before giving up the
ghost she would comfort her dear mistress by assuring her
that she could have perfect confidence in her sister, who
was laundress in the hotel, and was willing to let herself
be chopped as up small as sausage-meat to please Madame.
This she was the most adroit and roguish woman in the
neighbourhood, and renowned from the council chamber to
the Trahoir cross among the common people, as fertile in
invention for the desperate cases of love.

Then, while weeping for the decease of her good chamber-woman, the countess sent for the laundress, made her leave her tubs and join her in rummaging the bag of good tricks, wishing to save Savoisy, even at the price of her future salvation.

First of all the two women determined to let him know their lord and master's suspicions, and beg him to be careful.

Now behold the good washerwoman who, carrying her tub like a mule, attempts to leave the hotel. But at the porch she found a man-at-arms who turned a deaf ear to all the blandishments of the wash-tub. Then she resolved, from her great devotion, to take the soldier on his weak side, and she tickled him so with her fondling that he romped very well with her, although he was armour-plated ready for battle ; but when the game was over he still refused to let her go into the street, and although she tried to get herself a passport sealed by some of the handsomest, believing them more gallant : neither the archers, men-at-arms, nor others, dared open for her the smallest entrance of the house. "You are wicked and ungrateful wretches," said she, "not to render me a like service."

Luckily at this employment she learned everything, and came back in great haste to her mistress, to whom she re-counted the strange machinations of the count. The two women held a fresh council and had not considered, the time it takes to sing *Alleluia*, twice, these warlike ap-pearances, watches, defences, and equivocal, specious, and diabolical orders and dispositions before they recognised by the sixth sense with which all females are furnished, the special danger which threatened the poor lover.

Madame having learnt that she alone had leave to quit the house, ventured quickly to profit by her right, but she did not go the length of a bow-shot, since the con-stable had ordered four of his pages to be always on duty ready to accompany the countess, and two of the ensigns of his company not to leave her. Then the poor lady returned to her chamber, weeping as much as all the Magdalens one sees in the church pictures, could weep together.

" Alas !" said she, " my lover must then be killed, and I shall never see him again! . . . he whose words were so sweet, whose manners were so graceful, that lovely head that has so often rested on my knees, will now be bruised . . . What! can I not throw to my husband an empty and value-less head in place of the one full of charms and worth . . . a rank head for a sweet-smelling one ; a hated head for a head of love."

" Ah, Madame !" cried the washerwoman, " suppose we dress up in the garments of a nobleman, the steward's son who is mad for me, and wearies me much, and having thus accoutred him, we push him out through the postern."

Thereupon the two women looked at each other with assassinating eyes.

" This marplot," said she, " once slain, all those soldiers will fly away like geese."

" Yes, but will not the count recognise the wretch ?"

And the countess, striking her breast, exclaimed, shaking her head, " No, no, my dear, here it is noble blood that must be spilt without stint."

Then she thought a little, and jumping with joy, suddenly kissed the laundress, saying, " Because I have saved my lover's life by your counsel, I will pay you for his life until death."

Thereupon the countess dried her tears, put on the face of a bride, took her little bag and her prayer-book, and went towards the church of St. Pol, whose bells she heard ringing, seeing that the last Mass was about to be said. In this sweet devotion the countess never failed, being a showy woman, like all the ladies of the court. Now this was called the *full-dress Mass*, because none but fops, fashionables, young gentlemen and ladies puffed out and highly scented, were to be met there. In fact no dresses were seen there without armorial bearings, and no spurs that were not gilt.

So the Countess Bonne departed, leaving at the hotel the laundress much astonished, and charged to keep her eyes about her, and came with great pomp to the church, accom

This was called the *full-dress Mass*, because none but tops, fashionables, young gentlemen and ladies puffed out and highly scented were to be met there.

panied by her pages, the two ensigns and men-at-arms.
It is here necessary to say that among the band of gallant
knights who frisked round the ladies in church, the countess
had more than one whose joy she was, and who had given
his heart to her, after the fashion of youths who put
down enough and to spare upon their tablets, only in order to
make a conquest of at least one out of a great number.

Among these birds of fine prey who with open beaks
looked oftener between the benches and the paternosters than
towards the altar and the priests, there was one upon whom
the countess sometimes bestowed the charity of a glance,
because he was less trifling and more deeply smitten than all
the others.

This one remained
bashful, always stuck
against the same pillar,
never moving from it, but
readily ravished with the
sight alone of this lady
whom he had chosen as
his. His pale face was
softly melancholy. His
physiognomy gave proof
of a fine heart, one of
those which nourish ar-
dent passions and plunge
delightedly into the des-
pairs of a love without
hope. Of these people
there are few, because ordinarily one likes more a
certain thing than the
unknown felicities laying
and flourishing at the bot-
tommost depths of the soul ?

This said gentleman, although his garments were well
made, and clean and neat, having even a certain amount of
taste shown in the arrangement, seemed to the constable's
wife to be a poor knight seeking fortune, and come from afar,

with his nobility for his portion. Now partly from a suspicion
of his secret poverty, partly because she was well beloved
by him and a little because he had a good countenance, fine
black hair, and a good figure, and remained humble
and submissive in all, the constable had wished for him the
favour of women and of fortune, not to let his gallantry
stand idle, and from a good housewifely idea, she fired his
imagination according to her phantasies, by certain small
favours and little looks which serpented towards him like
biting adders, trifling with the happiness of this young life,
like a princess accustomed to play with objects more precious than a simple knight. In fact, her husband risked the
whole kingdom as you would a penny at piquet. Finally
it was only three days since, at the conclusion of vespers, that
the constable's wife, pointing out to the queen this follower
of love, said laughing—

" There's a man of quality."

This sentence remained in the fashionable language.
Later it became a custom so to designate the people of the
court. It was to the wife of the constable d'Armagnac, and
to no other source, that the French language is indebted for
this charming expression.

By a lucky chance the countess had surmised correctly
concerning this gentleman. He was a bannerless knight,
named Julien de Boys-Bourredon, who not having inherited
on his estate enough to make a toothpick, and knowing no
other wealth than the rich nature with which his dead mother
had opportunely furnished him, conceived the idea of deriving
therefrom both rent and profit at Court, knowing how fond
ladies are of these good revenues, and value them high
and dear, when they can stand being looked at between
two suns. There are many like him who have thus taken
the narrow road of women to make their way; but he, far
from arranging his love in measured quantities, spent funds
and all, as soon as, come to the full-dress Mass, he saw the
triumphant beauty of the Countess Bonne. Then he fell
really in love, which was a grand thing for his crowns, because he lost both thirst and appetite. This love is of the
worst kind, because it incites you to the love of diet, during

Then he fell really in love, which was a grand thing for his crowns, because
he lost both thirst and appetite.   This love is of the worst kind.

the diet of love ; a double malady, of which one is sufficient to extinguish a man.

Such was the young gentleman of whom the good lady had thought, and towards whom she came quickly to invite him to his death.

On entering, she saw the poor chevalier, who faithful to his pleasure, awaited her, his back against a pillar, as a sick man longs for the sun, the spring-time, and the dawn. Then she turned away her eyes, and wished to go to the queen and request her assistance in this desperate case, for she took pity on her lover, but one of the captains said to her, with great appearance of respect, " Madame, we have orders not to allow you to speak with man or woman, even though it should be the queen or your confessor. And remember that the lives of all of us are at stake."

" Is it not your business to die ?" said she.

" And also to obey," replied the soldier.

Then the countess knelt down in her accustomed place, and again regarding her faithful slave, found his face thinner and more deeply lined than ever it had been.

" Bah !" said she, " I shall have less remorse for his death ; he is half dead as it is."

With this paraphrase of her idea, she cast upon the said gentleman one of those warm little ogles that are only allowable in princesses and harlots, and the false love which her lovely eyes bore witness to, gave a pleasant pang to the gallant of the pillar. Who does not love the warm attack of life when it flows thus round the heart and engulfs everything.

Madame recognised with a pleasure, always fresh in the minds of women, the omnipotence of her magnificent regard by the answer which, without saying a word, the chevalier made to it. And in fact, the blushes which empurpled his cheeks spoke better than the best speeches of the Greek and Latin orators, and was also well understood. At this sweet sight, the countess, to make sure that it was not a freak of nature, took pleasure in experimentalizing how far the virtue of her eyes would go, and after having heated her slave more than thirty times, she was confirmed

in her belief that he would bravely die for her. This idea
so touched her, that from three repetitions between her
orisons she was tickled with the desire to put into a lump
all the joys of man, and to dissolve them for him in one
single glance of love, in order that she should not one
day be reproached with having not only dissipated the
life, but also the happiness of this gentleman. When the
officiating priest turned round to sing the *Off you go* to this
fine gilded flock, the constable's wife went out by the side
of the pillar where her courtier was, passed in front of him
and endeavoured to insinuate into his understanding by a
speaking glance that he was to follow her, and to make
positive the intelligence and significant interpretation of this
gentle appeal, the artful jade turned round again a little
after passing him to again request his company. She saw
that he had moved a little from his place, and dared not
advance, so modest was he, but upon this last sign, the
gentleman, sure of not being over-credulous, mixed with
the crowd with little and noiseless steps, like an innocent
who is afraid of venturing in one of those good places
people call bad ones. And whether he walked behind or
in front, to the right or to the left, my lady bestowed upon
him a glistening glance to allure him the more and the
better to draw him to her, like a fisher who gently jerks
the line in order to hook the gudgeon. To be brief: the
countess practised so well the profession of the daughters of
pleasure when they work to bring grist into their mills, that
one would have said nothing resembled a harlot so much as
a woman of high birth. And indeed, on arriving at the
porch of her hotel the countess hesitated to enter therein,
and again turned her face towards the poor chevalier
to invite him to accompany her, discharging at him
so diabolical a glance, that he ran to the queen of his
heart, believing himself to be called by her. Thereupon
she offered him her hand, and both boiling and trembling from contrary causes found themselves inside the
house. At this wretched hour, Madame d'Armagnac was
ashamed of having done all these harlotries to the profit
of death, and of betraying Savoisy the better to save him ;

And whether he walked behind or in front, to the right or to
the left, my lady bestowed upon him a glistening glance.

but this slight remorse was lame as the greater, and came tardily. Seeing everything ready, the countess leant heavily upon her vassal's arm, and said to him—

" Come quickly to my room; it is necessary that I should speak with you."

And he, not knowing that his life was in peril, found no voice wherewith to reply, so much did the hope of approach-ing happiness choke him.

When the laundress saw this handsome gentleman so quickly hooked, " Ah !" said she, " these ladies of the court are the best at such work." Then she honoured this courtier with a profound salutation, in which was depicted the ironical respect due to those who have the great courage to die for so little.

" Picard," said the constable's lady, drawing the laundress to her by the skirt, " I have not the courage to confess to him the reward with which I am about to pay his silent love and his charming belief in the loyalty of women."

" Bah ! Madame : why tell him ? Send him away well contented by the postern. So many men die in war for nothing, cannot this one die for something. I'll make another from him if that will console you."

" Come along," cried the countess, " I will confess all to him. That shall be the punishment for my sin."

Thinking that his lady was arranging with her servant certain trifling provisions and secret things in order not to be disturbed in the interview she had promised him, the unknown lover kept at a discreet distance, looking at the flies. Nevertheless, he thought that the countess was very bold, but also, as even a hunchback would have done, he found a thousand reasons to justify her, and thought himself quite worthy to inspire such recklessness. He was lost in these good thoughts when the constable's wife opened the door of her chamber, and invited the chevalier to follow her in. There his noble lady cast aside all the apparel of her lofty fortune, and falling at the feet of this gentleman, became a simple woman.

" Alas, sweet sir !" said she, " I have acted vilely towards you. Listen. On your departure from this house, you will

meet your death.   The love which I feel for another has
bewildered me, and without being able to hold his place here,
you will have to take it before his murderers.   This is the
joy to which I have bidden you."

"Ah !" replied Boys-Bourredon, interring in the depths of
his heart a dark despair, "I am grateful to you for having
made use of me as of something which belonged to you. . .
Yes, I love you so much that every day I have dreamed of
offering you in imitation of the ladies, a thing that can be
given but once.   Take, then, my life !"

And the poor chevalier, in saying this, gave her one glance
to suffice for all the time he would have been able to look
at her through the long days.   Hearing these brave and
loving words, Bonne rose suddenly.

"Ah! were it not for Savoisy, how I would love thee !"
said she.

"Alas ! my fate is then accomplished," replied Boys-
Bourredon.   " My horoscope predicted that I should die by
the love of a great lady.   Ah, God !" said he, clutching his
good sword, "I will sell my life dearly, but I shall die
content in thinking that my decease assures the happiness of
her I love.   I shall live better in her memory than in reality."
At the sight of the gesture and the beaming face of this
courageous man, the constable's wife was pierced to the
heart.   But soon she was wounded to the quick because he
seemed to wish to leave her without even asking of her the
smallest favour.

" Come, that I may arm you," said she to him, making an
attempt to kiss him.

" Ha ! my lady-love," replied he, moistening with a gentle
tear the fire of her eyes, " would you render my death impossible by attaching too great a value to my life ?"

" Come," cried she, overcome by this intense love, " I do
not know what the end of all this will be, but come—afterwards we will go and perish together at the postern."

The same flame leaped in their hearts, the same harmony
had struck for both, they embraced each other with rapture in
the delicious access of that mad fever which you know well
I hope ; they fell into a profound forgetfulness of the dangers

At the sight of the gesture and the beaming face of this courageous
man, the constable's wife was pierced to the heart.

of Savoisy, of themselves, of the constable, of death, of life, of everything.

Meanwhile the watchmen at the porch had gone to inform the constable of the arrival of the gallant, and to tell him how the enraged gentleman had taken no notice of the winks which, during Mass and on the road, the countess had given him in order to prevent his destruction. They met their master arriving in great haste at the postern, because on their side the archers of the quay had whistled to him afar off, saying to him—

" The Sire de Savoisy has passed in."

And indeed Savoisy had come at the appointed hour, and like all the lovers, thinking only of his lady, he had not seen the count's spies and had slipped in at the postern. This collision of lovers was the cause of the constable's cutting short the words of those who came from the Rue St. Antoine, saying to them with a gesture of authority, that they did not think wise to disregard—

" I know that the animal is taken."

Thereupon all rushed with a great noise through the said postern, crying, " Death to him ! death to him !" and men-at-arms, archers, the constable, and the captains, all rushed full tilt upon Charles Savoisy, the king's nephew, whom they attacked just under the countess's window, where by a strange chance, the groans of the poor young man were dolorously exhaled, mingled with the yells of the soldiers, at the same time as passionate sighs and cries were given forth by the two lovers, who hastened up in great fear.

" Ah," said the countess, turning pale from terror, " Savoisy is dying for me !"

" But I will live for you," replied Boys-Bourredon, " and shall esteem it a joy to pay the same price for my happiness as he has done."

" Hide yourself in the clothes chest," cried the countess ; " I hear the constable's footsteps."

And indeed M. d'Armagnac appeared very soon with a head in his hand, and putting it all bloody on the mantel-shelf, " Behold, Madame," said he, " a picture which will en-

"**Ah!**" said the countess, pale with terror, "Savoisy is dying for **me!**"

lighten you concerning the duties of a wife towards her husband."

"You have killed an innocent man," replied the countess, without changing colour. "Savoisy was not my lover."

And with this speech she looked proudly at the constable with a face marked by so much dissimulation and feminine audacity, that the husband stood looking as foolish as a girl who has allowed a note to escape her below, before a numerous company, and he was afraid of having made a mistake.

"Of whom were you thinking this morning?" asked he.

"I was dreaming of the king," said she.

"Then, my dear, why not have told me so?"

"Would you have believed me in the bestial passion you were in?"

The constable scratched his ear and replied—

"But how came Savoisy with the key of the postern?"

"I don't know," said she, curtly, "if you will have the goodness to believe what I have said to you."

And his wife turned lightly on her heel like a weather-cock turned by the wind, pretending to go and look after the household affairs. You can imagine that D'Armagnac was greatly embarrassed with the head of poor Savoisy, and that for his part Boys-Bourredon had no desire to cough while listening to the count, who was growling to himself all sorts of words. At length the constable struck two heavy blows over the table and said, "I'll go and attack the inhabitants of Poissy." Then he departed, and when the night was come Boys-Bourredon escaped from the house in some disguise or other.

Poor Savoisy was sorely lamented by his lady, who had done all that a woman could do to save her lover, and later he was more than wept, he was regretted ; and the countess having related this adventure to Queen Isabella, her majesty seduced Boys-Bourredon from the service of her cousin and put him to her own, so much was she touched with the qualities and firm courage of this gentleman.

Boys-Bourredon was a man whom danger had well recommended to the ladies. In fact he comported himself so

"Behold, madame," said he, "a picture which will enlighten you
concerning the duties of a wife towards her husband.

proudly in everything in the lofty fortune, which the queen
had made for him, that having badly treated King Charles

one day when the poor man was
in his proper senses, the courtiers, jealous of favour, informed
the king of his cuckoldom.
Then Boys-Bourredon was in
a moment sewn in a sack
and thrown into the Seine, near
the ferry at Charenton, as
every one knows. I have no
need to add, that since the
day when the constable took it into his head to play
thoughtlessly with knives, his good wife utilized so well the
two deaths he had caused and threw them so often in his
face, that she made him as soft as a cat's paw and put him in
the straight road of marriage; and he proclaimed her a
modest and virtuous constable's lady, as indeed she was.
As this book should, according to the maxims of great
ancient authors, join certain useful things to the good-laughs
which you will find therein and contains precepts of high
taste, I beg to inform you that the quintessence of this
story is this: That women need never lose their heads in
serious cases, because the God of Love never abandons them,
especially when they are beautiful, young, and of good
family: and that gallants when going to keep an amorous
assignation should never go there like giddy young men, but
carefully, and keep a sharp look-out near the burrow, to avoid
falling into certain traps and to preserve themselves; for
after a good woman the most precious thing is, certes, a pretty
gentleman.

THE MAID OF THILOUSE.

THE lord of Valennes, a pleasant place, of which the castle is not far from the town of Thilouse, had taken a mean wife, who by reason of taste or antipathy, pleasure or displeasure, health or sickness, allowed her good husband to abstain from those pleasures stipulated for in all contracts of marriage. In order to be just, it should be stated that the above mentioned lord was a dirty and ill-favoured person, always hunting wild animals and not more entertaining than is a room full of smoke. And what is more, the said sportsman was all sixty years of age, on which subject, however, he was as silent as an hempen widow on the subject of rope. But nature, which the crooked, the bandy-legged, the blind, and the ugly abuse so unmercifully here below, and have no more esteem for her than the well-favoured,— since, like workers of tapestry, they know not what they do,—gives the same appetite to all, and to all the same mouth for pudding. So every beast finds a mate, and from the same fact comes the proverb, " There is no pot, however ugly, that does not one day find a cover." Now the lord of Valennes searched everywhere for nice little pots to cover, and often in addition to wild,

Above all was she strict in keeping hands off the maiden.

he hunted tame animals ; but this kind of game was
scarce in the land, and it was an expensive affair to discover

a maid. At length, however, by reason of much ferreting
about and much inquiry, it happened that the lord of
Valennes was informed that in Thilouse was the widow of a
weaver who had a real treasure in the person of a little
damsel of sixteen years, whom she had never allowed to
leave her apronstrings, and whom, with great maternal
forethought, she always accompanied when the calls of
nature demanded her obedience ; she had her to sleep with
her in her own bed, watched over her, got her up in the
morning, and put her to such work that between the
twain they gained about eight pennies a day. On fête
days she took her to the church, scarcely giving her
a spare moment to exchange a merry word with the young
people ; above all was she
strict in keeping hands off
the maiden.

But the times were just
then so hard that the
widow and her daughter
had only bread enough to
save them from dying of
hunger, and as they lodged with one of their poor
relations, they often wanted wood in winter and clothes
in summer, owing enough rent to frighten sergeants of
justice, men who are not easily frightened at the debts

of others; in short, while the daughter was increasing in beauty, the mother was increasing in poverty and ran into debt on account of her daughter's virginity, as an alchemist will for the crucible in which his all is cast. As soon as his plans were arranged and perfect, one rainy day the said lord of Valennes by a mere chance came into the hovel of the two spinners, and in order to dry himself sent for some fagots to Plessis, close by. While waiting for them, he sat on a stool between the two poor women. By means of the grey shadows and half light of the cabin, he saw the sweet countenance of the Maid of Thilouse; her arms were red and firm, her breasts hard as bastions, which kept the cold from her heart, her waist round as a young oak, and all fresh and clean and pretty, like a first frost; green and tender as an April bud; in fact, she resembled all that is prettiest in the world. She had eyes of a modest and virtuous blue, with a look more coy than that of the Virgin, for she was less forward, never having had a child.

Had any one said to her, "Come, let us make love," she would have said, "Love! what is that?" she was so innocent and so little open to the comprehension of the thing.

The good old lord twisted about upon his stool, eyeing the maid and stretching his neck like a monkey trying to catch nuts, which the mother noticed, but said not a word, being in fear of the lord to whom the whole of the country belonged. When the fagot was put into the grate and flared up, the good hunter said to the old woman, " Ah ah ! that warms one almost as much as your daughter's eyes."

" But alas, my lord," said she, " we have nothing to cook on that fire."

" Oh yes," replied he.

" What ?"

" Ah, my good woman, lend your daughter to my wife, who has need of a good handmaiden; we will give you two fagots every day."

" Oh, my lord, what could I cook at such a good fire ?"

"Why," replied the old rascal, "good broth, for I will give you a measure of corn in season."

"Then," replied the old hag, "where shall I put it?"

"In your dish," answered the purchaser of innocence.

"But I have neither dish nor flour-bin, nor anything."

"Well, I will give you dishes and flour-bins, saucepans, flagons, a good bed with curtains, and everything."

"Yes," replied the good widow, "but the rain would spoil them, I have no house."

"You can see from here," replied the lord, "the house of La Tourbellière, where lived my poor huntsman Pillegrain, who was ripped up by a boar?"

"Yes," said the old woman.

"Well, you can make yourself at home there for the rest of your days."

"By my faith!" cried the mother, letting fall her distaff, "do you mean what you say?"

"Yes."

"Well, then, what will you give my daughter?"

All that she is willing to gain in my service."

"Oh! my lord, you are joking."

" No," said he.

" Yes," said she.

" By St. Gatien, St. Eleuther, and by the thousand million saints who move in heaven, I swear that——"

" Ah! well; if you are not jesting I should like those fagots to pass through the hands of the notary."

" By the blood of Christ and the charms of your daughter am I not a gentleman ? is not my word good enough ?"

" Ah ! well, I don't say that it is not; but as true as I am a poor spinner I love my child too much to leave her; she is too young and weak at present, she would break down in service. Yesterday, in his sermon, the vicar said that we should have to answer to God for our children."

" There ! there !" said the lord, "go and find the notary."

An old woodcutter ran to the scrivener, who came and drew up a contract, to which the lord of Valennes put his cross, not knowing how to write, and when all was signed and sealed—

" Well, old lady," said he, " now you are no longer answerable to God for the virtue of your child."

" Ah ! my lord, the vicar said until the age of reason, and my child is quite reasonable." Then turning towards her, she added, " Marie Fiquet, that which is dearest to you is your honour, and there where you are going every one, without counting my lord, will try to rob you of it, but you see well what it is worth ; for that reason do not lose it save willingly and in a proper manner. Now in order not to contaminate your virtue before God and before man, except for a legitimate motive, take heed that your chance of marriage be not damaged beforehand, otherwise you will go to the bad."

" Yes, dear mother," replied the maid.

And thereupon she left the poor abode of her relation, and came to the chateau of Valennes, there to serve my lady, who found her both pretty and to her taste.

When the people of Valennes, Saché, Villaines, and other places, learned the high price given for the maid of Thilouse, the good housewives recognising the fact that nothing is more profitable than virtue, endeavoured to nourish

and bring up their daughters virtuous ; but the business was as
risky as that of rearing silkworms, which are liable to perish,
since innocence is like a medlar, and ripens quickly on the
straw.   There were, however, some girls noted for it in
Touraine, who passed for virgins in the convents of the
religious, but I cannot vouch for these, not having proceeded
to verify them in the manner laid down by Verville, in order to
make sure of the perfect virtue of women.   However, Marie
Fiquet followed the wise counsel of her mother, and would
take no notice of the soft requests, honied words, or apish
tricks of her master, unless they were flavoured with a
promise of marriage.

When the old lord tried to kiss her, she would put her
back up like a cat at the approach of a dog, crying out, " I
will tell Madame!" In short, at the end of six months he had
not even recovered the price of a single faggot.   From her
labour La Fiquet became harder and firmer.   Sometimes she
would reply to the gentle request of her master, " When you
have taken it from me will you give it me back again ?"
Another time she would say, "If I were as full of holes as a
sieve not one should be for you, so ugly do I think you."

The good old man took these village sayings for flowers
of innocence, and ceased not to make little signs to her,
long harangues and a hundred vows and sermons, for by
reason of seeing the fine breasts of the maid, her plump hips,

which at certain movements came into prominent relief, and
by reason of admiring other things capable of inflaming the
mind of a saint, this dear man became enamoured of her
with an old man's passion, which augments in geometrical

proportions as opposed to the passions of young men, because the old
men love with their weakness which
grows greater, and the young with
their strength which grows less.   In
order to leave this headstrong girl no
loophole for refusal, the old lord took
into his confidence the steward, whose
age was seventy odd years, and made
him understand that he ought to
marry in order to keep his body
warm, and that Marie Fiquet was
the very girl to suit him.   The old

steward, who had gained three hundred pounds by different services about the house, desired to live quietly without opening the front door again ; but his good master begged him to marry to please him, assuring him that he need not trouble about his wife. So the good steward wandered out of sheer good nature into this marriage. The day of the wedding, bereft of all her reasons, and not able to find objections to her pursuer, she made him give her a fat settlement and dowry as the price of her conquest, and then gave the old knave leave to wink at her as often as he could, promising him as many embraces as he had given grains of wheat to her mother. But at his age a bushel was sufficient.

The festivities over, the lord did not fail, as soon as his wife had retired, to wend his way towards the well-glazed, well-carpeted, and pretty room where he had lodged his lass, his money, his faggots, his house, his wheat, and his steward. To be brief, know that he found the maid of Thilouse the sweetest girl in the world, as pretty as anything, by the soft light of the fire which was gleaming in the chimney, snug between the sheets, with a sweet odour about her, as a young maiden should have, and in fact he had no regret for the great price of this jewel. Not being able to restrain himself from hurrying over the first mouthfuls of this royal morsel, the lord treated her more as a past master than a young beginner. So the happy man by too much gluttony, managed badly, and in fact knew nothing of the sweet business of love. Finding which, the good wench said, after a minute or two, to her old cavalier, " My lord, if you are there, as I think you are, give a little more swing to your bells."

From this saying, which became spread about, I know not how, Marie Fiquet became famous, and it is still said in our country, " She is a maid of Thilouse," in mockery of a bride, and to signify a " fricquenelle."

" Fricquenelle" is said of a girl I do not wish you to find in your arms on your wedding night, unless you have been brought up in the philosophy of Zeno, which puts up with anything, and there are many people obliged to be Stoics in this funny situation, which is often met with, for Nature turns, but changes not, and there are always good maids of

Thilouse to be found in Touraine, and elsewhere. Now if you ask me in what consists, or where comes in, the moral of this tale? I am at liberty to reply to the ladies; that the Cent Contes Drolatiques are made more to teach the moral of pleasure than to procure the pleasure of pointing a moral. But if it were a used up old rascal who asked me, I should say to him, with all the respect due to his yellow or grey locks; that God wished to punish the lord of Valennes, for trying to purchase a jewel made to be given.

THE BROTHER-IN-ARMS.

A T the commencement of the reign of King Henry, second of the name, who loved so well the fair Diana, there existed still a ceremony of which the usage has since become much weakened, and which has altogether disappeared, like an infinity of the good things of the olden times. This fine and noble custom was the choice which all knights made of a brother-in-arms. After having recognised each other as two loyal and brave men, each one of this pretty couple was married for life to the other; both became brothers, the one had to defend the other in battling against the enemies who threatened him, and at Court against the friends who slandered him. In the absence of his companion the other was expected to say to one who should have accused his good brother of any disloyalty, wickedness or dark felony, " You have lied by your throat," and so go into the field instantly, so sure was the one of the honour of the other. There is no need to add, that the one was always the second of the other in all affairs, good or evil, and that they shared all good or evil fortune. They were better than the brothers who are only united by the hazard of nature, since they were fraternized by the bonds of an especial sentiment, involuntary and mutual, and thus the fraternity of

"Thou my Seraphim,
 You my soul,
 Thou my God,
 You my morning and evening star."

arms has produced splendid characters, as brave as those of
the ancient Greeks, Romans, or others. . . . . . But this
is not my subject; the history of these things has been written
by the historians of our country, and every one knows
them.

Now at this time two young gentlemen of Touraine, of
whom one was the Cadet of Maillé, and the other the
Sieur de Lavallière, became brothers-in-arms on the day they
gained their spurs. They were leaving the house of Monsieur
de Montmorency, where they had been nourished with the
good doctrines of this great Captain, and had shown how
contagious is valour in such good company, for at the battle
of Ravenna they merited the praises of the oldest knights.

It was in the thick of this fierce fight that Maillé, saved by
the said Lavallière, with whom he had had a quarrel or two,
perceived that this gentleman had a noble heart. As they had
each received slashes in their doublets, they baptized their
fraternity with their blood, and were ministered to together
in one and the same bed under the tent of Monsieur de
Montmorency their master. It is necessary to inform you
that, contrary to the custom of his family, which was always
to have a pretty face, the Cadet of Maillé was not of a pleasing

physiognomy, and had scarcely any beauty but that of the devil. For the rest, he was lithe as a greyhound, broad-shouldered and strongly built as King Pepin, who was a terrible antagonist. On the other hand, the Sieur de Chateau-Lavallière was a dainty fellow, for whom seemed to have been invented rich laces, silken hose, and cancellated shoes. His long dark locks were pretty as a lady's ringlets, and he was, to be brief, a child with whom all the women would be glad to play. One day the Dauphine, niece of the Pope, said laughingly to the Queen of Navarre, who did not dislike these little jokes, " that this page was a plaster to cure every ache," which caused the pretty little Tourainian to blush, because, being only sixteen, he took this gallantry as a reproach.

Now on his return from Italy the Cadet of Maillé found the slipper of marriage ready for his foot, the which his mother had obtained for him in the person of Mademoiselle d'Annebaut, who was a graceful maiden of good appearance, and well furnished with everything, having a splendid hotel in the Rue Barbette, with handsome furniture and Italian paintings and many considerable lands to inherit. Some days after the death of King Francis—a circumstance which planted terror in the hearts of every one, because his said Majesty had died in consequence of an attack of the Neapolitan sickness, and that for the future there would be no security even with princesses of the highest birth—the above-named Maillé was compelled to quit the Court in order to go and arrange certain affairs of great importance in Piedmont. You may be sure that he was very loth to leave his good wife, so young, so delicate, so sprightly, in the midst of the dangers, temptations, snares and pitfalls of this gallant assemblage, which comprised so many handsome fellows, bold as eagles, proud of mien, and as fond of women as the people are partial to Paschal hams. In this state of intense jealousy everything made him ill at ease ; but by dint of much thinking, it occurred to him to make sure of his wife

in the manner about to be related. He invited his good
brother-in-arms to come at daybreak on the morning of his
departure. Now directly he heard Lavallière's horse in the
courtyard, he leaped out of the bed, leaving his sweet and
fair better-halt sleeping that gentle, dreamy, dozing sleep
so beloved by dainty ladies and lazy people. Lavallière
came to him, and the two companions, hidden in the
embrasure of the window, greeted each other with a loyal
clasp of the hand, and immediately Lavallière said to
Maillé—

" I should have been here last night in answer to thy
summons, but I had a love suit on with my lady, who
had given me an assignation; I could in no way fail to keep
it, but I quitted her at dawn. Shall I accompany thee? I
have told her of thy departure, she has promised me to
remain without any amour; we have made a compact. If
she deceive me—well, a friend is worth more than a
mistress !"

" Oh ! my good brother," replied Maillé, quite overcome
with these words, " I wish to demand of thee a still higher
proof of thy brave heart. Wilt thou take charge of my wife,
defend her against all, be her guide, keep her in check and
answer to me for the integrity of my head? Thou canst
stay here during my absence, in the green-room, and be my
wife's cavalier."

Lavallière knitted his brow and said—

" It is neither thee nor thy wife that I fear. but evil-
minded people, who will take advantage of this to entangle
us like skeins of silk."

" Do not be afraid of me," replied Maillé, clasping
Lavallière to his breast. " If it be the divine will of the
Almighty that I shall have the misfortune to be a cuckold, I
should be less grieved if it were to your advantage. But by
my faith I should die of grief, for my life is bound up in my
good, young, virtuous wife."

Saying which, he turned away his head, in order that
Lavallière should not perceive the tears in his eyes; but the
fine courtier saw this flow of water, and taking the hand of
Maillé—

"Brother, said he to him, "I swear to thee on my honour as a man, that before any one lays a finger on thy wife, he shall have felt my dagger in the depth of his veins! And, unless I should die, thou shalt find her on thy return, intact in body if not in heart, because thought is beyond the control of gentlemen."

"It is then decreed above!" exclaimed Maillé, "that I shall always be thy servant and thy debtor!"

Thereupon the comrade departed, in order not to be inundated with the tears, exclamations, and other expressions of grief which ladies make use of when saying "Farewell." Lavallière having conducted him to the gate of the town, came back to the hotel, waited until Marie d'Annebaut was out of bed, informed her of the departure of her good husband, and offered to place himself at her orders, in such a graceful manner, that the most virtuous woman would have been tickled with a desire to keep such a knight to herself. But there was no need of this fine paternoster to indoctrinate the lady, seeing that she had listened to the discourse of the two friends, and was greatly offended at her husband's doubt. Alas! God alone is perfect! In all the ideas of men there is always a bad side, and it is therefore a great science in life, but an impossible science, to take hold of everything, even a stick by the right end. The cause of the great difficulty there is in pleasing the ladies is, that there is in them a thing which is more woman than they are, and but for the respect which is due to them, I would use another word. Now we should never awaken the phantasy of this malevolent thing. The perfect government of women is a task to rend a man's heart, and we are compelled to remain in perfect submission to them ; that is, I imagine, the best manner in which to solve the most agonizing enigma of marriage.

Now Marie d'Annebaut was delighted with the bearing and offers of the gallant ; but there was something in her smile which indicated a malicious idea, and, to speak plainly, the intention of putting her young guardian between honour and pleasure ; to regale him so with love, to surround him with so many little attentions, to pursue him with such warm glances, that he would be faithless to friendship, to the advantage of gallantry.

Everything was in perfect trim for the carrying out of her design, because of the companionship which the Sire de Lavallière would be obliged to have with her during his stay in the hotel, and as there is nothing in the world can turn a woman from her whim, at every turn the artful jade was ready to catch him in a trap.

At times she would make him remain seated near her by the fire, until twelve o'clock at night, singing soft refrains, and at every opportunity showing her fair shoulders, and the white temptations of which her corset was full, and casting upon him a thousand piercing glances, all without showing in her face the thoughts that surged in her brain.

At times she would walk with him in the morning, in the gardens of the hotel, leaning heavily upon his arm, pressing it, sighing, and making him tie the laces of her little shoes, which were always coming undone in that particular place. Then it would be those soft words and things which the ladies understand so well, little attentions paid to a guest, such as coming in to see if he were comfortable, if his bed were well made, the room clean, if the ventilation were good, if he felt any draughts in the night, if the sun came in during the day, and asking him to forego none of his usual fancies and habits, saying—

" Are you accustomed to take anything in the morning in bed, such as honey, milk, or spice? Do the meal times suit you? I will conform mine to yours : tell me. You are afraid to ask me. Come——"

She accompanied these coddling little attentions with a hundred affected speeches ; for instance, on coming into the room she would say—

"I am intruding, send me away. You want to be left alone—I will go." And always was she graciously invited to remain.

And the cunning Madame always came lightly attired, showing samples of her beauty, which would have made a patriarch neigh, even were he as much battered by time as must have been Mr. Methuselah, with his nine hundred and sixty years.

The good knight being as sharp as a needle, let the lady go on with her tricks, much pleased to see her occupy herself with him, since it was so much gained; but like a loyal brother, he always called her absent husband to the lady's mind.

Now one evening—the day had been very warm— Lavallière suspecting the lady's games, told her that Maillé loved her dearly, that she had in him a man of honour, a gentleman who doated on her, and was ticklish on the score of his crown.

" Why then, if he is so ticklish in this matter, has he placed you here ?"

" Was it not a most prudent thing?" replied he. " Was it not necessary to confide you to some defender of your virtue ? not that it needs one save to protect you from wicked men."

" Then you are my guardian ?" said she.

" I am proud of it !" exclaimed Lavallière.

" Ah !" said she, " he has made a very bad choice."

This remark was accompanied by a little look, so lewdly lascivious that the good brother-in-arms put on, by way of reproach, a severe countenance, and left the fair lady alone, much piqued at this refusal to commence love's conflict.

She remained in deep meditation, and began to search for the real obstacle that she had encountered, for it was impossible that it should enter the mind of any lady, that a gentleman could despise that bagatelle which is of such great price, and so high value. Now these thoughts knitted and joined together so well, one fitting into the other, that out of little pieces she constructed a perfect whole, and found herself desperately in love ; which should teach ladies never to play with a man's weapons, seeing that like glue, they always stick to the fingers.

By this means Marie d'Annebaut came to a conclusion which she should have known at the commencement—viz., that to keep clear of her snares, the good knight must be

smitten with some other lady, and looking around her, to
see where her young guest could have found a needle-case
to his taste, she thought of the fair Limeuil, one of Queen
Catherine's maids, of Mesdames de Nevers, d'Estrées, and de
Giac, all of whom were declared friends of Lavallière's, and
of the lot he must love one to distraction.

From this belief, she added the motive of jealousy to the
others which tempted her to seduce her Argus, whom she
did not wish to wound, but to perfume, kiss his head, and
treat kindly.

She was certainly more beautiful, young, and more appetizing
and gentle than her rivals ; at least, that was the melodious
decree of her imagination. So, urged on by the chords and
springs of conscience, and physical causes which affect
women, she returned to the charge, to commence a fresh
assault upon the heart of the chevalier, for the ladies like to
take that which is well fortified.

Then she played the pussy-cat, and nestled up close to
him, became so sweetly sociable, and wheedled him so gently,
that one evening when she was in a desponding state,
although merry enough in her inmost soul, her guardian-
brother asked her—

" What is the matter with you ?"

To which she replied to him dreamily, being listened to
by him as the sweetest music—

That she had married Maillé against her heart's will,
and that she was very unhappy; that she knew not the
sweets of love ; that her husband did not understand her,
and that her life was full of tears. In fact, that she was
a maiden in heart and all, since she confessed that in
marriage she had experienced nothing but the reverse of
pleasure. And she added, that surely this holy state should
be full of the sweetmeats and dainties of love, because all
the ladies hurried into it, and hated and were jealous of
those who out-bid them, for it cost certain people pretty
dear ; that she was so curious about it that for one good
day or night of love, she would give her life, and always
be obedient to her lover without a murmur ; but that he
with whom she would sooner than all others try the ex-

periment would not listen to her; that, nevertheless, the secret of their loves might be kept eternally, so great was her husband's confidence in him, and that finally if he still refused, it would kill her.

And all these paraphrases of the common canticle known to the ladies at their birth were ejaculated between a thousand pauses, interrupted with sighs torn from the heart, ornamented with quiverings, appeals to heaven, up-turned eyes, sudden blushings and clutchings at her hair. In fact, no ingredient of temptation was lacking in the dish, and at the bottom of all these words there was a nipping desire which embellished even its blemishes. The good knight fell at the lady's feet, and weeping took them and kissed them, and you may be sure the good woman was quite delighted to let him kiss them, and even without looking too carefully to see what she was going to do, she abandoned her dress to him, knowing well that to keep it from sweeping the ground it must be taken at the bottom to raise it; but it was written that for that evening she should be good, for the handsome Lavallière said to her with despair—

" Ah, madame, I am an unfortunate man, and a wretch."

" Not at all," said she.

" Alas, the joy of loving you is denied to me."

" How ?" said she.

" I dare not confess my situation to you !"

" Is it then very bad ?"

" Ah, you will be ashamed of me !"

"Speak, I will hide my face in my hands," and the cunning madam hid her face in such a way that she could look at her well-beloved between her fingers.

" Alas!" said he, " the other evening when you addressed me in such gracious words, I was so treacherously inflamed, that not knowing my happiness to be so near, and not daring to confess my flame to you, I ran to a Bordel where all the gentlemen go, and there for love of you, and to save the honour of my brother whose head I should blush to dishonour, I was so badly infected that I am in great danger of dying of the Italian sickness."

The lady, seized with terror, gave vent to the cry of a

woman in labour, and with great emotion, repulsed him with a gentle little gesture. Poor Lavallière, finding himself in so pitiable a state, went out of the room, but he had not even reached the tapestries of the door, when Marie d'Annebaut again contemplated him, saying to herself, " Ah ! what a pity !" Then she fell into a state of great melancholy, pitying in herself the gentleman, and became the more in love with him because he was fruit three times forbidden.

" But for Maillé," said she to him, one evening that she thought him handsomer than usual, " I would willingly take your disease. Together we should then have the same terrors."

" I love you too well," said the brother, " not to be good."

And he left her to go to his beautiful Limeuil. You can imagine that being unable to refuse to receive the burning glances of the lady, during meal times, and the evenings, there was a fire nourished that warmed them both, but she was compelled to live without touching her cavalier, otherwise than with her eyes. Thus occupied, Marie d'Annebaut was fortified at every point against the gallants of the Court, for there are no bounds so impassable as those of love, and no better guardian; it is like the devil, he whom it has in its clutches it surrounds with flames. One evening, Lavallière having escorted his friend's wife to a dance given by Queen Catherine, he danced with the fair Limeuil, with whom he was madly in love. At that time the knights carried on their amours bravely two by two, and even in troops. Now all the ladies were jealous of La Limeuil, who at that time

was thinking of yielding to the handsome Lavallière. Before taking their places in the quadrille, she had given him the sweetest of assignations for the morrow, during the

hunt.   Our great Queen Catherine, who from political
motives fomented these loves and stirred them up, like
pastrycooks make their oven fires burn by poking, glanced
at all the pretty couples interwoven in the quadrille, and
said to her husband—

"When they combat here, can they conspire against
you, eh?"

"Ah! but the Protestants?"

"Bah! have them here as well," said she, laughing. "Why,
look at Lavallière, who is suspected to be a Huguenot; he is
converted by my dear little Limeuil, who does not play her
cards badly for a young lady of sixteen.   He will soon have
her name down in his list."

"Ah, Madame! do not believe it," said Marie d'Annebaut,
"he is ruined through that same sickness of Naples which
made you queen."

At this artless confession, Catherine, the fair Diana, and
the king, who were sitting together, burst out laughing, and
the thing ran round the room.   This brought endless
shame and mockery upon Lavallière. The poor gentleman,
pointed at by every one, soon wished somebody else in his
shoes, for La Limeuil, whom his rivals had not been slow
laughingly to warn of her danger, appeared to shrink from
her lover, so rapid was the spread, and so violent the apprehensions of this nasty disease.   Thus Lavallière found himself abandoned by every one like a leper.   The king made
an offensive remark, and the good knight quitted the ball-
room, followed by poor Marie in despair at the speech. She
had in every way ruined the man she loved; she had destroyed
his honour, and marred his life, since the physicians and
master surgeons advanced as a fact, incapable of contradic-
tion, that persons Italianized by this love sickness, lost
through it their greatest attractions, as well as their generative
powers, and their bones went black.

Thus no woman would bind herself in legitimate marriage
with the finest gentleman in the kingdom if he were only
suspected of being one of those whom Master Francis
Rabelais named "*his very precious scabby ones. . . .*"

As the handsome knight was very silent and melancholy,

his companion said to him on the road home from Hercules House, where the fête had been held—

"My dear lord, I have done you a great mischief."

"Ah, madame!" replied Lavallière, "my hurt is curable; but into what a predicament have you fallen? You should not have been aware of the danger of my love."

"Ah!" said she, "I am sure now always to have you to myself; in exchange for this great obloquy and dishonour, I will be for ever your friend, your hostess, and your lady-love—more than that, your servant. My determination is to devote myself to you and efface the traces of this shame; to cure you by watch and ward; and if the learned in these matters declare that the disease has such hold of you that it will kill you like our defunct Sovereign, I must still have your company in order to die gloriously in dying of your complaint. Even then," said she, weeping, "that will not be penance enough to atone for the wrong I have done you."

These words were accompanied with big tears; her virtuous heart waxed faint, she fell to the ground exhausted. Lavallière, terrified, caught her and placed his hand upon her heart, above a breast of matchless beauty. The lady revived at the warmth of this beloved hand, experiencing such exquisite delights as nearly to make her again unconscious.

"Alas!" said she, "this sly and superficial caress will be for the future the only pleasure of our love. It will still be a hundred times better than the joys which poor Maillé fancies he is bestowing on me. . . .
Leave your hand there," said she; "verily is it upon my soul, and touches it."

At these words the knight was in a pitiful plight, and innocently confessed to the lady that he experienced so much pleasure at this touch that the pains of his malady increased, and that death was preferable to this martyrdom.

"Let us die then," said she.

But the litter was in the courtyard of the hotel, and as the means of death were not handy, each one slept far from the other, heavily weighed down with love, Lavallière having lost his fair Limeuli, and Marie d'Annebaut having gained pleasures without parallel.

From this affair, which was quite unforeseen, Lavallière found himself under the ban of love and marriage and dared no longer appear in public, and he found how much it costs to guard the virtue of a woman; but the more honour and virtue he displayed the more pleasure did he experience in these great sacrifices offered at the shrine of brotherhood. Nevertheless his duty was very bitter, very ticklish, and intolerable to perform, towards the last days of his guard. And in this way.

The confession of her love, which she believed was returned, the wrong done by her to her cavalier, and the experience of an unknown pleasure, emboldened the fair Marie, who fell into a platonic love, gently tempered with those little indulgences in which there is no danger. From this cause sprang the diabolical pleasures of the game invented by the ladies, who since the death of Francis the First feared the contagion, but wished to gratify their lovers. To these cruel delights, in order properly to play his part, Lavallière could not refuse his sanction. Thus every evening the mournful Marie would attach her guest to her petticoats, holding his hands, kissing him with burning glances, her cheek placed gently against his, and during this virtuous embrace, in which the knight was held like the devil by a holy water brush, she told him of her great love, which was boundless since it stretched through the infinite spaces of unsatisfied desire. All the fire with which ladies endow their substantial amours, when the night has no other lights than their eyes, she transferred into the mystic motions of her head, the exultations of her soul, and the ecstacies of her heart. Then, naturally, and with the delicious joy of two angels united by thought alone, they intoned together those sweet litanies repeated by the lovers of the period in honour of love—anthems which the Abbot of Theleme has paragraphically saved from oblivion by engraving them on the walls of his abbey, situated, according to master Alcofribas, in our land of Chinon, where I have seen them in Latin, and have translated them for the benefit of Christians.

"Alas!" said Marie d'Annebaut, "thou art my strength and my life, my joy and my treasure."

"And you," replied he, "you are a pearl, an angel."

"Thou art my seraphim."

"You my soul."

"Thou my God."

"You my evening star and morning star, my honour, my beauty, my universe."

"Thou my great my divine master."

"You my glory, my faith, my religion."

"Thou my gentle one, my handsome one, my courageous one, my dear one, my cavalier my defender, my king, my love."

"You my fairy, the flower of my days, the dream of my nights."

"Thou my thought at every moment."

"You the delight of my eyes."

"Thou the voice of my soul."

"You my light by day."

"Thou my glimmer in the night."

"You the best beloved among women."

"Thou the most adored of men."

"You my blood, a myself better than myself."

"Thou my heart, my lustre."

"You my saint, my only joy."

"I yield thee the palm of love, and how great soe'er mine be, I believe thou lovest me still more, for thou art the lord."

"No; the palm is yours, my goddess, my Virgin Marie."

"No; I am thy servant, thine handmaiden, a nothing thou canst crush to atoms."

"No, no; it is I who am your slave, your faithful page, whom you use as a breath of air, upon whom you can walk as on a carpet. My heart is your throne."

"No, dearest, for thy voice transfigures me."

"Your regard burns me."

" I see but thee."

" I love but you."

" Oh, put thine hand upon my heart—only thine hand—and thou wilt see me pale, when my blood shall have taken the heat of thine."

Then during these struggles their eyes, already ardent, flamed still more brightly, and the good knight was a little the accomplice of the pleasure which Marie d'Annebaut took in feeling his hand upon her heart. Now, as in this light embrace all their strength was put forth, all their desires strained, all their ideas of the thing concentrated, it happened that the knight's transport reached a climax. Their eyes wept warm tears, they seized each other hard and fast as fire seizes houses; but that was all. Lavallière had promised to return safe and sound to his friend the body only, not the heart.

When Maillé announced his return, it was quite time, since no virtue could avoid melting upon this gridiron ; and the less licence the lovers had, the more pleasure they had in their fantasies.

Leaving Marie d'Annebaut, the good companion in arms went as far as Bondy to meet his friend, to help him to pass through the forest without accident, and the two brothers slept together, according to the ancient custom, in the village of Bondy.

There, in their bed, they recounted to each other, one the adventures of his journey, the other the gossip of the camp, stories of gallantry, and the rest. But Maillé's first question was touching Marie d'Annebaut, whom Lavallière swore to be intact in that precious place where the honour of hus-bands is lodged ; at which the amorous Maillé was highly delighted.

On the morrow they were all three re-united, to the great disgust of Marie, who, with the high jurisprudence of women, made a great fuss with her good husband, but with her finger she indicated her heart in an artless manner to Lavallière, as one who said, " This is thine !"

At supper Lavallière announced his departure for the wars. Maillé was much grieved at this resolution, and wished to accompany his brother : but Lavallière refused him point blank.

" Madame," said he to Marie d'Annebaut, " I love you more than life, but not more than honour."

He turned pale, saying this, and Madame de Maillé blanched hearing him, because never in their amorous dalliance had there been so much true love as in this speech. Maillé insisted upon keeping his friend company as far as Meaux. When he came back, he was talking over with his wife the unknown reasons and secret causes of this departure, when Marie, who suspected the grief of poor Lavallière, said, " I know : he is ashamed to stop here because he has the Neapolitan sickness."

" He !" said Maillé, quite astonished. " I saw him when we were in bed together at Bondy the other evening, and yesterday at Meaux. There's nothing the matter with him ; he is as sound as a bell."

The lady burst into tears, admiring this great loyalty, the sublime resignation to his oath, and the extreme sufferings of this internal passion. But as she still kept her love in the recesses of her heart, she died when Lavallière fell before Metz, as has been elsewhere related by Messire Bourdeilles de Brantôme in his tittle-tattle.

Never did those who came to ask for wool at the vicarage go away
shorn, for his hand was always in his pocket.

THE VICAR OF AZAY-LE-RIDEAU.

I N those days the priests no longer took any woman in
legitimate marriage, but kept good mistresses as pretty
as they could get; which custom has since been interdicted
by the council, as every one knows, because, indeed, it was
not pleasant that the private confessions of people should
be retold to a wench who would laugh at them, besides the
other secret doctrines, ecclesiastical arrangements, and spe-
culations which are part and parcel of the politics of the
Church of Rome.   The last priest in our country who
theologically kept a woman in his parsonage, regaling her
with his scholastic love, was a certain Vicar of Azay-le-
Ridel, a place later on most aptly named Azay-le-Brulé,
and now Azay-le-Rideau, whose castle is one of the marvels
of Touraine.   Now this said period, when the women were
not averse to the odour of the priesthood, is not so far
distant as some may think, for Monsieur D'Orgemont, son
of the preceding bishop, still held the see of Paris, and the
great quarrels of the Armagnacs had not finished.   To tell
the truth, this vicar did well to have his vicarage in that age,
since he was well shapen, of a high colour, stout, big, strong,
eating and drinking like a convalescent, and, indeed, was
always rising from a little malady that attacked him at
certain times ; and, later on, he would have been his own

executioner, had he determined to observe the canonical continence. Add to this that he was a Tourainian, *id est*, dark, and had in his eyes flame to light, and water to quench all the domestic furnaces that required lighting or quenching; and never since at Azay has been such vicar seen ! A handsome vicar was he, square-shouldered, fresh-coloured, always blessing and chuckling, preferring weddings and christenings to funerals, a good joker, pious in church, and a man in everything. There have been many vicars who have drunk well and eaten well ; others who have blessed abundantly and chuckled consumedly ; but all of them together would hardly make up the sterling worth of this aforesaid vicar; and he alone has worthily filled his post with benedictions, has held it with joy, and in it has consoled the afflicted, all so well, that no one saw him come out of his house without wishing to be in his heart, so much was he beloved. It was he who first said in a sermon that the devil was not so black as he was painted, and who for Madame de Candé transformed partridges into fish, saying that the perch of the Indre were partridges of the river, and, on the other hand, partridges perch in the air. He never played artful tricks under the cloak of morality, and often said, jokingly, he would rather be in a good bed than in anybody's will, that he had plenty of everything, and wanted nothing. As for the poor and suffering, never did those who came to ask for wool at the vicarage go away shorn, for his hand was always in his pocket, and he melted (he who in all else was so firm) at the sight of all this misery and infirmity, and he endeavoured to heal all their wounds. There have been many good stories told concerning this king of vicars. It was he who caused such hearty laughter at the wedding of the lord of Valennes, near Sacché. The mother of the said lord had a good deal to do with the victuals, roast meats and other delicacies, of which there was sufficient quantity to feed a small town at least, and it is true, at the same time, that people came to the wedding from Montbazon, from Tours, from Chinon, from Langeais, and from everywhere, and stopped eight days.

Now the good vicar, as he was going into the room

where the company were enjoying themselves, met a little kitchen boy, who wished to inform Madame that all the elementary substances and fat rudiments, syrups, and sauces, were in readiness for a pudding of great delicacy, the secret compilation, mixing, and manipulation of which she wished herself to superintend, intending it as a special treat for her daughter-in-law's relations. Our vicar gave the boy a tap on the cheek, telling him that he was too greasy and dirty to show himself to people of high rank, and that he himself would deliver the said message. The merry fellow pushes open the door, shapes the fingers of his left hand into the form of a sheath, and moves gently therein the middle finger of his right, at the same time looking at the lady of Valennes, and saying to her, "Come, all is ready." Those who did not understand the affair burst out laughing, to see Madame get up and go to the vicar, because she knew he referred to the pudding, and not to that which the others imagined.

But a true story is that concerning the manner in which this worthy pastor lost his mistress, to whom the ecclesiastical authorities allowed no successor; but, as for that, the vicar did not want for domestic utensils. In the parish every one thought it an honour to lend him theirs, the more readily because he was not the man to spoil anything, and was careful to clean them out thoroughly, the dear man. But here are the facts. One evening the good man came home to supper with a melancholy face, because he had just put into the ground a good farmer, whose death came about in a strange manner, and is still frequently talked about in Azay. Seeing that he only ate with the end of his teeth, and turned up his nose at a dish of tripe, which had been cooked in his own especial manner, his good woman said to him—

"Have you passed before the Lombard (see MASTER CORNELIUS *passim*), met two black crows, or seen the dead man turn in his grave, that you are so upset?"

"Oh! oh!"

"Has any one deceived you?"

"Ha! ha!"

"Come, tell me!"

"My dear, I am still quite overcome at the death of poor Cochegrue, and there is not at the present moment a good housewife's tongue or a virtuous cuckold's lips that are not talking about it."

"And what was it?"

"Listen! This poor Cochegrue was returning from market, having sold his corn and two fat pigs. He was riding his pretty mare, who, near Azay, commenced to caper about without the slightest cause, and poor Cochegrue trotted and ambled along counting his profits. At the corner of the old road of the Landes de Charlemagne they came upon a stallion kept by the Sieur de la Carte, in a field, in order to have a good breed of horses, because the said animal was fleet of foot, as handsome as an abbot, and so high and mighty that the admiral who came to see it, said it was a beast of the first quality. This cursed horse scented the pretty mare; like a cunning beast, neither neighed nor gave vent to any equine ejaculation, but when she was close to the road, leaped over forty rows of vines and galloped after her, pawing the ground with his iron shoes, discharging the artillery of a lover who longs for an embrace, giving forth sounds to set the strongest teeth on edge, and so loudly, that the people of Champy heard it and were much terrified thereat. Cochegrue, suspecting the affair, makes for the moors, spurs his amorous mare, relying upon her rapid pace, and indeed the good mare understands, obeys, and flies—flies like a bird, but a bowshot off follows the blessed horse, thundering along the road like a blacksmith beating iron, and at full speed, his mane flying in the wind, replying to the sound of the mare's swift gallop with his terrible pat-a-pan! pat-a-pan! Then the good farmer, feeling death following him in the love of the beast, spurs anew his mare, and harder still she gallops, until at last, pale and half dead with fear, he reaches the outer yard of his farmhouse, but finding the door of the stable shut he

cries ' Help here ! wife !' Then he turned round on his mare, thinking to avoid the cursed beast whose love was burning, who was wild with passion, and growing more amorous every moment, to the great danger of the mare. His family, horrified at the danger, did not go to open the stable door, fearing the strange embrace and the kicks of the iron-shod lover. At last Cochegrue's wife went, but just as the good mare was half way through the door, the cursed stallion seized her, squeezed her, gave a wild greeting, with his two legs gripped her, pinched her and held her tight, and at the same time so kneaded and knocked about poor Cochegrue, that there was only found of him a shapeless mass, crushed like a nut after the oil has been distilled from it. It was shocking to see him squashed alive and mingling his cries with the loud love-sighs of the horse."

"Oh ! the mare !" exclaimed the vicar's good wench.

"What !" said the priest, astonished.

"Certainly. You men wouldn't have cracked a plum-stone for us."

"There," answered the vicar, "you wrong me." The good man threw her angrily upon the bed, attacked and treated her so violently that she split into pieces, and died immediately without either surgeons or physicians being able to determine the manner in which the solution of

continuity was arrived at, so violently disjointed were the
hinges and mesial partitions.   You can imagine that he was
a proud man, and a splendid vicar as has been previously
stated.

The good people of the country, even the women, agreed
that he was not to blame, but that his conduct was warranted
by the circumstances.

From this perhaps came the proverb so much in use at
that time, *Que l'aze le saille!*   The which proverb is really
so much coarser in its actual wording, that out of respect for
the ladies I will not mention it.   But this was not the only
clever thing this great and noble vicar achieved, for before
this misfortune he did such a stroke of business that no
robbers dare ask him how many angels he had in his pocket,
even had they been twenty strong and over to attack him.
One evening, when his good woman was still with him,
after supper, during which he had enjoyed his goose, his
wench, his wine and everything, and was reclining in his
chair thinking where he could build a new barn for the
tithes, a message came for him from the lord of Sacché,
who was giving up the ghost and wished to reconcile himself
with God, receive the Sacrament, and go through the usual
ceremonies.   " He is a good man and loyal lord.   I will
go," said he.   Thereupon he passed into the church,
took the silver box where the blessed bread is, rang the
little bell himself in order not to wake his clerk, and went
lightly and willingly along the road.   Near the Gué-droit,
which is a valley leading to the Indre across the moors,
our good vicar perceived a high toby.   And what is a
high toby?   It is a clerk of St. Nicholas.   Well, what is
that?   That means a person who sees clearly on a dark
night, instructs himself by examining and turning over
purses, and takes his degrees on the high road.   Do you
understand now?   Well then, this high toby waited for the
silver box, which he knew to be of great value.

" Oh ! oh !" said the priest, putting down the sacred vase
on a stone at the corner of the bridge, " stop thou there
without moving."

Then he walked up to the robber, tripped him up, seized his loaded stick, and when the rascal got up to struggle with him, he gutted him with a blow well planted in the middle of his stomach. Then he picked up the viaticum again, saying bravely to it, "Ah, if I had relied upon thy providence, we should have been lost." Now to utter these impious words upon the high road to Sacché was mere waste of breath, seeing that he addressed them not to God, but to the Archbishop of Tours, who had once severely rebuked him, threatened him with suspension, and admonished him before the Chapter for having publicly told certain lazy people that a good harvest was not due to the grace of God, but to skilled labour and hard work—a doctrine which smelt of the faggot. And indeed he was wrong, because the fruits of the earth have need both of one and the other; but he died in this heresy, for he could never understand how crops could come without digging, if God so willed it—a doctrine that learned men have since proved to be true, by showing that formerly wheat grew very well without the aid of man. I cannot leave this splendid model of a pastor without giving here one of the acts of his life, which proves with what fervour he imitated the saints in the division of their goods and mantles, which they gave formerly to the poor and the passers-by. One day, returning from Tours, where he had been paying his respects to the official, mounted on his mule, he was nearing Azay. On the way, just outside Ballan, he met a pretty girl on foot, and was grieved to see a woman travelling like a dog; the more so as she was visibly fatigued, and could scarcely raise one foot before the other. He whistled to her softly, and the pretty wench turned round and stopped. The good priest, who was too good a sportsman to frighten the birds, especially the hooded ones, begged her so gently to ride behind him on his mule, and in so polite a fashion, that the lass got up; not without making those little excuses and grimaces that they all make when one invites them to eat, or to take what they like. The sheep paired off with the shepherd, the mule jogged along after the fashion of mules,

while the girl slipped now this way now that, riding so un-
comfortably that the priest pointed out to her, after leaving

Ballan, that she had better hold on to him;
and immediately my lady put her plump
arms round the waist of her cavalier, in a
modest and timorous manner.

" There, you don't slip about now. Are
you comfortable?" said the vicar.

" Yes, I am comfortable.   Are you?"

" I?" said the priest; " I am better than
that."

And, in fact, he was quite at his ease,
and was soon gently warmed in the back
by two projections which rubbed against it, and at last
seemed as though they wished to
imprint themselves between his
shoulder blades, which would have
been a pity, as that was not the
place for this white merchandize.
By degrees the movement of the
mule brought into conjunction the
internal warmth of these two good
riders, and their blood coursed more

quickly through their veins, seeing that it felt the motion
of the mule as well as their own ; and thus the good wench
and the vicar finished by knowing each other's thoughts,
but not those of the mule.   When they were both acclima-
tized, he with her and she with him, they felt an internal
disturbance which resolved itself into secret desires.

" Ah !" said the vicar, turning round to his companion,
" here is a fine cluster of trees which has grown very
thick."

" It is too near the road," replied the girl.   " Bad boys
have cut the branches, and the cows have eaten the young
leaves."

" Are you not married?" asked the vicar, trotting his
animal again.

" No," said she.

" Not at all ?"

"I' faith! No!"

"What a shame, at your age!"

"You are right, sir; but you see, a poor girl who has had a child is a bad bargain."

Then the good vicar taking pity on such ignorance, and knowing that the canons say among other things that pastors should indoctrinate their flock and show them the duties and responsibilities of this life, he thought he would only be discharging the functions of his office by showing her the burden she would one day have to bear. Then he begged her gently not to be afraid, for if she would have faith in his loyalty no one should ever know of the marital experiment which he proposed then and there to perform with her; and as, since passing Ballan the girl had thought of nothing else; as her desire had been carefully sustained and augmented by the warm movements of the animal, she replied harshly to the vicar, "If you talk thus I will get down." Then the good vicar continued his gentle requests so well that on reaching the wood of Azay the girl wished to get down, and the priest got down there too, for it was not across a horse that this discussion could be finished. Then the virtuous maiden ran into the thickest part of the wood to get away from the vicar, calling out, "Oh, you wicked man, you shan't know where I am."

The mule arrived in a glade where the grass was good, the girl tumbled down over a root and blushed. The good vicar came to her, and there as he had rung the bell for mass he went through the service for her, and both freely discounted the joys of paradise. The good priest had it in his heart to thoroughly instruct her, and found his pupil very docile, as gentle in mind as soft in the flesh, a perfect jewel. Therefore was he much grieved at having so much abridged the lesson by giving it at Azay, seeing that he would have been quite willing to recommence it, like all preceptors who say the same thing over and over again to their pupils.

"Ah, little one," cried the good man, "why did you make so much fuss that we only came to an understanding close to Azay?"

" Ah !" said she, " I belong to Ballan."

To be brief, I must tell you that when this good man died in his vicarage there was a great number of people, children and others, who came, sorrowful, afflicted, weeping, and grieved, and all exclaimed, " Ah ! we have lost our father." And the girls, the widows, the wives and the little girls looked at each other, regretting him more than a friend, and said, " He was more than a priest, he was a man !" Of these vicars the seed is cast to the winds, and they will never be reproduced in spite of the seminaries.

Why even the poor, to whom his savings were left, found themselves still the losers, and an old cripple whom he had succoured hobbled into the churchyard, crying, " I don't die ! I don't !" meaning to say, " Why did not death take me in his place ?" This made some of the people laugh, at which the shade of the good vicar would certainly not have been displeased.

THE REPROACH.

THE fair laundress of Portillon-les-Tours, of whom a
droll saying has already been given in this book,
was a girl blessed with as much cunning as if she had stolen
that of six priests and three women at least. She did not
want for sweethearts, and had so many that one would have
compared them, seeing them around her, to bees swarming
of an evening towards their hive. An old silk
dyer, who lived in the Rue Montfumier, and
there possessed a house of scandalous magnifi-
cence, coming from his place at La Grenadière, situated on the fair borders of St. Cyr,
passed on horseback through Portillon in order
to gain the Bridge of Tours. By reason of the
warmth of the evening, he was seized with a wild desire on
seeing the pretty washerwoman sitting upon her door-step.
Now as for a very long time he had dreamed of this merry
maid, his resolution was taken to make her his wife, and in
a short time she was transformed from a washerwoman into a
dyer's wife, a good townswoman with laces, fine linen, and furniture to spare, and was happy in spite of the dyer, seeing that
she knew very well how to manage him. The good dyer had

for a crony a silk machinery manufacturer, who was small in stature, deformed for life, and full of wickedness. So on the wedding-day he said to the dyer, " You have done well to marry, my friend, *we* shall have a pretty wife ;" and a thousand sly jokes, such as it is usual to address to a bridegroom.

In fact, this said hunchback courted the dyer's wife, who from her nature caring little for badly built people, laughed to scorn the request of the mechanician, and joked him about the springs, engines, and spools of which his shop was full. However, this great love of the hunchback was rebuffed by nothing, and became so irksome to the dyer's wife that she resolved to cure it by a thousand practical jokes. One evening, after the sempiternal pursuit, she told her lover to come to the back-door and towards midnight she would open everything to him. Now note, this was on a winter's night ; the Rue Montfumier is close by the Loire, and in this corner there continually blow in winter, winds sharp as a hundred needle-points. The good hunchback, well muffled up in his mantle, failed not to come, and trotted up and down to keep himself warm while waiting the appointed hour. Towards midnight he was half frozen, as fidgety as thirty-two devils caught in a stole, and was about to give up his happiness, when a feeble light passed by the cracks of the window and came down towards the little door.

" Ah, it is she !" said he.

And this hope warmed him once more. Then he got close to the door, and heard a little voice—

" Are you there ?" said the dyer's wife to him.

" Yes."

" Cough, that I may see."

The hunchback began to cough.

" It is not you."

Then the hunchback said aloud—

" How do you mean, it is not I ? Do you not recognise my voice ? Open the door !"

"Who's there?" said the dyer, opening his window.

"There, you have awaked my husband, who returned from Amboise unexpectedly this evening."

Thereupon the dyer, seeing by the light of the moon a man at his door, threw a good big pot of cold water over him, and cried out, " Thieves ! thieves !" in such a manner that the hunchback was forced to run away; but in his fear he failed to clear the chain stretched across the bottom of the road, and fell into the common sewer, which the sheriff had not then replaced by a sluice to discharge the mud into the Loire. In this bath the mechanician expected every moment to breathe his last, and cursed the fair Tascherette, for her husband's name being Taschereau, so was she called by way of a little joke by the people of Tours.

Carandas—for so was named the manufacturer of machines to weave, to spin, to spool, and wind the silk—was not sufficiently smitten to believe in the innocence of the dyer's wife, and swore a devilish hate against her. But some days afterwards, when he had recovered from his wetting in the dyer's drain, he came to sup with his old comrade. Then the dyer's wife reasoned with him so well, flavoured her words with so much honey, and wheedled him with so many fair promises, that he dismissed his suspicions. He asked for a fresh assignation, and the fair Tascherette, with the face of a woman whose mind is dwelling on the subject, said to him, " Come to-morrow evening ; my husband will be staying some days at Chenonceaux. The queen wishes to have some of her old dresses dyed and would settle the colours with him. It will take some time."

Carandas put on his best clothes, failed not to keep the appointment, appeared at the time fixed, and found a good supper prepared, lampreys, wine of Vouvray, fine white napkins—for it was not necessary to remonstrate with the dyer's wife on the colour of her linen—and everything so well prepared that it was quite pleasant to him to see the dishes of fresh eels, to smell the good odour of the meats, and to admire a thousand nameless little things about the room, and La Tascherette fresh and appetizing as an apple on a hot day. Now the mechanician, excited to excess by these warm preparations, was on the point of attacking the charms of the dyer's wife, when Master Tachereau gave a loud knock at the street door.

" Ha !" said madame, " what has happened ? Put yourself in the clothes-chest, for I have been much abused respecting you ; and if my husband finds you, he may undo you ; he is so violent in his temper."

And immediately she thrust the hunchback into the chest, and went quickly to her good husband, who she knew well would be back from Chenonceaux to supper. Then the dyer was kissed warmly on both his eyes and on both his ears, and he caught his good wife to him and bestowed upon her two hearty smacks with his lips that sounded all over the room. Then the pair sat down to supper, talked together, and finished by going to bed ; and the mechanician heard all, though obliged to remain crumpled up, and not to cough or to make a single movement. He was in with the linen, crushed up as close as a sardine in a box, and had about as much air as he would have had at the bottom of a river ; but he had, to divert him, the music of love, the sighs of the dyer, and the little jokes of La Tascherette. At last, when he fancied his old comrade was asleep, he made an attempt to get out of the chest.

" Who is there ?" said the dyer.

" What is the matter, my little one ?" said his wife, lifting her nose above the counterpane.

" I heard a scratching," said the good man.

" We shall have rain to-morrow ; it's the cat," replied his wife.

The good husband put his head back upon the pillow after having been gently embraced by his spouse. " There, my dear, you are a light sleeper. It's no good trying to make a proper husband of you. There, be good. Oh ! oh ! my little papa, your nightcap is on one side. There, put it on the other way, for you must look pretty even when you are asleep. There ! are you all right ?"

" Yes."

" Are you asleep ?" said she, giving him a kiss.

" Yes,"

In the morning the dyer's wife came softly and let out the mechanician, who was whiter than a ghost.

"Give me air, give me air !" said he.

And away he ran, cured of his love, but with as much hate in his heart as a pocket could hold of black wheat. The said hunchback left Tours and went to live in the town of Bruges, where certain merchants had sent for him to arrange the machinery for making hauberks.

During his long absence, Carandas, who had Moorish blood in his veins, since he was descended from an ancient Saracen left half dead after the great battle which took place between the Moors and the French in the commune of Ballan (which is mentioned in the preceding tale), in which place are the Landes of Charlemagne, where nothing grows because of the cursed wretches and infidels there interred, and where the grass disagrees even with the cows— this Carandas never rose up or lay down in the foreign land without thinking of how he could give strength to his desires of vengeance ; and he was dreaming always of it, and wished nothing less than the death of the fair washerwoman of Portillon, and often would cry out, "I will eat her flesh ! I will cook one of her breasts, and swallow it without sauce !" It was a tremendous hate of good constitution—a cardinal hate—a hate of a wasp or old maid. It was all known hates moulded into one single hate, which boiled itself, concocted itself, and resolved itself into an elixir of wicked and diabolical sentiments, warmed at the fire of the most flaming furnaces of hell—it was, in fact, a master hate.

Now one fine day, the said Carandas came back into Touraine with much wealth, that he brought from the country of Flanders, where he had sold his mechanical secrets. He bought a splendid house in the Rue Montfumier, which is still to be seen, and is the astonishment of the passers-by, because it has certain very queer round humps fashioned upon the stones of the wall. Carandas the hater, found many notable changes at the house of his friend the dyer, for the good man had two sweet children, who, by a curious chance, presented no resemblance either to the mother or to the father. But as

it is necessary that children bear a resemblance to some
one, there are certain people who look for the features of their ancestors, when they are good looking—the
flatterers. So it was found by the good husband that his
two boys were like one of his uncles, formerly a priest at
Notre Dame de l'Egrinolles, but, according to certain jokers,
these two children were the living portraits of a good-
looking shaven crown officiating in the church of Notre Dame
la Riche, a celebrated parish situated between Tours and
Plessis. Now believe one thing, and inculcate it in your
minds, and when in this book you shall only have
gleaned, gathered, extracted, and learned this one principle
of truth, look upon yourself as a lucky man—namely, that a
man can never dispense with his nose, *id est*, that a man will

always be snotty—that is to say, he will
remain a man, and thus will continue
throughout all future centuries to laugh
and drink, to find himself in his shirt
without feeling either better or worse
there, and will have the same occupations.
But these preparatory ideas are to better
fix in the understanding that this two-
footed soul will always accept as true
those things which flatter his passions,
caress his hates, or serve his amours : from
this comes logic. So it was that, the first day the above-
mentioned Carandas saw his old comrade's children, saw
the handsome priest, saw the beautiful wife of the dyer,
saw Le Taschereau, all seated at the table, and saw to his
detriment the best piece of lamprey given with a certain
air by La Tascherette to her friend the priest, the mechanician said to himself, " My old friend is a cuckold, his wife
intrigues with the little confessor, and the children have
been begotten with his holy water. I'll show them that
the hunchbacks have something more than other men."

And this was true—as true as it is that Tours has always
had its feet in the Loire, like a pretty girl who bathes
herself and plays with the water, making a flick-flack, by
beating the waves with her fair white hands ; for this town is

And be sure if you go there you will find, in the centre of it, a sweet place, in which is a delicious street where every one promenades, where there is always a breeze, shade, sun, rain, and love.

more smiling, merry, loving, fresh, flowery, and fragrant than all the other towns of the world, which are not worthy to comb her locks, or to buckle her waistband. And be sure if you go there you will find, in the centre of it, a sweet place, in which is a delicious street where every one promenades, where there is always a breeze, shade, sun, rain, and love. Ha! ha! laugh away, but go there. It is a street always new, always royal, always imperial—a patriotic street, a street with two paths, a street open at both ends, a wide street, a street so large that no one has ever cried, "Out of the way!" there. A street which does not wear out, a street which leads to the abbey of Grand-Mont, and to a trench, which works very well with the bridge, and at the end of which is a fine fair ground. A street well paved, well built, well washed, as clean as a glass, populous, silent at certain times, a coquette with a sweet nightcap on in its pretty blue tiles —to be short, it is the street where I was born; it is the queen of streets, always between the earth and the sky; a street with a fountain; a street which lacks nothing to be celebrated among streets; and, in fact, it is the real street, the only street of Tours. If there are others, they are dark, muddy, narrow, and damp, and all come respectfully to salute this noble street, which commands them. Where am I? For once in this street no one cares to come out of it, so pleasant it is. But I owed this filial homage, this descriptive hymn sung from the heart, to my natal street, at the corners of which there are wanting only the brave figures of my good master, Rabelais, and of Monsieur Descartes, both unknown to the people of the country. To resume: the said Carandas was, on his return from Flanders, entertained by his comrade, and by all those by whom he was liked for his jokes, his drollery, and quaint remarks. The good hunchback appeared cured of his old love, embraced the children, and when he was alone with the dyer's wife recalled the night in the clothes-chest, and the night in the sewer, to her memory, saying to her, "Ha! ha! what games you used to have with me."

"It was your own fault," said she, laughing. "If you had allowed yourself by reason of your great love to be ridiculed, made a fool of, and bantered a few more times, you might have made an impression on me, like the others." Thereupon Carandas commenced to laugh, though inwardly raging all the time. Seeing the chest where he had nearly been suffocated, his anger increased the more violently because the sweet creature had become still more beautiful, like all those who are permanently youthful from bathing in the waters of youth, which waters are naught less than the sources of love. The mechanician studied the proceedings in the way of cuckoldom at his neighbour's house, in order to revenge himself, for as many houses as there are so many varieties of manner are there in this business ; and although all amours resemble each other in the same manner that all men resemble each other, it is proved to the abstractors of true things, that for the happiness of women, each love has its especial physiognomy, and if there is nothing that resembles a man so much as a man, there is also nothing differs from a man so much as a man. That it is, which confuses all things, or explains the thousand fantasies of women, who seek the best men with a thousand pains and a thousand pleasures, perhaps more the one than the other. But how can I blame them for their essays, changes, and contradictory aims? Why, Nature frisks and wriggles, twists and turns about, and you expect a woman to remain still ! Do you know if ice is really cold ? No. Well then, neither do you know that cuckoldom is not a lucky chance, the produce of brains well furnished and better made than all others. Seek something better than ventosity beneath the sky. This will help to spread the philosophic reputation of this eccentric book. Oh yes ; go on. He who cries " vermin powder," is more advanced than those who occupy themselves with Nature, seeing that she is a proud jade and a capricious one, and only allows herself to be seen at certain times. Do you understand ? So in all languages does she belong to the feminine gender, being a thing essentially changeable and fruitful and fertile in tricks.

Now Carandas soon recognised the fact that among cuckoldoms the best understood and the most discreet is ecclesiastical cuckoldom. This is how the good dyer's

wife had laid her plans. She went always towards ner
cottage at Grenadière-les-St.-Cyr on the eve of the Sabbath,
leaving her good husband to finish his work, to count
up and check his books, and to pay his workmen; then
Taschereau would join her there on the morrow, and always
found a good breakfast ready and his good wife gay, and
always brought the priest with him. The fact is, this
damnable priest crossed the Loire the night before in a
small boat, in order to keep the dyer's wife warm, and to
calm her fancies, in order that she might sleep well during
the night, a duty which young men understand very well.
Then this fine curber of phantasies got back to his house
in the morning by the time Taschereau came to invite
him to spend the day at La Grenadière, and the cuckold
always found the priest asleep in his bed. The boatman
being well paid, no one knew anything of these goings on,
for the lover journeyed the night before after nightfall, and
on the Sunday in the early morning. As soon as Carandas had verified the arrangement and constant practice of
these gallant diversions, he determined to wait for a day when
the lovers would meet, hungry one for the other, after some
accidental abstinence. This meeting took place very soon,
and the curious hunchback saw the boatman waiting below
the square, at the Canal St. Antoine, for the young priest,
who was handsome, blond, slender, and well-shaped, like
the gallant and cowardly hero of love, so celebrated by
Monsieur Ariosto. Then the mechanician went to find the
old dyer, who always loved his wife and always believed
himself the only man who had a finger in her pie.

"Ah! good evening, old friend," said Carandas to Taschereau; and Taschereau made him a bow.

Then the mechanician relates to him all the secret fes-
tivals of love, vomits words of peculiar import, and pricks
the dyer on all sides.

At length, seeing he was ready to kill both his wife and
the priest, Carandas said to him, "My good neighbour, I
have brought back from Flanders a poisoned sword, which
will instantly kill any one, if it only make a scratch upon

him. Now, directly you shall have merely touched your wench and her paramour, they will die."

" Let us go and fetch it," said the dyer.

Then the two merchants went in great haste to the house of the hunchback, to get the sword and rush off to the country.

" But shall we find them *in flagrante delicto ?*" asked Taschereau.

" You will see," said the hunchback, jeering his friend. In fact, the cuckold had not long to wait to behold the joy of the two lovers.

The sweet wench and her well-beloved were busy trying to catch, in a certain lake that you probably know, that little bird that sometimes makes his nest there, and they were laughing and trying, and still laughing.

" Ah, my darling !" said she, clasping him, as though she wished to take an outline of him on her chest, " I love thee so much I should like to eat thee ! Nay, more than that, to have you in my skin, so that you might never quit me."

" I should like it too," replied the priest, " but as you can't have me altogether, you must try a little bit at a time."

It was at this moment that the husband entered, his sword unsheathed and flourished above him. The beautiful Tascherette, who knew her lord's face well, saw what would be the fate of her well-beloved, the priest. But suddenly she sprang towards the good man, half naked, her hair streaming over her, beautiful with shame but more beautiful with love, and cried to him, " Stay, unhappy man ! Wouldst thou kill the father of thy children ?" Thereupon the good dyer staggered by the paternal majesty of cuckoldom, and perhaps also by the fire of his wife's eyes, let the sword fall upon the foot of the hunchback, who had followed him, and thus killed him.

This teaches us not to be spiteful.

H ERE ends the first volume of these Tales, a roguish
sample of the works of that merry Muse, born ages
ago, in our fair land of Touraine, the which Muse is a good
wench, and knows by heart that fine saying of her friend
Verville, written in LE MOYEN DE PARVENIR: *It is only necessary to be bold to obtain favours.* Alas! mad little one, get
thee to bed again, sleep; thou art panting from thy journey;
perhaps thou hast been farther than the present time. Now
dry thy fair naked feet, stop thine ears, and return to love.
If thou dreamest other poesy interwoven with laughter to
conclude these merry inventions, heed not the foolish
clamour and insults of those who, hearing the carol of a
joyous lark of other days, exclaim: Ah, the horrid bird!

 END OF THE FIRST TEN TALES.

The Second Ten.

THE SECOND TEN.

Prologue.

The Three Clerks of St. Nicholas.

The Continence of King Francis the First.

The Merry Tattle of the Nuns of Poissy.

How the Chateau d'Azay came to be built.

The False Courtesan.

The Danger of being too Innocent.

The Dear Night of Love.

The Sermon of the Merry Vicar of Meudon.

The Succubus.

Despair in Love.

Epilogue.

CERTAIN persons have reproached the Author for knowing no more about the language of the olden times than hares do of telling stories. Formerly these people would have been villified, called cannibals, churls, and sycophants, and Gomorrah would have been hinted at as their natal place. But the Author consents to spare them these flowery epithets of ancient criticism; he contents himself with wishing not to be in their skin, for he would be disgusted with himself, and esteem himself the vilest of scribblers thus to calumniate a poor little book which is not in the style of any spoil-paper of these times. Ah! ill-natured wretches! you should save your breath to cool your own porridge! The Author consoles himself for his want of success in not pleasing every one by remembering that an old Tourainian, of eternal memory, had to put up with such contumely, that, losing all patience, he declared in one of his prologues, that he *would never more put pen to paper*. Another age, but the same manners. Nothing changes, neither God above nor men below. Therefore the Author continues his task with a light heart, relying upon the future to reward his heavy labours.

And certes, it is a hard task to invent A HUNDRED DROLL TALES, since not only have ruffians and envious men opened fire upon him, but his friends have imitated their example, and come to him, saying, " Are you mad? Do you think it possible? No man ever had in the depths of his imagination a hundred such tales. Change the hyperbolic title of your budget. You will never finish it." These people are neither misanthropes nor cannibals ; whether they are ruffians I know not; but for certain they are kind, good-natured friends ; friends who have the courage to tell you disagreeable things all your life long, who are rough and sharp as currycombs, under the pretence that they are yours to command, in all the mishaps of life, and in the hour of extreme unction, all their worth will be known. If such people would only keep to these sad kindnesses : but they will not. When their terrors are proved to have been idle, they exclaim triumphantly, " Ha! ha! I knew it. I always said so."

In order not to discourage fine sentiments, intolerable though they be, the Author leaves to his friends his old shoes, and in order to make their minds easy; assures them that he has, legally protected and exempt from seizure, seventy droll stories, in that reservoir of nature, his brain. By the gods! they are precious yarns, well rigged out with phrases, carefully furnished with catastrophes, amply clothed with original humour, rich in diurnal and nocturnal effects, nor lacking that plot which the human race has woven each minute, each hour, each week, month, and year of the great ecclesiastical computation, commenced at a time when the sun could scarcely see, and the moon waited to be shown her way. These seventy subjects, which he gives you leave to call bad subjects, full of tricks and impudence, lust, lies, jokes, jests, and ribaldry, joined to the two portions here given, are, by the prophet! a small instalment of the aforesaid hundred.

Were it not now a bad time for bibliopolists, bibliomaniacs, bibliographers, and *bibliothèques* which hinder bibliolatry, he would have given them in a bumper, and not drop by drop as if he were afflicted with dysury of the brain. He cannot possibly be suspected of this infirmity, since he often gives good weight, putting several stories into one, as is clearly demonstrated by several in this volume. You may rely on it, that he has chosen for the finish, the best and most ribald of the lot, in order that he may not be accused of a senile discourse. Put then more likes with your dislikes, and dislikes with your likes. Forgetting the niggardly behaviour of nature to story-tellers, of whom there are not more than seven perfect in the great ocean of human writers, others, although friendly, have been of opinion that, at a time when every one went about dressed in black, as if in mourning for something, it was necessary to concoct works either wearisomely serious, or seriously wearisome; that a writer could only live henceforward by enshrining his ideas in some vast edifice, and that those who were unable to reconstruct cathedrals and castles of which neither stone nor cement could be moved, would die unknown, like the Pope's slippers. These friends were requested to declare which they liked best, a pint of good wine, or a tun of cheap rubbish; a diamond of twenty-two carats, or a flint-stone weighing a hundred pounds; the ring of Hans Carvel, as told by Rabelais, or a modern narrative pitifully expectorated by a schoolboy. Seeing them dumbfoundered and abashed, it was calmly said to them, " Do you thoroughly understand, good people? Then go your ways, and mind your own businesses."

The following, however, must be added, for the benefit of all whom it may concern :—The good man to whom we owe fables and stories of sempiternal authority has only used his tool on them, having taken his material from others ; but the workmanship expended on these little figures has given them a high value ; and although he was, like M. Louis Ariosto, vituperated for thinking of idle pranks and trifles, there is a certain insect engraved by him which has since become a monument of perennity more assured than that of the most solidly built works. In the especial jurisprudence of wit and wisdom the custom is to esteem more dearly a leaf wrested from the book of Nature and Truth, than all the indifferent volumes from which, however fine they be, it is impossible to extract either a laugh or a tear. The author has licence to say this without any impropriety, since it is not his intention to stand upon tiptoe in order to obtain an unnatural height, but because it is a question of the majesty of his art, and not of himself—a poor clerk of the court, whose business it is to have ink in his pen, to listen to the gentlemen on the bench, and take down the sayings of each witness in this case. He is responsible for the workmanship, Nature for the rest, since from the Venus of

Phidias the Athenian, down to the little old fellow Godenot, commonly called the Sieur Breloque, a character carefully elaborated by one of the most celebrated authors of the present day, everything is studied from the eternal model of human imitations which belongs to all. At this honest business, happy are the robbers that are not hanged, but esteemed and beloved. But he is a triple fool, a fool with ten horns on his head, who struts, boasts, and is puffed up at an advantage due to the hazard of dispositions, because glory lies only in the cultivation of the faculties, in patience and courage.

As for the soft-voiced and pretty-mouthed ones, who have whispered delicately in the author's ear, complaining to him that they have disarranged their tresses and spoiled their petticoats in certain places, he would say to them, " Why did you go there?" To these remarks he is compelled, through the notable slanders of certain people, to add a notice to the well-disposed, in order that they may use it, and end the calumnies of the aforesaid scribblers concerning him.

These droll tales are written—according to all authorities —at that period when Queen Catherine, of the house of Medicis, was hard at work ; for during a great portion of the reign, she was always interfering with public affairs to the advantage of our holy religion. The which time has seized many people by the throat, from our defunct master, Francis, first of the name, to the Assembly at Blois, where fell M. de Guise. Now, even schoolboys who play at chuck-farthing, know that at this period of insurrections, pacifications, and disturbances, the language of France was a little disturbed also, on account of the inventions of the poets, who at that time, as at this, used each to make a language for himself, besides the strange Greek, Latin, Italian, German, and Swiss words, foreign phrases, and Spanish jargon, introduced by foreigners, so that a poor writer has plenty of elbow room in this Babelish language, which has since been taken in hand by Messieurs de Balzac, Blaise Pascal, Furetière, Menage, St. Evremond, de Malherbe, and others, who first cleaned out the French language, sent foreign words to the rightabout, and gave the right of citizenship to legitimate words used and known by every one, but of which the Sieur Ronsard was ashamed.

Having finished, the author returns to his lady-love, wishing every happiness to those by whom he is beloved; to the others, misfortune according to their deserts. When the swallows fly homeward, he will come again, not without the third and fourth volume, which he here promises to the Pantagruelists, merry knaves, and honest wags of all degrees, who have a wholesome horror of the sadness, sombre meditation and melancholy of literary croakers.

THE THREE CLERKS

OF

SAINT NICHOLAS.

THE Inn of the Three Barbels was formerly at Tours, the best place in the town for sumptuous fare ; and the landlord, reputed the prince of cooks, went to prepare wedding breakfasts as far as Chatelherault, Loches, Vendôme, and Blois. This said man, an old fox, perfect in his business, never lighted lamps in the daytime, knew how to skin a flint, charged for wool, leather, and feathers, had an eye to everything, did not easily let any one pay with chaff instead of coin, and for a penny less than his account would have affronted even a prince. For the rest, he was a good banterer, drinking and laughing with his regular customers, hat in hand always before the persons furnished with plenary indulgences entitled *Sit nomen Domini benedictum*, running them into expense, and proving to them, if need were, by sound argument, that wines were dear, and that whatever they might think, nothing was given away in Touraine, everything had to be bought, and, at the same time, paid for. In short, if he could without disgrace have done so, he would have reckoned so much for the good air, and so much for the view of the country. Thus he built up a tidy fortune with other people's money,

The Landlord of The Three Barbels.

became as round as a butt, larded with fat, and was called
Monsieur. At the time of the last fair three young fellows,
who were apprentices in knavery, in whom there was more
of the material that makes thieves than saints, and who knew
just how far it was possible to go without catching their
necks in the branches of trees, made up their minds to amuse
themselves, and live well, condemning certain hawkers or
others in all the expenses. Now these limbs of Satan gave
the slip to their masters, under whom they had been
studying the art of parchment scrawling, and came to stay
at the hotel of the Three Barbels, where they demanded
the best rooms, turned the place inside out, turned up their
noses at everything, bespoke all the lampreys in the market,
and announced themselves as first-class merchants, who
never carried their goods with them, and travelled only
with their persons. The host bustled about, turned the
spits, got out the best of everything, and prepared a glorious
repast for these three dodgers, who had already made noise
enough for a hundred crowns, and who most certainly
would not even have given up the copper coins which one
of them was jingling in his pocket. But if they were hard
up for money they did not want for ingenuity, and all three
arranged to play their parts like thieves at a fair. Theirs
was a farce in which there was plenty of eating and drinking,
since for five days they so heartily attacked every kind of
provision, that a party of German soldiers would have
spoilt less than they obtained by fraud. These three
cunning fellows made their way to the fair after breakfast,
well primed, gorged, and big in the belly, and did as they
liked with the greenhorns and others, robbing, filching,
playing, and losing, taking down the writings and signs and
changing them, putting that of the toyman over the jeweller's,
and that of the jeweller outside the shoemaker's, turning
the shops inside out, making the dogs fight, cutting the
ropes of tethered horses, throwing cats among the crowd,
crying " Stop thief !" and saying to every one they met, " Are
you not Monsieur D'Entrefesse, of Angiers ?" Then they
hustled every one, making holes in the sacks of flour, look-

ing for their handkerchiefs in ladies' pockets, raising their
skirts, crying, looking for a lost jewel, and saying to them—
" Ladies, it has fallen into a hole !"

They directed the little children wrongly, slapped the
stomachs of those who were gaping in the air, and prowled
about, fleecing and annoying every one. In short, the devil
would have been a gentleman in comparison with these
blackguard students, who would have been hanged rather
than do an honest action ; as well have expected charity
from two angry litigants. They left the fair, not fatigued,
but tired of ill-doing, and spent the remainder of their
time over their dinner until the evening, when they re-
commenced their pranks by torchlight. After the pedlars
they commenced operations on the ladies of the town, to
whom, by a thousand dodges, they gave only that which they
received, according to the axiom of Justinian : *Cuicum jus
tribuere.* " To every one his own juice ;" and afterwards
jokingly said to the poor wenches—

" We are in the right and you in the wrong."

At last, at supper-time, having nothing else to do, they
began to knock each other about, and, to keep the game alive,
complained of the flies to the landlord, remonstrating with
him that elsewhere the innkeepers had them caught in order
that gentlemen of position might not be annoyed with them.
However, towards the fifth day, which is the critical day of
fevers, the host not having seen, although he kept his eyes
wide open, the royal surface of a crown, and knowing that
if all that glittered were gold it would be cheaper, began to
knit his brows and go more slowly about that which his high
class merchants required of him. Fearing that he had made
a bad bargain with them, he tried to sound the depth of their
pockets ; perceiving which the three clerks ordered him, with
the assurance of a provost hanging his man, to serve them
quickly with a good supper, as they had to depart immediately. Their merry countenances dismissed the host's suspicions. Thinking that rogues without money would certainly
look grave, he prepared a supper worthy a canon, wishing
even to see them drunk, in order the more easily to clap

them into gaol in the event of an accident. Not knowing
how to make their escape from the room, in which they were
about as much at their ease as are fish upon straw, the three
companions ate and drank immoderately, looking at the situation of the windows, waiting the moment to decamp, but not
getting the opportunity. Cursing their luck, one of them
wished to go and undo his waistcoat in the garden, on account
of a colic, the other to fetch a doctor to the third, who did his
best to faint. The cursed landlord kept dodging about from
the kitchen into the room, and from the room into the kitchen,
watching the nameless ones, going a step forward to save
his crowns, and going a step back to save his crown, in
case they should be real gentlemen ; and he acted like a
brave and prudent host who likes halfpence and objects to
kicks ; but under pretence of properly attending to them, he
always had an ear in the room and a foot in the court ;
fancied he was always being called by them, came every
time they laughed, showing them a face with an unsettled
look upon it, and always said, " Gentlemen, what is your
pleasure ?" This was an interrogatory in reply to which they
would willingly have given him ten inches of his own spit in
his stomach, because he appeared as if he knew very well
what would please them at this juncture, seeing that to have
twenty crowns, full weight, they would each of them have
sold a third of his eternity. You can imagine they sat on
their seats as if they were gridirons, that their feet itched
and their posteriors were rather warm. Already the host had
put the pears, the cheese, and the preserves near their noses,
but they, sipping their liquor and picking at the dishes,
looked at each other to see if either of them had found a
good piece of roguery in his sack, and they all began to
enjoy themselves rather wofully. The most cunning of
the three clerks, who was a Burgundian, smiled and said,
seeing the hour of payment arrived, " This must stand over
for a week," as if they had been at the Palais de Justice.
The two others, in spite of the danger, began to laugh.

" What do we owe ?" asked he who had in his belt the
heretofore mentioned twelve sols, and he turned them about
as though he would make them breed little ones by this

excited movement. He was a native of Picardy, and very passionate; a man to take offence at anything in order that he might throw the landlord out of the window in all security of conscience. Now he said these words with the air of a man of immense wealth.

"Six crowns, gentlemen," replied the host, holding out his hand.

"I cannot permit myself to be entertained by you alone, Viscount," said the third student, who was from Anjou, and as artful as a woman in love.

"Neither can I," said the Burgundian.

"Gentlemen! gentlemen!" replied the Picardian, "you are jesting. I am yours to command."

"Sambreguoy!" cried he of Anjou. "You will not let us pay three times; our host would not suffer it."

"Well then," said the Burgundian, "whichever of us shall tell the worst tale shall satisfy the landlord."

"Who will be the judge?" asked the Picardian, dropping his twelve sols to the bottom of his pocket.

"Pardieu! our host. He should be capable, seeing that he is a man of taste," said he of Anjou. "Come along, great *chef*, sit you down, drink, and lend us both your ears. The audience is open."

Thereupon the host sat down, but not until he had poured out a good gobletful of wine.

"My turn first," said the Anjou man. "I commence."

"In our duchy of Anjou, the country people are very faithful servants to our holy Catholic religion, and none of them would lose his portion of paradise for lack of doing penance or killing a heretic. If a professor of heresy passed that way, he quickly found himself under the grass, without knowing whence his death had proceeded. A good man of Larzé, returning one night from his evening prayer to the wine flasks of the Pomme-de-Pin, where he had left his understanding and memory, fell into a ditch full of water near his house, and found he was up to his neck. One of the neighbours finding him shortly afterwards nearly frozen, for it was winter time, said jokingly to him—

"'Holloa! what are you waiting for there?'

" 'A thaw,' said the tipsy fellow, finding himself held by the ice.

"Then Godenot, like a good Christian, released him from his dilemma, and opened the door of the house to him, out of respect to the wine, which is lord of this country. The good man then went and got into the bed of the maidservant, who was a young and pretty wench. The old bungler, bemuddled with wine, went ploughing in the wrong land, fancying all the time it was his wife by his side, and thanking her for the youth and freshness she still retained. On hearing her husband, the wife began to cry out, and by her horrible shrieks the man was awakened to the fact that he was not in the road to salvation, which made the poor labourer sorrowful beyond expression.

" 'Ah !' said he ; ' God has punished me for not going to vespers at church.'

"And he began to excuse himself as best he could, saying, that the wine had muddled his understanding, and getting into his own bed he kept repeating to his good wife, that for his best cow he would not have had this sin upon his conscience.

" ' My dear,' said she, ' go and confess the first thing to-morrow morning, and let us say no more about it.'

" The good man trotted to confessional, and related his case with all humility to the rector of the parish, who was a good old priest, capable of being up above, the slipper of the holy foot.

" 'An error is not a sin,' said he to the penitent. ' You will fast to-morrow, and be absolved.'

" ' Fast !—with pleasure,' said the good man. ' That does not mean go without drink.'

" ' Oh !' replied the rector, ' you must drink water, and eat nothing but a quarter of a loaf and an apple.'

"Then the good man, who had no confidence in his memory, went home, repeating to himself the penance ordered. But having loyally commenced with a quarter of a loaf and an apple, he arrived at home, saying, a quarter of apples, and a loaf.

" Then, to purify his soul, he set about accomplishing his

fast, and his good woman having given him a loaf from the
safe, and unhooked a string of apples from the beam, he set
sorrowfully to work. As he heaved a sigh on taking the last
mouthful of bread, hardly knowing where to put it, for he
was full to the chin, his wife remonstrated with him, that
God did not desire the death of a sinner, and that for lack
of putting a crust of bread in his belly, he would not be
reproached for having put things in their wrong places.

"'Hold your tongue, wife!' said he. 'If it chokes me,
I must fast.'"

"I've paid my share, it's your turn, Viscount," added he
of Anjou, giving the Picardian a knowing wink.

"The goblets are empty. Hi, there! More wine."

"Let us drink," cried the Picardian. "Moist stories slip
out easier."

At the same time he tossed off a glassful without leaving
a drop at the bottom, and after a preliminary little cough,
he related the following :—

"You must know that the maids of Picardy, before
setting up housekeeping, are accustomed honestly to gain
their linen, vessels, and chests; in short, all the needed
household utensils. To accomplish this, they go into service in Peronne, Abbeville, Amiens, and other towns, where
they are tire-women, wash up glasses, clean plates, fold
linen, and carry up the dinner, or anything that there is to
be carried. They are all married as soon as they possess
something else besides that which they naturally bring to
their husbands. These women are the best housewives, because they understand the business, and everything else
thoroughly. One belonging to Azonville, which is the land
of which I am lord by inheritance, having heard speak of
Paris, where the people did not put themselves out of the
way for any one, and where one could subsist for a whole
day by passing the cooks' shops and smelling the steam,
so fattening was it, took it into her head to go there.
She trudged bravely along the road, and arrived with a
pocket full of emptiness. There she fell in, at the Porte
St. Denis, with a company of soldiers, placed there for a
time as a vidette, for the Protestants had assumed a dan-

gerous attitude. The sergeant seeing this hooded linnet coming, stuck his headpiece on one side, straightened his feather, twisted his moustache, cleared his throat, rolled his eye, put his hands on his hips, and stopped the Picardian to see if her ears were properly pierced, since it was forbidden to girls to enter otherwise into Paris. Then he asked her, by way of a joke, but with a serious face, what brought her there, he pretending to believe she had come to take the keys of Paris by assault. To which the poor innocent replied, that she was in search of a good situation, and had no evil intentions, only desiring to gain something.

" ' Very well ; I will employ you,' said the wag. ' I am from Picardy, and will get you taken in here, where you will be treated as a queen would often like to be, and you will be able to make a good thing of it.'

" Then he led her to the guard-house, where he told her to sweep the floor, polish the saucepans, stir the fire, and keep a watch on everything, adding that she should have thirty sols a head for the men if their service pleased her. Now seeing that the squad was there for a month, she would be able to gain ten crowns, and at their departure would find fresh arrivals who would make good arrangements with her, and by this means she would be able to take back money and presents to her people. The girl cleaned the room and prepared the meals so well, singing and humming, that this day the soldiers found in their den the look of a monk's refectory. Then all being well content, each of them gave a sol to their handmaiden. Well satisfied, they put her into the bed of their commandant, who was in the town with his lady, and they petted and caressed her after the manner of philosophical soldiers, that is, soldiers partial to that which is good. She was soon comfortably ensconced between the sheets. But to avoid quarrels and strife, my noble warriors drew lots for their turn, arranged themselves in single file, playing well at Pique hardie, saying not a word, but each one taking at least twenty-six sols' worth of the girl's society. Although not accustomed to work for so many, the poor girl did her best, and by this means never closed her eyes the whole night. In the morning, seeing the soldiers were fast asleep, she rose happy at bearing no marks of the sharp skirmish, and although slightly fatigued, managed to get across the fields into the open country with her thirty sols. On the route to Picardy, she met one of her friends, who, like herself, wished to try service in Paris, and was hurrying thither, and seeing her, asked what sort of places they were.

" ' Ah! Perrine ; do not go. You want to be made of iron, and even if you were it would soon be worn away,' was the answer.

" Now, big-belly of Burgundy," said he, giving his neighbour a hearty slap, " spit out your story or pay !"

" By the queen of Antlers !" replied the Burgundian, " by my faith, by the saints, by God ! and by the devil, I know only stories of the Court of Burgundy, which are only current coin in our own land."

" Eh, ventre Dieu ! are we not in the land of Bauffre-mont ?" cried the other, pointing to the empty goblets.

" I will tell you, then, an adventure well known at Dijon, which happened at the time I was in command there, and was worth being written down. There was a sergeant of justice named Franc-Taupin, who was an old lump of mischief, always grumbling, always fighting ; stiff and starchy, and never comforting those he was leading to the hulks, with little jokes by the way ; and in short, he was just the man to find lice in bald heads, and bad behaviour in the Almighty. This said Taupin, spurned by every one, took unto himself a wife, and by chance he was blessed with one as mild as the peel of an onion, who, noticing the peculiar humour of her husband, took more pains to bring joy to his house than would another to bestow horns upon him. But although she was careful to obey him in all things, and to live at peace would have tried to excrete gold for him, had God permitted it, this man was always surly and crabbed, and no more spared his wife blows, than does a debtor promises to the bailiff's man. This unpleasant treatment continuing in spite of the carefulness and angelic behaviour of the poor woman, she being unable to accustom herself to it, was compelled to inform her relations, who thereupon came to the house. When they arrived, the husband declared to them that his wife was an idiot, that she displeased him in every possible way, and made his life almost unbearable ; that she would wake him out of his first sleep, never

came to the door when he knocked, but would leave him out in the rain and the cold, and that the house was always untidy. His garments were buttonless, his laces wanted tags. The linen was spoiling, the wine turning sour, the wood damp, and the bed was always creaking at unseasonable moments. In short, everything was going wrong. To this tissue of falsehoods, the wife replied by pointing to the clothes and things, all in a state of thorough repair. Then the sergeant said that he was very badly treated, that his dinner was never ready for him, or if it was, the broth was thin or the soup cold, either the wine or the glasses were forgotten, the meat was without gravy or parsley, the mustard had turned, he either found hairs in the dish or the cloth was dirty and took away his appetite, indeed nothing did she ever get for him that was to his liking. The wife, astonished, contented herself with stoutly denying the faults imputed to her. 'Ah,' said he, ' you dirty hussy ! You deny it, do you ! Very well then, my friends, you come and dine here to-day, you shall be witnesses of her misconduct. And if she can for once serve me properly, I will confess myself wrong in all I have stated, and will never lift my hand against her again, but will resign to her my halberd and my breeches, and give her full authority here."

" ' Oh, well,' said she, joyfully, ' I shall then henceforth be both wife and mistress !' "

"Then the husband, confident of the nature and imperfections of his wife, desired that the dinner should be served under the vine arbour, thinking he would be able to shout at her if she did not hurry quickly enough from the table to the pantry. The good housewife set to work with a will. The plates were clean enough to see one's face in, the mustard was fresh and well made, the dinner beautifully cooked, as appetizing as stolen fruit ; the glasses were clear, the wine was cool, and everything so nice, so clean and white, that the repast would have done honour to a bishop's chatterbox. Just as she was standing before the table, casting that last glance which all good housewives like to give to everything, her husband knocked at the door. At that very moment a cursed

hen, who had taken it into her head to get on the top of the arbour to gorge herself with grapes, let fall a large lump of dirt right in the middle of the cloth. The poor woman

was half dead with fright; so great was her despair, she
could think of no other way of remedying the thoughtless-
ness of the fowl than by covering the unseemly patch with
a plate in which she put the fine fruits taken at random from
her pocket, losing sight altogether of the symmetry of the
table.   Then, in order that no one should notice it, she instantly fetched the soup, seated every one in his place, and
begged them to enjoy themselves.

" Now, all of them seeing everything so well arranged,
uttered exclamations of pleasure, except the diabolical husband, who remained moody and sullen, knitting his brows
and looking for a straw on which to hang a quarrel with his
wife.   Thinking it safe to give him one for himself, her
relations being present, she said to him, ' Here's your
dinner, nice and hot, well served, the cloth is clean, the
salt-cellars full, the plates clean, the wine fresh, the bread
well baked.   What is there lacking?   What do you require?
What do you desire?   What else do you want ?'

" ' Oh, filth !' said he, in a great rage.

" The good woman instantly lifted the plate, and replied—

" ' There you are, my dear !'

" Seeing which, the sergeant was dumbfoundered, thinking
that the devil was in league with his wife.   He was immediately gravely reproached by the relations, who declared
him to be in the wrong, abused him, and made more jokes
at his expense than a recorder writes words in a month.
From that time forward the sergeant lived comfortably and
peaceably with his wife, who at the least appearance of temper
on his part, would say to him—

" ' Do you want some filth ?' "

" Who has told the worst now?" cried the Anjou man,
giving the host a tap on the shoulder.

" He has ! he has !" said the two others.   Then they
began to dispute among themselves, like the holy fathers in
council; seeking, by creating a confusion, throwing the
glasses at each other, and jumping about, a lucky chance,
to make a run of it.

" I'll settle the question," cried the host, seeing that

whereas they had all three been ready with their own accounts, not one of them was thinking of his.

They stopped terrified.

" I will tell you a better one than all, then you will have to give me ten sols a head."

" Silence for the landlord," said the one from Anjou.

" In our faubourg of Notre-Dame la Riche, in which this inn is situated, there lived a beautiful girl, who besides her natural advantages, had a good round sum in her keeping. Therefore, as soon as she was old enough, and strong enough to bear the matrimonial yoke, she had as many lovers as there are sols in St. Gatien's money-box on the Paschal-day. This girl chose one who, saving your presence, was as good a worker, night and day, as any two monks together. They were soon betrothed, and the marriage was arranged ; but the joy of the first night did not draw near without occasioning some slight apprehensions to the lady, as she was liable, through an infirmity, to expel vapours, which came out like bombshells. Now, fearing that when thinking of something else, during the first night, she might give the reins to her eccentricities, she stated the case to her mother, whose assistance she invoked. That good lady informed her that this faculty of engendering wind was inherent in the family ; that in her time she had been greatly embarrassed by it, but only in the earlier period of her life. God had been kind to her, and since the age of seven, she had evaporated nothing except on the last occasion, when she had bestowed upon her dead husband a farewell blow. ' But,' said she to her daughter, ' I have a sure specific, left to me by my mother, which brings these surplus explosions to nothing, and exhales them noiselessly. By this means these sighs become odourless, and scandal is avoided.'

" The girl, much pleased, learned how to sail close to the wind, thanked her mother, and danced away merrily, storing up her flatulence like an organ-blower waiting the first note of mass. Entering the nuptial chamber, she determined to expel it when getting into bed, but the fantastic element was beyond control. The husband came; I leave you to imagine how love's conflict sped. In the middle of the night, the bride arose under a false pretext, and quickly returned again; but when climbing into her place, the pent-up force went off with such a loud discharge, that you would have thought with me that the curtains were split.

" ' Ha ! I've missed my aim !' said she.

" ''Sdeath, my dear,' I replied, ' then spare your powder. You would earn a good living in the army with that artillery.' "

" It was my wife."

" Ha ! ha ! ha !" went the clerks.

And they roared with laughter, holding their sides and complimenting their host.

" Did you ever hear a better story, Viscount?"

" Ah, what a story !"

" That is a story !"

" A master story !"

" The king of stories !"

" Ha ! ha ! It beats all the other stories hollow. After that I say there are no stories like the stories of our host."

" By the faith of a Christian, I never heard a better story in my life."

" Why, I can hear the report."

" I should like to kiss the orchestra."

" Ah, gentlemen," said the Burgundian, gravely, " we cannot leave without seeing the hostess, and if we do not ask to kiss this famous wind-instrument, it is out of respect for so good a story-teller."

Thereupon they all exalted the host, his story, and his wife's trumpet so well that the old fellow, believing in these knaves' laughter and pompous eulogies, called to his wife. But she not coming, the clerks said, not without frustrative intention, "Let us go to her."

Thereupon they all went out of the room. The host took the candle and went upstairs first, to light them and show them the way ; but seeing the street door ajar, the rascals took to their heels, and were off like shadows, leaving the host to take in settlement of his account another of his wife's offerings.

THE CONTINENCE

KING FRANCIS THE FIRST.

EVERY one knows through what adventure King
Francis, the first of that name, was taken like a silly
bird and led into the town of Madrid, in Spain. There the
Emperor Charles V. kept him carefully locked up, like an

article of great value, in one of his
castles, in the which our defunct sire,
of immortal memory, soon became
listless and weary, seeing that he
loved the open air, and his little
comforts, and no more understood
being shut up in a cage than a cat
would folding up lace. He fell
into moods of such strange melancholy that his letters having been
read in full council, Madame d'An-
goulême, his mother ; Madame Catherine, the Dauphine,
Monsieur de Montmorency, and those who were at the head
of affairs in France, knowing the great lechery of the king,

determined, after mature deliberation, to send Queen Marguerite to him, from whom he would doubtless receive alleviation of his sufferings, that good lady being much loved by him, and merry, and learned in all necessary wisdom. But she, alleging that it would be dangerous for her soul, because it was impossible for her, without great danger, to be alone with the king in his cell, a sharp secretary, the Sieur de Fizes, was sent to the Court of Rome, with orders to beg of the Pontiff a papal brief of special indulgences, containing proper absolutions for the petty sins which, looking at their consanguinity, the said queen might commit with a view to cure the king's melancholy.

At this time, Adrian VI., the Dutchman, still wore the tiara, who, a good fellow, for the rest did not forget, in spite of the scholastic ties which united him to the emperor, that the eldest son of the Catholic Church was concerned in the affair, and was good enough to send to Spain an express legate, furnished with full powers, to attempt the salvation of the queen's soul, and the king's body, without prejudice to God. This most urgent affair made the gentlemen very uneasy, and caused an itching in the feet of the ladies, who, from great devotion to the crown, would all have offered to go to Madrid, but for the dark distrust of Charles the Fifth, who would not grant the king permission to see any of his subjects, nor even the members of his family. It was therefore necessary to negotiate the departure of the Queen of Navarre. Then, nothing else was spoken about but this deplorable abstinence, and the lack of amorous exercise so vexatious to a prince who was much accustomed to it. In short, from one thing to another, the women finished by thinking more of the king's condition, than of the king himself. The queen was the first to say that she wished she had wings. To this Monseigneur Odet de Châtillon replied, that she had no need of them to be an angel. One, that was Madame l'Amirale, blamed God that it was not possible to send by a messenger that which the poor king so much required; and every one of the ladies would have lent it in her turn.

"God has done very well to fix it," said the Dauphine,

quietly; "for our husbands would leave us rather badly off during their absence."

So much was said and so much thought upon the subject, that at her departure the Queen of all Marguerites was charged, by these good Christians, to kiss the captive heartily for all the ladies of the realm ; and if it had been permissible to prepare pleasure like mustard, the queen would have been laden with enough to sell to the two Castiles.

While Madame Marguerite was, in spite of the snow, crossing the mountains, by relays of mules, hurrying on to these consolations as to a fire, the king found himself harder pressed by unsatisfied desire than he ever had been before, or would be again. In this reverberation of nature, he opened his heart to the Emperor Charles, in order that he might be provided with a merciful specific, urging upon him that it would be an everlasting disgrace to one king to let another die for lack of gallantry. The Castilian showed himself to be a generous man. Thinking that he would be able to recuperate himself for the favour granted, out of his guest's ransom, he hinted quietly to the people commissioned

to guard the prisoner, that they might gratify him in this respect. Thereupon, a certain Don Hiios de Lara y Lopez Barra di Ponto, a poor captain, whose pockets were empty in spite of his genealogy, and who had been for some time thinking of seeking his fortune at the court of France, fancied that by procuring his majesty a soft cataplasm of warm flesh, he would open for himself an honestly fertile door; and, indeed, those who know the character of the good king and his court, can decide if he deceived himself.

When the above mentioned captain came in his turn into the chamber of the French king, he asked him respectfully if it was his good pleasure to permit him an interrogation on a subject concerning which he was as curious as about papal indulgences ? To which the prince, casting aside his hypochondriacal demeanour, and twisting round on the chair in which he was seated, gave a sign of consent. The captain begged him not to be offended at the licence of his language, and confessed to him, that he the king was said to be one of the most amorous men in France, and he would be glad to learn from him if the ladies of his court were expert in the science of love. The poor king, calling to mind his many adventures, gave vent to a deep-drawn sigh, and exclaimed, that no woman of any country, including those of the moon, knew better than the ladies of France the secrets of this alchemy; and at the remembrance of the savoury, gracious, and vigorous fondling of one alone, he felt himself the man, were she then within his reach, to clasp her to his heart, even on a rotten plank a hundred feet above a precipice.

Saying which, this good king, a ribald fellow, if ever there was one, shot forth so fiercely life and light from his eyes, that the captain, although a brave man, felt a quaking in his inside so fiercely flamed the sacred majesty of royal love. But recovering his courage he began to defend the Spanish ladies, declaring that in Castile alone was love properly understood, because it was the most religious place in Christendom, and the more fear the women had of damning themselves by yielding to a lover, the more their souls were in the affair, because they knew they must take their pleasure then against eternity. He further added, that if the Lord King would wager one of the best and most profitable manors in the kingdom of France, he would give him a Spanish night of love, in which a casual quean should, unless he took care, draw his soul from his body."

"Done," said the king, jumping up from his chair. "I will give thee, by God, the manor of Ville-aux-Dames in my province of Touraine, with full privilege of chase, of high and low jurisdiction."

Then the captain, who was acquainted with the Donna of the Cardinal Archbishop of Toledo, requested her to smother the King of France with kindness, and demonstrate to him the great advantage of the Castilian imagination over the simple movement of the French. To which the Marchesa of Amaesguy consented for the honour of Spain, and also for the pleasure of knowing of what paste God made kings, a matter in which she was ignorant, having experience only of the princes of the church. Thus she came passionate as a lion that has broken out of his cage, and made the bones of the king crack, in a manner that would have killed any other man. But the above named lord was so well furnished, so greedy, and so well bitten, that he no longer felt a bite ; and from this terrible duel the Marchesa emerged abashed, believing that she had had the devil to confess.

The captain, confident in his agent, came to salute his lord, thinking to do homage for his fief. Thereupon the king said to him, in a jocular manner, that the Spanish ladies were of a passable temperature, and their system a fair one, but that when gentleness was required they substituted frenzy ; that he kept fancying each thrill was a sneeze, or a case of violence ; in short, that the embrace of a Frenchwoman brought back the drinker more thirsty than ever, tiring him never ; and that with the ladies of his court, love was a gentle pleasure without parallel, and not the labour of a master baker in his kneading trough.

The poor captain was strangely piqued at this language. In spite of the nice sense of honour which the king pretended to possess, he fancied that his majesty wished to bilk him like a student, stealing a slice of love at a brothel in Paris. Nevertheless, not knowing for the matter of that, if the Marchesa had not over-spanished the king, he demanded his revenge from the captive, pledging him his word, that he should have for certain a veritable fay, and that he would yet gain the fief. The king was too courteous and gallant a knight to refuse this request, and even made a pretty and right royal speech, intimating his desire to lose the wager. Then, after vespers, the guard passed fresh and

With the ladies of his Court, love was a gentle pleasure,
without parallel.

warm into the king's chamber, a lady most dazzlingly white—most delicately wanton, with long tresses and velvet hands, filling out her dress at the least movement, for she was gracefully plump, with a laughing mouth, and eyes moist in advance, a woman to beautify hell, and whose first word had such cordial power that the king's garment was cracked by it. On the morrow, after the fair one had slipped out after the king's breakfast, the good captain came radiant and triumphant into the chamber.

At sight of him the prisoner exclaimed—

" Baron de la Ville-aux-Dames ! God grant you joys like to mine ! I like my goal ! By'r lady, I will not judge between the love of our lands, but pay the wager."

" I was sure of it," said the captain.

" How so ?" said the king.

" Sire, it was my wife."

This was the origin of Larray de la Ville-aux-Dames in our country, since from corruption of the names, that of Lara-y Lopez, finished by becoming Larray. It was a good family, delighting in serving the kings of France, and it multiplied exceedingly. Soon after, the Queen of Navarre came in due course to the king, who, weary of Spanish customs, wished to disport himself after the fashion of France ; but the remainder is not the subject of this narrative. I reserve to myself the right to relate elsewhere how the legate managed to sponge the sin of the thing off the great slate, and the delicate remark of our Queen of Marguerites, who merits a saint's niche in this collection ; she who first concocted such good stories. The morality of this one is easy to understand.

In the first place, kings should never let themselves be taken in battle any more than their archetype in the game of the Grecian chief Palamedes. But from this, it appears the captivity of its king is a most calamitous and horrible evil to fall upon the populace. If it had been a queen, or even a princess, what worse fate ? But I believe the thing could not happen again, except with cannibals. Can there ever be a reason for imprisoning the flower of a realm ? I think too well of Ashtaroth, Lucifer, and others, to imagine that did they reign, they would hide the joy of all the beneficent light, at which poor sufferers warm themselves. And it was necessary that the worst of devils, *id est*, a wicked old heretic woman, should find herself upon a throne, to keep a prisoner sweet Mary of Scotland, to the shame of all the knights of Christendom, who should have come without previous assignation to the foot of Fotheringay, and have left thereof no single stone.

THE MERRY TATTLE

OF

THE NUNS OF POISSY.

T HE Abbey of Poissy has been rendered famous by old authors as a place of pleasure, where the misconduct of the nuns first began, and whence proceeded so many good stories calculated to make laymen laugh at the expense of our holy religion. The said abbey by this means became fertile in proverbs, which none of the clever folks of our day understand, although they sift and chew them in order to digest them.

If you ask one of them what the *olives of Poissy* are, they will answer you gravely that it is a periphrase relating to truffles, and that *the way to serve them*, of which one formerly spoke, when joking with these virtuous maidens, meant a peculiar kind of sauce. That's the way these scribblers hit on truth once in a hundred times. To return to these good recluses, it was said—by way of a joke, of course—that they preferred finding a harlot in their chemises to a good woman. Certain other jokers reproached them with imitating the lives of the saints, in their own fashion, and said that all they admired in Mary of Egypt was her fashion of paying the boatmen. From whence the raillery, *To honour the saints after the fashion of Poissy.* There is still the *crucifix of Poissy*, which kept the stomach warm ; and *the matins of Poissy*, which concluded with a little chorister. Finally, of a hearty jade, well acquainted with the ways of love, it was said— *She is a nun of Poissy.* That property of a man which he can only lend, was *The key of the Abbey of Poissy.* What the *gate* of the said abbey was can easily be guessed. This gate, door, wicket, opening, or road was always half open, was easier to open than to shut, and cost much in repairs. In short, at that period, there was no fresh device in love invented, that had not its origin in the good convent of Poissy. You may be sure there is a good deal of untruth and hyperbolical emphasis, in these proverbs, jests, jokes, and idle tales. The nuns of the said Poissy were good young ladies, who now this way, now that, cheated God to the profit of the devil, as many others did, which was but natural, because our nature is weak; and although they were nuns, they had their little imperfections. They found themselves barren in a certain particular, hence the evil. But the truth of the matter is, all these wickednesses were the deeds of an abbess who had fourteen children, all born alive, since they had been perfected at leisure. The fantastic amours and the wild conduct of this woman, who was of royal blood, caused the convent of Poissy to become fashionable; and thereafter no pleasant adventure happened in the abbeys of France which was not credited to these poor girls, who would have been well satisfied with a tenth of them. Then the abbey was reformed, and these holy sisters were deprived of the little happiness and liberty which they had enjoyed. In an old cartulary of the abbey of Turpenay, near Chinon, which in these later troublous times had found a resting place in the library of Azay, where the custodian was only too glad to receive it, I met with a fragment under the head of *The Hours of Poissy*, which had evidently been put together by a merry abbot of Turpenay for the diversion of his neighbours of Ussé, Azay, Mongaugar, Sacchez, and other places of this province. I give them under the authority of the clerical garb, but altered to my own style, because I have been compelled to turn them from Latin into French. I commence :—At Poissy the nuns were accustomed, when Mademoiselle, the king's daughter, their abbess, had gone to bed . . . . It was she who first called it *faire la petite oie*, to stick to the preliminaries of love, the prologues, prefaces, protocols, warnings, notices, introductions, summaries, prospectuses, arguments, notes, epigraphs, titles, false-titles, current titles, scholia, marginal remarks, frontispieces, observations, gilt edges, bookmarks, reglets, vignettes, tail pieces and engravings, without once opening the merry book to read, re-read, and study to apprehend and comprehend the contents. And she gathered together in a body, all these extra-judicial little pleasures of that sweet language, which comes indeed from the lips, yet makes no noise, and practised them so well, that she died a virgin and perfect in shape. This gay science was afterwards deeply studied by the ladies of the court, who took lovers for *la petite oie*, others for honour, and at times also certain ones who had over them the right of high and low jurisdiction, and were masters of everything— a state of things much preferred. But to continue : When this virtuous princess was naked and shameless between the sheets, the said girls (those whose cheeks were unwrinkled and their hearts gay) would steal noiselessly out of their cells, and hide themselves in that of one of the sisters who was much liked by all of them. There they would have cosy little chats, enlivened with sweetmeats, pastries, liqueurs, and girlish quarrels, worry their elders, imitating them grotesquely, innocently mocking them, telling stories that made them laugh till the tears came, and playing a thousand pranks. At times they would measure their feet, to see whose were smallest, compare the white plumpness of their arms, see whose nose had the infirmity of blushing after supper, count their freckles, tell each other where their skin marks were situated, dispute whose complexion was the clearest, whose hair the prettiest colour, and whose figure the best. You can imagine that among these figures sanctified to God there were fine ones, stout ones, lank ones, thin ones, plump ones, supple ones, shrunken ones, and figures of all kinds. Then they would quarrel amongst themselves as to who took the least stuff to make a girdle, and she who spanned the least was pleased without knowing why. At times they would relate their dreams, and what they had seen in them.

Often one or two, at times all of them, had dreamed they had tight hold of the keys of the abbey. Then they would consult each other about their little ailments. One had scratched her finger, another had a whitlow; this one had risen in the morning with the white of her eye bloodshot; that one had put her finger out, telling her beads. All had some little thing the matter with them.

"Ah! you have lied to our mother; your nails are marked with white," said one to her neighbour.

"You stopped a long time at confession this morning, sister," said another. "You must have had a good many little sins to confess."

As there is nothing resembles a pussy-cat so much as a tom-cat, they would swear eternal friendship, quarrel, sulk, dispute, and make it up again; would be jealous, laugh and pinch, pinch and laugh, and play tricks upon the novices.

At times they would say, "Suppose a gendarme came here one rainy day, where should we put him?"

"With Sister Ovide ; her cell is so big he could get into it with his helmet on."

"What do you mean?" cried Sister Ovide, "are not all our cells alike ?"

Thereupon my girls burst out laughing like ripe figs. One evening they increased their council by a little novice, about seventeen years of age, who appeared innocent as a new-born babe, and would have had the host without confession. This maiden's mouth had long watered for these secret confabulations, little feasts and rejoicings by which the young nuns softened the holy captivity of their bodies, and had wept at not being admitted to them.

"Well," said Sister Ovide to her, "have you had a good night's rest, little one ?"

"Oh no !" said she, "I have been bitten by fleas."

"Ha ! you have fleas in your cell? But you must get rid of them at once. Do you know how the rules of our order enjoin them to be driven out, so that never again during her conventual life shall a sister see so much as the tail of one ?"

"No," replied the novice.

" Well then, I will teach you. Do you see any fleas here?
do you notice any trace of fleas? do you smell an odour of
fleas? Is there any appearance of fleas in my cell? Look !"

" I can't find any," said the little novice, who was Mademoiselle de Fiennes, "and smell no other odour than our
own."

" Do as I am about to tell you, and be no more bitten.
Directly you feel yourself pricked, you must strip yourself,
lift your chemise, and be careful not to sin while looking
all over your body; think only of the cursed flea, looking
for it, in good faith, without paying any attention to other
things; trying only to catch the flea, which is a difficult
job, as you may easily be deceived by the little black
spots on your skin, which you were born with. Have you
any, little one ?"

" Yes," cried she. " I have two dark freckles, one on my
shoulder and one on my back, rather low down, but it is
hidden in a fold of the flesh."

" How did you see it ?" asked Sister Perpétue."

" I did not know it. It was Monsieur de Montresor who
found it out."

" Ha ! ha !" said the sister, "is that all he saw?"

" He saw everything," said she, " I was quite little ;
he was about nine years old, and we were playing
together. . . ."

The nuns hardly being able to restrain their laughter,
Sister Ovide went on—

" The above-mentioned flea will jump from your legs to
your eyes, will try and hide himself in apertures and crevices,
will leap from valley to mountain, endeavouring to escape
you ; but the rules of the house order you
courageously to pursue, repeating *aves*. Ordinarily at the third *ave* the beast is taken."

" The flea ?" asked the novice.

" Certainly, the flea," replied Sister Ovide ;
" but in order to avoid the dangers of this
chase, you must be careful in whatever spot
you put your finger on the beast, to touch
nothing else . . . Then without regarding its cries, plaints,

groans, efforts and writhings, and the rebellion which frequently it attempts, you will press it under your thumb or other finger of the hand engaged in holding it, and with the other hand you will search for a veil to bind this flea's eyes and prevent it from leaping, as the beast seeing no longer clearly will not know where to go. Nevertheless, as it will still be able to bite you, and will be getting terribly enraged, you must gently open its mouth and delicately insert therein a twig of the blessed brush that hangs over your pillow. Thus the beast will be compelled to behave properly. But, remember, that the discipline of our order allows you to retain no property, and the beast cannot belong to you. You must take into consideration that it is one of God's creatures, and strive to render it more agreeable. Therefore, before all things, it is necessary to verify three serious things—viz., if the flea be a male, if it be female, or if it be a virgin; supposing it to be a virgin, which is extremely rare, since these beasts have no morals, are all wild hussies, and yield to the first seducer who comes, you will seize her hinder feet, and drawing them under her little caparison you must bind them with one of her hairs, and carry it to the superior, who will decide upon its fate after having consulted the chapter. If it be a male——"

"How can one tell that a flea is a virgin?"* asked the curious novice.

"First of all," replied Sister Ovide, "she is sad and melancholy, does not laugh like the others, does not bite so sharp, has her mouth less wide open, and blushes when touched—you know where."

"In that case," replied the novice, "I have been bitten by a male."

At this the sisters burst out laughing so heartily that one of them sounded a base note, and voided a little water; and Sister Ovide, pointing to it on the floor, said—

"You see there's never wind without rain."

The novice laughed herself, thinking that these chuckles were caused by the sister's exclamation.

---

* "A quoy peut-on veoir qu'une puce est pucelle?" demanda la curieuse novice.

"Now," went on Sister Ovide, "if it be a male flea, you take your scissors, or your lover's dagger, if by chance he has given you one as a souvenir, previous to your entry into the convent. In short, furnished with a cutting instrument, you carefully slit open the flanks of the flea. Expect to hear him howl, cough, spit, beg your pardon ; to see him twist about, sweat, make sheep's eyes, and anything that may come into his head to put off this operation. But be not astonished ; pluck up your courage, by thinking that you are acting thus, to bring a perverted creature into the way of salvation. Then you will dexterously take the reins, the liver, the heart, the gizzard, and noble parts, and dip them all several times into the holy water, washing and purifying them there, at the same time imploring the Holy Ghost to sanctify the interior of the beast. Afterwards you will replace all these intestinal things in the body of the flea, who will be anxious to get them back again. Being by this means baptized, the soul of the creature has become Catholic. Immediately you will get a needle and thread, and sew up the belly of the flea with great care, with such regard and attention as is due to a fellow Christian ; you will even pray for it—a kindness to which you will see it is sensible by its genuflexions and the attentive glances which it will bestow upon you. In short, it will cry no more, and have no further desire to kill you ; and fleas are often encountered who die from pleasure at being thus converted to our holy religion. You will do the same to all you can catch ; and the others perceiving it, after staring at the convert, will go away, so perverse are they, and so terrified at the idea of becoming Christians."

"And they are, therefore, wicked," said the novice. "Is there any greater happiness than to be in the bosom of the Church ?"

"Certainly," answered Sister Ursula, "here we are sheltered from the dangers of the world and of love, in which there are so many."

"Is there any other danger than that of having a child at an unseasonable time ?" asked a young sister.

"During the present reign," replied Ursula, raising her

head, "love has inherited leprosy, St. Anthony's fire, the Ardennes' sickness, and the red rash, and has heaped up all the fevers, agonies, drugs, and sufferings of the lot in his pretty mortar, to draw out therefrom a terrible complaint, of which the devil has given the receipt, luckily for convents, because there are a great number of frightened ladies, who become virtuous for fear of this love."

Thereupon they all huddled up close together, alarmed at these words, but wishing to know more.

"And is it enough to love, to suffer?" asked a sister.

"Oh yes!" cried Sister Ovide.

"You love just for one little once a pretty gentleman," replied Ursula, "and you have the chance of seeing your teeth go one by one, your hair fall off, your cheeks grow pallid, and your eyebrows drop, and the disappearance of your prized charms will cost you many a sigh. There are poor women who have scabs come upon their noses, and others who have a horrid animal with a hundred claws, which gnaws their tenderest parts. The Pope has at last been compelled to excommunicate this kind of love."

"Ah! how lucky I am to have had nothing of that sort," cried the novice.

Hearing this souvenir of love, the sisters suspected that the little one had gone astray through the heat of a *crucifix of Poissy*, and had been joking with the Sister Ovide, and drawing her out. All congratulated themselves on having so merry a jade in their company, and asked her to what adventure they were indebted for that pleasure.

"Ah!" said she, "I let myself be bitten by a big flea, who had not been baptized."

At this speech, the sister of the bass note could not restrain a second sigh.

"Ah!" said Sister Ovide, "you are bound to give us the third. If you spoke that language in the choir, the abbess would diet you like Sister Petronille; so put a sordine in your trumpet."

"Is it true that you knew in her lifetime that Sister Petronille, on whom God bestowed the gift of only going twice a year to the bank of deposit?" asked Sister Ursula.

" Yes," replied Ovide. "And one evening it happened she had to remain enthroned until matins, saying, 'I am here by the will of God.' But at the first verse, she was delivered, in order that she should not miss the office. Nevertheless, the late abbess would not allow that this was an especial favour, granted from on high, and said that God did not look so low. Here are the facts of the case. Our defunct sister, whose canonization the order are now endeavouring to obtain at the court of the Pope, and would have had it if they could have paid the proper costs of the papal brief; this Petronille, then, had an ambition to have her name in-cluded in the Calendar of Saints, which was in no way pre-judicial to our order. She lived in prayer alone, would remain in ecstasy before the altar of the Virgin, which is on the side of the fields, and pretend so distinctly to hear the angels flying in Paradise, that she was able to hum the tunes they were singing. You all know that she took from them the chant of *Adoremus*, of which no man could have invented a note. She remained for days with her eye fixed like a star, fasting, and putting no more nourishment into her body than I could into my eye. She had made a vow never to taste meat, either cooked or raw, and ate only a crust of bread a day; but on great feast days she would add thereto a morsel of salt fish, without any sauce. On this diet she became dreadfully thin, yellow as saffron, and dry as an old bone in a cemetery; for she was of an ardent disposition, and any one who had had the happiness of knocking up against her, would have drawn fire as from a flint. However, little as she ate, she could not escape an infirmity to which, luckily or unluckily, we are all more or less subject. If it were otherwise, we should be very much embarrassed. The affair in question, is the obligation of expelling after eating, like all the animals, matter more or less agreeable, according to constitution. Now Sister Petronille differed from all others, because she expelled matter such as is left by a deer, and these are the hardest substances that any gizzard produces, as you must know, if you have ever put your foot upon them in the forest glade, and from their hardness they are called bullets, in the language of forestry. This peculiarity of Sister

Petronille's was not unnatural, since long fasts kept her temperament at a permanent heat. According to the old sisters, her nature was so burning, that when water touched her, she went *frist!* like a hot coal. There are sisters who have accused her of secretly cooking eggs, in the night, between her toes, in order to support her austerities. But these were scandals, invented to tarnish this great sanctity of which all the other nunneries were jealous. Our sister was piloted in the way of salvation and divine perfection by the Abbot of St. Germain-des-Près de Paris—a holy man, who always finished his injunctions with a last one, which was to offer to God all our troubles, and submit ourselves to His will, since nothing happened without His express commandment. This doctrine, which appears wise at first sight, has furnished matter for great controversies, and has been finally condemned on the statement of the Cardinal of Chatillon, who declared that then there would be no such thing as sin, which would considerably diminish the revenues of the Church. But Sister Petronille lived imbued with this feeling, without knowing the danger of it. After Lent, and the fasts of the great jubilee, for the first time for eight months she had need to go to the little room, and to it she went. There bravely lifting her dress, she put herself into position to do that which we poor sinners do rather oftener. But Sister Petronille could only manage to expectorate the commencement of the thing, which kept her puffing without the remainder making up its mind to follow. In spite of every effort, pursing of lips and squeezings of body, her guest preferred to remain in her blessed body, merely putting his head out of window, like a frog taking the air, and felt no inclination to fall into the vale of misery among the others, alleging that he would not there be in the odour of sanctity. And his idea was a good one for a sample lump of dirt like himself. The good saint having used all methods of coercion, having over-stretched her muscles, and tried the nerves of her thin face till they bulged out, recognised the fact that no suffering in the world was so great, and her anguish attaining the apogee of sphincterial terrors, she exclaimed, ' Oh ! my God, to Thee I offer it !' At this orison, the stony

matter broke off short, and fell like a flint against the walls
of the privy, making a croc, croc, croooc, paf! You can
easily understand, my sisters, that she had no need of a
torch-cul, and drew back the remainder."

"Then did she see angels?" asked one.

"'Have they a behind?" asked another.

"Certainly not," said Ursula. "Do you not know that
one general meeting day, God having ordered them to be
seated, they answered Him that they had not the wherewithal."

Thereupon they went off to bed, some alone, others nearly
alone. They were good girls, who harmed only themselves.

I cannot leave them without relating an adventure which
took place in their house, when Reform was passing a sponge
over it, and making them all saints, as before stated. At that
time, there was in the episcopal chair of Paris a veritable
saint, who did not brag about what he did, and cared for
naught but the poor and suffering, whom the dear old bishop
lodged in his heart, neglecting his own interests for theirs,
and seeking out misery in order that he might heal it with
words, with help, with attentions, and with money, according to the case: as ready to solace the rich in their misfortunes as the poor, patching up their souls and bringing
them back to God; and tearing about hither and thither,
watching his troop, the dear shepherd! Now the good
man went about careless of the state of his cassocks,
mantles, and breeches, so that the naked members of his
church were covered. He was so charitable that he would
have pawned himself, to save an infidel from distress. His
servants were obliged to look after him carefully. Ofttimes
he would scold them when they changed unasked his tattered
vestments for new; and he used to have them darned and
patched, as long as they would hold together. Now this
good archbishop knew that the late Sieur de Poissy had left
a daughter, without a sou or a rag, after having eaten, drunk,
and gambled away her inheritance. This poor young lady
lived in a hovel, without fire in winter or cherries in spring;
and did needlework, not wishing either to marry beneath her
or sell her virtue. Awaiting the time when he should be able

to find a young husband for her, the prelate took it into his head to send her the outside case of one to mend, in the person of his old breeches, a task which the young lady, in her present position, would be glad to undertake. One d°y that the archbishop was thinking to himself that he must go to the convent of Poissy, to see after the reformed inmates, he gave to one of his servants, the oldest of his nether garments, which was sorely in need of stitches, saying, " Take this, Saintot, to the young ladies of Poissy," meaning to say, " the young lady of Poissy." Thinking of affairs connected with the cloister, he did not inform his varlet of the situation of the lady's house ; her desperate condition having been by him discreetly kept a secret. Saintot took the breeches and went his way towards Poissy, gay as a grasshopper, stopping to chat with friends he met on the way,

slaking his thirst at the wayside inns, and showing many things to the breeches during their journey that might hereafter be useful to them. At last he arrived at the convent, and informed the abbess that his master had sent him to give her these articles. Then the varlet departed, leaving with the reverend mother, the garment accustomed to model in relief the archiepiscopal proportions of the continent nature of the good man, according to the fashion of the period, beside the image of those things of which the Eternal Father has deprived His angels, and which in the good prelate did not want for amplitude. Madame the abbess having informed the sisters of the precious message of the good archbishop, they came in haste, curious and hustling, as ants into whose republic a chestnut husk as fallen. When they undid the breeches, which gaped horribly, they shrieked out, covering their eyes with one hand, in great fear of seeing the devil come out, the abbess exclaiming, "Hide yourselves, my daughters! This is the abode of mortal sin!"

The mother of the novices, giving a little look between her fingers, revived the courage of the holy troop, swearing by an Ave that no living head was domiciled in the breeches. Then they all blushed at their ease, while examining this Habitavit, thinking that perhaps the desire of the prelate was that they should discover therein some sage admonition or evangelical parable. Although this sight caused certain ravages in the hearts of these most virtuous maidens, they paid little attention to the fluttering of their reins, but sprinkling a little holy water in the bottom of the abyss, one touched it, another passed her finger through a hole, and grew bolder looking at it. It has even been pretended that, their first stir over, the abbess found a voice sufficiently firm to say, "What is there at the bottom of this? With what idea has our father sent us that which consummates the ruin of women?"

"It's fifteen years, dear mother, since I have been permitted to gaze upon the demon's den."

"Silence, my daughter. You prevent me thinking what is best to be done."

Then so much were these archiepiscopal breeches turned and twisted about, admired and re-admired, pulled here, pulled there, and turned inside out—so much were they talked about, fought about, thought about, dreamed about, night and day, that on the morrow a little sister said, after having sung the matins, to which the convent had a verse and two responses—"Sisters, I have found out the parable of the archbishop. He has sent us as a mortification his garment to mend, as a holy warning to avoid idleness, the mother abbess of all the vices.'

Thereupon there was a scramble to get hold of the breeches; but the abbess, using her high authority, reserved to herself the meditation over this patchwork. She was occupied during ten days, praying, and sewing the said breeches, lining them with silk, and making double hems, well sewn, and in all humility. Then the chapter being assembled, it was arranged that the convent should testify by a pretty souvenir to the said archbishop their delight that he thought of his daughters in God. Then all of them, to the very youngest, had to do some work on these blessed breeches, in order to do honour to the virtue of the good man.

Meanwhile, the prelate had had so much to attend to, that he had forgotten all about his garment. This is how it came about. He made the acquaintance of a noble of the court, who, having lost his wife—a she-fiend and sterile— said to the good priest, that he had a great ambition to meet with a virtuous woman, confiding in God, with whom he was not likely to quarrel, and was likely to have pretty children. Such a one he desired to hold by the hand, and have confidence in. Then the holy man drew such a picture of Mademoiselle de Poissy, that this fair one soon became Madame de Genoilhac. The wedding was celebrated at the archiepiscopal palace, where was a feast of the first

quality, and a table bordered with ladies of the highest lineage, and the fashionable world of the court, among whom the bride appeared the most beautiful, since it was certain that she was a virgin, the archbishop guaranteeing her virtue.

When the fruits, conserves, and pastry were, with many ornaments, arranged on the cloth, Saintot said to the arch- bishop, "Monseigneur, your well-beloved daughters of Poissy send you a fine dish for the centre."

" Put it there," said the good man, gazing with admiration at an edifice of velvet and satin, embroidered with wire ribbon, in the shape of an ancient vase, the lid of which exhaled a thousand superfine odours.

Immediately the bride, uncovering it, found therein sweetmeats, cakes, and those delicious confections to which the ladies are so partial. But one of them—some curious devotee—seeing a little piece of silk, pulled it towards her, and exposed to view the habitation of the human compass, to the great confusion of the prelate, for laughter rang round the table like a discharge of artillery.

"Well have they made the centre dish," said the bridegroom. " These young ladies are of good understanding. Therein are all the sweets of matrimony."

Can there be any better moral than that deduced by Monsieur de Genoilhac? Then no other is needed.

HOW THE CHÂTEAU D'AZAY
CAME TO BE BUILT.

JEHAN, son of Simon Fourniez, called Simonnin, a
citizen of Tours—originally of the village of Moulinot,
near to Beaune, whence, in imitation of certain persons,
he took the name when he became steward to Louis the
Eleventh—had to fly one day into Languedoc with his wife,
having fallen into great disgrace, and left his son Jacques
penniless in Touraine. This youth, who possessed nothing
in the world except his good looks, his sword, and spurs, but
whom worn-out old men would have considered very well
off, had in his head a firm intention to save his father, and
make his fortune at the court, then holden in Touraine. At
early dawn this good Tourainian left his lodging, and, enveloped in his mantle, all except his nose, which he left
open to the air, and his stomach empty, walked about the
town without any trouble of digestion. He entered the
churches, thought them beautiful, looked into the chapels,
flicked the flies from the pictures, and counted the columns all
after the manner of a man who knew not what to do with
his time or his money. At other times he feigned to recite
his paternosters, but really made mute prayers to the ladies,
offered them holy water when leaving, followed them afar
off, and endeavoured by these little services to encounter

some adventure, in which at the peril of his life he would
find for himself a protector or a gracious mistress. He had
in his girdle two doubloons which he spared far more than
his skin, because that would be replaced, but the doubloons
never. Each day he took from his little hoard the price of

a roll and a few apples, with which he sustained life, and
drank at his will and discretion of the water of the Loire.
This wholesome and prudent diet, besides being good for
his doubloons, kept him frisky and light as a greyhound,
gave him a clear understanding and a warm heart, for the
water of the Loire is of all syrups the most strengthening,
because having its course afar off it is invigorated by its
long run, through many strands, before it reaches Tours. So
you may be sure that the poor fellow imagined a thousand
and one good fortunes and lucky adventures, and what is
more, almost believed them true. Oh! the good times!
One evening Jacques de Beaune (he kept the name although
he was not lord of Beaune), was walking along the embankment, occupied[1] in cursing his star and everything, for his
last doubloon was with scant respect upon the point of quitting him ; when at the corner of a little street, he nearly ran

He determined to follow her, in order to ascertain whither she would
lead him—to Paradise or to the limbo of hell—to a gibbet or to an abode
of love. Anything was a gleam of hope to him, in the depth of his misery.

against a veiled lady, whose sweet odour gratified his amorous
senses. This fair pedestrian was bravely mounted on pretty

pattens, wore a beautiful dress
of Italian velvet, with wide
slashed satin sleeves ; while
as a sign of her great fortune,
through her veil a white diamond of reasonable size shone
upon her forehead like the rays
of the setting sun among her
tresses, which were so delicately rolled, built up, and so neat,
that they must have taken her maids quite three hours to arrange. She walked like a lady who was only accustomed to a
litter. One of her pages followed her, well armed. She was
evidently some light o' love belonging to a noble of high
rank, or a lady of the court, since she held
her dress high off the ground, and bent her
back like a woman of quality. Lady or
courtesan she pleased Jacques de Beaune,
who, far from turning up his nose at her,
conceived the wild idea of attaching himself
to her for life. With this in view he determined to follow her in order to ascertain
whither she would lead him—to Paradise or
to the limbo of hell—to a gibbet or to an
abode of love. Anything was a gleam of

hope to him in the depth of his misery. The lady strolled
along the bank of the Loire toward Plessis, inhaling like a
fish the fine freshness of the water, toying, sauntering like a

little mouse who wishes to see and taste
everything. When the page perceived that
Jacques de Beaune persistently followed
his mistress in all her movements, stopped
when she stopped, and watched her trifling, in a barefaced fashion, as if he had a
right so to do, he turned brusquely round
with a savage and threatening face, like that of a dog who
says, "Stand back, sir !" But the good Tourainian had his wits
about him. Believing that if a cat may look at a king, he, a

She said nothing, but looked at the sky, which was putting on its
nightcap, the stars, and everything which could give her pleasure. So
things went on.

baptized Christian, might certainly look at a pretty woman; he stepped forward, and feigning to grin at the page, he strutted now behind and now before the lady. She said nothing, but looked at the sky, which was putting on its nightcap, the stars, and everything which could give her pleasure. So things went on. At last, arrived opposite Portillon, she stood still, and in order to see better, cast her veil back over her shoulder, and in so doing cast upon the youth the glance of a clever woman who looks around to see if there is any danger of being robbed.

I may tell you that Jacques de Beaune was a thorough ladies' man, could walk by the side of a princess without disgracing her, had a brave and resolute air which pleased the sex, and if he was a little

browned by the sun from being so much in the open air, his skin would look white enough under the canopy of a bed. The glance, keen as a needle, which the lady threw him, appeared to him more animated than that with which she would have honoured her prayer-book. Upon it he built the hope of a windfall of love, and resolved to push the adventure to the very edge of the petticoat, risking to go still further, not only his lips, which he held of little account, but his two ears and something else besides. He followed into the town the lady, who returned by the Rue des Trois-Pucelles, and led the gallant through a labyrinth of little streets, to the square in which is at the present time situated the Hôtel de la Crouzille. There she stopped at the door of a splendid mansion, at which the page knocked. A servant opened it, and the lady went in and closed the door, leaving the Sieur de Beaune open-mouthed, stupefied, and as foolish as Monseigneur St. Denis when he was trying to pick up his head. He raised his nose in the air to see if some token of favour would be thrown him, and saw nothing except a light which went up the stairs, through the rooms, and rested before a fine window, where probably the lady was also. You can believe that the poor lover remained melancholy and dreaming, and knowing not what to do. The window gave a sudden creak and broke his reverie. Fancying that his lady was about to call him, he looked up again, and but for the friendly shelter of the balcony, which was a helmet to him, he would have received a stream of water and the utensil which contained it, since the handle only remained in the grasp of the person who delivered the deluge. Jacques de Beaune, delighted at this, did not lose the opportunity, but flung himself against the wall, crying, "I am killed," with a feeble voice. Then stretch-ing himself upon the fragments of broken china, he lay as if dead, awaiting the issue. The ser-vants rushed out in a state of alarm, fearing their mistress, to whom they had confessed their fault, and picked up the wounded man, who could hardly restrain his laughter at being then carried up the stairs.

"He is cold," said the page.

"He is covered with blood," said the butler, who while feeling his pulse had wetted his hand.

"If he revives," said the guilty one, "I will pay for a mass to Saint Gatien."

"Madame takes after her late father, and if she does not have thee hanged, the least mitigation of thy penalty will be that thou wilt be kicked out of her house and service," said another. "Certes, he's dead enough, he is so heavy."

"Ah! I am in the house of a very great lady," thought Jacques.

"Alas! is he really dead?" de-manded the author of the calamity. While with great labour the Tourai-nian was being carried up the stairs, his doublet caught on a projection, and the dead man cried, "Ah, my doublet!"

The Physicians and Master Surgeons.

"He groans," said the culprit, with a sigh of relief.

The Regent's servants (for this was the house of the Regent, the daughter of King Louis XI. of virtuous memory) brought Jacques de Beaune into a room, and laid him stiff and stark upon a table, not thinking for a moment that he could be saved.

"Run and fetch a surgeon," cried Madame de Beaujeu. "Run here, run there !"

The servants were down the stairs in a trice. The good lady Regent despatched her attendants for ointment, for linen to bind the wounds, for goulard-water, for so many things, that she remained alone. Gazing upon this splendid and senseless man, she cried aloud, admiring his presence and his features, handsome even in death, "Ah, God wishes to punish me. Just for one poor little time in my life has there been born in me, and taken possession of me, a naughty idea, and my patron saint is angry, and deprives me of the sweetest gentleman I have ever seen. By the rood, and by the soul of my father, I will hang every man who had a hand in this !"

"Madame," cried Jacques de Beaune, springing from the table, and falling at the feet of the Regent, "I will live to serve you, and am so little bruised that I promise you this night as many joys as there are months in the year, in imitation of the Sieur Hercules, a pagan baron. For the last twenty days," he went on (thinking that matters would be smoothed by a little lying), "I

have met you again and again. I fell madly in love with
you, yet dared not, by reason of my great respect for
your person, make an advance. You can imagine how
intoxicated I must have been with your royal beauties, to
have invented the trick to which I owe the happiness of
being at your feet."

Thereupon he kissed her amorously, and gave her a look
that would overcome any scruples. The Regent, by means
of time, which respects not queens, was, as every one knows,
in her middle age. In this critical and autumnal season,
women formerly virtuous and loverless desire now here, now
there, to enjoy, unknown to the world, certain hours of love,
in order that they may not arrive in the other world with
hands and heart alike empty, through having left the fruit
of the tree of knowledge untasted. The lady of Beaujeu,
without appearing to be astonished while listening to the
promises of this young man, since royal personages ought
to be accustomed to having them by dozens, kept this
ambitious speech in the depths of her memory, or of her

registry of love, which caught fire at his
words. Then she raised the Tourainian, who
still found in his misery the courage to smile
at his mistress, who had the majesty of a
full-blown rose, ears like shoes, and the
complexion of a sick cat, but was so well
dressed, so fine in figure, so royal of foot,
and so queenly in carriage, that he might still find in this
affair means to gain his original object.

"Who are you?" said the Regent, putting on the stern
look of her father.

"I am your very faithful subject, Jacques de Beaune, son
of your steward, who has fallen into disgrace in spite of
his faithful services."

"Ah, well," replied the lady, "lay yourself on the table
again. I hear some one coming; and it is not fit that
my people should think me your accomplice in this farce
and mummery."

The good fellow perceived, by the soft sound of her

voice, that he was pardoned the enormity of his love. He
lay down upon the table again, and remembered how certain
lords had ridden to court in an old stirrup—a thought which
perfectly reconciled him to his present position.

"Good," said the Regent to her maid-
servants; "nothing is needed. This gentleman is better; thanks to heaven and the
Holy Virgin, there will have been no murder
in my house."

Thus saying, she passed her hand through
the locks of the lover who had fallen to her
from the skies, and taking a little reviving water she bathed
his temples, undid his doublet, and, under pretence of
aiding his recovery, verified better than an expert how soft
and young was the skin of this young fellow and bold
promiser of bliss, and all the bystanders, men and women,
were amazed to see the Regent act thus. But humanity
never misbecomes those of royal blood. Jacques stood up,
and appeared to come to his senses, thanked the Regent
most humbly, and dismissed the physicians, master surgeons,

and other imps in black, saying
that he had thoroughly recovered. Then he gave his name,
and saluting Madame de Beaujeu, wished to depart, as
though afraid of her on account
of his father's disgrace, but no
doubt horrified at his terrible
vow.

"I cannot permit it," said
she. "Persons who come to
my house should not meet with
such treatment as you have encountered. The Sieur de Beaune
will sup here," she added to her major domo. "He who
has so unduly insulted him will be at his mercy if he makes
himself known immediately; otherwise, I will have him found
out and hanged by the provost."

Hearing this, the page who had attended the lady during her promenade stepped forward.

"Madame," said Jacques, "at my request pray both pardon and reward him, since to him I owe the felicity of seeing you, the favour of supping in your company, and perhaps that of getting my father re-established in the office to which it pleased your glorious father to appoint him."

"Well said," replied the Regent. "D'Estouteville," said she, turning towards the page, "I give thee command of a company of archers. But for the future do not throw things out of the window."

Then she, delighted with De Beaune, offered him her hand, and led him most gallantly into her room, where they conversed freely together while supper was being prepared. There the Sieur Jacques did not fail to exhibit his talents, justify his father, and raise himself in the estimation of the lady, who, as is well known, was like her father in disposition, and did everything at random. Jacques de Beaune thought to himself that it would be rather difficult for him to remain all night with the Regent. Such matters are not so easily arranged as the amours of cats, who have always a convenient refuge upon the housetops for their moments of dalliance. So he rejoiced that he was known to the Regent without being compelled to fulfil his rash promise, since for this to be carried out it was necessary that the servants and others should be out of the way, and her reputation safe. Nevertheless, suspecting the powers of intrigue of the good lady, at times he would ask himself if he were equal to the task. But beneath the surface of conversation, the same thing was in the mind of the Regent, who had already managed affairs quite as difficult, and she began most cleverly to arrange the means. She sent for one of her secretaries, an adept in all arts necessary for the perfect government of a kingdom, and ordered him to give her secretly a false message during supper. Then came the repast, which the lady did not touch, since her heart had swollen like a sponge and so diminished her stomach, for she kept thinking of this handsome and desirable man, having no appetite save for him. Jacques did not fail to make a good meal for many reasons. The messenger came, madame began to storm, to knit her brows after the manner of the late king, and to say, "Is there never to be peace in this land? Pasques Dieu! can we not have one quiet evening?" Then she arose, and strode about the room. "Ho there! my horse! Where is Monsieur de Vieilleville, my squire? Ah, he is in Picardy. D'Estoute-ville, you will rejoin me with my household at the Château d'Amboise. . . ." And looking at Jacques, she said, "You shall be my squire, Sieur de Beaune. You wish to serve the State. The occasion is a good one. Pasques Dieu! come. There are rebels to subdue, and faithful knights are needed."

In less time than an old beggar would have taken to say thank you, the horses were bridled, saddled, and ready. Madame was on her mare, and the Tourainian at her side, gal-loping at full speed to her castle of Amboise, followed by the men-at-arms. To be brief and come to the facts without further commentary, De Beaune was lodged not twenty yards from Madame, far from prying eyes. The courtiers

and the household, much astonished, ran about inquiring from what quarter the danger might be expected; but our hero, taken at his word, knew well enough where to find it. The virtue of the Regent, well known in the kingdom, saved her from suspicion, since she was supposed to be as impregnable as the Château de Péronne. At curfew, when everything was shut, both ears and eyes, and the castle silent, Madame de Beaujeu sent away her handmaid, and called for her squire. The squire came. Then the lady and

the adventurer sat side by side upon a velvet couch, in the shadow of a lofty fireplace, and the curious Regent, with a tender voice, asked of Jacques, "Are you not bruised? It was very wrong of me to make a knight, wounded by one of my servants, ride twelve miles. I was so anxious about it that I would not go to bed without having seen you. Do you suffer?"

"I suffer with impatience," said he of the dozen, thinking I would not do to appear reluctant. "I see well," continued he, "my noble and beautiful mistress, that your servant has found favour in your sight."

"There, there," replied she; "did you not tell a story when you said——"

"What?" said he.

"Why, that you had followed me dozens of times to churches, and other places to which I went."

"Certainly," said he.

" I am astonished," replied the Regent, " never to have seen until to-day a noble youth whose courage is so apparent in his countenance. I am not ashamed of that which you heard me say when I believed you dead. You are agreeable to me, you please me, and you wish to do well."

Then the hour of the dreaded sacrifice having struck, Jacques fell at the knees of the Regent, kissed her feet, her hands, and everything, it is said ; and while kissing her, previous to retirement, proved by many arguments to the aged virtue of his sovereign, that a lady bearing the burden of the state had a perfect right to enjoy herself —a theory which was not directly admitted by the Regent, who determined to be forced, in order to throw the burden of the sin upon her lover. This notwithstanding, you may be sure she had highly perfumed and elegantly attired herself for the night, and shone with desire of embraces, for desire lent her a high colour which greatly improved her complexion ; and in spite of her feeble resistance she was, like a young girl, carried by assault in her royal couch, where the good lady and her young dozener conscientiously embraced each other. Then from play to quarrel, from quarrel to riot, from riot to ribaldry, from thread to needle, the Regent declared that she believed more in the virginity of the Holy Mary than in the promised dozen. Now, by chance, Jacques de Beaune did not find this great lady so very old between the sheets, since everything is metamorphosed by the light of the lamps of the night. Many women of fifty by day are twenty at midnight, as others are twenty at mid-day and a hundred after vespers. Jacques, happier at this sight than at that of the king on a hanging day, renewed his undertaking. Madame, herself astonished, promised every assistance on her part. The manor of Azay-le-Brulé, with good title thereto, she undertook to confer upon her cavalier, as well as the pardon of his father, if from this encounter she came forth vanquished. Then the clever fellow said to himself, " This is to save my father from punishment ! this for the fief ! this for the letting and selling ! this for the forest of Azay ! item for the right of fishing ! another for the isles of the Indre ! this for the meadows ! I may as well release from confiscation our land of La Carte, so dearly bought by my father ! Once more for a place at court ! Arriving without hindrance at this point, he believed his dignity involved, and fancied that having France under him, it was a question of the honour of the crown. In short, at the cost of a vow which he made to his patron, Monsieur Saint Jacques, to build him a chapel

 at Azay, he presented his liege homage to the Regent in eleven clear, clean, limpid, and genuine periphrases. Concerning the epilogue of this slow conversation, the Tourainian had the great self-confidence to wish excellently to regale the Regent, keeping for her on her waking the salute of an honest man,

as it was necessary for the lord of Azay to thank his sovereign, which was wisely thought. But when nature is oppressed, she acts like a spirited horse, lies down, and will die under the whip sooner than move until it pleases her to rise reinvigorated. Thus, when in the morning the seignior of the castle of Azay desired to salute the daughter of King Louis XI., he was constrained, in spite of his courtesy, to make the salute as royal salutes should be made—with blank cartridge only. Therefore the Regent, after getting up, and while she was breakfasting with Jacques, who called himself the legitimate lord of Azay, seized the occasion of this insufficiency to contradict her esquire, and pretended, that as he had not gained his wager, he had not earned the manor.

" Ventre-Saint-Paterne ! I have been near enough," said Jacques. " But my dear lady and noble sovereign, it is not proper for either you or me to judge in this cause. The case being an allodial case, must be brought before your council, since the fief of Azay is held from the crown."

" Pasques Dieu !" replied the Regent, with a forced laugh. " I give you the place of the Sieur de Vieilleville in my house. Don't trouble about your father. I will give you Azay, and will place you in a royal office, if you can, without

injury to my honour, state the case in full council; but if
one word falls to the damage of my reputation as a virtuous
woman, I——"

" May I be hanged," said Jacques, turning the thing into
a joke, because there was a shade of anger in the face of
Madame de Beaujeu.

In fact, the daughter of King Louis thought more of her
royalty than of the roguish dozen, which she considered as
nothing, since fancying she had had her night's amusement
without loosening her purse-strings, she preferred the difficult
recital of his claim to another dozen offered her by the
Tourainian.

"Then, my lady," replied her good companion, " I shall
certainly be your squire."

The captains, secretaries, and other persons holding office
under the regency, astonished at the sudden departure of
Madame de Beaujeu, learnt the cause of her anxiety, and
came in haste to the castle of Amboise to discover whence
proceeded the rebellion, and were in readiness to hold a
council when her majesty had arisen. She called them together. not to be suspected of having deceived them, and
gave them certain falsehoods to consider, which they considered most wisely. At the close of the sitting, came the
new squire to accompany his mistress. Seeing the councillors rising, the bold Tourainian begged them to decide a
point of law which concerned both himself and the property
of the crown.

" Listen to him," said the Regent. " He speaks truly."

Then Jacques de Beaune, without being nervous at the
sight of this august court, spoke as follows, or thereabouts:—
"Noble lords, I beg you, although I am about to speak to you
of walnut shells, to give your attention to this case, and pardon
me the trifling nature of my language. One lord was walking with another in a fruit garden, and noticed a fine walnut
tree, well planted, well grown, worth looking at, worth keeping, although a little empty ; a nut tree always fresh, sweet-
smelling, a tree which you would not leave if you once saw
it, a tree of love which seemed the tree of good and evil,
forbidden by the Lord, through which were banished our

mother Eve and the gentleman her husband. Now, my lords, this said walnut tree was the subject of a slight dispute between the two, and of one of those many wagers which are occasionally made between friends. The younger boasted that he could throw twelve times through it a stick which he had in his hand at the time—as many people have who walk in a garden—and with each flight of the stick he would send a nut to the ground——"

"That is, I believe, the knotty point of the case," said Jacques, turning towards the Regent.

"Yes, gentlemen," replied she, surprised at the craft of her squire.

"The other wagered to the contrary," went on the pleader. "Now the first-named throws his stick with such precision of aim, so gently and so well that both derived pleasure therefrom, and by the joyous protection of the saints, who no doubt were amused spectators, with each throw there fell a nut; in fact, there fell twelve. But by chance the last of the fallen nuts was empty, and had no nourishing pulp from which could have come another nut tree, had the gardener planted it. Has the man with the stick gained his wager? I have finished. Judge."

"The thing is clear enough," said Messire Adam Fumée, a Tourainian, who at that time was the keeper of the seals. "There is only one thing for the other to do."

"What is that?" said the Regent.

"To pay the wager, madame."

"He is rather too clever," said she, tapping her squire on the cheek. "He will be hanged one of these days."

She meant this as a joke. But these words were the real horoscope of the steward, who mounted the gallows by the ladder of royal favour, through the vengeance of another old woman, and the notorious treason of a man of Ballan, his secretary, whose fortune he had made, and whose name was Prévost, and not René Gentil, as certain persons have wrongly called him. This Ganelon and bad servant gave,

it is said, to Madame d'Angoulême the receipt for the
money which had been given him by Jacques de Beaune,
then become baron of Samblançay, lord of La Carte and
Azay, and one of the foremost men in the State. Of his two
sons, one was Archbishop of Tours, the other Minister of
Finance and Governor of Touraine. But this is not the subject of the present history.

Now that which concerns the present narrative, is that
Madame de Beaujeu, to whom the pleasure of love had
come rather late in the day, well pleased with the great
wisdom and knowledge of public affairs which her chance
lover possessed, made him Lord of the Privy Purse, in
which office he behaved so well, and added so much to the
contents of it, that his great renown procured for him one
day the handling of the revenues which he superintended and
controlled most admirably, and with great profit to himself,
which was but fair. The good Regent paid the bet, and
handed over to her squire the manor of Azay-le-Brulé, of
which the castle had long before been demolished by the
first bombarders who came into Touraine, as every one
knows. For this powdery miracle, but for the intervention
of the king, the said engineers would have been condemned
as heretics and abettors of Satan, by the ecclesiastical tribune
of the chapter.

At this time there was being built with great care by
Messire Bohier, Minister of Finance, the Castle of Chenonceaux, which, as a curiosity and novel design, was placed
right across the river Cher.

Now the Baron de Samblançay, wishing to oppose the
said Bohier, determined to lay this foundation of his at the
bottom of the Indre, where it still stands, the gem of this
fair green valley, so solidly was it placed upon the piles.
It cost Jacques de Beaune thirty thousand crowns, not
counting the work done by his vassals. You may take it
for granted this castle is one of the finest, prettiest, most
exquisite, and most elaborate castles of our sweet Touraine,
and laves itself in the Indre like a princely creature, gaily
decked with pavilions and lace-curtained windows, with fine

weather-beaten soldiers on her vanes, turning which ever way the wind blows, as all soldiers do. But Samblançay was hanged before it was finished, and since that time no one has been found with sufficient money to complete it. Nevertheless, his master, King Francis the First, was once his guest, and the royal chamber is still shown there. When the king was going to bed, Samblançay, whom the king called "old fellow," in honour of his white hairs, hearing his royal master, to whom he was devotedly attached, remark, "Your clock has just struck twelve, old fellow!" replied, "Ah, sire, to twelve strokes of a hammer, an old one now, but years ago a good one, at this hour of the clock do I owe my lands, the money spent on this place, and the honour of being in your service."

The king wished to know what his minister meant by these strange words; and when his majesty was getting into bed, Jacques de Beaune narrated to him the history with which you are acquainted. Now Francis the First, who was partial to these spicy stories, thought the adventure a very droll one, and was the more amused thereat because at that time his mother, the Duchess d'Angoulême, in the decline of life, was pursuing the constable of Bourbon, in order to obtain of him one of these dozens. Wicked love of a wicked woman, for therefrom proceeded the peril of the kingdom, the capture of the king, and the death—as has been before mentioned—of poor Samblançay.

I have here endeavoured to relate how the Château d'Azay came to be built, because it is certain that thus was commenced the great fortune of that Samblançay who did so much for his natal town, which he adorned; and also spent such immense sums upon the completion of the towers of the cathedral. This lucky adventure has been handed down from father to son, from lord to lord, in the said place of Azay-le-Ridel, where the story frisks still under the curtains of the king, which have been curiously respected down to the present day. It is, therefore, the falsest of falsities which attributes the dozen of the Tourainian to a German knight, who by this deed would have secured the domains of Austria to the House of Hapsburgh. The author of our days, who brought this history to light, although a learned man, has allowed himself to be deceived by certain chroniclers, since the archives of the Roman Empire make no mention of an acquisition of this kind. I am angry with him for having believed that a " braguette," nourished with beer, could have been equal to the alchemical operations of the Chinonian " braguettes,"* so much esteemed by Rabelais. And I have for the advantage of the country, the glory of Azay, the conscience of the castle, and the renown of the House of Beaune, from which sprang the Sauves and the Noirmoutiers, re-established the facts in all their veritable, historical, and admirable beauty. Should any ladies pay a visit to the castle, there are still *dozens* to be found in the neighbourhood, but they can only be procured retail.

---

* *Braguettes*, haut-de-chausses, culottes, et plus particulièrement la partie de devant de ce vêtement, le pont.—*Translator*.

THE FALSE COURTESAN.

THAT which certain people do not know, is the truth concerning the decease of the Duke of Orleans, brother of King Charles VI., a death which proceeded from a great number of causes, one of which will be the subject of this narrative. This prince was for certain the most lecherous of all the royal race of Monseigneur St. Louis (who was in his lifetime King of France), without even putting on one side some of the most debauched of this fine family, which was so concordant with the vices and especial qualities of our brave and pleasure-seeking nation, that you could more easily imagine Hell without Satan than France without her valorous, glorious, and jovial kings. So you can laugh as loudly at those muckworms of philosophy who go about saying, "Our fathers were better," as at the good, philanthropical old bunglers who pretend that mankind is on the right road to perfection. These are old blind bats, who observe neither the plumage of oysters nor the shells of birds, which change no more than do our ways. Hip, hip, huzzah then! make merry while you're young. Keep your throats wet and your eyes dry, since an hundred weight of melancholy is worth less than an ounce of jollity. The

wrong doings of this lord, lover of Queen Isabella, whom
he doated upon, brought about pleasant adventures, since
he was a great wit, of an Alcibiadescal nature, and a chip of
the old block. It was he who first conceived the idea of

a relay of sweethearts, so that when he went from Paris to
Bordeaux, every time he unsaddled his nag he found ready
for him a good meal, and a bed with as much lace inside as
out. Happy prince! who died on horseback, for he was
always across something in-doors and out. Of his comical
jokes our most excellent King Louis the Eleventh has given
a splendid sample in the book of the "Cent Nouvelles
Nouvelles," written under his superintendence during his
exile, at the court of Burgundy, where, during the long
evenings, in order to amuse themselves, he and his cousin
Charolois would relate to each other the good tricks and
jokes of the period; and when they were hard up for true
stories each of the courtiers tried who could invent the best
one. But out of respect for the blood royal, the Dauphin
has credited a townsman with that which happened to the
Lady of Cany. It is given under the title of *La Médaille à
revers*, in the collection of which it is one of the brightest
jewels, and commences the hundred. But now for mine.

The Duc d'Orléans had in his suite a lord of the province
of Picardy, named Raoul d'Hocquetonville, who had taken
for a wife, to the future trouble of the prince, a young lady
related to the house of Burgundy, and rich in domains.
But, an exception to the general run of heiresses, she was

The modest and virtuous Lady D'Hocquetonville.

of so dazzling a beauty, that all the ladies of the court, even
the queen and Madame Valentine, were thrown into the
shade ; nevertheless, this was as nothing in the lady of
Hocquetonville, compared with her Burgundian consanguinity, her inheritances, her prettiness, and gentle nature,
because these rare advantages received a religious lustre
from her supreme innocence, sweet modesty, and chaste
education. The duke had not long gazed upon this heaven-
sent flower before he was seized with the fever of love. He
fell into a state of melancholy, frequented no bad places,
and only with regret now and then did he take a bite at his
royal and dainty German morsel Isabella. He became
passionate, and swore either by sorcery, by force, by trickery,
or with her consent, to enjoy the favours of this gentle lady,
who, by the sight of her sweet body, forced him to the last
extremity, during his now long and weary nights. At first,
he pursued her with honied words, but he soon knew by her
untroubled air that she was determined to remain virtuous,
for without appearing astonished at his proceedings, or
getting angry like certain other ladies, she replied to him,
" My lord, I must inform you that I do not desire to trouble
myself with the love of other persons, not that I despise the
joys which are therein to be experienced (and supreme they
must be, since so many ladies cast into the abyss of love
their homes, their honour, their future, and everything), but
from the love I bear my children. Never would I be the
cause of a blush upon their cheeks, for in this idea will I
bring up my daughters—that in virtue alone is true happiness to be found. For, my lord, if the days of our old age
are more numerous than those of our youth, of them must
we think. From those who brought me up I learned to
properly estimate this life, and I know that everything
therein is transitory, except the security of the natural affections. Thus I wish for the esteem of every one, and above
all that of my husband, who is all the world to me. Therefore do I desire to appear honest in his sight. I have
finished, and I entreat you to allow me unmolested to
attend to my household affairs, otherwise I will unhesi-

tatingly refer the matter to my lord and master, who will quit your service."

This brave reply rendered the king's brother more amorous than ever, and he endeavoured to ensnare this noble woman in order to possess her, dead or alive, and he never doubted a bit that he would have her in his clutches, relying upon his dexterity at this kind of sport, the most joyous of all, in which it is necessary to employ the weapons of all other kinds of sport, seeing that this sweet game is taken running, by taking aim, by torchlight, by night, by day, in the town, in the country, in the woods, by the waterside, in nets, with falcons, with the lance, with the horn, with the gun, with the decoy bird, in snares, in the toils, with a bird call, by the scent, on the wing, with the cornet, in slime, with a bait, with the lime-twig—indeed, by means of all the snares invented since the banishment of Adam. And gets killed in various different ways, but generally is overridden.

The artful fellow ceased to mention his desires, but had a post of honour given to the Lady of Hocquetonville in the queen's household. Now, one day that the said Isabella went to Vincennes, to visit the sick king, and left him master of the Hôtel St. Paul, he commanded the *chef* to have a delicate and royal supper prepared, and to serve it in the queen's apartments. Then he sent for his obstinate lady by express command, and by one of the pages of the household. The Countess d'Hocquetonville, believing that she was desired by Madame Isabella for some service appertaining to her post, or invited to some sudden amusement, hastened to the room. In consequence of the precautions taken by the disloyal lover, no one had been able to inform the noble dame of the princess's departure, so she hastened to the splendid chamber, which, in the Hôtel St. Paul, led into the queen's bedchamber; there she found the Duc d'Orléans alone. Suspecting some treacherous plot, she went quickly into the other room, found no queen, but heard the prince give vent to a hearty laugh.

"I am undone!" said she. Then she endeavoured to run away.

But the good lady-killer had posted about devoted

attendants, who, without knowing what was going on, closed the hotel, barricaded the doors, and in this mansion, so large that it equalled a fourth of Paris, the Lady d'Hocquetonville was as in a desert, with no other aid than that of her patron saint and God. Then, suspecting the truth, the poor lady trembled from head to foot, and fell into a chair ; and then the working of this snare, so cleverly conceived, was, with many a hearty laugh, revealed to her by her lover. Directly the duke made a movement to approach her this woman rose and exclaimed, arming herself first with her tongue, and flashing a thousand maledictions from her eyes—

"You will possess me—but dead ! Ha ! my lord, do not force me to a struggle which must become known to certain people. I may yet retire, and the Sire d'Hocquetonville shall be ignorant of the sorrow with which you have for ever tinged my life. Duke, you look too often in the ladies' faces to find time to study men's, and you do not therefore know your man. The Sire d'Hocquetonville would let himself be hacked to pieces in your service, so devoted is he to you, in memory of your kindness to him, and also because he is partial to you. But as he loves so does he hate ; and I believe him to be the man to bring his mace down upon your head, to take his revenge, if you but compel me to utter one cry. Do you desire both my death and your own ? But be assured that, as an honest woman, whatsoever happens to me, good or evil, I shall keep no secret. Now, will you let me go ?"

The bad fellow began to whistle. Hearing his whistling, the good woman went suddenly into the queen's chamber, and took from a place known to her therein, a sharp stiletto. Then, when the duke followed her to ascertain what this flight meant, "When you pass that line," cried she, pointing to a board, " I will kill myself."

My lord, without being in the least terrified, took a chair, placed it at the very edge of the plank in question, and commenced a glowing description of certain things, hoping to influence the mind of this brave woman, and work her to that point that her brain, her heart, and everything

should be at his mercy. Then he commenced to say to
her, in that delicate manner to which princes are accustomed, that, in the first place, virtuous women pay dearly
for their virtue, since in order to gain the uncertain blessings of the future, they lose all the sweetest joys of the
present, because husbands were compelled, from motives of
conjugal policy, not to show them all the jewels in the
shrine of love, since the said jewels would so affect their
hearts, were so rapturously delicious, so titillatingly voluptuous, that a woman would no longer consent to dwell in
the cold regions of domestic life ; and he declared this
marital abomination to be a great felony, because the least
thing a man could do in recognition of the virtuous life of a
good woman and her great merits, was to overwork himself,
to exert, to exterminate himself, to please her in every way,
with fondlings and kissings and wrestling, and all the
delicacies and sweet confectionery of love ; and that, if she
would taste a little of the seraphic joys of these little ways
to her unknown, she would believe all the other things of
life as not worth a straw ; and that, if such were her wish,
he would for ever be as silent as the grave, and thus no
scandal would besmear her virtue. And the lewd fellow,
perceiving that the lady did not stop her ears, commenced
to describe to her, after the fashion of arabesque pictures,
which at that time were much esteemed, the wanton inventions of debauchery. Then did his eyes shoot flame, his
words burn, and his voice ring, and he himself took great
pleasure in calling to mind the various ways of his ladies,
naming them to Madame d'Hocquetonville, and even revealing to her the tricks, caresses, and amorous ways of
Queen Isabella, and he made use of an expression so gracious and so ardently inciting, that, fancying it caused the
lady to relax her hold upon the stiletto a little, he made as
if to approach her. But she, ashamed to be found buried
in thought, gazed proudly at the diabolical leviathan who
tempted her, and said to him, " Fine sir, I thank you.
You have caused me to love my husband all the more, for
from your discourse I learn how much he esteems me by
holding me in such respect that he does not dishonour his

couch with the tricks of street-walkers and bad women. I should think myself for ever disgraced, and should be contaminated to all eternity if I put my foot in those sloughs where go these shameless hussies. A man's wife is one thing, and his mistress another."

" I will wager," said the duke, smiling, " that, nevertheless, for the future you spur the Sire d'Hocquetonville to a little sharper pace."

At this the good wife trembled, and cried, " You are a wicked man. Now I both despise and abominate you ! What ! unable to rob me of my honour, you attempt to poison my mind ! Ah, my lord, this night's work will cost you dear :—

> If I forgive it, yet,
> God will not forget.

" Are not those verses yours ?"

" Madame," said the duke, turning pale with anger, " I can have you bound——"

" Oh no ! I can free myself," replied she, brandishing the stiletto.

The rapscallion began to laugh.

" Never mind," said he. " I have a means of plunging you into the sloughs of these brazen hussies, as you call them."

" Never, while I live."

" Head and heels you shall go in—with your two feet, two hands, your two ivory breasts, and two other things white as snow—your teeth, your hair, and everything. You will go of your own accord ; you shall enter into it lasciviously, and in a way to crush your cavalier, as a wild horse does its rider—stamping, leaping, and snorting. I swear it by Saint Castud !"

Instantly he whistled for one of his pages. And when the page came, he secretly ordered him to go and seek the Sire d'Hocquetonville, Savoisy, Tanneguy, Cypierre, and other members of his band, asking them to these rooms to supper, not without at the same time inviting to meet his guests a pretty petticoat or two.

Then he came and sat down in his chair again, ten paces

from the lady, off whom he had not taken his eye while giving his commands to the page in a whisper.

"Raoul is jealous," said he. "Now let me give you a word of advice. In this place," he added, pointing to a secret door, "are the oils and superfine perfumes of the queen ; in this other little closet she performs her ablutions and little feminine offices. I know by much experience that each of you gentle creatures has her own special perfume, by which she is smelt and recognised. So if, as you say, Raoul is overwhelmingly jealous with the worst of all jealousies, you will use these fast hussies' scents, because your danger approaches fast."*

"Ah, my lord, what do you intend to do ?"

"You will know when it is necessary that you should know. I wish you no harm, and pledge you my honour, as a loyal knight, that I will most thoroughly respect you, and be for ever silent concerning my discomfiture. In short, you will know that the Duc d'Orléans has a good heart, and revenges himself nobly on ladies who treat him with disdain, by placing in their hands the key of Paradise. Only keep your ears open to the joyous words that will be handed from mouth to mouth in the next room, and cough not if you love your children."

Since there was no egress from the royal chamber, and the bays crossing hardly left room to put one's head through, the good prince closed the door of the room, certain of keeping the lady a safe prisoner there, and again impressed upon her the necessity of silence. Then came the merry blades in great haste, and found a good and substantial supper smiling at them from the silver plates upon the table, and the table well arranged and well lighted, loaded with fine silver cups, and cups full of royal wine. Then said their master to them—

"Come ! come ! to your places my good friends. I was becoming very weary. Thinking of you, I wished to arrange

---

* *Vous userez de ces senteurs de bourbeteuse, puisque bourbier y ha.* *Bourbeteuse* is a dirty woman ; and *bourbier*, danger or scrape. The exact play upon the word cannot be preserved in the translation.

with you a merry feast after the ancient method, when the
Greeks and the Romans said their *Pater noster* to Master
Priapus, and the learned god called in all countries Bacchus.
The feast will be a proper and right hearty one, since at
our libation there will be present some pretty crows with
three beaks, of which I know from great experience the best
one to kiss."

Then all of them recognising their master in all things,
took pleasure in this gay discourse, except Raoul d'Hocquetonville, who advanced and said to the prince—

"My lord, I will aid you willingly in any battle but that
of the petticoats, in that of spear and axe, but not of the
wine flasks. My good companions here present have not
wives at home, it is otherwise with me. I have a sweet
wife, to whom I owe my company, and an account of all my
deeds and actions."

"Then, since I am a married man I am to blame?" said
the duke.

"Ah! my dear master, you are a prince, and can do as
you please."

These brave speeches made, as you can imagine, the
heart of the lady prisoner hot and cold.

"Ah! my Raoul," thought she, "thou art a noble man!"

"You are," said the duke, "a man whom I love, and
consider more faithful and praiseworthy than any of my
people. The others," said he, looking at the three lords,
"are wicked men. But, Raoul," he continued, "sit
thee down. When the linnets come—they are linnets of
high degree—you can make your way home. S'death! I
had treated thee as a virtuous man, ignorant of the extra-
conjugal joys of love, and had carefully put for thee in that
room the queen of raptures—a fair demon, in whom is concentrated all feminine inventions. I wished that once in
thy life thou, who hast never tasted the essence of love, and
dreamed but of war, should know the secret marvels of the
gallant amusement, since it is shameful that one of my followers should serve a fair lady badly."

Thereupon the Sire d'Hocquetonville sat down to the
table in order to please his prince as far as he could lawfully

do so. Then they all commenced to laugh, joke, and talk about the ladies; and, according to their custom, they related to each other their good fortunes and their love adventures, sparing no woman except the queen of the

house, and betraying the little habits of each one, to which followed horrible little confidences, which increased in treachery and lechery as the contents of the goblets grew less. The duke, gay as an universal legatee, drew the guests out, telling lies himself to learn the truth from them; and his companions ate at a trot, drank at full gallop, and their tongues rattled away faster than either.

Now, listening to them, and heating his brain with wine, the Sire d'Hocquetonville unharnessed himself little by little from his reluctance. In spite of his virtues, he indulged certain desires, and became soaked in these impurities like a saint who defiles himself while saying his prayers. Perceiving which, the prince, on the alert to satisfy his ire and his bile, began to say to him, joking him—

"By St. Castud, Raoul, we are all tarred with the same brush, all discreet away from here. Go; we will say nothing to Madame. By heaven! man, I wish thee to taste of the joys of paradise. There," said he, tapping the door of the room in which was Madame d'Hocquetonville, "in there is a lady of the court and a friend of the queen, but the greatest priestess of Venus that ever was, and her equal is not to be found in any courtesan, harlot, dancer, doxy, or hussy. She was engendered at a moment when paradise was radiant with joy, when nature was procreating, when the planets were whispering vows of love, when the beasts were frisking and capering, and everything was aglow with desire. Although the woman to make an altar her bed, she is nevertheless too great a lady to allow herself to be seen, and too well known to utter any words but the sounds of love. No light will you need, for her eyes flash fire, and attempt no conversation, since she speaks only with movements and twistings more rapid than those of a deer surprised in the forest. Only, my dear Raoul, with so merry a nag look to your stirrups, sit light in the saddle, since with one plunge she would hurl thee to the ceiling, if you are not careful. She burns always, and is always longing, for male society. Our poor dead friend, the young Sire de Giac, met his death through her; she drained his marrow in one springtime. God's truth! to know such bliss as that of which she rings the bells and lights the fires, what man would not forfeit a third of his future happiness? and he who has known her once would for a second night forfeit without regret eternity."

"But," said Raoul, "in things which should be so much alike, how is it there is so great a difference?"

"Ha! ha! ha!"

Thereupon the company burst out laughing, and animated by the wine and a wink from their master, they all commenced relating droll and quaint conceits, laughing, shouting, and making a great noise. Now, knowing not that an innocent scholar was there, these jokers, who had drowned their sense of shame in the wine-cups, said things to make the figures on the mantel shake, the walls and the ceilings blush; and the duke surpassed them all, saying, that the lady who was in bed in the next room awaiting a gallant should be the empress of these warm imaginations, because she practised them every night. Upon this, the flagons being empty, the duke pushed Raoul, who let himself be pushed willingly, into the room, and by this means the prince compelled the lady to deliberate by which dagger she would either live or die. At midnight the Sire d'Hocquetonville came out gleefully, not without remorse at having been

Our poor dear friend, the young Sire de Giac, met his
death through her.

false to his good wife. Then the Duc d'Orléans led Madame d'Hocquetonville out by a garden door, so that she gained her residence before her husband arrived there. "This," said she, in the prince's ear, as she passed the postern, "will cost us all dear."

One year afterwards, in the old Rue du Temple, Raoul d'Hocquetonville, who had quitted the service of the duke for that of Jehan of Burgundy, gave the king's brother a blow on the head with a club, and killed him, as every one knows. In the same year died the Lady d'Hoc- quetonville, having faded like a flower deprived of air and eaten by a worm. Her good husband had engraved upon her marble tomb, which is in one of the cloisters of Péronne, the following inscription :—

HERE LIES

BERTHA DE BOURGONGNE,

THE NOBLE AND COMELY WIFE

OF

RAOUL, SIRE DE HOCQUETONVILLE.

ALAS ! PRAY NOT FOR HER SOUL.

SHE

BLOSSOMED AGAIN IN PARADISE,

THE ELEVENTH DAY OF JANUARY,

IN THE YEAR OF OUR LORD MCCCCVIII.,

IN THE TWENTY-THIRD YEAR OF HER AGE,

LEAVING TWO SONS AND HER LORD SPOUSE

INCONSOLABLE.

✠

The just death of this rascal nevertheless caused many serious
rebellions, which finally Louis XI., losing all patience, put down
with fire and sword,

This epitaph was written in elegant Latin, but for the convenience of all it was necessary to translate it, although the word *comely* is feeble beside that of *formosa*, which signifies *beautiful in shape.* The Duke of Burgundy, called the Fearless, to whom previous to his death the Sire d'Hocquetonville confided the troubles cemented with lime and sand in his heart, used to say, in spite of his hard-heartedness in these matters, that this epitaph plunged him into a state of melancholy for a month, and that among all the abominations of his cousin of Orleans, there was one for which he would kill him over again if the deed had not already been done, because this wicked man had villanously defaced with vice the most divine virtue in the world and had prostituted two noble hearts, the one by the other. When saying this he would think of the lady of Hocquetonville and of his own, whose portrait had been unwarrantably placed in the cabinet where his cousin placed the likenesses of his wenches.

This adventure was so extremely shocking, that when it was related by the Count de Charolois to the Dauphin, afterwards Louis XI., the latter would not allow his secretaries to publish it in his collection, out of respect for his great-uncle the Duke of Orleans, and for Dunois his old comrade, the son of the same. But the person of the lady of Hocquetonville is so sublimely virtuous, so exquisitely melancholy, that in her favour the present publication of this narrative will be forgiven, in spite of the diabolical invention and vengeance of Monseigneur d'Orléans. The just death of this rascal nevertheless caused many serious rebellions, which finally Louis XI., losing all patience, put down with fire and sword.

This shows us that there is a woman at the bottom of everything, in France as elsewhere, and that sooner or later we must pay for our follies.

THE DANGER

OF

BEING TOO INNOCENT.

THE lord of Moncontour was a brave soldier of Tours, who, in honour of the battle gained by the Duke of Anjou, afterwards our right glorious king, caused to be built at Vouvray the castle thus named, for he had borne himself most bravely in that affair, where he overcame the greatest of heretics, and from that was authorized to take the name. Now this said captain had two sons, good Catholics, of whom the eldest was in favour at court. After the peace, which was concluded before the stratagem arranged for St. Bartholomew's day, the good man returned to his manor, which was not ornamented as it is at the present day. There he received the sad announcement of the death of his son, slain in a duel by the lord of Villequier. The poor father was the more cut up at this, as he had arranged a capital marriage for this said son with a young lady of the male branch of Amboise. Now, by this death most piteously inopportune, vanished all the future and advantages of his family, of which he wished to make a great and noble house.

With this idea, he had put his other son in a monastery, under the guidance and government of a man renowned for his holiness, who brought him up in a Christian manner, according to the desire of his father, who wished from high ambition to make of him a cardinal of renown. For this the good abbot kept the young man in a private house, had him to sleep by his side in his cell, allowed no evil weeds to grow in his mind, brought him up in purity of soul and true contrition, as all priests should be. This said clerk, when turned nineteen years, knew no other love than the love of God, no other nature than that of the angels who have not our carnal properties, in order that they may live in purity, seeing that otherwise they would make good use of them. The which the King on High, who wished to have His pages always proper, was afraid of. He has done well, because his good little people cannot drink in dram shops or riot in brothels as ours do. He is divinely served ; but then, remember, He is Lord of all. Now in this plight the lord of Moncontour determined to withdraw his second son from the cloister, and invest him with the purple of the soldier and the courtier, in the place of the ecclesiastical purple ; and determined to give him in marriage to the maiden, affianced to the dead man, which was wisely determined, because wrapped round with continence and sobriety in all ways as was the little monk, the bride would be as well used and happier than she would have been with the elder, already well hauled over, upset, and spoilt by the ladies of the court. The befrocked unfrocked, and very sheepish in his ways, followed the sacred wishes of his father, and consented to the said marriage without knowing what a wife, and—what is more curious—what a girl was. By chance, his journey having been hindered by the troubles and marches of conflicting parties, this innocent—more innocent than it is lawful for a man to be innocent—only came to the castle of Moncontour the evening before the wedding, which was performed with dispensations bought in the archbishopric of Tours. It is necessary here to describe the bride. Her mother, long time a widow, lived in the house of M. de Braguelongne, civil lieutenant of the

Chatelet de Paris, whose wife lived with the lord of Lig-
nieres, to the great scandal of the period. But every one
then had so many joists in his own eye that he had no
right to notice the rafters in the eyes of others. Now, in
all families people go to perdition, without noticing their
neighbours, some at an amble, others at a gentle trot, many
at a gallop, and a small number walking, seeing that the
road is all down hill. Thus in these times the devil had
many a good orgie in all things, since that misconduct was
fashionable. The poor old lady Virtue had retired trembling, no one knew whither, but now here, now there, lived
miserably in company with honest women.

In the most noble house of Amboise there still lived the
dowager of Chaumont, an old woman of well proved virtue,
in whom had retired all the religion and good conduct of
this fine family. The said lady had taken to her bosom,
from the age of ten years, the little maiden who is concerned
in this adventure, and who never caused Madame Amboise
the least anxiety, but left her free in her movements, and
she came to see her daughter once a year, when the court
passed that way. In spite of this high maternal reserve,
Madame Amboise was invited to her daughter's wedding,
and also the lord of Braguelongne, by the good old soldier,
who knew his people. But the dear dowager came not to
Moncontour, because she could not obtain leave from her
sciatica, her cold, nor the state of her legs, which gambolled
no longer. Over this the good woman cried copiously. It
hurt her much to let go into the dangers of the court
and of life this gentle maiden, as pretty as it was possible
for a pretty girl to be, but she was obliged to give her her
wings. But it was not without promising her many masses
and orisons every evening for her happiness. And comforted a little, the good old lady began to think that the
staff of her old age was passing into the hands of a quasi-
saint, brought up to do good by the above-mentioned abbot,
with whom she was acquainted, the which had aided considerably in the prompt exchange of spouses. At length,
embracing her with tears, the virtuous dowager made those
last recommendations to her that ladies make to young

brides, as that she ought to be respectful to his mother, and obey her husband in everything.

Then the maid arrived with a great noise, conducted by servants, chamberlains, grooms, gentlemen, and people of the house of Chaumont, so that you would have imagined her suite to be that of a cardinal legate. So arrived the two spouses the evening before their marriage. Then, the feasting over, they were married with great pomp on the Lord's Day, a mass being said at the castle by the Bishop of Blois, who was a great friend of the lord of Moncontour; in short, the feasting, the dancing, and the festivities of all sorts lasted till the morning. But on the stroke of midnight the bridesmaids went to put the bride to bed, according to the custom of Touraine; and during this time they kept quarrelling with the innocent husband, to prevent him going to this innocent wife, who sided with them from ignorance. However, the good lord of Moncontour interrupted the jokers and the wits, because it was necessary that his son should occupy himself in well-doing. Then went the innocent into the chamber of his wife, whom he thought more beautiful than the Virgin Marys painted in Italian, Flemish, and other pictures, at whose feet he had said his prayers. But you may be sure he felt very much embarrassed at having so soon become a husband, because he knew nothing of his business, and saw that certain forms had to be gone through concerning which, from great and modest reserve, he had not time to question even his father, who had said sharply to him—

" You know what you have to do; be valiant therein."

Then he saw the gentle girl who was given him, comfortably tucked up in the bedclothes, terribly curious, her head buried under, but hazarding a glance as at the point of a halberd, and saying to herself—

" I must obey him."

And knowing nothing, she awaited the will of this slightly ecclesiastical gentleman, to whom, in fact, she belonged. Seeing which, the Chevalier de Moncontour came close to the bed, scratched his ear, and knelt down, a thing in which he was expert.

" Have you said your prayers ?" said he.

" No," said she ; " I have forgotten them. Do you wish me to say them ?"

Then the young couple commenced the business of housekeeping by imploring God, which was not at all out of place. But unfortunately the devil heard, and at once replied to their requests, God being much occupied at that time with the new and abominable reformed religion.

" What did they tell you to do ?" said the husband.

" To love you," said she, in perfect innocence.

" That has not been told to me ; but I love you, I am ashamed to say, better than I love God."

This speech did not at all alarm the bride.

" I should like," said the husband, " to repose myself in your bed, if it will not disturb you."

" I will make room for you willingly, because I am to submit myself to you."

" Well," said he, " don't look at me, then. I'm going to take my clothes off, and come."

At this virtuous speech, the young damsel turned herself towards the wall in great expectation, seeing that it was for the very first time that she was about to find herself separated from a man by the confines of a shirt only. Then came the innocent, gliding into the bed, and thus they found themselves, so to speak, united, but far from you can imagine what. Did you ever see a monkey brought from across the seas, who for the first time is given a nut to crack ? This ape, knowing by high apish imagination how delicious is the food hidden under the shell, sniffs and twists himself about in a thousand apish ways, saying, I know not what, between his chattering jaws. Ah ! with what affection he studies it, with what study he examines it, in what examination he holds it, then throws it, rolls and tosses it about with passion, and often, when it is an ape of low extraction and intelligence, leaves the nut. As much did the poor innocent who, towards the dawn, was obliged to confess to his dear wife that, not knowing how to perform his office, or what that office was, or where to obtain the said office, it would be necessary for him to inquire concerning it, to have help and aid.

"Yes," said she; "since, unhappily, I cannot instruct you."

In fact, in spite of their efforts, essays of all kinds—in spite of a thousand things which the innocents invent, and which the wise in matters of love know nothing about—the pair dropped off to sleep, wretched at having been unable to discover the secret of marriage. But they wisely agreed to say that they had done so. When the wife got up, still a maiden, seeing that she had not been crowned, she boasted of her night, and said she had the king of husbands, and went on with her chattering and repartees as briskly as those who know nothing of these things. Then every one found the maiden a little too sharp, since for a two-edged joke a lady of Roche-Corbon having incited a young maiden, de la Bourdaisière, who knew nothing of such things, to ask the bride—

" How many loaves did your husband put in the oven ?"

" Twenty-four," she replied.

Now, as the bridegroom was roaming sadly about, thereby distressing his wife, who followed him with her eyes, hoping to see his state of innocence come to an end, the ladies believed that the joy of that night had cost him dear, and that the said bride was already regretting having so quickly ruined him. And at breakfast came the bad jokes, which at that time were relished as excellent. One said that the bride had an open expression ; another, that there had been some good strokes of business done that night in the castle; this one, that the oven had been burned ; that one, that the two families had lost something that night that they would never find again. And a thousand other jokes, stupidities, and double meanings that, unfortunately, the husband did not understand. But on account of the great affluence of the relations, neighbours, and others, no one had been to bed ; all had danced, rollicked, and frolicked, as is the custom at noble weddings.

At this was quite contented my said Sieur de Braguelongne, upon whom my lady of Amboise, excited by the
thought of the good things which were happening to her
daughter, cast the glances of a falcon in matters of gallant
assignation.   The poor lieutenant civil, learned in bailiffs'
men and serjeants, and who nabbed all the pickpockets
and scamps of Paris, pretended not to see his good fortune,
although his good lady required him to.   You may be sure
this great lady's love weighed heavily upon him, so he
only kept to her from a spirit of justice, because it was not
seeming in a lieutenant criminal to change his mistresses
as often as a man at court, because he had under his charge
morals, the police, and religion.   This notwithstanding his
rebellion must come to an end.   On the day after the
wedding a great number of the guests departed; then
Madame d'Amboise and Monsieur de Braguelongne could
go to bed, their guests having decamped.   Sitting down
to supper, the lieutenant received a half-verbal summons
to which it was not becoming, as in legal matters, to oppose
any reasons for delay.

During supper the said lady d'Amboise made more than
a hundred little signs in order to draw the good Braguelongne from the room where he was with the bride, but out
came instead of the lieutenant the husband, to walk about
in company with the mother of his sweet wife.   Now, in the
mind of this innocent there had sprung up like a mushroom
an expedient—namely, to interrogate this good lady, whom
he considered discreet, for remembering the religious precepts of his abbot, who had told him to inquire concerning all
things of old people expert in the ways of life, he thought of
confiding his case to my said lady d'Amboise.   But he made
first awkwardly and shyly certain twists and turns, finding no
terms in which to unfold his case.   And the lady was also
perfectly silent, since she was outrageously struck with the
blindness, deafness, and voluntary paralysis of the lord of
Braguelongne ; and said to herself, walking by the side of
this delicate morsel, a young innocent of whom she did not
think, little imagining that this cat so well provided with
young bacon could think of old—

"This Ho, Ho, with a beard of flies' legs, a flimsy, old, grey, ruined, shaggy beard—a beard without comprehension, beard without shame, without any feminine respect— beard which pretends neither to feel nor to hear nor to see, a pared away beard, a beaten down, disordered, gutted beard. May the Italian sickness deliver me from this vile joker with a squashed nose, fiery nose, frozen nose, nose without religion, nose dry as a lute table, pale nose, nose without a soul, nose which is nothing but a shadow; nose which sees not, nose wrinkled like the leaf of the vine; nose that I hate, old nose, nose full of mud—dead nose. Where have my eyes been to attach myself to this truffle nose, to this old hulk that no longer knows his way? I give my share to the devil of this old juiceless beard, of this old grey beard, of this monkey face, of these old tatters, of this old rag of a man, of this—I know not what; and I'll take a young husband who'll marry me properly, and . . . and often—every day—and well——"

In this wise train of thought was she when the innocent began his anthem to this woman, so warmly excited, who at the first paraphrase took fire in her understanding, like a piece of old touchwood from the carbine of a soldier; and finding it wise to try her son-in-law, said to herself—

"Ah! young beard, sweet scented! ah! pretty new nose—fresh beard—innocent nose—virgin beard—nose full of joy—beard of springtime, small key of love!"

She kept on talking the round of the garden, which was

long, and then arranged with the Innocent that, night come, he should sally forth from his room and get into hers, where

she engaged to render him more learned than ever was his father. And the husband was well content, and thanked Madame d'Amboise, begging her to say nothing of this arrangement.

During this time the good old Braguelongne had been growling and saying to himself, " Old ha, ha! old ho, ho! may the plague take thee! may a cancer eat thee!— worthless old currycomb! old slipper, too big for the foot! old arquebus! ten year old codfish! old spider that spins no more! old death with open eyes! old devil's cradle! vile lantern of an old town-crier! old wretch whose look kills! old moustache of an old theriacler! old wretch to make dead men weep ! old organ-pedal ! old sheath with a hundred knives ! old church porch, worn out by the knees ! old poor-box in which every one has dropped. I'll give all my future to be quit of thee !" As he finished these gentle thoughts the pretty bride, who was thinking of her young husband's great sorrow at not knowing the particulars of that essential item of marriage, and not having the slightest idea what it was, thought to save him much tribulation, shame, and labour by instructing herself. And she counted upon much astonishing and rejoicing him the next night when she should say to him, teaching him his duty, " That's the thing, my love !" Brought up in great respect of old people by her dear dowager, she thought of inquiring of this good man in her sweetest manner to distil for her the sweet mysteries of the commerce. Now, the lord of Braguelongne, ashamed of being lost in sad contemplation of his evening's work, and of saying nothing to his gay companion, put this summary interrogation to the fair bride—" If she was not happy with so good a young husband——"

" He is very good," said she.

" Too good, perhaps," said the lieutenant, smiling.

To be brief, matters were so well arranged between them that the lord of Braguelongne engaged to spare no pains to enlighten the understanding of Madame d'Amboise's daughter-in-law, who promised to come and study her lesson in his room. The said lady d'Amboise pretended after supper to play terrible music in a high key to Monsieur de Braguelongne, saying that he had no gratitude for the blessings she had brought him—her position, her wealth, her fidelity, &c. In fact, she talked for half an hour without having exhausted a quarter of her ire. From this a hundred knives were drawn between them, but they kept the sheaths. Meanwhile the spouses in bed were arranging to themselves how to get away, in order to please each other. Then the innocent began to say he felt quite giddy, he knew not from what, and wanted to go into the open air. And his maiden wife told him to take a stroll in the moonlight. And then the good fellow began to pity his wife in being left alone a moment. At her desire, both of them at different times left their conjugal couch and came to their preceptors, both very impatient, as you can well believe; and good instruction was given to them. How? I cannot say, because every one has his own method and practice, and of all sciences this is the most variable in principle. You may be sure that never did scholars receive more gaily the precepts of any language, grammar, or lessons whatsoever. And the two spouses returned to their nest, delighted at being able to communicate to each other the discoveries of their scientific peregrinations.

"Ah, my dear," said the bride, " you already know more than my master!"

From these curious tests came their domestic joy and perfect fidelity; because immediately after their entry into the married state they found out how much better each of them was adapted for love than any one else, their masters included. Thus for the remainder of their days they kept to the legitimate substance of their own persons; and the lord of Moncontour said in old age to his friends—

" Do like me, be cuckolds in the blade, and not in the sheaf."

Which is the true morality of the conjugal condition.

THE DEAR NIGHT OF LOVE.

IN that winter when commenced that first taking up of arms by those of the religion, which was called the Riot of Amboise, an advocate, named Avenelles, lent his house, situated in the Rue des Marmousets for the interviews and conventions of the Huguenots, being one of them, without knowing, however, that the Prince of Condé, La Regnaudie, and others, intended to carry off the king.

This said Avenelles wore a nasty red beard, as shiny as a stick of liquorice, and was devilishly pale, as are all the rogues who take refuge in the darknesses of the law ; in short, the most evil-minded advocate that has ever lived, laughing at the gallows, selling everybody, and a true Judas. According to certain authors of great experience in subtle rogues, he was in this affair half knave, half fool, as is abundantly proved by this narrative. This *procureur* had married a very lovely lady of Paris, of whom he was jealous enough to kill her for a pleat in the sheets, for which she could not

account, which would have been wrong, because honest
creases are often met with.   But she folded her clothes very

well, so there's an end of the matter.
Be sure that, knowing the murderous
and evil nature of this man, his wife
was faithful enough to him, always
ready, like a candlestick, arranged
for her duty like a chest which never
moves, and opens to order.   Nevertheless, the advocate had placed her
under the guardianship and pursuing
eye of an old servant, a duenna as
ugly as a pot without a handle, who
had brought up the Sieur Avenelles,
and was very fond of him.   His poor
wife, for all pleasure in her cold domestic life, used to go to the church
of St. Jehan, on the Place de Grève, where, as every one
knows, the fashionable world was accustomed to meet;
and while saying her
paternosters to God
she feasted her eyes
upon all these gallants,
curled, adorned, and
starched, young, come-
ly, and flitting about
like true butterflies,
and finished by pick-
ing out from among
the lot a good gen-
tleman, lover of the
queen-mother, and a
handsome Italian, with
whom she was smitten

because he was in the May of his age, nobly dressed, a graceful
mover, brave in mien, and was all that a lover should be to
bestow a heart full of love upon an honest woman too tightly
squeezed by the bonds of matrimony, which torment her,
and always excite her to unharness herself from the conjugal

yoke. And you can imagine that the young gentleman grew to admire Madame, whose silent love spoke secretly to him, without either the devil or themselves knowing how. Both one and the other had their correspondences of love. At first the advocate's wife adorned herself only to come to church, and always came in some new sumptuosity; and instead of thinking of God, she made God angry by thinking of her handsome gentleman, and leaving her prayers, she gave herself up to the fire which consumed her heart, and moistened her eyes, her lips, and everything, seeing that this fire always dissolves itself in water; and often said she to herself: "Ha! I would give my life for a single embrace with this pretty lover who loves me." Often, too, in place of saying her litanies to Madame the Virgin, she thought in her heart. "To feel the glorious youth of this gentle lover, to have the full joys of love, to taste all in one moment, little should I mind the flames into which the heretics are thrown." Then the gentleman gazing at the charms of this good wife, and her burning blushes when he glanced at her, came always close to her stool, and addressed to her those requests which the ladies understand so well. Then he said aside to himself: "By the double horn of my father I swear to have that woman, though it cost me my life."

And when the duenna turned her head, the two lovers squeezed, pressed, breathed, ate, devoured, and kissed each other by a look which would have set light to the match of a musketeer, if the musketeer had been there. It was certain that a love so far advanced in the heart should have an end. The gentleman, dressed as a scholar of Montaign, began to regale the clerks of the said Avenelles, and to joke in their company, in order to learn the habits of the husband, his hours of absence, his journeys, and everything, watching for an opportunity to stick his horns on. And this was how, to his injury, the opportunity occurred. The advocate, obliged to follow the course of this conspiracy, and, in case of failure, intending to revenge himself upon the Guises, determined to go to Blois, where the court then was in great danger of being carried off. Knowing this, the gentleman came first to the town of Blois, and there arranged

a master-trap, into which the Sieur Avenelles should fall, in
spite of his cunning, and not come out until steeped in a
crimson cuckoldom.   This said Italian, intoxicated with
love, called together all his pages and vassals, and posted
them in such a manner that on the arrival of the advocate, his wife, and her duenna, it was stated to them at
all the hostelries at which they wished to put up that the
hostelry being full, in consequence of the sojourn of the
court, they must go elsewhere.   Then the gentleman made
such an arrangement with the landlord of the Soleil Royal,
that he had the whole of the house, and occupied it, without
any of the usual servants of the place remaining there.   For
greater security, my lord sent the said master and his people
into the country, and put his own in their places, so that the
advocate should know nothing of this arrangement.   Behold
my good gentleman who lodges his friends come to the court
in the hostelry, and for himself keeps a room situated above
those in which he intends to put his lovely mistress, her
advocate, and the duenna, not without first having cut a
trap in the boards.   And his steward being charged to play
the part of the innkeeper, his pages dressed like guests, and
his female servants like servants of the inn, he waited for
spies to convey to him the dramatis personæ of this farce—
viz., wife, husband, and duenna, none of whom failed to
come.   Seeing the immense wealth of the great lords,
merchants, warriors, members of the service, and others,
brought by the sojourn of the young king, of two queens, the
Guises, and all the court, no one had a right to be
astonished or to talk of the roguish trap, or of the confusion
come to the Soleil Royal.   Behold now the Sieur Avenelles,
on his arrival, bundled about, he, his wife and the duenna
from inn to inn, and thinking themselves very fortunate in
being received at the Soleil Royal, where the gallant was
getting warm, and love was burning.   The advocate being
lodged, the lover walked about in the courtyard, watching and
waiting for a glance from his lady ; and he did not have to
wait very long, since the fair Avenelles, looking soon into
the court, after the custom of the ladies, there recognised,
not without great throbbing of the heart, her gallant and

well-beloved gentleman. At that she was very happy ; and if by a lucky chance both had been alone together for an ounce of time, the good gentleman would not have had to wait for his good fortune, so burning was she from head to foot.

" How warm it is in the rays of this lord." said she, meaning to say sun, since it was then shining fiercely.

Hearing this, the advocate sprang to the window, and beheld my gentleman.

" Ha ! you want lords, my dear, do you ?" said the advocate, dragging her by the arm, and throwing her like one of his bags on to the bed. " Remember that if I have a pencase at my side instead of a sword, I have a penknife in this pencase, and the penknife will go into your heart on the least suspicion of conjugal impropriety. I believe I have seen that gentleman somewhere."

The advocate was so terribly spiteful that the lady rose, and said to him—

" Well, kill me. I am afraid of deceiving you. Never touch me again, after having thus menaced me. And from to-day I shall never think of sleeping save with a lover more gentle than are you."

" There, there, my little one !" said the advocate, surprised. " We have gone a little too far. Kiss me, chick-a-biddy, and forgive me."

" I will neither kiss nor pardon you," said she. " You are a wretch !"

Avenelles, enraged, wished to take by force that which his wife denied him, and from this resulted a combat, from which the husband emerged clawed all over. But the worst of it was, that the advocate, covered with scratches, being expected by the conspirators, who were holding a council, was obliged to quit his good wife, leaving her to the care of the old woman.

The knave having departed, the gentleman putting one of his servants to keep watch at the corner of the street, mounts to his blessed trap, lifts it noiselessly, and calls the lady by a gentle *psit ! psit !* which was understood by the heart, which generally understands everything. The lady lifts her head, and sees her pretty lover four flea jumps above her. Upon a sign, she takes hold of two cords of black silk, to which were attached loops, through which she passes her arms, and in the twinkling of an eye is translated by two pulleys from her bed through the ceiling into the room above, and the trap closing as it had opened, left the old duenna in a state of great flabbergastation, when, turning her head, she neither saw robe nor woman, and perceived that the woman had been robbed. How? by whom? in what way? where?—Presto! Foro! Magico! As much knew the alchemists at their furnaces reading Herr Trippa. Only the old woman knew well the crucible, and the great work—the one was cuckoldom, and the other the private property of Madame Advocate. She remained dumbfoundered, watching for the Sieur Avenelles—as well say death, for in his rage he would attack everything, and the poor duenna could not run away, because with great prudence the jealous man had taken the keys with him. At first sight, Madame Avenelles found a dainty supper, a good fire in the grate, but a better in the heart of her lover, who seized her, and kissed her, with tears of joy, on the eyes first of all, to thank them for their sweet glances during devotion at the church of St. Jehan en Grève. Nor did the glowing better half of the lawyer refuse her little mouth to his love, but allowed herself to be properly pressed, adored, caressed, delighting to be properly pressed, admirably adored, and calorously caressed after the manner of eager lovers. And both agreed to be all in all to each other the whole night long, no matter what the result might be, she counting the future as a fig in comparison with the joys of this night, he relying upon his cunning and his sword to obtain many another. In short, both of them caring little for life, because at one stroke they consummated a thousand lives, enjoyed with each other a thousand delights, giving to each other the double of their own—believing, he and she, that they were falling into an abyss, and wishing to roll there closely clasped, hurling all the love of their souls with rage in one throw. Therein they loved each other well. Thus they know not love, the poor citizens, who live mechanically with their good wives, since they know not the fierce beat-

ing of the heart, the hot gush of life, and the vigorous clasp
as do two young lovers, closely united and glowing with passion, who embrace in face of the danger of death. Now the
youthful lady and the gentleman ate little supper, but retired
early to rest. Let us leave them there, since no words,
except those of paradise unknown to us, would describe
their delightful agonies, and agonizing delights. Meanwhile,
the husband, so well cuckolded that all memory of marriage had been swept away by love,—the said Avenelles
found himself in a great fix. To the council of the Huguenots came the Prince of Condé, accompanied by all the
chiefs and bigwigs, and there it was resolved to carry off the
queen-mother, the Guises, the young king, the young queen,
and to change the government. This becoming serious,
the advocate seeing his head at stake, did not feel the ornaments being planted there, and ran to divulge the conspiracy to the cardinal of Lorraine, who took the rogue to the
duke his brother, and all three held a consultation, making
fine promises to the Sieur Avenelles, whom with the greatest
difficulty they allowed, towards midnight, to depart, at
which hour he issued secretly from the castle. At this
moment the pages of the gentleman and all his people were
having a right jovial supper in honour of the fortuitous
,wedding of their master. Now, arriving at the height of the
festivities, in the middle of the intoxication and joyous
huzzahs, he was assailed with jeers, jokes, and laughter that
turned him sick when he came into his room. The poor
servant wished to speak, but the advocate promptly planted
a blow in her stomach, and by a gesture commanded her to
be silent. Then he felt in his valise, and took therefrom a
good poniard. While he was opening and sharpening it,
a frank, naïve, joyous, amorous, pretty, celestial roar of
laughter, followed by certain words of easy comprehension,
came down through the trap. The cunning advocate, blow-
ing out his candle, saw through the cracks in the boards
caused by the shrinking of the door a light, which vaguely
explained the mystery to him, for he recognised the voice
of his wife and that of the combatant. The husband
took the duenna by the arm, and went softly up the stairs

searching for the door of the chamber in which were the
lovers, and did not fail to find it. Fancy! that like a
horrid, rude advocate, he burst open the door, and with
one spring was on the bed, in which he surprised his wife,
half dressed, in the arms of the gentleman.

"Ah !" said she.

The lover having avoided the blow, tried to snatch the
poniard from the hands of the knave, who held it firmly.
Now, in this struggle of life and death, the husband finding
himself hindered by his lieutenant, who clutched him tightly
with his fingers of iron, and bitten by his wife, who tore
away at him with a will, gnawing him as a dog gnaws a bone,
he thought instantly of a better way to gratify his rage.
Then this devil, newly horned, maliciously ordered, in his
patois, the servant to tie the lovers with the silken cords of
the trap, and throwing the poniard away, he helped the
duenna to make them fast. And the thing thus done in a
moment, he rammed some linen into their mouths to stop
their cries, and ran to his good poniard without saying a
word. At this moment there entered several officers of the
Duke of Guise, whom during the struggle no one had heard

turning the house upside down, looking for the Sieur Avenelles. These soldiers, suddenly warned by the cries of the

pages of the lord, bound, gagged and half killed, threw
themselves between the man with the poniard and the lovers,
disarmed him, and accomplished their mission by arresting
him and marching him off to the castle prison, he, his wife,
and the duenna. At the same time the people of the Guises,
recognising one of their master's friends, with whom at this
moment the queen was most anxious to consult, and whom
they were enjoined to summon to the council, invited him
to come with them. Then the gentleman soon untied,
dressing himself, said aside to the chief of the escort, that
on his account, for the love of him, he should be careful to
keep the husband away from his wife, promising him his
favour, good advancement, and even a few deniers, if he
were careful to obey him on this point. And for greater
surety he explained to him the why and the wherefore of
the affair, adding that if the husband found himself within
reach of this fair lady he would give her for certain a blow
in the belly from which she would never recover. Finally
he ordered him to place the lady in the gaol of the castle,
in a pleasant place level with the gardens, and the advocate
in a safe dungeon, not without chaining him hand and foot.
The which the said officer promised, and arranged matters
according to the wish of the gentleman, who accompanied
the lady as far as the courtyard of the castle, assuring her
that this business would make her a widow, and that he would
perhaps espouse her in legitimate marriage. In fact, the
Sieur Avenelles was thrown into a damp dungeon without air,
and his pretty wife placed in a room above him, out of consideration for her lover, who was the Sieur Scipion Sardini,
a noble of Lucca, exceedingly rich, and, as has before been
stated, a friend of Queen Catherine de Medicis, who at that
time did everything in concert with the Guises. Then he
went up quickly to the queen's apartments, where a great
secret council was then being held, and there the Italian
learned what was going on, and the danger of the court.
Monseigneur Sardini found the privy councillors much embarrassed and surprised at this dilemma, but he made
them all agree, telling them to turn it to their own advantage; and to his advice was due the clever idea of

lodging the king in the castle of Amboise, in order to catch the heretics there like foxes in a bag, and there to slay them all. Indeed, every one knows how the queen-mother and the Guises dissimulated, and how the riot of Amboise terminated. This is not, however, the subject of the present narrative. When in the morning every one had quitted the chamber of the queen-mother, where everything had been arranged, Monseigneur Sardini, in no way oblivious of his love for the fair Avenelles, although he was at the time deeply smitten with the lovely Limeuil, a girl belonging to the queen-mother, and her relation by the house of La Tour de Turenne, asked why the good Judas had been caged. Then the Cardinal of Lorraine told him that his intention was not in any way to harm the rogue, but that fearing his repentance, and for greater security of his silence until the end of the affair, he had put him out of the way, and would liberate him at the proper time.

"Liberate him!" said the Luccanese. "Never! Put him in a sack, and throw the old black gown into the Loire. In the first place I know him; he is not the man to forgive you his imprisonment, and will return to the Protestant Church. Thus this will be a work pleasant to God, to rid him of a heretic. Then no one will know your secrets, and not one of his adherents will think of asking you what has become of him, because he is a traitor. Let me procure the escape of his wife and arrange the rest; I will take it off your hands."

"Ha! ha!" said the cardinal; "you give good counsel. Now I will, before distilling your advice, have them both more securely guarded. Hi, there!"

Came an officer of police, who was ordered to let no person, whoever he might be, communicate with the two prisoners. Then the cardinal begged Sardini to say at his hotel that the said advocate had departed from Blois to return to his causes in Paris. The men charged with the arrest of the advocate, had received verbal orders to treat him as a man of importance, so they neither stripped nor robbed him. Now the advocate had kept thirty gold crowns in his purse, and re-solved to lose them all to assure his vengeance, and proved by good arguments to the gaolers that it was allowable for him to see his wife, on whom he doted, and whose legitimate embrace he desired. Monseigneur Sar-dini, fearing for his mistress the danger of the proximity of this red learned rogue, and for her having great fear of certain evils,

determined to carry her off in the night, and put her in a place of safety. Then he hired some boatmen and also their boat, placing them near the bridge, and ordered three of his most active servants to file the bars of the cell, seize the lady, and conduct her to the wall of the gardens, where he would await her.

These preparations being made, and good files bought, he obtained an interview in the morning with the queen-mother, whose apartments were situated above the stronghold in which lay the said advocate and his wife, believing that the queen would willingly lend herself to this flight. Presently he was received by her, and begged her not to think it wrong that, at the instigation of the cardinal and of the Duke of Guise, he should deliver this lady; and besides this, urged her very strongly to tell the cardinal to throw the man into the water. To which the queen said, "Amen." Then the lover sent quickly to his lady a letter in a plate of cucumbers, to advise her of her approaching widowhood, and the hour of flight, with all of which was the fair citizen well content. Then at dusk the soldiers of the watch being got out of the way by the queen, who sent them to look at a ray of the moon, which frightened her, behold the servants raised the grating, and called the lady, who came quickly enough, and was led to the house to Monseigneur Sardini.

But the postern closed, and the Italian outside with the

He had time to jump into the boat and push off in great haste.

lady, behold the lady throw aside her mantle, see the lady change into an advocate, and see my said advocate seize his cuckolder by the collar, and half strangle him, dragging him towards the water to throw him to the bottom of the Loire ; and Sardini begin to defend himself, to shout, and to struggle, without being able, in spite of his dagger, to shake off this devil in long robes. Then he was quiet, falling into a slough under the feet of the advocate, whom he recognised through the mists of this diabolical combat, and by the light of the moon, his face plashed with the blood of his wife. The enraged advocate quitted the Italian, believing him to be dead, and also because servants, armed with torches, came running up. But he had time to jump into the boat and push off in great haste.

Thus poor Madame Avenelles died alone, since Monseigneur Sardini badly strangled, was found, and revived from this murder ; and later, as every one knows, married the fair Limeuil after this sweet girl had been brought to bed in the queen's cabinet—a great scandal, which from friendship the queen-mother wished to conceal, and which from great love Sardini, to whom Catherine gave the splendid estate of Chaumont-sur-Loire. and also the castle, covered with marriage.

But he had been so brutally used by the husband, that he did not make old bones, and the fair Limeuil was left a widow in her spring time. In spite of her misdeeds the advocate was not searched after. He was cunning enough eventually to get included in the number of those conspirators who were not prosecuted, and returned to the Huguenots, for whom he worked hard in Germany.

Poor Madame Avenelles, pray for her soul ! for she was hurled no one knew where, and had neither the prayers of the Church nor Christian burial. Alas ! shed a tear for her, ye ladies lucky in your loves.

That good philosophy to which we shall always be obliged
to return.

THE SERMON

OF

THE MERRY VICAR OF MEUDON.

WHEN, for the last time, came Master Francis Rabelais to the court of King Henry the Second of the name, it was in that winter when the will of nature compelled him to quit for ever his fleshly garb, and live for ever in his writings resplendent with that good philosophy to which we shall always be obliged to return. The good man had, at that time, counted as nearly as possible seventy flights of the swallow. His Homeric head was but scantily ornamented with hair, but his beard was still perfect in its flowing majesty; there was still an air of spring-time in his quiet smile, and wisdom on his ample brow. He was a fine old man according to the statement of those who had the happiness to gaze upon his face, to which Socrates and Aristophanes, formerly enemies, but there become friends,

contributed their features. Hearing his last hour tinkling in his ears, he determined to go and pay his respects to the King of France, because he having just at that time arrived in

his castle of Tournelles, the good man's house being situated
in the gardens of St. Paul, was not a stone's throw distant
from the court. He soon found himself in the presence of
Queen Catherine, Madame Diana, whom she received from
motives of policy, the king, the constable, the cardinals of
Lorraine and Bellay, Messieurs de Guise, the Sieur de
Birague, and other Italians, who at that time stood well at
court in consequence of the queen's protection ; the admiral,
Montgomery, the officers of the household, and certain
poets, such as Melin de St. Gelays, Philibert de l'Orme, and
the Sieur Brantôme.

Perceiving the good man, the king, who knew his wit,
said to him, with a smile, after a short conversation—

"Hast thou ever delivered a sermon to thy parishioners
of Meudon?"

Master Rabelais, thinking that the king was joking, since
he had never troubled himself further about his post than to
collect the revenues accruing from it, replied—

"Sire, my listeners are in every place, and my sermons
heard throughout Christendom."

Then glancing at all the courtiers, who, with the exception
of Messieurs du Bellay and Chatillon, considered him to be
nothing but a learned merry-andrew, while he was really the
king of all wits, and a far better king than he whose crown
only the courtiers venerate, there came into the good man's
head the malicious idea to philosophically pump over their
heads, just as it pleased Gargantua to give the Parisians a
bath from the turrets of Notre Dame, so he added—

"If you are in a good humour, sire, I can regale you with
a capital little sermon, always appropriate, and which I have
kept under the tympanum of my left ear in order to deliver
it in a fit place, by way of an aulic parable.

"Gentlemen," said the king, "Master Francis Rabelais
has the ear of the court, and our salvation is concerned in
his speech. Be silent, I pray you, and give heed; he is
fruitful in evangelical drolleries."

"Sire," said the good vicar, "I commence."

All the courtiers became silent, and arranged themselves
into a circle, pliant as osiers before the father of Panta-

gruel, who unfolded to them the following tale, in words the illustrious eloquence of which it is impossible to equal. But since this tale has only been verbally handed down to us, the author will be pardoned if he write it after his own fashion.

"In his old age Gargantua took to strange habits, which greatly astonished his household, but the which he was forgiven since he was seven hundred and four years old, in spite of the statement of St. Clement of Alexandria in his *Stromates*, which makes out that at this time he was a quarter of a day less, which matters little to us. Now this paternal master, seeing that everything was going wrong in his house, and that every one was fleecing him, conceived a great fear that he would in his last moments be stripped of everything, and resolved to invent a more perfect system of management in his domains, and he did well. In a cellar of Gargantuan abode he hid away a fine heap of red wheat, besides twenty jars of mustard and several delicacies, such as plums and Tourainian rolls, articles of dessert, Olivet cheese, goat cheese, and others, well known between Langeais and Loches, pots of butter, hare pasties, preserved ducks, pigs' trotters in bran, boatloads and pots full of crushed peas, pretty little pots of Orleans quince preserve, hogsheads of lampreys, measures of green sauce, river game, such as francolins, teal, sheldrake, heron, and flamingo, all preserved in sea-salt, dried raisins, tongues smoked in the manner invented by Happe-Mousche, his celebrated ancestor, and sweetstuff for Gargamelle on feast days ; and a thousand other things which are detailed in the records of the Ripuary laws and in certain folios of the Capitularies, Pragmatics, royal establishments, ordinances and institutions of the period. To be brief, the good man, putting his spectacles on his nose or his nose in his spectacles, looked about for a fine flying dragon or unicorn to whom the guard of this precious treasure could be committed. With this thought in his head he strolled about the gardens. He did not desire Coquecigrue,* because the Egyptians were afraid of them, as it appeared in the Hieroglyphics. He dismissed the idea of engaging the legions of Caucquemarres,† because emperors disliked them and also the Romans according to that sulky fellow Tacitus. He rejected the Pechrocholiers in council assembled, the Magi, the Druids, the legion of Papimania, and the Massorets, who grew like quelch-grass and overran all the land, as he had been told by his son, Pantagruel, on his return from his journey. The good man calling to mind old stories, had no confidence in any race, and if it had been permissible would have implored the Creator for a new one, but not daring to trouble Him about such trifles, did not know whom to choose, and was thinking that his wealth would be a great trouble to him, when he met in his path a pretty little shrew-mouse of the noble race of shrew-mice, who bear all gules on an azure ground. By the gods ! be sure that it was a splendid

---

* Coquecigrue—an imaginary animal. The word is probably compounded of *coq*, *cygne*, and *grue*. There is a French saying still in vogue, " A la venue des coquecigrues"—that is to say, never.

† Caucquemarre—also an imaginary animal. The name was **also** given occasionally to sorcerers.

animal, with the finest tail of the whole family, and was strutting about in the sun like a brave shrew-mouse. It was proud of having been in this world since the Deluge, according to letters-patent of indisputable nobility, registered by the parliament of the universe, since it appears from the Ecumenical Inquiry a shrew-mouse was in Noah's ark." Here Master Alcofribas raised his cap slightly, and said, reverently, " It was Noah, my lords, who planted the vine, and first had the honour of getting drunk upon the juice of its fruit."

" For it is certain," he continued, " that a shrew-mouse was in the vessel from which we all came ; but the men have made bad marriages ; not so the mice, because they are more jealous of their coat of arms than any other animals, and would not receive a field-mouse among them, even though he had the especial gift of being able to convert grains of sand into fine fresh hazel nuts. This fine gentlemanly character so pleased the good Gargantua, that he decided to give the post of watching his granaries to the shrew-mouse, with the most ample powers—of justice, *committimus, missi dominici,* clergy, men-at-arms, and all. The shrew-mouse promised faithfully to accomplish his task, and to do his duty as a loyal beast, on condition that he lived on a heap of grain, which Gargantua thought perfectly fair. The shrew-mouse began to caper about in his domain as happy as a prince who is happy, reconnoitring his immense empire of mustard, countries of sugar, provinces of ham, duchies of raisins, counties of chitterlings, and baronies of all sorts, scrambling on to the heap of grain, and frisking his tail against everything. To be brief, everywhere was the shrew-mouse received with honour by the pots, which kept a respectful silence, except two golden tankards, which knocked against each other like the bells of a church ringing a tocsin, at which he was much pleased, and thanked them, right and left, by a nod of the head, while promenading in the rays of the sun, which were illuminating his domain. Therein so splendidly did the brown colour of his hair shine forth, that one would have thought him a northern king in his sable furs. After his twists, turns, jumps, and capers, he munched two grains of corn, sat upon the heap like a king in full court, and fancied himself the most illustrious of shrew-mice. At this moment there came from their accustomed holes the gentlemen of the night-prowling court, who scamper with their little feet across the floors; these gentlemen being the rats, mice, and other gnawing, thieving, and crafty animals, of whom the citizens and housewives complain. When they saw the shrew-mouse they took fright, and all remained shily at threshold of their dens. Among these common people, in spite of the danger, one old infidel of the trotting, nibbling race of mice, advanced a little, and putting his nose in the air, had the courage to stare my lord shrew-mouse full in the face, although the latter was proudly squatted upon his rump, with his tail in the air; and he came to the conclusion that he was a devil, from whom nothing but scratches were to be gained. And from these facts, Gargantua, in order that the high authority of his lieutenant might be universally known by all the shrew-mice, cats, weasels, martins, field-mice, mice, rats, and other bad characters of the same kidney, had lightly dipped his muzzle, pointed as a larding pin, in oil of musk, which all shrew-mice have since inherited, because this one, in spite of the sage advice of Gargantua, rubbed himself against others of his breed. From this sprang the troubles in Muzaraignia, of which I will give you a good account in an historical book when I get an opportunity.

"Then an old mouse, or rat—the rabbis of the Talmud have not yet agreed concerning the species—perceiving by this perfume that this shrew-mouse was appointed to guard the grain of Gargantua, and had been sprinkled with virtues, invested with full powers, and armed at all points, was alarmed lest he should no longer be able to live, according to the custom of mice, upon the meats, morsels, crusts, crumbs, leavings, bits, atoms, and fragments of this Canaan of rats. In this dilemma the good mouse, artful as an old courtier who had lived under two regencies and three kings, resolved to try the mettle of the shrew-mouse, and devote

himself to the salvation of the jaws of his race. This would
have been a laudable thing in a man, but it was far more so in
a mouse, belonging to a tribe who live for themselves alone,
barefacedly and shamelessly, and in order to gratify themselves would defile a consecrated wafer, gnaw a priest's stole
without shame, and would drink out of a Communion cup,
caring nothing for God. The mouse advanced with many
a bow and scrape, and the shrew-mouse let him advance
rather near — for, to tell the truth, these animals are
naturally short-sighted. Then this Curtius of nibblers
made his little speech, not in the jargon of common mice,
but in the polite language of shrew-mice : — ' My lord, I
have heard with very much concern of your glorious family,
of which I am one of the most devoted slaves. I know the
legend of your ancestors, who were thought much of by
the ancient Egyptians, who held them in great veneration,
and adored them like other sacred birds. Nevertheless,
your fur robe is so royally perfumed, and its colour is so
splendiferously tanned, that I am doubtful if I recognise
you as belonging to this race, since I have never seen any
of them so gorgeously attired. However, you have swallowed the grain after the antique fashion. Your proboscis
is a proboscis of sapience ; you have kicked like a learned
shrew-mouse ; but if you are a true shrew-mouse, you should
have in I know not what part of your ear—I know not what
special auditorial channel, which I know not, what wonderful door, closes I know not how, and I know not with what
movements, by your secret commands to give you, I know
not why, licence not to listen to I know not what things,
which would be displeasing to you, on account of the
special and peculiar perfection of your faculty of hearing
everything, which would often pain you.'

" ' True,' said the shrew-mouse, ' the door has just fallen.
I hear nothing !'

" ' Ah, I see,' said the old rogue.

" And he made for the pile of corn, from which he commenced to take his store for the winter.

" ' Do you hear anything ?' asked he.

" ' I hear the pit-a-pat of my heart.'

" ' Kouick !' cried all the mice ; 'we shall be able to hoodwink him.'

" The shrew-mouse, fancying that he had met with a faithful vassal, opened the trap of his musical orifice, and heard the noise of the grain going towards the hole. Then, without having recourse to forfeiture, the justice of commissaries, he sprang upon the old mouse and squeezed him to death. Glorious death ! for this hero died in the thick of the grain, and was canonized as a martyr. The shrew-mouse took him by the ears and placed him on the door of the granary, after the fashion of the Ottoman Porte, where my good Panurge was within an ace of being spitted. At the cries of the dying wretch the rats, mice, and others made for their holes in great haste. When the night had fallen they came to the cellar, convoked for the purpose of holding a council to consider public affairs; to which meeting, in virtue of the Papirian and other laws, their lawful wives were admitted. The rats wished to pass before the mice, and serious quarrels about precedence nearly spoilt everything ; but a big rat gave his arm to a mouse, and the gaffer rats and gammer mice being paired off in the same way, all were soon seated on their rumps, tails in air, muzzles stretched whiskers stiff, and their eyes brilliant as those of a falcon.

Then commenced a deliberation, which finished up with insults and a confusion worthy of an ecumenical council of holy fathers. One said this, and another said that, and a cat passing by took fright and ran away, hearing those strange noises : 'Bou, bou, frou, ou, ou, houic, houic, briff, briffnac, nac, nac, fouix, fouix, trr, trr, trr, trr, za, za, zaaa, brr, brrr, raaa, ra, ra, ra, ra, fouix !' so well blended together in a Babel of sound, that a council at the Hôtel de Ville could not have made a greater hubbub. During this tempest a little mouse, who was not old enough to enter parliament, thrust through a chink her inquiring snout, the hair on which was as downy as that of all mice, too downy to be caught. As the tumult increased, by degrees her body followed her nose, until she came to the hoop of a cask, against which she so dexterously squatted that she might have been mistaken for a work of art carved in antique bas-relief. Lifting his eyes to heaven to implore a remedy for the misfortunes of the State, an old rat perceived this pretty mouse, so gentle and shapely, and declared that the State might be saved by her. All the muzzles turned to this Lady of Good Help, became silent, and agreed to let her loose upon the shrew-mouse, and in spite of the anger of certain envious mice, she was triumphantly marched round the cellar, where, seeing her walk mincingly, mechanically move her tail, shake her cunning little head, twitch her diaphanous ears, and lick with her little red tongue the hairs just sprouting on her cheeks, the old rats fell in love with her, and wagged their wrinkled, white-whiskered jaws with delight at the sight of her, as did formerly the old men of Troy, admiring the lovely Helen returning from her bath. Then the maiden was conducted to the granary, with instructions to make a conquest of the shrew-mouse's heart, and save the fine red grain, as did formerly the fair Hebrew, Esther, for the chosen people, with the Emperor Ahasuerus, as it is written in the master-book, for *Bible* comes from the Greek word *Biblos,* as if to say the only book. The mouse promised to deliver the granaries, for by a lucky chance she was the queen of mice, a fair, plump, pretty little mouse, the most delicate little lady that ever scampered merrily across the floors, scratched between the walls, and gave utterance to little cries of joy at finding nuts, meal, and crumbs of bread in her path ; a true fay, pretty and playful, with an eye clear as crystal, a little head, sleek skin, amorous body, rosy feet, and velvet tail—a high born mouse and polished speaker, with a natural love of bed and idleness—a merry mouse, more cunning than an old doctor of Sorbonne fed on parch-

ment, lively, white bellied, streaked on the back, with
sweetly moulded breasts, pearl-white teeth, and of a frank,
open nature—in fact, a true king's morsel."

This portraiture was so bold — the mouse appearing
to have been the living image of Madame Diana, then
present—that the courtiers stood aghast.   Queen Catherine smiled, but the king was in no laughing humour.
But Rabelais went on without paying any attention to the
winks of the Cardinal Bellay and de Chatillon, who were terrified for the good man,

" The pretty mouse," said he, continuing, " did not beat
long about the bush, and from the first moment that she
trotted before the shrew-mouse, she had enslaved him for ever
by her coquetries, affectations, friskings, provocations, little
refusals, piercing glances, and wiles of a maiden who desires
yet dares not, amorous oglings, little caresses, preparatory
tricks, pride of a mouse who knows her value, laughings
and squeakings, triflings and other endearments, feminine,
treacherous, and captivating ways, all traps which are abundantly used by the females of all nations.   When, after
many wrigglings, smacks in the face, nose lickings, gallantries of amorous shrew-mice, frowns, sighs, serenades, tit-
bits, suppers and dinners on the pile of corn, and other attentions, the superintendent overcame the scruples of his
beautiful mistress, he became the slave of this incestuous and
illicit love, and the mouse, leading her lord by the snout,
became queen of everything, nibbled his cheese, ate the
sweets, and foraged everywhere.   This the shrew-mouse
permitted to the empress of his heart, although he was ill at
ease, having broken his oath made to Gargantua, and betrayed the confidence placed in him.   Pursuing her advantage with the pertinacity of a woman, one night that they
were joking together, the mouse remembered the dear old
fellow her father, and desiring that he should make his meals
off the grain, she threatened to leave her lover cold and
lonely in his domain if he did not allow her to indulge her
filial piety.   In the twinkling of a mouse's eye he had granted
letters patent, sealed with a green seal, with tags of crimson
silk, to his wench's father, so that the Gargantuan palace

was open to him at all hours, and he was at liberty to see
his good virtuous daughter, kiss her on the forehead, and
eat his fill, but always in a corner. Then there arrived a
venerable old rat, weighing about twenty-five ounces, with a
white tail, marching like the president of a court of justice,
wagging his head, and followed by fifteen or twenty nephews,
all with teeth sharp as saws, who demon-
strated to the shrew-mouse by little speeches
and questions of all kinds that they, his relations, would soon be loyally attached to
him, and would help him to count the
things committed to his charge, arrange
and ticket them, in order that when Gargantua came to visit them he would find
everything in perfect order.   There was an
air of truth about these promises. The poor shrew-mouse
was, however, in spite of this speech, troubled by ideas from
on high, and serious pricking of his shrew-mousian conscience.   Seeing that he turned up his nose at everything,
went about slowly and with a careworn face, one morning
the mouse, who was pregnant by him, conceived the idea of
calming his doubts and easing his mind by a Sorbonnical consultation, and sent for the doctors of the tribe.   During the
day she introduced to him one, the Sieur Evegault, who had
just stepped out of a cheese where he lived in perfect abstinence, an old confessor of high degree, a merry fellow of
good appearance, with a fine black skin, firm as a rock,
and slightly tonsured on the head by the pat of a cat's claw.
He was a grave rat, with a monastical paunch, having much
studied scientific authorities by nibbling at their works in
parchments, papers, books, and volumes of which certain
fragments had remained upon his grey beard.   In honour
of and great reverence for his great virtue and wisdom, and
his modest life, he was accompanied by a black troop of
black rats, all bringing with them pretty little mice, their
sweethearts, for not having adopted the canons of the
council of Chesil, it was lawful for them to have respectable
women for concubines. These beneficed rats being arranged ː two lines, you might have fancied them a pro-

The Merry Vicar of Meudon.

cession of the university authorities going to Lendit. And
they all began to sniff the victuals.

" When the ceremony of placing them all was complete,
the old cardinal of the rats lifted up his voice, and in a
good rat-latin oration pointed out to the guardian of the

grain that no one but God was superior to him ; and that to
God alone he owed obedience, and he entertained him with
many fine phrases, stuffed with evangelical quotations, to disturb the principal and fog his flock ; in fact, fine arguments
interlarded with much sound sense. The discourse finished
with a peroration full of high sounding words in honour of
shrew-mice, among whom his hearer was the most illustrious
and best beneath the sun ; and this oration considerably
bewildered the keeper of the granaries.

" This good gentleman's head was thoroughly turned, and
he installed this fine speaking rat and his tribe in his manor,
where night and day his praises and little songs in his
honour were sung, not forgetting his lady, whose little paw
was kissed and little tail was sniffed at by them all.
Finally the mistress, knowing that certain young rats were
still fasting, determined to finish her work. Then she kissed
her lord tenderly, loading him with love, and performing
those little endearing antics of which one alone was sufficient to send a beast to perdition ; and said to the shrew-
mouse that he wasted the precious time due to their love by

travelling about, that he was always going here or there, and
that she never had her proper share of him ; that when she
wanted his society he was either on the leads chasing the
cats, and that she wished him always to be ready to her
hand like a lance, and kind as a bird.   Then in her great
grief she tore out a grey hair, declaring herself, weepingly,
to be the most wretched little mouse in the world.   The
shrew-mouse pointed out to her that she was mistress of
everything, and wished to resist, but after the lady had shed

a torrent of tears he implored a truce and considered her
request.   Then instantly drying her tears, and giving him
her paw to kiss, she advised him to arm some soldiers,
trusty and tried rats, old warriors, who would go the rounds
and keep watch.   Everything was thus wisely arranged.
The shrew-mouse had the rest of the day to dance, play,
and amuse himself, listen to the roundelays and ballads
which the poets composed in his honour, play the lute and
the mandore, make acrostics, eat, drink, and be merry.
One day his mistress having just risen from her confinement,
after having given birth to the sweetest little mouse-sorex
or sorex-mouse, I know not what name was given to this
mongrel fruit of love, whom you may be sure the gentlemen
of the long robe would manage to legitimatize" (the constable
of Montmorency, who had married his son to a legitimatized
bastard of the king's, here put his hand to his sword and
clutched the handle fiercely), " a grand feast was given in the

granaries, to which no court festival or gala can be compared, not even that of the Field of the Cloth of Gold. In every corner mice were making merry. Everywhere there were dances, concerts, banquets, sarabands, music, joyous songs, and epithalamia. The rats had broken open the pots, uncovered the jars, lapped the gallipots, and unpacked the stores. The mustard was strewn over the place, the hams were mangled and the corn scattered. Everything was rolling, tumbling, and falling about the floor, and the little rats dabbled in puddles of green sauce, the mice navigated oceans of sweetmeats, and the old folks carried off the pasties. There were mice astride

on salt tongues. Field-mice were swimming in the pots, and the most cunning of them were carrying the corn into their private holes, profiting by the confusion to make ample provision for themselves. No one passed the quince confection of Orleans without saluting it with one nibble, and oftener with two. It was like a Roman carnival. In short, any one with a sharp ear might have heard the frizzling frying-pans, the cries and clamours of the kitchens, the crackling of the furnaces, the noise of turnspits, the creaking of baskets, the haste of the confectioners, the click of the meat-jacks, and the noise of the little feet scampering thick as hail over the floor. It was a bustling wedding-feast, where people come and go, footmen, stablemen, cooks, musicians, buffoons, where every one pays compliments and makes a noise. In short, so great was the delight that they all kept up a general wagging of the head to celebrate this eventful night. But suddenly there was heard the horrible foot-fall of Gargantua, who was ascending the stairs of his house to visit the granaries, and made the planks, the beams, and everything else tremble. Certain old rats asked each other what might mean this seignorial footstep, with which they were unacquainted, and some of them decamped, and they did well, for the lord and master entered suddenly. Perceiving the confusion these gentlemen had made, seeing his preserves eaten, his mustard unpacked, and everything dirtied and scratched about, he

put his feet upon these lively vermin without giving them time to squeak, and thus spoiled their best clothes, satins, pearls, velvets, and rubbish, and upset the feast."

"And what became of the shrew-mouse?" said the king, waking from his reverie.

"Ah, sire!" replied Rabelais, "herein we see the injustice of the Gargantuan tribe. He was put to death, but being a gentleman he was beheaded. That was ill done, for he had been betrayed."

"You go rather far, my good man," said the king.

"No, sire," replied Rabelais, "but rather high. Have you not sunk the crown beneath the pulpit? You asked me for a sermon; I have given you one which is gospel."

"My fine vicar," said Madame Diana, in his ear, "suppose I were spiteful?"

"Madame," said Rabelais, "was it not well then of me to warn the king, your master, against the queen's Italians, who are as plentiful here as cockchafers?"

"Poor preacher," said Cardinal Odet, in his ear, "go to another country."

"Ah, monsieur," replied the old fellow, "ere long I shall be in another land."

"God's truth! Mr. Scribbler," said the constable (whose son, as every one knows, had treacherously deserted Mademoiselle de Piennes, to whom he was betrothed, to espouse Diana of France, daughter of the mistress of certain high personages and of the king), "who made thee so bold as to slander persons of quality? Ah, wretched poet, you like to raise yourself high; well, then, I promise to put you in a good high place."

"We shall all go there, my lord constable," replied the old man; "but if you are friendly to the State and to the king you will thank me for having warned him against the hordes of Lorraine, who are evils that will devour everything."

"My good man," whispered Cardinal Charles of Lorraine, "if you need a few gold crowns to publish your fifth book of Pantagruel you can come to me for them, because you have put the case clearly to this enemy, who has bewitched the king, and also to her pack."

"Well, gentlemen," said the king, "what do you think of the sermon?"

"Sire," said Mellin de Saint-Gelais, seeing that all were well pleased, "I have never heard a better pantagruelian prognostication. Much do we owe to him who made these leonine verses in the abbey of Theleme:—

> ' Cy vous *entrez*, qui le saint Evangile
> En sens *agile* annoncez, quoy qu'on gronde,
> Céans *aurez* une refuge et bastille
> Contre l'*hostile* erreur qui tant postille
> Par son faux *style* empoisonner le monde.' "

All the courtiers having applauded their companion, each one complimented Rabelais, who took his departure accompanied with great honour by the king's pages, who, by express command, held torches before him.

Some persons have charged Francis Rabelais, the imperial honour of our land, with spiteful tricks and apish pranks,

unworthy of his Homeric philosophy, of this prince of wisdom, of this fatherly centre, from which have issued since the rising of his subterranean light a good number of marvellous works. Out upon those who would defile this divine head! All their life long may they find grit between their teeth, those who have ignored his good and moderate nourishment.

Dear drinker of pure water, faithful servant of monachal abstinence, wisest of wise men, how would thy sides ache with laughter, how wouldst thou chuckle, if thou couldst come again for a little while to Chinon, and read the idiotic mouthings and the maniacal babble of the fools who have interpreted, commentated, torn, disgraced, misunderstood, betrayed, defiled, adulterated, and meddled with thy peerless book. As many dogs as Panurge found busy with his lady's robe at church, so many two-legged academic puppies have busied themselves with befouling the high marble pyramid in which is cemented for ever the seed of all fantastic and comic inventions, besides magnificent instruction in all things. Although rare are the pilgrims who have the breath to follow thy bark in its sublime peregrinations through the ocean of ideas, methods, varieties, religions, wisdom, and human trickeries, at least their worship is unalloyed, pure, and unadulterated, and thine omnipotence, omniscience, and omni-language are by them bravely recognised. Therefore has a poor son of our merry Touraine here been anxious, however unworthily, to do thee homage by magnifying thine image, and glorifying thy works of eternal memory, so cherished by those who love the concentrative works wherein the universal moral is contained, wherein are found, pressed like fresh sardines in their boxes, philosophical ideas on every subject, science, art, and eloquence, as well as theatrical mummeries.

The Succubus.

CONTENTS OF THE SUCCUBUS.

number of persons of the noble country of Touraine, considerably edified by the warm search which the author is making into the antiquities, adventures, good jokes, and pretty tales of that blessed land, and believing for certain that he should know everything, have asked him (after drinking with him of course understood), if he had discovered the etymological reason, concerning which all the ladies of the town are so curious, and from which a certain street in Tours is called the Rue Chaude. By him was it replied, that he was much astonished to see that the ancient inhabitants had forgotten the great number of convents situated in this street, where the severe continence of the monks and the nuns might have caused the walls to be made, so hot that no woman of position should increase in size from walking too slowly along them to vespers. A troublesome fellow, wishing to appear learned, declared that formerly all the scandalmongers of the neighbourhood were wont to meet in this place. Another entangled himself in the minute suffrages of science, and poured forth golden words without being understood, qualifying words, harmonizing the melodies of the ancient and the modern, congregating customs, distilling verbs, alchemizing all languages since the Deluge, of the Hebrews, Chaldeans, Egyptians, Greeks, Latins, and of Turnus, the ancient founder of Tours ; and the good man finished by declaring the Chaude or Chaulde, with the exception of the H and the L, came from *Cauda*, and that there was a tail in the affair, but the ladies only understood the end of it. An old man observed that in this same place was formerly a source of thermal water, of which his great great grandfather had drunk. In short, in less time than it takes a fly to embrace its sweetheart, there had been given a pocketful of etymologies, in which the truth of the matter had been less easily found than a louse in the filthy beard of a Capuchin friar. But a man learned and well informed, through having left his footprint in many monasteries, consumed much midnight oil, and manured his brain with many a volume—himself more cumbered with pieces, dyptic fragments, boxes, charters, and registers concerning the history of Touraine than is a gleaner with stalks of straw in the month of August—this man, old, infirm, and gouty, who had been drinking in his corner without saying a word, smiled the smile of a wise man and knitted his brows, the said smile finally resolving itself into a *pish !* well articulated, which the Author heard and understood it to be big with an adventure historically good, the delights of which he would be able to unfold in this sweet collection.

To be brief, on the morrow this gouty old fellow said to him, " By your poem, which is called ' The Venial Sin,' you have for ever gained my esteem, because everything therein is true from head to foot,—which I believe to be a precious superabundance in like matters. But doubtless you do not know what became of the Moor placed in religion by the said knight, Bruyn de la Roche-Corbon. I

The Rue Chaude at Tours.

know very well. Now if this etymology of the street harass you, and also the Egyptian nun, I will lend you a curious and antique parchment, found by me in the *Olim* of the episcopal palace, of which the libraries were a little knocked about at a period when none of us knew if he would have the pleasure of his head's society on the morrow. Now will not this yield you a perfect contentment ?"

" Good !" said the author.

Then this worthy collector of truths gave certain rare and dusty parchments to the author, the which he has, not without great labour, translated into French, and which were fragments of a most ancient ecclesiastical process. He has believed that nothing would be more amusing than the actual resurrection of this antique affair, wherein shines forth the illiterate simplicity of the good old times. Now, then, give ear. This is the order in which were the manuscripts, of which the author has made use in his own fashion, because the language was devilishly difficult.

THE SUCCUBUS.

I.

WHAT THE SUCCUBUS WAS.

✠ *In nomine Patris, et Filii, et Spiritûs Sancti. Amen.*

IN the year of our Lord one thousand two hundred and seventy-one, before me, HIEROME CORNILLE, grand inquisitor and ecclesiastical judge (thereto commissioned by the members of the chapter of Saint Maurice, the cathedral of Tours, having of this deliberated in presence of our lord Jehan de Monsoreau, archbishop—namely, the grievances and complaints of the inhabitants of the said town, whose request is here subjoined), have appeared certain noblemen, citizens, and inhabitants of the diocese, who have stated the following facts concerning a demon suspected of having taken the features of a woman, who has much afflicted the minds of the diocese, and is at present a prisoner in the gaol of the chapter; and in order to arrive at the truth of the said charge we have opened the present court, this Monday, the eleventh day of December, after mass, to communicate the evidence of each witness to the said demon,

HIEROME CORNILLE,
Grand Inquisitor and Ecclesiastical Judge.

to interrogate her upon the said crimes to her imputed, and
to judge her according to the laws enforced *contra dæmonios.*

In this inquiry has assisted me to write the evidence
therein given, Guillaume Tournebouche, rubrican of the
chapter, a learned man.

Firstly has come before us one Jehan, surnamed Tortebras,
a citizen of Tours, keeping by licence the hostelry of La
Cigoygne, situate on the Place
du Pont, and who has sworn by
the salvation of his soul, his
hand upon the holy Evangelists,
to state no other thing than that
which by himself hath been
seen and heard. He hath stated
as here followeth :—

" I declare that about two
years before the feast of St.
Jehan, upon which are the grand
illuminations, a gentleman, at
first unknown to me, but belonging without doubt to our
lord the King, and at that time
returned into our country from
the Holy Land, came to me with
the proposition that I should
let to him at a rental a certain
country-house by me built, in the quit rent of the chapter
over against the place called of St. Etienne, and the which
I let to him for nine years, for the consideration of three
besans of fine gold. In the said house was placed by the
said knight a fair wench having the appearance of a woman,
dressed in the strange fashion of the Saracens and Ma-
homedans, whom he would allow by none to be seen or to
be approached within a bowshot, but whom I have seen
with mine own eyes, weird feathers upon her head, and eyes
so flaming that I cannot adequately describe them, and from
which gleamed forth a fire of hell. The defunct knight
having threatened with death whoever should appear to spy
about the said house, I have by reason of great fear left

GUILLAUME TOURNEBOUCHE,

Rubrican of the Chapter, a Learned Man.

But whom I have seen with mine own eyes, weird feathers upon her head and eyes so flaming that I cannot adequately describe them, and from which gleamed forth a fire of Hell.

the said house, and I have until this day secretly kept in my
mind certain presumptions and doubts concerning the bad
appearance of the said foreigner, who was more strange
than any woman, her equal not having as yet by me
been seen.

"Many persons of all conditions having at the time believed
the said knight to be dead, but kept upon his feet by virtue
of certain charms, philtres, spells, and diabolical sorceries of
this seeming woman, who wished to settle in our country, I
declare that I have always seen the said knight so ghastly
pale that I can only compare his face to the wax of a Paschal
candle, and to the knowledge of all the people of the hostelry of La Cigoygne, this knight was interred nine days after
his first coming.   According to the statement of his groom,
the defunct had been chalorously coupled with the said
Moorish woman during seven whole days shut up in my
house, without coming out from her, the which I heard him
horribly avow upon his deathbed.   Certain persons at the
present time have accused this she-devil of holding the
said gentleman in her clutches by her long hair, the which
was furnished with certain warm properties by means of

which are communicated to Christians the flames of hell in
the form of love, which work in them until their souls are
by this means drawn from their bodies and possessed by

Satan. But I declare that I have seen nothing of this excepting the said dead knight, bowelless, emaciated, wishing, in spite of his confessor, still to go to this wench; and then he has been recognised as the lord de Bueil, who was a Crusader, and who was, according to certain persons of the town, under the spell of a demon whom he had met in the Asiatic country of Damascus or elsewhere.

" Afterward I have left my house to the said unknown lady, according to the clauses of the deed of lease. The said lord of Bueil, being defunct, I have nevertheless been into my house in order to learn from the said foreign woman if she wished to remain in my dwelling, and after great trouble was led before her by a strange, half-naked black man, whose eyes were white.

" Then I have seen the said Moorish woman in a little room, shining with gold and jewels, lighted with strange lights, upon an Asiatic carpet, where she was seated, lightly attired, with another gentleman, who was there imperilling his soul; and I had not the heart bold enough to look upon her, seeing that her eyes would have incited me immediately to yield myself up to her, for already her voice thrilled into my very belly, filled my brain, and debauched my mind. Finding this, from the fear of God, and also of hell, I have departed with swift feet, leaving my house to her as long as she liked to retain it, so dangerous was it to behold that Moorish complexion from which radiated diabolical heats, besides a foot smaller than it was lawful in a real woman to possess; and to hear her voice, which pierced into one's heart! And from that day I have lacked the courage to enter my house from great fear of falling into hell. I have said my say."

To the said Tortebras we have then shown an Abyssinian, Nubian or Ethiopian, who, black from head to foot, had been found wanting in certain virile properties with which all good Christians are usually furnished who, having persevered in his silence, after having been tormented and tortured many times, not without much moaning, has persisted in being unable to speak the language of our country. And the said Tortebras has recognised the said Abyssinian heretic

as having been in his house in company with the said demoniacal spirit, and is suspected of having lent his aid to
her sorcery.

And the said Tortebras has confessed his great faith in
the Catholic religion, and declared no other things to be
within his knowledge save certain rumours which were
known to every one, of which he had been in no way a
witness except in the hearing of them.

In obedience to the citation served upon him, has appeared,
then, Matthew, surnamed Cognefestu, a day-labourer of St.

Etienne, whom, after hav-
ing sworn by the holy
Evangelists to speak the
truth, has confessed to us
always to have seen a
bright light in the dwelling
of the said foreign woman,
and heard much wild and
diabolical laughter on the
days and nights of feasts
and fasts, notably during
the days of the holy
and Christmas weeks, as if
a great number of people
were in the house. And
he has sworn to have
seen by the windows of
the said dwellings, green
buds of all kinds in the
winter, growing as if by magic, especially roses in a time of
frost, and other things for which there was need of great
heat; but of this he was in no way astonished, seeing that
the said foreigner threw out so much heat that when she
walked in the evening by the side of his wall he found on
the morrow his salad grown; and on certain occasions she
had, by the touching of her petticoats, caused the trees to
put forth leaves and hastened the buds. Finally, the said
Cognefestu has declared to us to know no more, because

he worked from early morning, and went to bed at the same hour as the fowls.

Afterwards the wife of the aforesaid Cognefestu has by us been required to state also upon oath the things come to her cognizance in this process, and has avowed naught save praises of the said foreigner, because since her coming her man had treated her better in consequence of the neighbourhood of this good lady, who filled the air with love as the sun did light, and other incongruous nonsense, which we have not committed to writing.

To the said Cognefestu and to his wife we have shown the said unknown African, who has been seen by them in the gardens of the house, and is stated by them for certain to belong to the said demon. In the third place, has advanced Harduin V., lord of Maillé, who being by us reverentially begged to enlighten the religion of the church, has expressed his willingness so to do, and has, moreover, engaged his word, as a gallant knight, to say no other thing than that which he has seen. Then he has testified to have known in

the army of the Crusades the demon in question, and in the town of Damascus to have seen the knight of Bueil, since defunct, fight at close quarters to be her sole possessor. The above-mentioned wench, or demon, belonged at that time to the knight Geoffroy IV., lord of Roche-Pozay, by whom she was said to have been brought from Touraine, although she was a Saracen; concerning which the knights of France marvelled much, as well as at her beauty, which made a great noise and a thousand scandalous ravages in

the camp.   During the voyage this wench was the cause of
many deaths, seeing that Roche-Pozay had already discomfited certain Crusaders, who wished to keep her to
themselves, because she shed, according to certain knights
petted by her in secret, joys around her comparable to none
others.   But in the end the knight of Bueil, having killed
Geoffroy de la Roche-Pozay, became lord and master of

this young murderess, and placed her in a convent, or harem,
according to the Saracen custom.   About this time one used
to see her and hear her chattering at her entertainments
many foreign dialects, such as the Greek of the Latin
empire, Moorish, and, above all, French better than any of
those who knew the languages of France best in the Christian
host, from which sprang the belief that she was demoniacal.

The said knight Harduin has confessed to us not to have
tilted for her in the Holy Land, not from fear, coldness, or
other cause, so much as that he believed the time had
arrived for him to bear away a portion of the true cross, and
also he had belonging to him a noble lady of the Greek
country, who saved him from this danger in denuding him
of love, morning and night, seeing that she took all of it
substantially from him, leaving him none in his heart or
elsewhere for others.

And the said knight has assured us that the woman living
in the country house of Tortebras, was really the said Saracen
woman, come into the country from Syria, because he had
been invited to a midnight feast at her house by the young
lord of Croixmare, who expired the seventh day afterwards,
according to the statement of the Dame de Croixmare, his

mother, ruined at all points by the said wench, whose commerce with him had consumed his vital spirit, and whose
strange phantasies had squandered his fortune.

Afterwards questioned in his quality of a man full of prudence, wisdom, and authority in this country, upon the ideas
as entertained concerning the said woman, and summoned by
us to open his conscience, seeing that it was question of a
most abominable case of Christian faith and divine justice,
answer has been made by the said knight :—

That by certain of the host of Crusaders it has been
stated to him that always this she-devil was a maid to him
who embraced her, and that Mammon was for certain occupied in her, making for her a new virtue for each of her lovers,
and a thousand other foolish sayings of drunken men, which
were not of a nature to form a fifth Gospel. But for a fact
he, an old knight on that turn of life, and knowing nothing
more of the aforesaid, felt himself again a young man in
that last supper with which he had been regaled by the lord
of Croixmare ; then the voice of this demon went straight to
his heart before flowing into his ears, and had awakened so
great a love in his body that his life was ebbing from the
place whence it should flow, and that eventually, but for
the assistance of Cyprus wine, which he had drunk to blind
his sight, and his getting under the table in order no longer
to gaze upon the fury eyes of his diabolical hostess, and
not to rend his heart for her, without doubt he would
have fought the young Croixmare, in order to enjoy for a
single moment this supernatural woman. Since that he had
had absolution from his confessor for the wicked thought.
Then, by advice from on high, he had carried back to his
spouse his portion of the true cross, and had remained in
his own manor, where, in spite of his Christian precautions, the said voice still at certain times tickled his brain,
and in the morning often had he in remembrance this
demon, warm as brimstone ; and because the look of this
wench was so warm that it made him burn like a young
man, he half dead, and because it cost him then many
transhipments of the vital spirit, the said knight has requested us not to confront him with this empress of love

to whom, if it were not the devil, God the Father had granted strange liberties with the minds of men. Afterwards, he retired, after reading over his statement, not without having first recognised the above-mentioned African to be the servant and page of the lady.

In the fourth place, upon the faith pledged by us in the name of the Chapter and of our Lord Archbishop, that he should not be tormented, tortured, nor harassed in any manner, nor further cited after his statement, in consequence of his commercial journeys, and upon the assurance that he should retire in perfect freedom, has come before us a Jew, named Salomon al Rastchild, who, in spite of the infamy of his person and his Judaism, has been heard by us to this one end, to know everything concerning the conduct of the aforesaid demon. Thus he has not been required to take any oath this Salomon, seeing that he is beyond the pale of the Church, separated from us by the blood of our Saviour (*trucidatus Salvator inter nos.*) Interrogated by us as to why he appeared without the green cap upon his head, and the yellow wheel in the apparent locality of the heart in his garment, according to the ecclesiastical and royal ordonnances, the said de Rastchild has exhibited to us letters patent of dispensation granted by our lord the king, and recognised by the seneschal of Touraine and Poitou. Then the said Jew has declared to us to have done a large business for the lady dwelling in the house of the innkeeper Tortebras, to have sold to her golden chandeliers with many branches, minutely engraved, plates of red silver, cups enriched with stones, emeralds and rubies; to have brought for her from the Levant a number of rare stuffs, Persian carpets, silks, and fine linen; in fact, things so magnificent that no queen in Christendom could say she was so well furnished with jewels and household goods; and that he had for his part received from her three hundred thousand pounds for the rarity of the purchases in which he had been employed, such as Indian flowers, popinjays, birds' feathers, spices, Greek wines, and diamonds. Requested by us the judge to say if he had furnished certain ingredients of magical conjuration, the blood of new-born children, conjuring books, and things generally and whatsoever made use of by sorcerers, giving him licence to state his case without that thereupon he should be subject to any further inquest or inquiry, the said Al Rastchild has sworn by his Hebrew faith never to have had any such commerce; and has stated that he was involved in too high interests to give himself to such miseries, seeing that he was the agent of certain most powerful lords, such as the Marquis de Montferrat, the King of England, the King of Cyprus and Jerusalem, the Count of Provence, the lords of Venice, and many German gentlemen; to have belonging to him merchant galleys of all kinds, going into Egypt with the permission of the Sultan, and he trafficking in precious articles of silver and of gold, which took him often into the exchange of Tours. Moreover, he has declared that he considered the said lady, the subject of inquiry, to be a right loyal and natural woman, with the sweetest limbs, and the smallest he has ever seen. That in consequence of her renown for a diabolical spirit, pushed by a wild imagination, and also because that he was smitten with her, he had once that she was husbandless, proposed to her to be her gallant, to which proposition she willingly acceded. Now although from that night, he long felt his bones disjointed and his bowels crushed, he had not experienced, as certain persons say, that who once yielded was free no more; he went to his fate as lead into the crucible of the alchemist. Then the said Salomon, to whom we have granted his liberty according to the safe conduct, in spite of this statement, which proves abundantly his commerce with the devil, because he has been safely there where all Christians have succumbed, has submitted to us an agreement concerning the said demon. To make known that he made an offer to the chapter of the cathedral to give for the said semblance of a woman such a ransom, if she were condemned to be burned alive, that the highest of the towers of the church of Saint Maurice, at present in course of construction, could therewith be finished.

The which we have noted to be deliberated upon at an opportune time by the assembled chapter. And the said Salomon has taken his departure without being willing to indicate his residence, and has told us that he can be informed of the deliberation of the chapter by a Jew of the synagogue of Tours, named Tobias Nathaneus. The said Jew has before his departure been shown the African, and has recognised him as the page of the demon, and has stated the Saracens to have the custom of mutilating their slaves thus, to commit to them the task of guarding their women by an ancient usage, as it appears in the profane histories of Narsez, general of Constantinople, and others.

On the morrow after mass has appeared before us the most noble and illustrious lady of Croixmare. The same has sworn her faith in the holy Evangelists, and has related

to us with tears how she had placed her eldest son beneath the earth, dead by reason of his extravagant amours with this female demon. The which noble gentleman was three-and-twenty years of age; of good complexion, very manly and well bearded, like his defunct sire. Notwithstanding his great vigour, in ninety days he had little by little withered, ruined by his commerce with the Succubus of the Rue Chaude, according to the statement of the common people; and her maternal authority over this son had been powerless. Finally, in his latter days he appeared like a

Finally, in his latter days, he appeared like a poor dried-up worm, such as housekeepers meet with in a corner when they clean out the dwelling rooms.

poor dried up worm, such as housekeepers meet with in a corner when they clean out the dwelling-rooms. And always, so long as he had the strength to go, he went to shorten his life with this cursed woman; where, also, he emptied his cash-box. When he was in his bed, and knew his last hour to be come, he swore at, cursed, and threatened and heaped upon all—his sister, his brother, and upon her his mother—a thousand insults, rebelled in the face of his

chaplain; denied God, and wished to die in damnation; at which were much afflicted the retainers of the family, who, to save his soul and pluck it from hell, have founded two annual masses in the cathedral. And, in order to have him buried in consecrated ground, the house of Croixmare has undertaken to give to the chapter, during one hundred years, the wax candles for the chapels and the church, upon the day of the Paschal feast. And, in conclusion, saving the wicked words heard by that reverend person, Dom Loys Pot, a nun of Marmoustiers, who came to assist in his last hours, the said Baron de Croixmare affirms never to have heard any words offered by the defunct, touching the demon who had undone him.

And therewith has retired the noble and illustrious lady in deep mourning.

In the sixth place has appeared before us, after adjournment, Jacquette, called Vieux-Oing, a kitchen scullion, going to houses to wash dishes, residing at present in the Fishmarket, who, after having pledged her word to say

And always, as long as he had the strength to go, he went
to shorten his life with this accursed woman.

nothing she did not hold to be true, has declared as here follows :—Namely, that one day she, being come into

the kitchen of the said demon, of whom she had no fear, because she was wont to regale herself only upon males, she had the opportunity of seeing in the garden this female demon, superbly attired, walking in company with a knight, with whom she was laughing, like a natural woman. Then she had recognised in this demon the true likeness of the Moorish woman placed as a nun in the convent of Notre-Dame de l'Egrignolles by the defunct seneschal of Touraine and Poitou, Messire Bruyn, Count of Roche-Corbon, the which Moorish woman had been left in the situation and place of the image of our Lady the Virgin, the mother of our blessed Saviour, stolen by the Egyptians about eighteen years since. Of this time, in

She had the opportunity of seeing, in the garden, this female
demon superbly attired, walking in company with a knight,
with whom she was laughing like a natural woman.

consequence of the troubles come about in Touraine, no record has been kept.   This girl, aged about twelve years, was saved from the stake at which she should have been burned by being baptized ; and the said defunct and his wife had then been godfather and godmother to this child of hell.   Being at that time laundress at the convent, she who bears witness has remembrance of the flight which the said Egyptian took twenty months after her entry into the convent, so subtilely that it has never been known how or by what means she escaped.   At that time, it was thought by

all, that with the devil's aid she had flown away in the air, seeing that notwithstanding much search, no trace of her flight was found in the convent, where everything remained in its accustomed order.

The African having been shown to the said scullion, she has declared not to have seen him before, although she was curious so to do, as he was commissioned to guard the place in which the Moorish woman combated with those whom she drained through the spigot.

In the seventh place has been brought before us Hugues

du Fou, son of the Sieur de Bridoré, who, aged twenty
years, has been placed in the hands of his father, under
caution of his estates, and by him is represented in this process, whom it concerns if he should be duly attainted and
convicted of having, assisted by several unknown and bad
young men, laid siege to the gaol of the archbishop and of
the chapter, and of having lent himself to disturb the force of
ecclesiastical justice, by
causing the escape of the
demon now under con-
sideration. In spite of
his evil disposition we
have commanded the
said Hugues du Fou to
testify truly, touching the
things he should know
concerning the said de-
mon, with whom he is

vehemently reputed to have had commerce, pointing out to
him that it was a question of his salvation and of the life
of the said demon. He, after having taken oath, has
said :—

"I swear by my eternal salvation and by the holy Evangelists here present under my hand, to hold the woman
suspected of being a demon to be an angel, a perfect
woman, and even more so in mind than in body, living in
all honesty, full of the migniard charms and delights of
love, in no way wicked, but most generous, assisting greatly
the poor and suffering. I declare that I have seen her
weeping veritable tears for the death of my friend the
knight of Croixmare. And because on that day she had
made a vow to our Lady the Virgin no more to receive the
love of young noblemen too weak in her service ; she has
to me constantly and with great courage denied the enjoyment of her body, and has only granted to me love, and the
possession of her heart, of which she has made me sovereign.
Since this gracious gift, in spite of my increasing flame I
have remained alone in her dwelling, where I have spent
the greater part of my days, happy in seeing and in hearing

her. Oh ! I would eat near her, partaking of the air which
entered into her lungs, of the lights which shone in her
sweet eyes, and found in this occupation more joy than have
the lords of paradise. Elected by me to be for ever my
lady, chosen to be one day my dove, my wife, and only sweetheart, I, poor fool, have received from her no advances on
the joys of the future, but, on the contrary, a thousand
virtuous admonitions ; such as that I should acquire renown
as a good knight, become a strong man and a fine one, fear
nothing except God ; honour the ladies, serve but one and
love them in memory of that one ; that when I should be
strengthened by the work of war, if her heart still pleased
mine, at that time only would she be mine, because she
would be able to wait for me, loving me so much."

So saying the young Sire Hugues wept, and weeping
added :—

" That thinking of this graceful and feeble woman, whose
arm seemed scarcely large enough to sustain the light
weight of her golden chains, he did not know how to con-
tain himself while fancying the irons which would wound
her, and the miseries with which she would traitorously be
loaded, and from this cause came his rebellion. And that he
had licence to express his sorrow before justice, because his
life was so bound up with that of his delicious mistress and
sweetheart that on the day when evil came to her he would
surely die."

And the said young man has vociferated a thousand
other praises of the said demon, which bear witness to the
vehement sorcery practised upon him, and prove, moreover,
the abominable, unalterable, and incurable life and the
fraudulent witcheries to which he is at present subject, concerning which our lord the archbishop will judge, in order
to save by exorcisms and penitences this young soul from
the snares of hell, if the devil have not gained too strong a
hold of it.

Then we have handed back the said young nobleman
into the custody of the noble lord his father, after that by
the said Hugues, the African has been recognised as the
servant of the accused.

In the eighth place, before us, have the footguards of our lord the archbishop led in great state the MOST HIGH AND REVEREND LADY JACQUELINE DE CHAMPCHEVRIER, ABBESS OF THE CONVENT OF NOTRE-DAME, under the invocation of Mount Carmel, to whose control had been submitted by the late seneschal of Touraine, father of Monseigneur the Count of Roche-Corbon, present advocate of the said convent, the Egyptian, named at the baptismal font Blanche Bruyn.

To the said abbess we have shortly stated the present cause, in which is involved the holy church, the glory of God, and the eternal future of the people of the diocese afflicted with a demon, and also the life of a creature who it was possible might be quite innocent. Then the cause elaborated, we have requested the said noble abbess to testify that which was within her knowledge concerning the magical disappearance of her daughter in God, Blanche Bruyn, espoused by our Saviour under the name of Sister Claire.

Then has stated the very high, very noble, and very illustrious lady abbess as follows :—

" The Sister Claire, of origin to her unknown, but suspected to be of an heretic father and mother, people inimical to God, had truly been placed in religion in the

convent of which the government had canonically come to
her in spite of her unworthiness ; that the said sister had
properly concluded her novitiate, and made her vows
according to the holy rule of the order. That the vows
taken, she had fallen into great sadness and had much
drooped. Interrogated by her, the abbess, concerning her
melancholy malady, the said sister had replied with tears
that she herself did not know the cause. That one thousand
and one tears engendered themselves in her at feeling no
more her splendid hair upon her head ; that besides this she
thirsted for air, and could not resist her desire to jump up
into the trees, to climb and to tumble about according to her
wont during her open air life ; that she passed her nights in
tears, dreaming of the forests under the leaves of which in
other days she slept ; and in remembrance of this she
abhorred the quality of the air of the cloisters, which
troubled her respiration ; that in her inside she was filled
with evil vapours ; that at times she was inwardly diverted
in church by thoughts which made her lose her countenance. Then I have repeated over and over again to the

poor creature the holy directions of the church, have re-
minded her of the eternal happiness which women without
sin enjoy in paradise, and how transitory was life here

She thirsted for air, and could not resist her desire to jump.
up into the trees, to climb and to tumble about according to
her wont during her open air life.

below, and certain the goodness of God, who for certain bitter pleasures lost, kept for us a love without end. In spite of this wise maternal advice the evil spirit has persisted in the said sister; and always would she gaze upon the leaves of the trees and grass of the meadows through the windows of the church during the offices and times of prayer; and persisted in becoming as white as linen in order that she might stay in her bed, and at certain times would run about the cloisters like a goat broken loose from its fastening. Finally, she has grown thin, lost much of her great beauty, and shrunk away to nothing. While in this condition by us, the abbess her mother, was she placed in the sick-room, we daily expecting her to die. One winter's morning the said sister has fled, without leaving any trace of her steps, without breaking of door, forcing of locks, or opening of windows, nor any sign whatever of the manner of her passage; a frightful adventure which was believed to have taken place by the aid of the demon who had annoyed and tormented her. For the rest it was settled by the authorities of the metropolitan church that the mission of this daughter of hell was to divert the nuns from their holy ways, and blinded by their perfect lives, she had returned through the air on the wings of the sorcerer, who had left her for mockery of our holy religion, in the place of the Virgin Mary."

The which having said, the lady abbess was, with great honour, and according to the command of our lord the archbishop, accompanied as far as the convent of Mount Carmel.

In the ninth place, before us has come, agreeably to the citation served upon him, Joseph, called Leschalopier, a money-changer, living on the bridge at the sign of the Besant d'Or, who, after having pledged his Catholic faith to say no other thing than the truth, and that known to him, touching the process before the ecclesiastical tribunal,

PREDHOMME

The which having said, the lady abbess was, with great
honour, and according to the command of our lord the archbishop, accompanied as far as the convent of Mount Carmel.

has testified as follows :—" I am a poor father, much afflicted by the sacred will of God: Before the coming of

the Succubus of the Rue Chaude, I had, for all good, a son as handsome as a noble, learned as a clerk, and having made more than a dozen voyages into foreign lands ; for the rest a good Catholic : keeping himself on guard against the needles of love, because he avoided marriage, knowing himself to be the support of my old days, the love of my eyes, and the constant delight of my heart. He was a son of whom the king of France might have been proud—a good and courageous man, the light of my commerce, the joy of my roof, and, above all, an inestimable blessing, seeing that I am alone in the world, having had the misfortune to lose my wife, and being too old to take another. Now, monseigneur, this treasure without equal has been taken from me, and cast into hell by the demon. Yes, my lord judge, directly he beheld this mischievous jade, this she-devil, in whom is a whole workshop of perdition, a conjunction of pleasure and delectation, and whom nothing can satiate, my poor child stuck himself fast in the glue-pot of love, and afterward lived only between the columns of Venus, and there did not live long, because in that place lies so great a heat that nothing can satisfy the thirst of this gulf, not even should you plunge therein the germs of the entire world. Alas ! then, my poor boy—his fortune, his generative hopes, his eternal future, his entire self, more than himself, have been engulfed in this sewer, like a grain of corn in the jaws of a bull. By this means become an old orphan, I, who speak, shall have no greater joy than to see burning, this demon, nourished with blood and gold. This Arachne, who has drawn out and sucked more marriages, more families in the seed, more hearts, more

She has all the fire of hell in her, the strength of Samson in
her hair, and the sound of celestial music in her voice.

Christians than there are lepers in all the lazar-houses of Christendom. Burn, torment this fiend—this vampire who feeds on souls, this tigrish nature that drinks blood, this amorous lamp in which burns the venom of all the vipers. Close this abyss, the bottom of which no man can find. . . . I offer my deniers to the chapter for the stake, and my arm to light the fire. Watch well, my lord judge, to surely guard this devil, seeing that she has a fire more flaming than all other terrestrial fires ; she has all the fire of hell in her, the strength of Samson in her hair, and the sound of celestial music in her voice. She charms to kill the body and the soul at one stroke ; she smiles to bite, she kisses to devour ; in short, she would wheedle an angel, and make him deny his God. My son ! my son ! where is he at this hour? The flower of my life—a flower cut by this feminine needle-case as with scissors. Ha, lord ! why have I been called? Who will give me back my son, whose soul has been absorbed by a womb which gives death to all, and life to none ? The devil alone copulates, and engenders not. This is my evidence, which I pray Master Tournebouche to write without omitting one iota, and to grant me a schedule, that I may tell it to God every evening in my prayer, to this end to make the blood of the innocent cry aloud into His ears, and to obtain from His infinite mercy the pardon of my son."

Here followed twenty and seven other statements, of which the transcription in their true objectivity, in all their quality of space, would be over-fastidious, would draw to a great length, and divert the thread of this curious process— a narrative which, according to ancient precepts, should go straight to the fact, like a bull to his principal office. Therefore here is, in a few words, the substance of these testimonies.

A great number of good Christians, townsmen and townswomen, inhabitants of the noble town of Tours, testified the demon to have held every day wedding feasts and royal festivities, never to have been seen in any church, to have cursed God, to have mocked the priests, never to have crossed herself in any place ; to have spoken

To have been met many times in the fields mounted upon an
unknown animal which went before the clouds

all the languages of the earth—a gift which has only been
granted by God to the blessed Apostles; to have been
many times met in the fields, mounted upon an unknown
animal who went before the clouds; not to grow old, and

to have always a youthful face; to have received the father
and the son on the same day, saying that her door sinned
not; to have visible malign influences which flowed from
her, for that a pastrycook, seated on a bench at his door,
having perceived her one evening, received such a gust of
warm love that, going in and getting to bed, he had with
great passion embraced his wife, and was found dead
on the morrow, that the old men of the town went to
spend the remainder of their days and of their money
with her, to taste the joys of the sins of their youth, and
that they died like fleas on their bellies, and that certain of
them, while dying, became black as Moors; that this
demon never allowed herself to be seen neither at dinner,
nor at breakfast, nor at supper, but ate alone, because she
lived upon human brains; that several had seen her during
the night go to the cemeteries, and there embrace the
young dead men, because she was not able to assuage
otherwise the devil who worked in her entrails, and there
raged like a tempest, and from that came the astringent
biting, nitrous shooting, precipitant, and diabolical movements, squeezings, and writhings of love and voluptuousness, from which several men had emerged bruised, torn,
bitten, pinched, and crushed; and that since the coming of

Several had seen her during the night go to the cemeteries,
and there embrace the young dead men.

our Saviour, who had imprisoned the master devil in the
bellies of the swine, no malignant beast had ever been seen
in any portion of the earth so mischievous, so venomous,
and so clutching ; so much so that if one threw the town of
Tours into this field of Venus, she would there transmute
it into the grain of cities, and this demon would swallow it
like a strawberry.

And a thousand other statements, sayings, and depositions,
from which was evident in perfect clearness the infernal
generation of this woman, daughter, sister, niece, spouse, or
brother of the devil, besides abundant proofs of her evil
doing, and of the calamity spread by her in all families.
And if if it were possible to put them here conformably with
the catalogue preserved by the good man to whom is due the
discovery, it would seem like a sample of the horrible cries
which the Egyptians gave forth on the day of the seventh
plague.   Also this examination has covered with great
honour Messire Guillaume Tournebouche, by whom are
quoted all the memoranda.   In the tenth vacation was thus
closed this inquest, arrived at a maturity of proof, furnished
with authentic testimony and sufficiently engrossed with the
particulars, plaints, interdicts, contradictions, charges, assign-
ments, withdrawals, confessions public and private, oaths,
adjournments, appearances, and controversies, to which the
said demon must reply.   And the townspeople say everywhere that were she really a she-devil, and furnished with
internal horns planted in her nature, with which she drank
the men, and broke them, this woman might swim a long
time in this sea of writing before being landed safe and
sound in hell.

II.

THE PROCEEDINGS TAKEN RELATIVE TO THIS FEMALE VAMPIRE.

✠ *In nomine Patris, et Filii, et Spiritûs Sancti.   Amen.*

In the year of our Lord one thousand two hundred and seventy-one, before us, Hiérome Cornille, grand penitentiary and ecclesiastical judge to this. canonically appointed, have appeared—

The Sire Philippe d'Idré, bailiff of the town and city of Tours and province of Touraine, living in his hotel in the Rue de la Rotisserie, in Chateauneuf; Master Jehan Ribou, provost of the brotherhood and company of drapers, residing on the Quay de Bretaingne, at the image of St. Pierre-es-liens; Messire Antoine Jehan, alderman and chief of the brotherhood of Changers, residing in the Place du Pont, at the image of St. Mark—counting-tournoise-pounds; Master Martin Beaupertuys, captain of the archers of the town re siding at the castle; Jehan Rabelais, a ships' painter and boat maker residing at the port of the isle of St. Jacques, treasurer of the brotherhood of the mariners of the Loire; Mark Hiérome, called Maschefer, hosier, at the sign of Saint-Sébastien, president of the trades council; and Jacques, called de Villedomer, master tavern-keeper and vine-dresser, re-

siding in the High Street, at the Pomme de Pin ; to the said
Sire d'Idré, and to the said citizens, we have read the following petition by them, written, signed, and deliberated
upon, to be brought under the notice of the ecclesiastical
tribunal :—

PETITION.

We, the undersigned, all citizens of Tours, are come into
the hotel of his worship the Sire d'Idré, bailiff of Touraine,
in the absence ot our mayor, and have requested him to hear
our plaints and statements concerning the following facts,
which we intend to bring before the tribunal of the archbishop, the judge of ecclesiastical crimes, to whom should be
deferred the conduct of the cause which we here expose :—

A long time ago there came into this town a wicked
demon in the form of a woman, who lives in the parish of
Saint-Etienne, in the house of the innkeeper Tortebras,
situated in the quit-rent of the chapter, and under the temporal jurisdiction of the archiepiscopal domain. The which
foreigner carries on the business of a gay woman in a pro-
digal and abusive manner, and with such increase of infamy
that she threatens to ruin the Catholic faith in this town,
because those who go to her come back again their souls
lost in every way, and refuse the assistance of the Church
with a thousand scandalous discourses.

Now considering that a great number of those who yielded
to her are dead, and that arrived in our town with no other
wealth than her beauty, she has, according to public clamour,
infinite riches and right royal treasure, the acquisition of
which is vehemently attributed to sorcery, or at least to
robberies committed by the aid of magical attractions and
her supernaturally amorous person ;

Considering that it is a question of the honour and security of our families, and that never before has been seen in
this country a woman wild of body or a daughter of pleasure,
carrying on with such mischief her vocation of light o' love,
and menacing so openly and bitterly the life, the savings,
the morals, chastity, religion, and the everything of the
inhabitants of this town ;

Considering that there is need of an inquiry into her person, her wealth, and her deportment, in order to verify if these effects of love are legitimate, and do not proceed, as would seem indicated by her manners, from a bewitchment of Satan, who often visits Christianity under the form of a female, as appears in the holy books, in which it is stated that our blessed Saviour was carried away into a mountain, from which Lucifer or Astaroth showed him the fertile domains of Judæa, and that in many places have been seen succubi or demons having the faces of women, who, not wishing to return to hell, and having within them an insatiable fire, attempt to refresh and sustain themselves by sucking in souls ;

Considering that in the case of the said woman a thousand proofs of *diablerie* are met with, of which certain inhabitants speak openly, and that it is necessary for the repose of the said woman that the matter be sifted, in order that she shall not be attacked by certain people, ruined by the result of her wickednesses ;

For these causes we pray that it will please you to submit to our spiritual lord, father of this diocese, the most noble and blessed Archbishop Jehan de Monsoreau, the troubles of his afflicted flock, to the end that he may advise upon them.

By so doing you will fulfil the duties of your office, as we do those of preservers of the security of this town, each one according to the things of which he has charge in his locality.

And we have signed the present, in the year of our Lord one thousand two hundred and seventy-one, on All Saints' Day, after mass.

Master Tournebouche having finished the reading of this petition, by us, Hiérome Cornille, has it been said to the petitioners—

" Gentlemen, do you, at the present time, persist in these statements? have you proofs other than those come within our own knowledge, and do you undertake to maintain the truth of this before God, before man, and before the accused ?"

All, with the exception of Master Jehan Rabelais, have

persisted in their belief, and the aforesaid Rabelais has withdrawn from the process, saying that he considered the said Moorish woman to be a natural woman and a good wench who had no other fault than that of keeping up a very high temperature of love.

Then we, the judge appointed, have, after mature deliberation, found matter upon which to proceed in the petition of the aforesaid citizens, and have commanded, that the woman at present in the gaol of the chapter shall be proceeded against by all legal methods, as written in the canons and ordinances, *contra dæmonios.* The said ordonnance, embodied in a writ, shall be published by the town crier in all parts, and with the sound of a trumpet, in order to make it known to all, and that each witness may, according to his knowledge, be confronted with the said demon, and finally the said accused to be provided with a defender, according to custom, and the interrogations, and the process to be congruously conducted.

(Signed)   HIEROME CORNILLE.

And, lower down,

TOURNEBOUCHE.

✠ *In nomine Patris, et Filii, et Spiritûs Sancti. Amen.*

In the year of our Lord one thousand two hundred and seventy-one, the 10th day of February, after mass, by command of us, Hiérome Cornille, ecclesiastical judge, has been brought from the gaol of the chapter and led before us the woman taken in the house of the innkeeper Tortebras, situated in the domain of the chapter and the cathedral of St. Maurice, and thus subject to the temporal and seigneurial justice of the Archbishop of Tours ; besides which, in consequence of the nature of the crimes imputed to her, she is liable to the tribunal and council of ecclesiastical justice, the which we have made known to her, to the end that she should not ignore it.

And after a serious reading, entirely and well understood by her, in the first place of the petition of the town ; then of the statements, plaints, accusations, and proceedings which were written in twenty-four quires by Master Tournebouche, and are above related, we have, with the invocation and assistance of God and the Church, resolved to ascertain the truth, first by interrogatories made to the said accused.

In the first interrogation we have requested the aforesaid to inform us in what land or town she had been born. By her who speaks was it answered : " In Mauritania."

We have then inquired : "If she had a father or mother, or any relations ?" By her who speaks has it been replied : "That she had never known them." By us requested to declare her name. By her who speaks has been replied : " Zulma," in the Arabian tongue.

By us has it been demanded : " Why she spoke our language ?" By her who speaks has it been said : " Because she had come into this country." By us has it been asked : " At what time ?" By her who speaks has it been replied : "About twelve years."

By us has it been asked : " What age she then was ?" By her who speaks has it been answered : " Fifteen years, or thereabout."

By us has it been said : " Then you acknowledge yourself to be twenty-seven years of age ?" By her who speaks has it been replied : " Yes."

By us has it been said to her : " That she was then the Moorish child found in the niche of Madame the Virgin, baptized by the archbishop, held at the font by the late Lord of Roche-Corbon and the Lady of Azy, his wife, afterwards by them placed in religion at the convent of Mount Carmel, where by her had been made vows of chastity, poverty, silence, and the love of God, under the divine assistance of St. Claire ?" By her who speaks has it been said : " That is true."

By us has it been asked her : " If, then, she allowed to be true the declarations of the very noble and illustrious lady the abbess of Mount Carmel, also the statement of Jacquette, called Vieux-Oing, being kitchen scullion ?" By the accused has it been answered : " These words are true in a great measure."

Then by us has it been said to her : " Then you are a

Christian ?" And by her who speaks has been answered :
" Yes, my father."

Then by us has she been requested to make the sign of
the cross, and to take holy water from a brush placed by
Master Tournebouche in her hand ; the which having done,
and by us having been witnessed, it has been admitted as an
indisputable fact, that Zulma, the Moorish woman, called in
our country Blanche Bruyn, a nun of the convent under the
invocation of Mount Carmel, there named Sister Claire, and
suspected to be the false appearance of a woman under
which is concealed a demon, has in our presence made act
of religion, and thus recognised the justice of the ecclesiastical tribunal.

Then by us have these words been said to her : " My
daughter, you are vehemently suspected to have had recourse to the devil from the manner in which you left the
convent, which was supernatural in every way." By her who
speaks has it been stated, that she at that time gained
naturally the fields by the street door after vespers,
enveloped in the robes of Jehan de Marsilis, visitor of the
convent, who had hidden her, the person speaking, in a
little hovel belonging to him, situated in the Cupidon Lane,
near a tower in the town. That there this said priest had
to her then speaking, at great length, and most thoroughly
taught the delights of love, of which she then speaking was
before in all points ignorant, for which delights she had a
great taste, finding them of good use. That the Sire
d'Amboise having perceived her then speaking at the
window of this retreat, had been smitten with a great love
for her. Then she loving him more heartily than the monk,
has fled from the hovel where she was detained for profit
of his pleasure by Don Marsilis. And then she has gone
in great haste to Amboise, the castle of the said lord,
where she had had a thousand pastimes, hunting, and
dancing, and beautiful dresses fit for a queen. One day
the Sire de la Roche-Pozay having been invited by the
Sire d'Amboise to come and feast and enjoy himself, the
Baron d'Amboise had allowed him to see her then speaking,
as she came out naked from her bath. That at this sight

the said Sire de la Roche-Pozay having fallen violently in
love with her, had on the morrow discomfited in single
combat the Sire d'Amboise, and by great violence had, in
spite of her tears taken her to the Holy Land, where she

who was speaking had led the life of a woman well beloved, and been held in great respect on account of her
great beauty. That after numerous adventures, she who
was speaking returned into this country in spite of her
apprehensions of misfortune, because such was the will of
her lord and master, the Baron de Bueil, who was dying
of grief in Asiatic lands, and desired to return to his
patrimonial manor. Now he had promised her who was
speaking to preserve her from all peril. Now she who
was speaking had faith and belief in him, the more so
as she loved him very much; but on his arrival in this
country the Sire de Bueil was seized with an illness, and
died deplorably, without taking any remedies, in spite of
the fervent requests which she who was speaking had
addressed to him, but without success, because he hated
physicians, master surgeons, and apothecaries; and that this
was the whole truth.

Then by us has it been said to the accused that she then
held to be true the statements of the good Sire Harduin
and of the innkeeper Tortebras. By her who speaks has it
been replied, that she recognised as evidence the greater
part, and also as malicious, calumnious, and imbecile certain portions.

Then by us has the accused been required to declare if
she had had pleasure and carnal commerce with all the men,

The Sire d'Amboise, having perceived her then speaking
at the window of the retreat, had been smitten with a great
love for her

The Sire de Roche-Pozay, having fallen violently in love with her, had on the morrow discomfited in single combat the Sire d'Amboise.

nobles, citizens, and others as set forth in the plaints and declarations of the inhabitants. To which by her who speaks has it been answered with great effrontery : " Pleasure, yes ! Commerce, I do not know."

By us has it been said to her, that all had died by her acts. By her who speaks has it been said that their deaths could not be the result of her acts, because she had always refused herself to them, and the more she fled from them the more they came and embraced her with infinite passion, and that when she who was speaking was taken by them she gave herself up to them with all her strength, by the grace of God, because she had in that more joy than in any other thing; and has stated, she who speaks, that she avows her secret sentiments solely because she has been requested by us to state the whole truth, and that she the speaker stood in great fear of the torments of the torturers.

Then by us has she been requested to answer, under pain of torture, in what state of mind she was when a young nobleman died in consequence of his commerce with her. Then by her speaking has it been replied, that she remained quite melancholy and wished to destroy herself; and prayed God, the Virgin, and the saints to receive her in Paradise, because never had she met with any but lovely and good hearts in which was no guile, and beholding them die she fell into great sadness, fancying herself to be an evil creature or subject to an evil fate, which she communicated like the plague.

Then by us has she been requested to state where she paid her orisons.

By her speaking has it been said that she prayed in her oratory on her knees before God, who, according to the evangelist, sees and hears all things and resides in all places.

Then by us has it been demanded why she never frequented the churches, the offices, nor the feasts. To this by her speaking has it been answered, that those who came to love her had elected the feast days for that purpose, and that she speaking did all things to their liking.

By us has it been remonstrated that, by so doing, she was submissive to man rather than to the commandments of God.

Then by her speaking has it been stated, that for those who loved her well she speaking would have thrown herself into a flaming pile, never having followed in her love any course but that of nature, and that for the weight of the world in gold she would not have lent her body or her love to a king, who did not love her with his heart, feet, head, hair, forehead, and all over. In short and moreover the speaker had never made act of harlotry in selling one single grain of love to a man whom she had not chosen to be hers, and that he who had held her in his arms one hour or kissed her on the mouth a little, possessed her for the rest of her days.

Then by us has she been requested to state whence proceeded the jewels, gold plate, silver, precious stones, regal furniture, carpets, *et cætera*, worth 200,000 doubloons, according to the inventory found in her residence and placed in the custody of the treasurer of the chapter. By the speaker answer has been made, that in us she placed all her hopes, even as much as in God, but that she dare not reply to this, because it involved the sweetest things of love upon which she had always lived. And interpellated anew, the speaker has said that if we the judge knew with what fervour she held him she loved, with what obedience she followed him in good or evil ways, with what study she submitted to him, with what happiness she listened to his desires, and inhaled the sacred words with which his mouth gratified her, in what adoration she held his person, even we, an old judge, would believe with her well-beloved, that no sum could pay for this great affection which all the men ran after. And the speaker has declared never from any man loved by her, to have solicited any present or gift, and that she rested perfectly contented to live in their hearts, that she would there curl herself up with indestructible and ineffable pleasure, finding herself richer with this heart than with anything, and thinking of no other thing than to give them more pleasure and happiness than she received from them. But in spite of the iterated refusals of the speaker her lovers persisted in graciously rewarding her. At times one came to her with a necklace of pearls, saying, " This is to show my darling that the satin of her skin did not falsely appear to me whiter than pearls;" and would put it on the speaker's neck, kissing her lovingly. The speaker would be angry at these follies, but could not refuse to keep a jewel that gave them pleasure to see it there where they placed it. Each one had a different fancy. At times another liked to tear the precious garments which the speaker wore to gratify him ; and another to deck out the speaker with sapphires on her arms, on her legs, on her neck, and in her hair ; another to seat her on the carpet, robed in silk or black velvet, and to remain for days together in ecstasy at the perfections of the speaker to whom the things desired by her lovers gave infinite pleasure, because these things rendered them quite happy. And the speaker has said, that as we love nothing so much as our pleasure, and wish that everything should shine in beauty and harmonize, outside as well as inside the heart, so they all wished to see the place inhabited by the speaker adorned with the handsomest objects, and from this idea all her lovers were pleased as much as she was in spreading thereabout gold, silks, and flowers. Now seeing that these lovely things spoil nothing, the speaker had no force or commandment by which to prevent a knight, or even a rich citizen beloved by her, having his will, and thus found herself constrained to receive rare perfumes and other satisfactions with which the speaker was loaded, and that such was the source of the gold plate, carpets, and jewels seized at her house by the officers of justice. This terminates the first interrogation made to the said Sister Claire, suspected to be a demon, because we the judge and Guillaume Tournebouche are greatly fatigued with having the voice of the aforesaid in our ears, and find our understanding in every way muddled.

By us the judge has the second interrogatory been appointed, three days from to-day, in order that the proofs of the possession and presence of the demon in the body of the aforesaid may be sought, and the accused, according to the order of the judge, has been taken back to the gaol under the conduct of Master Guillaume Tournebouche.

✠ *In nomine Patris, et Filii, et Spiritûs Sancti. Amen.*

On the thirteenth day following of the said month of February, before us, Hiérome Cornille, *et cætera*, has been produced the Sister Claire above-mentioned, in order to be interrogated upon the facts and deeds to her imputed, an^r of them to be convicted.

By us, the judge, has it been said to the accused that, looking at the diverse responses by her given to the preceding interrogatories, it was certain that it never had been in the power of a simple woman, even if she were authorized, if such licence were allowed, to lead the life of a loose woman, to give pleasure to all, to cause so many deaths, and to accomplish sorceries so perfect, without the assistance of a special demon lodged in her body, and to whom her soul had been sold by an especial compact. That it had been clearly demonstrated that under her outward appearance lies and moves a demon, the author of these evils, and that she was now called upon to declare at what age she had received

this demon, to avow the agreement existing between herself
and him, and to tell the truth concerning their common evil
doings. By the speaker was it replied that she would answer
us, man, as to God, who should be judge of all of us.   Then
has the speaker pretended never to have seen the demon,
neither to have spoken with him, nor in any way to desire to
see him ; never to have led the life of a courtesan, because
she, the speaker, had never practised the various delights
that love invents, other than those furnished by the pleasure
which the Sovereign Creator has put in the thing, and to
have always been incited more from the desire of being
sweet and good to the dear lord loved by her, than by
an incessantly raging desire. But if such had been her
inclination, the speaker begged us to bear in mind that
she was a poor African girl, in whom God had placed very
hot blood, and in her brain so easy an understanding of
the delights of love, that if a man only looked at her she
felt greatly moved in her heart. That if from desire of acquaintance an amorous gentleman touched the speaker on
any portion of the body, there passing his hand, she was, in
spite of everything, under his power, because her heart failed
her instantly. By this touch, the apprehension and remembrance of all the sweet joys of love woke again in her breast,
and there caused an intense heat, which mounted up, flamed
in her veins, and made her love and joy from head to foot.
And since the day when Don Marsilis had first awakened
the understanding of the speaker concerning these things,
she had never had any other thought, and thenceforth recognised love to be a thing so perfectly concordant with her
nature, that it had since been proved to the speaker that in default of love and natural relief she would have died, withered
at the said convent. As evidence of which, the speaker
affirms as a certainty, that after her flight from the said
convent she had not passed a single day or one particle
of time in melancholy and sadness, but always was she
joyous, and thus followed the sacred will of God, which she
believed to have been diverted during the time lost by her
in the convent.

To this was it objected by us, Hiérome Cornille, to the

said demon, that in this response she had openly blasphemed against God, because we had all been made to His greater glory, and placed in the world to honour and to serve Him, to have before our eyes His blessed commandments, and to live in sanctity, in order to gain eternal life, and not to be always in bed, doing that which even the beasts only do at a certain time. Then by the said sister has answer been made, that she honoured God greatly, that in all countries she had taken care of the poor and suffering, giving them both money and raiment, and that at the last judgment-day she hoped to have around her a goodly company of holy works pleasant to God, which would intercede for her. That but for her humility, a fear of being reproached and of displeasing the gentlemen of the chapter, she would with joy have spent her wealth in finishing the cathedral of St. Maurice, and there have established foundations for the welfare of her soul—would have spared therein neither her pleasure nor her person, and that with this idea she would have taken double pleasure in her nights, because each one of her amours would have added a stone to the building of this basilic. Also the more for this purpose, and for the eternal welfare of the speaker, would they have right heartily given their wealth.

Then by us has it been said to this demon that she could not justify the fact of her sterility, because in spite of so much commerce no child had been born of her, the which proved the presence of a demon in her. Moreover, Astaroth alone, or an apostle, could speak all languages, and she spoke after the manner of all countries, the which proved the presence of the devil in her. Thereupon the speaker has asked: "In what consisted the said diversity of languages?"—that of Greek she knew nothing save *Kyrie eleison*, of which she made great use; of Latin, nothing save *Amen*, which she said to God, wishing therewith to obtain her liberty. That for the rest the speaker had felt great sorrow, being without children, and if the good wives had them, she believed it was because they took so little pleasure in the business, and she, the speaker, a little too much. But that such was doubtless the will of

God, who thought that from too great happiness, the world would be in danger of perishing. Taking this into consideration, and a thousand other reasons, which sufficiently establish the presence of a devil in the body of the sister, because the peculiar property of Lucifer is to always find heretical arguments having the semblance of truth, we have ordered that in our presence the torture be applied to the said accused, and that she be well tormented, in order to reduce the said demon by suffering to submit to the authority of the Church, and have requested to render us assistance one François de Hangest, master surgeon and doctor to the chapter, charging him by a codicil hereunder written to investigate the qualities of the feminine nature (*virtutes vulvæ*) of the above-mentioned woman, to enlighten our religion upon the methods employed by this demon to lay hold of souls in that way, and to see if any artifice was there apparent.

Then the said Moorish woman has wept bitterly, tortured in advance, and, in spite of her irons, has knelt down imploring with cries and clamour the revocation of this order, objecting that her limbs were in such a feeble state, and her bones so tender, that they would break like a glass; and finally, has offered to purchase her freedom from this by the gift of all her goods to the chapter, and to quit incontinently the country.

Upon this, by us has she been required to voluntarily declare herself to be, and to have always been, a demon of the nature of a Succubus, which is a female devil whose business it is to corrupt Christians by the blandishments and flagitious delights of love. To this the speaker has replied that the affirmation would be an abominable falsehood, seeing that she had always felt herself to be a most natural woman.

Then her irons being struck off by the torturer, the aforesaid has removed her dress, and has maliciously and with evil design bewildered and attacked our understandings with the sight of her body, the which, for a fact, exercises upon a man supernatural coercion.

Master Guillaume Tournebouche has, by reason of nature, quitted the pen at this period, and retired, objecting that he was unable, without incredible temptations, which worked in his brain, to be a witness of this torture, because he felt the devil violently gaining his person.

This finishes the second interrogatory; and as the apparitor and janitor of the chapter have stated Master François de Hangest to be in the country, the torture and interrogations are appointed for to-morrow at the hour of noon after mass.

This has been written verbally by me, Hiérome, in the absence of Master Guillaume Tournebouche, on whose behalf it is signed.

HIEROME CORNILLE,
Grand Penitentiary.

PETITION.

To-day, the fourteenth day of the month of February, in the presence of me, Hiérome Cornille, have appeared the said Masters Jehan Ribou, Antoine Jahan, Martin Beaupertuys, Hiérome Maschefer, Jacques de Ville d'Omer, and the Sire d'Idré, in place of the Mayor of the city of Tours, for the time absent. All plaintiffs designated in the act of process made at the Town Hall, to whom we have, at the request of Blanche Bruyn (now confessing herself a nun of the convent of Mount Carmel, under the name of Sister Claire), declared the appeal made to the judgment of God by the said person accused of demoniacal possession, and her offer to pass through the ordeal of water and of fire, in presence of the Chapter and of the town of Tours, in order to prove her reality as a woman and her innocence.

To this request have agreed for their parts, the said accusers, who, on condition that the town is security for it, have engaged to prepare a suitable place and a pile, to be approved by the godparents of the accused.

Then by us, the judge, has the first day of the new year been appointed for the day of ordeal—which will be next

Paschal day—and we have indicated the hour of noon, after mass, each of the parties having acknowledged this delay to be sufficient.

And the present proclamation shall be cried, at the suit of each of them, in all the towns, boroughs, and castles of Touraine and the land of France, at their request and at their cost and suit.

HIEROME CORNILLE.

III.

WHAT THE SUCCUBUS DID TO SUCK OUT THE SOUL OF THE OLD JUDGE, AND WHAT CAME OF THE DIABOLICAL DELECTATION.

This is the act of extreme confession made the first day of the month of March, in the year one thousand two hundred and seventy-one, after the coming of our blessed Saviour, by Hiérome Cornille, priest, canon of the chapter of the cathedral of St. Maurice, grand penitentiary, of all acknowledging himself unworthy, who, finding his last hour to be come, and contrite of his sins, evil doings, forfeits, bad deeds, and wickednesses, has desired his avowal to be published to serve the preconisation of the truth, the glory of God, the justice of the tribunal, and to be an alleviation to him of his punishment, in the other world. The said Hiérome Cornille being on his deathbed, there have been convoked to hear his declarations, Jehan de la Haye (de Hago), vicar of the church of St. Maurice; Pietro Guyard, treasurer of the Chapter, appointed by our lord Jehan de Mon-

Jehan de la Haye.

soreau, Archbishop, to write his words; and Don Louis Pot,
a monk of maius MONASTERIUM *(Marmoustier), chosen by him*
for a spiritual father and confessor; all three assisted by the
great and illustrious Doctor Guillaume de Censoris, Roman
Archdeacon, at present sent into our diocese (LEGATUS) *by our*
Holy Father the Pope; and, finally, in presence of a great
number of Christians come to be witnesses of the death of the
said Hiérome Cornille, upon his known wish to make act
of public repentance, seeing that he was fast sinking, and that
his words might open the eyes of Christians about to fall into
Hell.

And before him, Hiérome, who, by reason of his great
weakness could not speak, has Don Louis Pot read the following confession, to the great agitation of the said company:—
" My brethren, until the seventy-first year of my age, which
is the one in which I now am, with the exception of the

little sins through which, all holy though he be, a Christian
renders himself culpable before God, but which it is allowed
to us to repurchase by penitence, I believe I led a Christian
life, and merited the praise and renown bestowed upon me
in this diocese, where I was raised to the high office of
grand penitentiary, of which I am unworthy. Now, struck
with the knowledge of the infinite glory of God, horrified
at the agonies which await the wicked and prevaricators in
hell, I have thought to lessen the enormity of my sins by

the greatest penitence I can show in the extreme hour at which I am. Thus I have prayed of the Church, whom I have deceived and betrayed, whose rights and judicial renown I have sold, to grant me the opportunity of accusing myself publicly in the manner of the ancient Christians. I hoped, in order to show my great repentance, to have still enough life in me to be reviled at the door of the cathedral by all my brethren, to remain there an entire day on my knees, holding a candle, a cord round my neck, and my feet naked, seeing that I had followed the ways of hell with regard to the sacred instincts of the Church. But in this great shipwreck of my fragile virtue, which will be to you a warning to fly from vice and the snares of the demon, and to take refuge in the Church, where all help is, I have been so bewitched by Lucifer that our Saviour Jesus Christ will take, by the intercession of all you whose help and prayers I request, pity on me, a poor abused Christian, whose eyes now stream with tears. So would I have another life to spend in works of penitence. Nor then listen and tremble with great fear! Elected by the assembled Chapter to carry out, instruct, and complete the process commenced against a demon, who had appeared in a feminine shape, in the person of a relapsed nun—an abominable person, denying God, and bearing the name of Zulma in the infidel country whence she comes; the which devil is known in the diocese under that of Claire, of the convent of Mount Carmel, and has much afflicted the town by putting herself under an infinite number of men to gain their souls to Mammon, Astaroth, and Satan—princes of hell, by making them leave this world in a state of mortal sin, and causing their death where life has its source, I have, I the judge, fallen in my latter days into this snare, and have lost my senses, while acquitting myself traitorously of the functions committed with great confidence by the Chapter to my cold senility. Hear how subtle the demon is, and stand firm against her artifices. While listening to the first response of the aforesaid Succubus, I saw with horror that the irons placed upon her feet and hands left no mark there, and was astonished at her hidden strength and

I listened to the music of her voice, which warmed me from head
to foot, and made me desire to be young.

at her apparent weakness. Then my mind was troubled suddenly at the sight of the natural perfections with which the devil was endowed. I listened to the music of her voice, which warmed me from head to foot, and made me desire to be young, to give myself up to this demon, thinking that for an hour passed in her company my eternal salvation was but poor payment for the pleasure of love tasted in those slender arms. Then I lost that firmness with which all judges should be furnished. This demon by me questioned, reasoned with me in such a manner that at the second interrogatory I was firmly persuaded I should be committing a crime in fining and torturing a poor little creature who cried like an innocent child. Then warned by a voice from on high to do my duty, and that these golden words, this music of celestial appearance, were diabolical mummeries, that this body, so pretty, so infatuating, would transmute itself into a bristly beast with sharp claws, those eyes so soft into flames of hell, her behind into a scaly tail, her pretty rosebud mouth and gentle lips into the jaws of a crocodile, I came back to my intention of having the said Succubus tortured until she avowed her mission, as this practice had already been followed in Christianity. Now when this demon showed herself stripped to me, to be put to the torture, I was suddenly placed in her power by magical conjurations. I felt my old bones crack, my brain received a warm light, my heart transshipped young and boiling blood. I was light in myself, and by virtue of the magic philter thrown into my eyes the snows of my forehead melted away. I lost all conscience of my Christian life and found myself a schoolboy, running about the country, escaped from class and stealing apples. I had not the power to make the sign of the cross, neither did I remember the Church, God the Father, nor the sweet Saviour of men. A prey to this design, I went about the streets thinking over the delights of that voice, the abominable, pretty body of this demon, and saying a thousand wicked things to myself. Then pierced and drawn by a blow of the devil's fork, who had planted himself already in my head as a serpent in an oak, I was conducted by this sharp prong towards the gaol, in spite of my guardian angel, who from time to time pulled me by the arm and defended me against these temptations, but in spite of his holy advice and his assistance I was dragged by a million claws stuck into my heart, and soon found myself in the gaol. As soon as the door was opened to me I saw no longer any appearance of a prison, because the Succubus had there, with the assistance of evil genii or fays, constructed a pavilion of purple and silk, full of perfumes and flowers, where she was seated, superbly attired with neither irons on her neck nor chains on her feet. I allowed myself to be stripped of my ecclesiastical vestments, and was put into a scent-bath. Then the demon covered me with a Saracen robe, entertained me with a repast of rare viands contained in precious vases, gold cups, Asiatic wines, songs, and marvellous music, and a thousand sweet sounds that tickled my soul by means of my ears. At my side kept always the said Succubus, and her sweet, detestable embrace distilled new ardour into my members. My guardian angel quitted me. Then I lived only by the terrible light of the Moorish woman's eyes, coveted the warm embraces of the delicate body, wished always to feel her red lips, that I believed natural, and had no fear of the bite of those teeth which drew one to the bottom of hell. I delighted to feel the unequalled softness of her hands without thinking that they were unnatural claws. In short, I acted like a husband desiring to go to his affianced without thinking that that spouse was everlasting death. I had no thought for the things of this world nor the interests of God, dreaming only of love, of the sweet breasts of this woman, who made me burn, and of the gate of hell in which I wished to cast myself. Alas! my brethren, during three days and three nights was I thus constrained to toil without being able to stop the stream which flowed from my reins, in which were plunged, like two pikes, the hands of the Succubus, which communicated to my poor old age and to my dried up bones, I know not what sweat of love. At first this demon, to draw me to her, caused to flow in my inside the softness of milk, then came poignant joys which pricked like a hundred needles my bones, my marrow, my brain, and my nerves.   Then all this gone all things became inflamed, my head, my blood, my nerves, my flesh, my bones, and then I burned with the real fire of hell, which caused me torments in my joints, and an incredible, intolerable, tearing voluptuousness which loosened the bonds of my life.   The tresses of this demon, which enveloped my poor body, poured upon me a stream of flame, and I felt each lock like a bar of red iron. During this mortal delectation I saw the ardent face of the said Succubus, who laughed and addressed to me a thousand exciting words; such as that I was her knight, her lord, her lance, her day, her joy, her hero, her life, her good, her rider, and that she would like to clasp me even closer, wishing to be in my skin or have me in hers.   Hearing which, under the prick of this tongue which sucked out my soul, I plunged and precipitated myself finally into hell without finding the bottom.   And then when I had no more a drop of blood in my veins, when my heart no longer beat in my body, and I was ruined at all points, the demon still fresh, white, rubicund, glowing, and laughing, said to me—

" ' Poor fool, to think me a demon ! Had I asked thee to sell me thy soul for a kiss, wouldst thou not give it me with all thy heart ?'

" ' Yes,' said I.

" ' And if always to act thus it were necessary for thee to nourish thyself with the blood of new-born children in order always to have new life to spend in my arms, would you not imbibe it willingly ?'

" ' Yes,' said I.

" ' And to be always my gallant horseman, gay as a man in his prime, feeling life, drinking pleasure, plunging to the depths of joy as a swimmer into the Loire, wouldst thou not deny God, wouldst thou not spit in the face of Jesus ?'

" ' Yes,' said I.

" ' If twenty years of monastic life could yet be given thee, wouldst thou not forfeit them for two years of this love which burns thee, and to be at this sweet occupation ?'

" ' Yes,' said I.

" Then I felt a hundred sharp claws which tore my diaphragm as if the beaks of a thousand birds there took their bellyfuls, shrieking. Then I was lifted suddenly above the earth upon the said Succubus, who had spread her wings, and cried to me—

" ' Ride, ride, my gallant rider ! Hold yourself firmly on the back of thy mule, by her mane, by her neck ; and ride, ride, my gallant rider—everything rides !' And then I saw, as a thick fog, the cities of the earth, where by a special gift I perceived each one coupled with a female demon, and tossing about, engendering in great concupiscence, all shrieking a thousand words of love and exclamations of all kinds, and all toiling away with ecstasy. Then my horse with the Moorish head pointed out to me, still flying and galloping beyond the clouds, the earth coupled with the sun in a conjunction, from which proceeded a germ of stars, and there each female world was embracing a male world ; but in place of the words used by creatures, the worlds were giving forth the howl of tempests, throwing out lightnings and crying thunders. Then still rising, I saw overhead the female nature of all things in love with the Prince of Movement. Now, by way of mockery, the Succubus placed me in the centre of this horrible and perpetual conflict, where I was lost as a grain of sand in the sea. Then still cried my white mare to me, ' Ride, ride, my gallant rider—all things ride !' Now, thinking how little was a priest in this torrent of the seed of worlds, nature always clasped together, and metals, stones, waters, airs, thunders, fish, plants, animals, men, spirits, worlds and planets, all embracing with rage, I denied the Catholic faith. Then the Succubus, pointing out to me the great patch of stars seen in the heavens, said to me, ' That way is a drop of celestial seed escaped from the great flow of the worlds in conjunction.' Thereupon I in-stantly clasped the Succubus with passion by the light of a thousand million of stars, and I wished in clasping her to feel the nature of those thousand million of creatures. Then by this great effort of love I fell impotent in every way, and heard a great infernal laugh. Then I found myself in my bed, surrounded by my servitors, who had had the courage to struggle with the demon, throwing into the bed where I

was stretched a basin full of holy water, and saying fervent
prayers to God. Then had I to sustain, in spite of this
assistance, a horrible combat with the said Succubus, whose
claws still clutched my heart, causing me infinite pains ; still,
while reanimated by the voice of my servitors, relations, and
friends, I tried to make the sacred sign of the cross ; the Succubus perched on my bed, on the bolster, at the foot, everywhere occupying herself in distracting my nerves, laughing,
grimacing, putting before my eyes a thousand obscene images,
and causing me a thousand wicked desires. Nevertheless,
taking pity on me, my lord the Archbishop caused the relics
of St. Gatien to be brought, and the moment the shrine had
touched my bed the said Succubus was obliged to depart,
leaving an odour of sulphur and of hell, which made the
throats of my servants, friends, and others sore for a whole
day. Then the celestial light of God having enlightened
my soul, I knew that I was, through my sins and my
combat with the evil spirit, in great danger of dying. Then
did I implore the especial mercy, to live just a little time
to render glory to God and to his Church, objecting the
infinite merits of Jesus dead upon the cross for the salvation
of Christians. By this prayer I obtained the favour of recovering sufficient strength to accuse myself of my sins, and
to beg of the members of the church of St. Maurice their aid
and assistance to deliver me from purgatory, where I am
about to atone for my faults by infinite agonies. Finally, I declare that my proclamation, wherein the said demon appeals
to the judgment of God by the ordeals of holy water and of
fire, is a subterfuge due to an evil design suggested by the
said demon, who would thus have had the power to escape
the justice of the tribunal of the Archbishop and of the
Chapter, seeing that she secretly confessed to me, to be able
to make another demon accustomed to the ordeal appear in
her place. And, in conclusion, I give and bequeath to the
Chapter of the church of St. Maurice my property of all
kinds, to found a Chapter in the said church, to build it
and adorn it and put it under the invocation of St. Hiérome
and St. Gatien, of whom the one is my patron and the other
the saviour of my soul."

This, heard by all the company, has been brought to the notice of the ecclesiastical tribunal by Jehan de la Haye Johannes de Haga).

We, Jehan de la Haye (Johannes de Haga), elected grand penitentiary of St. Maurice by the general assembly of the Chapter, according to the usage and custom of that church, and appointed to pursue afresh the trial of the demon Succubus, at present in the gaol of the Chapter, have ordered a new inquest, at the which will be heard all those of this diocese having cognisance of the facts relative thereto. We declare void the other proceedings, interrogations, and decrees, and annul them in the name of the members of the Church in general, and sovereign Chapter assembled, and declare that the appeal to God, traitorously made by the demon, shall not take place, in consequence of the notorious treachery of the devil in this affair. And the said judgment shall be cried by sound of trumpet in all parts of the diocese in which have been published the false edicts of the preceding month, all notoriously due to the instigations of the demon, according to the confession of the late Hiérome Cornille.

Let all good Christians be of assistance to our Holy Church, and to her commandments.

JEHAN DE LA HAYE.

IV.

HOW THE MOORISH WOMAN OF THE RUE CHAUDE TWISTED ABOUT SO BRISKLY, THAT WITH GREAT DIFFICULTY WAS SHE BURNED AND COOKED ALIVE, TO THE GREAT LOSS OF THE INFERNAL REGIONS.

This was written in the month of May, of the year 1360, after the manner of a testament.

" My very dear and well-beloved son, when it shall be lawful for thee to read this I shall be, I, thy father, reposing in the tomb, imploring thy prayers, and supplicating thee to conduct thyself in life as it will be commanded thee in this rescript, bequeathed for the good government of thy family, thy future, and safety; for I have done this at a period when I had my senses and understanding, still recently affected by the sovereign injustice of men. In my virile age I had a great ambition to raise myself in the Church, and therein to attain the highest dignities, because no life appeared to me more splendid. Now with this earnest idea, I learned to read and to write, and with great trouble became in a fit condition to enter the clergy. But because I had no protection, or good advice to superintend my training, I had an idea of becoming the writer, tabellion, and rubrican of the Chapter of St. Maurice, in which were the highest and richest personages of Christendom, since

the King of France is only therein a simple canon. Now
there I should be able better than elsewhere to find services
to render to certain lords, and thus to find a master or gain
patronage, and by this assistance enter into religion, and
be mitred and ensconced in an archiepiscopal chair, somewhere or other. But this first vision was over credulous,
and a little too ambitious, the which God caused me clearly
to perceive by the sequel. In fact, Messire Jehan de Villedomer, who afterwards became cardinal, was given this
appointment, and I was rejected, discomfited. Now in this
unhappy hour I received an alleviation of my troubles, by
the advice of the good old Hiérome Cornille, of whom I
have often spoken to you. This dear man induced me, by
his kindness, to become penman to the Chapter of St.
Maurice and the archbishop of Tours, the which offer
I accepted with joy, since I was reputed a good scrivener.
At the time I was about to enter into the presbytery commenced the famous process against the devil of the Rue
Chaude, of which the old folks still talk, and which, in its
time, has been recounted in every home in France. Now,
believing that it would be of great advantage to my ambition, and that for this assistance the Chapter would raise
me to some dignity, my good master had me appointed
for the purpose of writing all that should be in this grave
cause, subject to writing. At the very outset Monseigneur
Hiérome Cornille, a man approaching eighty years, of
great sense, justice, and sound understanding, suspected
some spitefulness in this cause, although he was not partial
to immodest girls, and had never been involved with a
woman in his life, and was holy and venerable, with a sanctity which had caused him to be selected as judge, all this
notwithstanding. As soon as the depositions were completed, and the poor wench heard, it remained clear that
although this merry doxy had broken her religious vows,
she was innocent of all devilry, and that her great wealth
was coveted by her enemies, and other persons, whom I
must not name to thee for reasons of prudence. At this
time every one believed her to be so well furnished with
silver and gold that she could have bought the whole

county of Touraine, if so it had pleased her. A thousand falsehoods and calumnious words concerning this girl, envied by all the honest women, were circulated and believed in as gospel. At this period Master Hiérome Cornille, having ascertained that no demon other than that of love was in this girl, made her consent to remain in a convent for the remainder of her days. And having ascertained from certain noble knights brave in war and rich in domains, that they would do everything to save her, he invited her secretly to demand of her accusers the judgment of God, at the same time giving her goods to the Chapter, in order to silence mischievous tongues. By this means would be saved from the stake the most delicate flower that ever heaven has allowed to fall upon our earth; the which flower yielded only from excessive tenderness and amiability to the malady of love, cast by her eyes into the hearts of all her pursuers. But the real devil, under the form of a monk, mixed himself up in this affair; in this wise: a great enemy of the virtue, wisdom, and sanctity of Monseigneur Hiérome Cornille, named Jehan de la Haye, having learned that in the gaol, the poor girl was treated like a queen, wickedly accused the grand penitentiary of connivance with her and of being her servitor, because, said this wicked priest, she makes him young, amorous, and happy, from which the poor old man died of grief in one day, knowing by this, that Jehan de la Haye had sworn his ruin and coveted his dignities. In fact, our lord the archbishop visited the gaol, and found the Moorish woman in a pleasant place, reposing comfortably, and without irons, because, having placed a diamond in a place where none would have believed she could have held it, she had purchased the clemency of her gaoler. At the time certain persons said that this goaler was smitten with her, and that from love, or perhaps in great fear of the young barons, lovers of this woman, he had planned her escape. The good man Cornille, being at the point of death, through the treachery of Jehan de la Haye, the Chapter thinking it necessary to make null and void the proceedings taken by the penitentiary, and also his decrees, the said Jehan de la Haye, at that time a simple vicar of the cathedral, pointed out that to do this it would be sufficient to obtain a public confession from the good man on his death-bed. Then was the moribund tortured and tormented by the gentlemen of the Chapter, those of Saint Martin, those of Marmoustiers, by the archbishop and also by the Pope's legate, in order that he might recant to the advantage of the Church, to which the good man would not consent. But after a thousand ills, his public confession was prepared, at which the most noteworthy people of the town assisted, and the which spread more horror and consternation than I can describe. The churches of the diocese held public prayers for this calamity, and every one expected to see the devil tumble into his house by the chimney. But the truth of it is that the good Master Hiérome had the fever, and saw cows in his room, and then was this recantation obtained of him. The access passed, the poor saint wept copiously on learning this trick from me. In fact, he died in my arms, assisted by his physician, heart-broken at this mummery, telling us that he was going to the feet of God to pray Him to prevent the consummation of this deplorable iniquity. This poor Moorish woman had touched him much by her tears and repentance, seeing that before making her demand for the judgment of God he had minutely confessed her, and by that means had disentangled the soul divine which was in her body, and of which he spoke as of a diamond worthy of adorning the holy crown of God, when she should have departed this life, after repenting her sins. Then, my dear son, knowing by the statements made in the town, and by the naïve responses of this unhappy wretch, all the trickery of this affair, I determined, by the advice of Master François de Hangest, physician of the Chapter, to feign an illness and quit the service of the church of St. Maurice and of the archbishopric, in order not to dip my hands in the innocent blood, which still cries and will continue to cry aloud unto God, until the day of the last judgment. Then was the gaoler dismissed, and in his place was put the second son of the torturer, who threw the Moorish woman into a dungeon, and inhumanly put upon her hands and feet irons weighing fifty pounds, beside a wooden waist-

bánd; and the gaol was watched by the crossbowmen of the
town and the people of the archbishop. The wench was
tormented and tortured, and her bones were broken; conquered by sorrow, she made an avowal according to the
wishes of Jehan de la Haye, and was instantly condemned
to be burned in the enclosure of St. Etienne, having been
previously placed in the portals of the church, attired in a
chemise of sulphur, and her goods given over to the Chapter,
et cætera. This order was the cause of great disturbances and
fighting in the town, because three young knights of Touraine
swore to die in the service of the poor girl, and to deliver
her in all possible ways. Then they came into the town, accompanied by thousands of sufferers, labouring people, old
soldiers, warriors, courtesans, and others, whom the said girl
had succoured, saved from misfortune, from hunger and
misery, and searched all the poor dwellings of the town
where lay those to whom she had done good. Thus all

were stirred up and called together
to the plain of Mont-Louis under
the protection of the soldiers of
the said lords; they had for companions all the scape-graces of
twenty leagues round, and came
one morning to lay siege to the
prison of the archbishop, de-
manding that the Moorish woman
should be given up to them as
though they would put her to
death, but in fact to set her free,
and to place her secretly upon a
swift horse, that she might gain
the open country, seeing that she
rode like a groom. Then in this frightful tempest of men
have we seen between the battlements of the archiepiscopal
palace and the bridges, more than ten thousand men swarming, besides those who were perched upon the roofs of the
houses and climbing on all the balconies to see the sedition; in short, it was easy to hear the horrible cries of
the Christians, who were terribly in earnest, and of those

This order was the cause of great disturbances and
fighting in the town.

who surrounded the gaol with the intention of setting the
poor girl free, across the Loire, to the other side of Saint
Symphorien.   The suffocation and squeezing of bodies was
so great in this immense crowd, bloodthirsty for the poor
creature at whose knees they would have fallen had they had
the opportunity of seeing her, that seven children, eleven
women, and eight citizens were crushed and smashed beyond
all recognition, since they were like splodges of mud; in
short, so wide open was the great mouth of this popular
Leviathan, this horrible monster, that the clamour was heard
at Montils-les-Tours.   All cried, ' Death to the Succubus!
Throw out the demon!   Ha! I'd like a quarter!   I'll have
her skin !   The foot for me, the mane for thee !   The head
for me !   The something for me !   Is it red ?   Shall we
see ?   Will it be grilled ?   Death to her ! death to her !'
Each one had his say.   But the cry, ' Largesse to God !
Death to the Succubus!' was yelled at the same time by the
crowd so hoarsely and so cruelly that one's ears and heart
bled therefrom ; and the other cries were scarcely heard in
the houses.   The archbishop decided, in order to calm this
storm which threatened to overthrow everything, to come
out with great pomp from the church, bearing the host,
which would deliver the Chapter from ruin, since the wicked
young men and the lords had sworn to destroy and burn the
cloisters and all the canons.   Now by this stratagem the
crowd was obliged to break up, and from lack of provisions
return to their houses.   Then the monks of Touraine, the
lords, and the citizens, in great apprehension of pillage on
the morrow, held a nocturnal council, and accepted the
advice of the Chapter.   By their efforts the men-at-arms,
archers, knights, and citizens, in a large number, kept
watch, and killed a party of shepherds, road menders, and
vagrants, who, knowing the disturbed state of Tours, came
to swell the ranks of the malcontents.   Messire Harduin de
Maillé, an old nobleman, reasoned with the young knights,
who were the champions of the Moorish woman, and argued
sagely with them, asking them if for so small a woman they
wished to put Touraine to fire and sword : that even if they
were victorious they would be masters of the bad characters

In this frightful tempest of men, have we seen between the battlements of the archiepiscopal palace and the bridges, more than ten thousand men swarming.

brought together by them ; that these said freebooters, after having sacked the castles of their enemies would turn to those of their chiefs. That the rebellion commenced had had no success in its first attack, because up to that time the place was untouched, could they have any over the Church, which would invoke the aid of the king ? and a thousand other arguments. To these reasons the young knights replied, that it was easy for the Chapter to aid the girl's escape in the night, and that thus the cause of the sedition would be removed. To this humane and wise request replied Monseigneur *de Censoris*, the Pope's legate, that it was necessary that strength should remain with the religion of the Church. And thereupon the poor wench paid for all, since it was agreed that no inquiry should be made concerning this sedition.

" Then the Chapter had full license to proceed to the penance of the girl, to which act and ecclesiastical ceremony the people came from twelve leagues round. So that on the day when, after divine satisfaction, the Succubus was to be delivered up to secular justice, in order to be publicly burned at a stake, not for a gold pound would a lord or even an abbot have found a lodging in the town of Tours. The night before many camped outside the town in tents, or slept upon straw. Provisions were lacking, and many who came with their bellies full, returned with their bellies empty, having seen nothing but the reflection of the fire in the distance. And the bad characters did good strokes of business by the way.

" The poor courtesan was half dead ; her hair had whitened. She was, to tell the truth, nothing but a skeleton, scarcely covered with flesh, and her chains weighed more than she did. If she had had joy in her life, she paid dearly for it at this moment. Those who saw her pass say that she wept and shrieked in a way that should have earned the pity of her hardest pursuers ; and in the church they were compelled to put a piece of wood in her mouth, which she bit as a lizard bites a stick. Then the executioner tied her to a stake to sustain her, since she let herself roll at times and fell for want of strength. Then she suddenly recovered

She was able to break her cords and escape into the church,
where, in remembrance of her old vocation, she climbed quickly
into the galleries above.

a vigorous handful, because, this notwithstanding, she was able, it is said, to break her cords and escape into the church, where, in remembrance of her old vocation, she climbed quickly into the galleries above, flying like a bird along the little columns and small friezes. She was about to escape on to the roof when a soldier perceived her, and thrust his spear in the sole of her foot. In spite of her foot half cut through, the poor girl still ran along the church without noticing it, going along with her bones broken and her blood gushing out, so great fear had she of the flames of the stake. At last she was taken and bound, thrown into a tumbrel and led to the stake, without being afterwards heard to utter a cry. The account of her flight in the church assisted in making the common people believe that she was the devil, and some of them said that she had flown in the air. As soon as the executioner of the town threw her into the flames, she made two or three horrible leaps and fell down into the bottom of the pile, which burned day and night. On the following evening I went to see if anything remained of this gentle girl, so sweet, so loving, but I found nothing but a fragment of the ' *os stomachal*,' in which, in spite of this, there still remained some moisture, and which some say still trembled like a woman does in the same place. It is impossible to tell, my dear son, the sadnesses, without number and without equal, which for about ten years weighed upon me ; always was I thinking of this angel burned by wicked men, and always I beheld her with her eyes full of love. In short the supernatural gifts of this artless child were shining day and night before me, and I prayed for her in the church where she had been martyred. At length I had neither the strength nor the courage to look without trembling upon the grand penitentiary Jehan de la Haye, who died eaten up by lice. Leprosy was his punishment. Fire burned his house and his wife ; and all those who had a hand in the burning had their own hand singed.

"This, my well-beloved son, was the cause of a thousand ideas, which I have here put into writing to be for ever the rule of conduct in our family.

" I quitted the service of the Church, and espoused your mother, from whom I received infinite blessings, and with whom I shared my life, my goods, my soul, and all. And she agreed with me in the following precepts—namely, Firstly, that to live happily, it is necessary to keep far away from Church people, to honour them much without giving them leave to enter your house, any more than to those who by right, just or unjust, are supposed to be superior to us. Secondly, to take a modest condition, and to keep oneself in it without wishing to appear in any way rich. To have a care to excite no envy, nor strike any onesoever in any manner, because it is needful to be as strong as an oak, which kills the plants at its feet, to crush envious heads, and even then would one succumb, since human oaks are especially rare, and that no Tournebouche should flatter himself that he is one, granting that he be a Tournebouche. Thirdly, never to spend more than one quarter of one's income, conceal one's wealth, hide one's goods and chattels, to undertake no office, to go to church like other people, and always keep one's thoughts to oneself, seeing that they belong to you and not to others, who twist them about, turn them after their own fashion, and make calumnies therefrom. Fourthly, always to remain in the condition of the Tournebouches, who are now and for ever drapers. To marry your daughters to good drapers, to send your sons to be drapers in other towns of France furnished with these wise precepts, and to bring them up to the honour of drapery, without leaving any dream of ambition in their minds. *A draper like a Tournebouche* should be their glory, their arms, their name, their motto, their life. Thus by being always drapers, they will be always Tournebouches, and rub on like the good little insects, who, once lodged in a beam, make their dens, and go on with security to the end of their ball of thread. Fifthly, never to speak any other language than that of drapery, and never to dispute concerning religion or government. And even though the government of the state, the province, religion, and God turn about, or have a fancy to go to the right or to the left, always in your

quality of Tournebouche, stick to your cloth. Thus un-
noticed by the others of the town, the Tournebouches will
live in peace with their little Tournebouches—paying the
tithes and taxes, and all that they are required by force
to give, be it to God or to the king, to the town or to the
parish, with all of whom it is unwise to struggle. Also
it is necessary to keep the patrimonial treasure, to have
peace and to buy peace, never to owe anything, to have
corn in the house, and enjoy yourselves with the doors and
windows shut.

" By this means none will take from the Tournebouches,
neither the State, nor the Church, nor the Lords, to
whom, should the case be that force is employed, you
will lend a few crowns without cherishing the idea of ever
seeing them again—I mean the crowns.

" Thus, in all seasons people will love the Tournebouches,
will mock the Tournebouches as poor people—as the slow
Tournebouches, as Tournebouches of no understanding.
Let the know-nothings say on. The Tournebouches will
neither be burned nor hanged, to the advantage of King
or Church, or other people ; and the wise Tournebouches
will have secretly money in their pockets, and joy in their
houses, hidden from all.

" Now, my dear son, follow this the counsel of a modest
and middle-class life. Maintain this in thy family as a county
charter ; and when you die, let your successor maintain it
as the sacred Gospel of the Tournebouches, until God wills
it that there be no longer Tournebouches in this world."

*This letter has been found at the time of the inventory made
in the house of François Tournebouche, lord of Veretz, chancellor to Monseigneur the Dauphin, and condemned at the time
of the rebellion of the said lord against the King to lose his
head, and have all his goods confiscated by order of the Parliament of Paris. The said letter has been handed to the Governor
of Touraine as an historical curiosity, and joined to the pieces
of the process in the archbishopric of Tours, by me, Pierre
Gaultier, Sheriff, President of the Trades Council.*

The author having finished the transcription and deciphering of these parchments, translating them from their strange language into French, the donor of them declared that the Rue Chaude at Tours was so called, according to certain people, because the sun remained there longer than in all other parts. But in spite of this version, people of lofty understanding will find, in the warm way of the said Succubus, the real origin of the said name. In which acquiesces the author. This teaches us not to abuse our body, but to use it wisely in view of our salvation.

DESPAIR IN LOVE.

AT the time when King Charles the Eighth took it into
his head to decorate the castle of Amboise, there came
with him certain workmen, master sculptors, good painters,
and masons, or architects, who ornamented the galleries with
splendid works, which, through neglect, have since been
much spoiled.

At that time the court was staying in this beautiful
locality, and, as every one knows, the king took great
pleasure in watching his people work out their ideas.
Among these foreign gentlemen was an Italian, named
Angelo Cappara, a most worthy young man, and, in spite
of his age, a better sculptor and engraver than any of them ;
and it astonished many to see one in the April of his life so
clever. Indeed, there had scarcely sprouted upon his
visage the hair which imprints upon a man virile majesty.
To this Angelo the ladies took a great fancy because he
was charming as a dream, and as melancholy as a dove left
solitary in its nest by the death of its mate. And this was

the reason thereof: this sculptor knew the curse of poverty, which mars and troubles all the actions of life; he lived miserably, eating little, ashamed of his pennilessness, and made use of his talents only through great despair, wishing by any means to win that idle life which is the best of all for those whose minds are occupied. The Florentine, out of bravado, came to the court gallantly attired, and from

the timidity of youth and misfortune dared not to ask his money from the king, who, seeing him thus dressed, believed him well furnished with everything. The courtiers and the ladies used all to admire his beautiful works, and also their author; but of money he got none. All, and the ladies above all, finding him rich by nature, esteemed him well off with his youth, his long black hair, and bright eyes, and did not give a thought to lucre, while thinking of these things and the rest. Indeed, they were quite right, since these ad-

vantages gave to many a rascal of the court lands, money, and
all. In spite of his youthful appearance, Master Angelo
was twenty years of age, and no fool, had a large heart, a
head full of poetry; and more than that, was a man of lofty
imaginings. But although he had little confidence in himself,
like all poor and unfortunate people, he was astonished at
the success of the ignorant. He fancied that he was ill-
fashioned, either in body or mind, and kept his thoughts to
himself. I am wrong, for he told them in the clear starlight
nights to the shadows, to God, to the devil, and everything about him. At such times he would lament his fate
in having a heart so warm, that doubtless the ladies avoided
him as they would a red hot iron ; then he would say to
himself how he would worship a beautiful mistress, how all
his life long he would honour her, with what fidelity he
would attach himself to her, with what affection serve
her, how studiously obey her commands, with what
sports he would dispel the light clouds of her melancholy
sadness on the days when the sky should be overcast.
Fashioning himself one out of his imagination, he would
throw himself at her feet, kiss, fondle, caress, bite, and clasp
her with as much reality as a prisoner scampers over the
grass when he sees the green fields through the bars of his
cell. Thus he would appeal to her mercy ; overcome with
his feelings, would stop her breath with his embraces, would
become daring in spite of his respect, and passionately

 bite the clothes of his bed, seeking this
celestial lady, full of courage when by himself, but abashed on the morrow if he
passed one by. Nevertheless, inflamed
by these amorous fancies, he would hammer away anew at his marble figures,
would carve beautiful breasts, to bring
the water into one's mouth at the sight
of these sweet fruits of love, without
counting the other things that he raised,
carved, and caressed with his chisels, smoothed down with
his file, and fashioned in a manner that would make their
use intelligible to the mind of a greenhorn, and stain his
verdure in a single day. The ladies would criticise these

He told his thoughts in the clear starlight nights, to the shadows,
to God, to the devil, and everything about him.

beauties, and all of them were smitten with the youthful Cappara. And the youthful Cappara would eye them up and down, swearing that the day one of them gave him her little finger to kiss, he would have his desire.

Among these high-born ladies there came one day one by herself to the young Florentine, asking him why he was so shy, and if none of the court ladies could make him sociable. Then she graciously invited him to come to her house that evening.

Master Angelo perfumes himself, purchases a velvet mantle with a double fringe of satin, borrows from a friend a cloak with wide sleeves, a slashed doublet, and silken hose, arrives at the house, and ascends the stairs with hasty feet, hope beaming from his eyes, knowing not what to do with his heart, which leapt and bounded like a goat ; and, to sum up so much, over head and ears in love, that the perspiration trickled down his back.

You may be sure the lady was beautiful, and Master Cappara was the more aware of it, since his profession he had studied the mouldings of the arms, the lines of the body, the secret surroundings of the sex, and other mysteries. Now this lady satisfied the especial rules of art ; and besides being fair and slender, she had a voice to disturb life in its source, to stir the fire of heart, brain, and everything ; in short, she put into one's imagination delicious images of love without thinking of it, which is the characteristic of these cursed women.

The sculptor found her seated by the fire in a high chair, and the lady immediately commenced to converse at her ease, although Angelo could find no other reply than "Yes" and "No," could get no other words from his throat nor idea in his brain, and would have beaten his head against the fireplace but for the happiness of gazing at and listening to his lovely mistress, who was playing there with a young fly in a ray of sunshine. Because, with this mute admiration, both remained until the middle of the night, wandering slowly down the flowery path of love, the good sculptor went away radiant with happiness. On the road, he concluded in his own mind, that if a noble lady kept him rather close to her skirts during four hours of the night, it would not matter a

straw if she kept him there the remainder. Drawing from
these premises certain sweet corollaries, he resolved to ask
her favours as a simple woman. Then he determined to kill
everybody—the husband, the wife, or himself—rather than
lose the distaff whereon to spin one hour of joy. Indeed,
he was so mad with love, that he believed life to be but a
small stake in the game of love, since one single day of it
was worth a thousand lives.

The Florentine chiselled away at his statues, thinking of
his evening, and thus spoiled many a nose thinking of something else. Noticing this, he left his work, perfumed himself, and went to listen to the sweet words of his lady, with
the hope of turning them into deeds ; but when he was in
the presence of his sovereign, her feminine majesty made
itself felt, and poor Cappara, such a lion in the street, looked
sheepish when gazing at his victim. This notwithstanding, towards the hour when desire becomes heated, he was almost in
the lady's lap and held her tightly clasped. He had obtained
a kiss, had taken it, much to his delight ; for, when they give
it, the ladies retain the right of refusal, but when they let it
be taken, the lover may take a thousand. This is the reason
why all of them are accustomed to let it be taken. The
Florentine had stolen a good number, and things were going
on admirably, when the lady, who had been thrifty with her
favours, cried, " My husband !"

And, in fact, my lord had just returned from playing
tennis, and the sculptor had to leave the place, but not
without receiving a warm glance from the lady interrupted
in her pleasure. This was all his substance, pittance, and
enjoyment during a whole month, since on the brink of his
joy always came the said husband, and he always arrived
wisely between a point-blank refusal and those little caresses
with which women always season their refusals—little things
which reanimate love and render it all the stronger. And
when the sculptor, out of patience, commenced, immediately
upon his arrival, the skirmish of the skirt, in order that
victory might arrive before the husband, to whom, no doubt,
these disturbances were not without profit, his fine lady,
seeing desire written in the eyes of her sculptor, commenced

endless quarrels and altercations : at first she pretended to be jealous, in order to rail against love ; then appeased the anger of the little one with the moisture of a kiss, then kept the conversation to herself, and kept on saying that her lover should be good, obedient to her will, otherwise she would not yield to him her life and soul ; that a desire was a small thing to offer a mistress ; that she was more courageous, because loving more she sacrificed more, and to his propositions she would exclaim, " Silence, sir !" with the air of a queen, and at times she would put on an angry look, to reply to the reproaches of Cappara : " If you are not as I wish you to be, I will no longer love you."

The poor Italian saw, when it was too late, that this was not a noble love, one of those which does not mete out joy as a miser his crowns ; and that this lady took delight in letting him jump about outside the hedge and be master of everything, provided he touched not the garden of love. At this business Cappara became savage enough to kill any one, and took with him trusty companions, his friends, to whom he gave the task of attacking the husband while walking home to bed after his game of tennis with the king. He came to his lady at the accustomed hour when the sweet sports of love were in full swing, which sports were long, lasting kisses, hair twisted and untwisted, hands bitten with passion, ears as well ; indeed, the whole business, with the exception of that especial thing which good authors rightly find abominable. The Florentine exclaims between two hearty kisses—

" Sweet one, do you love me more than anything ?"

" Yes," said she, because words never cost anything.

" Well, then," replied the lover, " be mine in deed as in word."

" But," said she, " my husband will be here directly."

" Is that the only reason ?" said he.

" Yes."

" I have friends who will cross him, and will not let him go unless I show a torch at this window. If he complain to the king, my friends will say they thought they were playing a joke on one of their own set."

" Ah, my dear," said she, " let me see if every one in the house is gone to bed."

She rose, and held the light to the window. Seeing which Cappara blew out the candle, seized his sword, and placing himself in front of this woman, whose scorn and evil mind he recognised.

" I will not kill you, madam," said he, " but I will mark your face in such a manner that you will never again

coquette with young lovers whose lives you waste. You have deceived me shamefully, and are not a respectable woman. You must know that a kiss will never sustain life in a true lover, and that a kissed mouth needs the rest. You have made my life for ever dull and wretched ; now I will make you remember for ever my death, which you have caused. You shall never again behold yourself in the glass without seeing there my face also." Then he raised his arm, and held the sword ready to cut off a good slice of the fresh fair cheek, where still the traces of his kiss remained. And the lady exclaimed, " You wretch !"

" Hold your tongue," said he ; " you told me that you loved me better than everything. Now you say otherwise ;

each evening have you raised me a little nearer to heaven; with one blow you cast me into hell, and you think that your petticoat can save you from a lover's wrath—No !"

"Ah, my Angelo ! I am thine," said she, marvelling at this man glaring with rage.

But he, stepping three paces back, replied, " Ah, woman of the court and wicked heart, thou lovest, then, thy face better than thy lover."

She turned pale, and humbly held up her face, for she understood that at this moment her past perfidity wronged her present love. With a single blow Angelo slashed her face, then left her house, and quitted the country. The husband not having been stopped by reason of that light which was seen by the Florentines, found his wife minus her left cheek. But she spake not a word in spite of her agony ; she loved her Cappara more than life itself. Nevertheless, the husband wished to know whence proceeded this wound. No one having been except the Florentine, he complained to the king, who had his workman hastily pursued, and ordered him to be hanged at Blois. On the day of execution a noble lady was seized with a desire to save this courageous man, whom she believed to be a lover of the right sort. She begged the king to give him to her, which he did willingly. But Cappara declaring that he belonged entirely to his lady, the memory of whom he could not banish entirely, entered the Church, became a cardinal and a great savant, and used to say in his old age that he had existed upon the remembrance of the joys tasted in those poor hours of anguish ; in which he was, at the same time, both very well and very badly treated by his lady. There are authors who say that afterwards he succeeded better with his old sweetheart, whose cheek healed ; but I cannot believe this, because he was a man of heart, who had a high opinion of the holy joys of love.

This teaches us nothing worth knowing, unless it be that there are unlucky meetings in life, since this tale is in every way true. If in other places the author has overshot the truth, this one will gain for him the indulgence of the conclave of lovers.

ALTHOUGH this second volume has on its frontispiece
an inscription which declares it to have been finished
in a time of snows and chills, it comes in the merry month
of June, when all is green and gay, because the poor muse,
whose slave the author is, has been more capricious than
the love of a queen, and has mysteriously wished to bring forth
her fruit in the time of flowers. No one can boast himself
master of this fay. At times, when grave thoughts occupy
the mind and grieve the brain, comes the jade whispering
her merry tales in the author's ear, tickling her lips with her
feathers, dancing sarabands, and making the house echo
with her laughter. If by chance the writer, abandoning
science for pleasure, says to her, "Wait a moment, little
one, till I come," and runs in great haste to play with the
madcap, she has disappeared. She has gone back into her
hole, hides herself there, rolls herself up, and retires.
Take the poker, take a staff, a cudgel, a cane, raise them,
strike the wench, and rave at her, she moans; strap her,
she moans; caress her, fondle her, she moans; kiss her,

say to her, " Here, little one," she moans.   Now she's cold,
now she is going to die; adieu to love, adieu to laughter,
adieu to merriment, adieu good stories.   Wear mourning
for her, weep and fancy her dead, groan.   Then she raises
her head, her merry laugh rings out again; she spreads her
white wings, flies one knows not wither, turns in the air,
capers, shows her impish tail, her woman's breasts, her
strong loins, and her angelic face, shakes her perfumed
tresses, gambols in the rays of the sun, shines forth in all
her beauty, changes her colours like the breast of a dove,
laughs until she cries, casts the tears of her eyes into the
sea, where the fishermen find them transmuted into pretty
pearls, which are gathered to adorn the foreheads of queens.
She twists about like a colt broken loose, exposing her
virgin charms, and a thousand things so fair that a pope
would peril his salvation for her at the mere sight of them.
During these wild pranks of the ungovernable beast you
meet fools and friends, who say to the poor poet, " Where
are your tales? Where are your new volumes? You're a
pagan prognosticator.   Oh yes, you are known.   You go
to fêtes and feasts, and do nothing between your meals.
Where's your work?"

Although I am by nature partial to kindness, I should
like to see one of these people impaled in the Turkish
fashion, and thus equipped, sent on the Love Chase.
Here endeth the second volume; may the devil give it
a lift with his horns, and it will be well received by a smiling
Christendom.

The Third Ten.

THE THIRD TEN.

CERTAIN persons have interrogated the author as to why there was such a demand for these tales that no year passes without his giving an instalment of them, and why he has lately taken to write commas mixed up with bad syllables, at which the ladies publicly knit their brows, and have put to him other questions of a like character. The author declares that these treacherous words, cast like pebbles in his path, have touched him in the very depths of his heart, and he is sufficiently cognizant of his duty not to fail to give to his special audience in this prologue certain reasons other than preceding ones, because it is always necessary to reason with children until they are grown up, understand things, and hold their tongues ; and because he perceives many mischievous fellows among this crowd of noisy people, who ignore at pleasure the real object of these volumes. In the first place know, that if certain virtuous ladies—I say virtuous because common and low class women do not read these stories, preferring those that are never published ; on the contrary, other citizens' wives and ladies, of high respectability and godliness, although doubtless dis-

gusted with the subject matter, read them piously to satisfy
an evil spirit, and thus keep themselves virtuous. Do you
understand, my good reapers of horns? It is better to be deceived by the tale of a book than cuckolded through the story
of a gentleman. You are saved the damage by this, poor fools!
besides which, often your lady becoming enamoured, is seized
with fecund agitations to your advantage, raised in her by the
present book. Therefore do these volumes assist to popu-
late the land and maintain it in mirth, honour, and health.
I say mirth, because much is to be derived from these tales.
I say honour, because you save your nest from the claws of
that youthful demon named cuckoldom in the language of
the Celts. I say health, because this book incites that
which was prescribed by the Church of Salerno, for the avoid-
ance of cerebral plethora. Can you derive a like proof in
any other typographically blackened folios? Ha! ha!
where are the books that make children? Think! Nowhere.
But you will find a glut of children making books which
beget nothing but weariness. But to continue. Now be it
known that when ladies, of a virtuous nature and talkative
turn of mind, converse publicly on the subject of these
volumes, a great number of them, far from reprimanding the
author, confess that they like him very much, esteeming him
a valiant man, worthy to be a monk in the Abbey of
Theleme. For as many reasons as there are stars in the
heavens, he does not drop the style which he has adopted in
these said tales, but lets himself be vituperated, and keeps
steadily on his way, because noble France is a woman who
refuses to yield, crying, twisting about, and saying, "No,
no; never! Oh, sir, what are you going to do? I wont
let you; you'd rumple me." And when the volume is done
and finished, all smiles, she exclaims, "Oh, my master, are
there any more to come?" You may take it for granted
that the author is a merry fellow, who troubles himself little
about the cries, tears, and tricks of the lady you call glory,
fashion, or public favour, for he knows her to be a wanton
who would put up with any violence. He knows that in
France her war cry is, *Mount Joy!* A fine cry, indeed, but
one which certain writers have disfigured, and which sig-

nifies, " Joy is not of the earth, it is there ; seize it, otherwise good-bye." The author has this interpretation from Rabelais, who told it to him. If you search history, has France ever breathed a word when she was joyously mounted, bravely mounted, passionately mounted, mounted and out of breath ? She goes furiously at everything, and likes this exercise better than drinking. Now, do you not see that these volumes are French, joyfully French, wildly French, French before, French behind, French to the backbone. Back then, curs ! strike up the music ; silence, bigots ! advance my merry wags, my little pages, put your soft hands into the ladies' hands and tickle them in the middle—of the hand of course. Ha ! ha ! these are high sounding and peripatetic reasons, or the author knows nothing of sound and the philosophy of Aristotle. He has on his side the crown of France and the oriflamme of the king and Monsieur St. Denis, who, having lost his head, said, " Mount-my-Joy !" Do you mean to say, you quadrupeds, that the word is wrong ? No. It was certainly heard by a great many people at the time ; but in these days of deep wretchedness you believe nothing concerning the good old saints.

The author has not finished yet. Know all ye who read these tales with eye and hand, feel them in the head alone, and love them for the joy they bring you, and which goes to your heart, know that the author having in an evil hour let his ideas, *id est*, his inheritance, go astray, and being un- able to get them together again, found himself in a state of mental nudity. Then he cried like the woodcutter in the prologue of the book of his dear master, Rabelais, in order to make himself heard by the gentleman on high, Lord Paramount of all things, and obtain from Him fresh ideas. This said Most High, still busy with the congress of the time, threw to him through Mercury an inkstand with two cups, on which was engraved, after the manner of a motto, these three letters, *Ave.* Then the poor fellow, perceiving no other help, took great care to turn over this said inkstand to find out the hidden meaning of it, thinking over the mysterious words and trying to find a key to them. First, he saw that God was polite, like a great Lord as He is, because the world is His, and He holds the title of it from no one. But since, in thinking over the days of his youth, he remembered no great service rendered to God, the author was in doubt concerning this hollow civility, and pondered long without finding out the real substance of this celestial utensil. By reason of turning and twisting it about, studying it, looking at it, feeling it, emptying it, knocking it in an interrogatory manner, smacking it down, standing it up straight, standing it on one side, and turning it upside down, he read backwards *Eva*. Who is Eva, if not all women in one? Therefore by the Voice Divine was it said to the author :—

Think of woman ; woman will heal thy wound, stop the waste-hole in thy bag of tricks. Woman is thy wealth ; have but one woman, dress, undress, and fondle that woman, make use of the woman—woman is everything—woman has an inkstand of her own ; dip thy pen in that bottomless inkpot. Woman likes love ; make love to her with the pen only, tickle her phantasies, and sketch merrily for her a thousand pictures of love in a thousand pretty ways. Woman is generous, and all for one, or one for all, must pay the painter, and furnish the hairs of the brush. Now, muse upon that which is written there. *Ave*-hail, *Eva*-woman ; or, *Eva*-woman, *Ave*-hail. Yes, she makes and unmakes. Heigh, then, for the inkstand! What does woman like best? What does she desire? All the special things of love ; and woman is right. To have children, to produce in imitation of nature, which is always in labour. Come to me, then, woman !—come to me, *Eva!* With this the author began to dip into that fertile inkpot, where there was a brain-fluid, concocted by virtues from on high in a talismanic fashion. From one cup there came serious things, which wrote themselves in brown ink ; and from the other trifling things, which merely gave a roseate hue to the pages of the manuscript. The poor author has often, from carelessness, mixed the inks now here, now there ; but as soon as the heavy sentences, difficult to smooth, polish, and brighten up, of some work suitable to the taste of the day are finished, the author, eager to amuse himself, in

spite of the small amount of merry ink remaining in the left
cup, steals and bears eagerly therefrom a few penfuls with
great delight. These said penfuls are, indeed, these same
Droll Tales, the authority of which is above suspicion,
because it flows from a divine source, as is shown in this
the author's naive confession.

Certain evil-disposed people will still cry out at this; but
can you find a man perfectly contented on this lump of
mud? Is it not a shame? In this the author has wisely
comported himself in imitation of a higher power; and he
proves it by *atqui.* Listen. Is it not most clearly demonstrated to the learned, that the sovereign Lord of worlds
has made an infinite number of heavy, weighty, and serious
machines with great wheels, large chains, terrible notches,
and frightfully complicated screws and weights like the
roasting-jack, but also has amused Himself with little trifles
and grotesque things light as zephyrs, and has also made
naïve and pleasant creations, at which you laugh directly you
see them. Is it not so? Then in all eccentric works, such as
the very spacious edifice undertaken by the author, in order
to model himself upon the laws of the above-named Lord,
it is necessary to fashion certain delicate flowers, pleasant
insects, fine dragons well twisted, imbricated, and coloured
—nay, even gilt, although he is often short of gold—and
throw them at the feet of his snow-clad mountains, piles of
rocks, and other cloud-capped philosophies, long and terrible works, marble columns, real thoughts carved in
porphyry. Ah! unclean beasts, who despise and repudiate
the figures, phantasies, harmonies, and roulades of the fair
muse of drollery, will you not pare your claws, so that you
may never again scratch her white skin, all azure with veins,
her amorous reins, her flanks of surpassing elegance,
her feet that stay modestly in bed, her satin face, her
lustrous features, her heart devoid of bitterness? Ah!
wooden-heads, what will you say when you find that this
merry lass springs from the heart of France, agrees with all
that is womanly in nature, has been saluted with a polite
Ave! by the angels in the person of their spokesman, Mercury, and finally, is the clearest quintessence of Art. In

this work are to be met with necessity, virtue, whim, the desire of a woman, the votive offering of a stout Pantagruelist, all are here. Hold your peace, then, drink to the author, and let his inkstand with the double cup endow the Gay Science with a hundred glorious Droll Tales.

Stand back then, curs; strike up the music! Silence, bigots; out of the way, dunces! Step forward my merry wags!—my little pages! give your soft hand to the ladies, and tickle theirs in the centre in a pretty manner, saying to them, "Read to laugh." Afterwards you can tell them some merry jest to make them roar, since when they are laughing their lips are apart, and they make but a faint resistance to love.

PERSEVERANCE IN LOVE.

URING the first years of the thirteenth century after
the coming of our Divine Saviour there happened in
the city of Paris an amorous adventure, through the deed of
a man of Tours, of which the town and even the king's court
were never tired of speaking. As to the clergy, you will see
by that which is related below the part they played in this
history, the testimony of which was by them preserved.
This said man, called the Tourainian by the common people,
because he had been born in our merry Touraine, had for his
true name that of Anseau. In his latter days the good man
returned into his own country and was mayor of St. Martin,
according to the chronicles of the abbey of that town; but
at Paris he was a great silversmith. But now in his prime,

And his heart leaped almost into his mouth.

"You have a fine cow," said he.

"Would you like a little milk?" replied she.

by his great honesty, his labours, and so forth, he became a
citizen of Paris and subject of the king, whose protection he
bought, according to the custom of the period. He had a
house built for him free of all quit-rent, close to the church
of St. Leu, in the Rue St. Denis, where his forge was well
known by those in want of fine jewels. Although he was a
Tourainian, and had plenty of spirit and animation, he kept
himself virtuous as a true saint, in spite of the blandishments
of the city, and had passed the days of his green season
without once dragging his good name through the mire.
Many will say this passes the bounds of that faculty of
belief which God has placed in us to aid that faith due to
the mysteries of our holy religion; so it is needful to demonstrate abundantly the secret cause of this silversmith's
chastity. And, first, remember that he came into the town
on foot, poor as Job, according to the old saying; and, like
all the inhabitants of our part of the country, who have but
one passion, he had a character of iron, and persevered in
the path he had chosen as steadily as a monk in vengeance.
As a workman, he laboured from morn to night; become a
master, he laboured still, always learning new secrets, seeking new receipts, and in seeking, meeting with inventions of
all kinds. Late idlers, watchmen, and vagrants saw always
a modest lamp shining through the silversmith's window,
and the good man tapping, sculping, rounding, chiselling,
modelling, and finishing, with his apprentices, his door
closed and his ears open. Poverty engendered hard work,
hard work engendered his wonderful virtue, and his virtue
engendered his great wealth. Take this to heart, ye children of Cain, who eat doubloons and micturate water. If
the good silversmith felt himself possessed with wild desires
which now in one way, now in another, seize upon an unhappy bachelor when the devil tries to get hold of him,
making the sign of the cross, the Tourainian hammered
away at his metal, drove out the rebellious spirits from his
brain by bending down over the exquisite works of art, little
engravings, figures of gold and silver forms, with which he
appeased the anger of his Venus. Add to this that this
Tourainian was an artless man, of simple understanding,

fearing God above all things, then robbers, next to that the
nobles, and more than all, a disturbance. Although he had
two hands, he never did more than one thing at a time.
His voice was as gentle as that of a bridegroom before marriage. Although the clergy, the military, and others gave
him no reputation for knowledge, he knew well his mother's
Latin, and spoke it correctly without waiting to be asked.
Latterly the Parisians had taught him to walk uprightly, not
to beat the bush for others, to measure his passions by the
rule of his revenues, not to let them take *his* leather to make
others' shoes, to trust no one farther than he could see them,
never to say what he did, and always to do what he said;
never to spill anything but water; to have a better memory
than flies usually have; to keep his hands to himself, to do
the same with his purse; to avoid a crowd at the corner of
a street, and sell his jewels for more than they cost him;
all things, the sage observance of which gave him as much
wisdom as he had need of to do business comfortably and
pleasantly. And so he did, without troubling any one else.
And watching this good little man unobserved, many said,
" By my faith, I should like to be this jeweller, even were I
obliged to splash myself up to the eyes with the mud of
Paris during a hundred years for it."

They might just as well have wished to be king of France,
seeing that the silversmith had great powerful nervous arms,
so wonderfully strong that when he closed his fist the
cleverest trick of the roughest fellow could not open it;
from which you may be sure that whatever he got hold of
he stuck to. More than this, he had teeth fit to masticate
iron, a stomach to dissolve it, a duodenum to digest it, a
sphincter to let it out again without tearing, and shoulders
that would bear a universe upon them, like that pagan
gentleman to whom the job was confided, and whom the
timely coming of Jesus Christ discharged from the duty.
He was, in fact, a man made with one stroke, and they are
the best, for those who have to be touched up are worth
nothing, being patched up and finished at odd times. In
short, Master Anseau was a thorough man, with a lion's face,
and under his eyebrows a glance that would melt his gold if

the fire of his forge had gone out, but a limpid water placed
in his eyes by the great Moderator of all things tempered
this great ardour, without which he would have burnt up
everything. Was he not a splendid specimen of a man?

With such a sample of his cardinal virtues, some persist in
asking why the good silversmith remained as unmarried as an
oyster, seeing that these properties of nature are of good use
in all places. But these opinionated critics, do they know
what it is to love? Ho! ho! Easy! The vocation of a
lover is to go, to come, to listen, to watch, to hold his
tongue, to talk, to stick in a corner, to make himself big, to
make himself little, to agree, to play music, to drudge, to go
to the devil wherever he be, to count the grey peas in the
dovecot, to find flowers under the snow, to say paternosters
to the moon, to pat the cat and pat the dog, to salute the
friends, to flatter the gout or the cold of the aunt, to say to
her at opportune moments, "You have good looks, and will
yet write the epitaph of the human race." To please all the
relations, to tread on no one's corns, to break no glasses, to
waste no breath, to talk nonsense, to hold ice in his hand, to
say, "This is good!" or, "Really, madam, you are very beautiful so." And to vary that in a hundred different ways. To
keep himself cool, to bear himself like a nobleman, to have a
free tongue and a modest one, to endure with a smile all
the evils the devil may invent on his behalf, to smother his

anger, to hold nature in control, to have the finger of God
and the tail of the devil, to reward the mother, the cousin,
the servant; in fact, to put a good face on everything. In
default of which the female escapes and leaves you in a fix,
without giving a single Christian reason. In fact, the lover
of the most gentle maid that God ever created in a good-
tempered moment, had he talked like a book, jumped like a
flea, turned about like dice, played like King David, and
built for the aforesaid woman the Corinthian order of the
columns of the devil, if he failed in the essential and hidden
thing which pleases his lady above all others, which often
she does not know herself and which he has need to
know, the lass leaves him like a red leper. She is quite right.
No one can blame her for so doing. When this happens
some men become ill-tempered, cross, and more wretched
than you can possibly imagine. Have not many of them
killed themselves through this petticoat tyranny. In this
matter the man distinguishes himself from the beast, seeing
that no animal ever yet lost his senses through blighted
love, which proves abundantly that animals have no souls.
The employment of a lover is that of a mountebank, of a
soldier, of a quack, of a buffoon, of a prince, of a ninny, of a
king, of an idler, of a monk, of a dupe, of a blackguard, of a
liar, of a braggart, of a sycophant, of a numskull, of a
frivolous fool, of a blockhead, of a know-nothing, of a knave.
An employment from which Jesus abstained, in imitation of
whom folks of great understanding likewise disdain it; it is
a vocation in which a man of worth is required to spend
above all things, his time, his life, his blood, his best words,
besides his heart, his soul, and his brain; things to which
the women are cruelly partial, because directly their tongues
begin to go, they say among themselves that if they have not
the whole of a man they have none of him. Be sure, also,
that there are cats who, knitting their eyebrows, complain
that a man does but a hundred things for them, for the
purpose of finding out if there be a hundred, and first seeing that in everything they desire the most through spirit
of conquest and tyranny. And this high jurisprudence has
always flourished among the customs of Paris, where the

women receive more wit at their baptism than in any other place in the world, and thus are mischievous by birth.

But our silversmith, always busy at his work, burnishing gold and melting silver, had no time to warm his love or to burnish and make shine his fantasies, nor to show off, gad about, waste his time in mischief, or to run after she-males. Now seeing that in Paris virgins do not fall into the beds of young men any more than roast pheasants into the streets, not even when the young men are royal silversmiths, the Tourainian had the advantage of having, as I have before observed, a continent member in his shirt. However, the good man could not close his eyes to the advantages of nature with which were so amply furnished the ladies with whom he dilated upon the value of his jewels. So it was that, after listening to the gentle discourse of the ladies, who tried to wheedle and to fondle him to obtain a favour from him, the good Tourainian would return to his home, dreamy as a poet, wretched as a restless cuckoo, and would say to himself, " I must take to myself a wife. She would keep the house tidy, keep the plates hot for me, fold the clothes for me, sew my buttons on, sing merrily about the house, tease me to do everything according to her taste, would say to me as they all say to their husbands when they want a jewel, ' Oh, my own pet, look at this, is it not pretty?' And every one in the quarter will think of my wife and then of me, and say, ' There's a happy man.' Then the getting married, the bridal festivities, to fondle Madame Silversmith, to dress her superbly, give her a fine gold chain, to worship her from crown to toe, to give her the whole management of the house, except the cash, to give her a nice little room upstairs, with good windows, pretty, and hung round with tapestry, with a wonderful chest in it and a fine large bed, with twisted columns and curtains of yellow silk. He would buy her beautiful mirrors, and there would always be a dozen or so of children, his and hers, when he came home to greet him." Then wife and children would vanish into the clouds. He transferred his melancholy imaginings to fantastic designs, fashioned his amorous thoughts into grotesque jewels that pleased their buyers well, they knowing not how

many wives and children were lost in the productions of the
good man, who, the more talent he threw into his art, the
more disordered he became.   Now if God had not had pity
upon him, he would have quitted this world without knowing
what love was, but would have known it in the other without
that metamorphosis of the flesh which spares it, according to
Monsieur Plato, a man of some authority, but who, not being
a Christian, was wrong.   But, there ! these preparatory digressions are the idle digressions and fastidious commentaries
which certain unbelievers compel a man to wind about a tale,
like swaddling clothes about an infant when it should run
about stark naked.   May the great devil give them a clyster
with his red-hot, three-pronged fork.   I am going on with my
story now without further circumlocution.   This is what happened to the silversmith in the one-and-fortieth year of his age.
One Sabbath-day, while walking on the left bank of the Seine,
led by an idle fancy, he ventured as far as that meadow
which has since been called the Pré-aux-Clercs, and which
at that time was in the domain of the abbey of Saint
Germain, and not in that of the University.   There, still
strolling on, the Tourainian found himself in the open fields,
and there met a poor young girl who, seeing that he was
well dressed, curtsied to him, saying, " Heaven preserve you,
monseigneur."   In saying this her voice had such sympa-
thetic sweetness that the silversmith felt his soul ravished by
this feminine melody, and conceived an affection for the
girl, the more so as, tormented with ideas of marriage as he
was, everything was favourable thereto.   Nevertheless, as he
had passed the wench by he dared not go back, because he
was as timid as a young maid who would die in her petticoats rather than raise them for her pleasure.   But when he
was a bowshot off he bethought him that he was a man who
for ten years had been a master silversmith, had become
a citizen, and was a man of mark, and could look a
woman in the face if his fancy so led him, the more so as
his imagination had great power over him.   So he turned
suddenly back, as if he had changed the direction of his
stroll, and came upon the girl, who held by an old cord her

poor cow, who was munching the grass that had grown on the border of a ditch at the side of the road.

"Ah, my pretty one," said he, "you are not over-burdened with the goods of this world that you thus work with your hands upon the Lord's Day. Are you not afraid of being cast into prison?"

"Monseigneur," replied the maid, casting down her eyes, "I have nothing to fear, because I belong to the abbey. The Lord Abbot has given me leave to exercise the cow after vespers."

"You love your cow, then, more than the salvation of your soul?"

"Ah, monseigneur, our beast is almost the half of our poor lives."

"I am astonished, my girl, to see you poor and in rags, clothed like a faggot, running barefoot about the fields on the Sabbath, when you carry about you more treasures than you could dig up in the grounds of the abbey. Do not the townspeople pursue you, and torment you with love?"

"Oh, never, monseigneur. I belong to the abbey," replied she, showing the jeweller a collar on her left arm like those that the beasts of the field have, but without the little bell, and at the same time casting such a deplorable glance at our townsman that he was stricken quite sad, for by the eyes are communicated contagions of the heart when they are strong.

"And what does this mean?" he said, wishing to hear all about it.

And he touched the collar, upon which was engraved the arms of the abbey very distinctly, but which he did not wish to see.

"Monseigneur, I am the daughter of an *homme de corps;* thus, whoever unites himself to me by marriage will become a bondsman, even if he were a citizen of Paris, and would belong body and goods to the abbey. If he loved me otherwise, his children would still belong to the domain. For this reason I am neglected by every one, abandoned like a poor beast of the field. But what makes me most unhappy is, that according to the pleasure of monseigneur the abbot, I shall be coupled at some time with a bondsman. And if I were less ugly than I am, at the sight of my collar the most amorous would flee from me as from the black plague."

So saying, she pulled her cow by the cord to make it follow her.

" And how old are you ?" asked the silversmith.

" I do not know, monseigneur ; but our master, the abbot, has kept account."

This great misery touched the heart of the good man, who had in his day eaten the bread of sorrow. He regulated his pace to the girl's, and they went together towards the water in painful silence. The good man gazed at the fine forehead, the round red arms, the queen's waist, the feet dusty, but made like those of a Virgin Mary ; and the sweet physiognomy of this girl, who was the living image of St. Genevieve, the patroness of Paris, and the maidens who live in the fields. And make sure that this Joseph suspected the pretty white of the sweet girl's breasts, which were by a modest grace carefully covered with an old rag, and looked at them as a schoolboy looks at a rosy apple on a hot day. Also, may you depend upon it that these little hillocks of nature denoted a wench fashioned with delicious perfection, like everything the monks possess. Now, the more it was forbidden our silversmith to touch them, the more his mouth watered for these fruits of love. And his heart leaped almost into his mouth.

" You have a fine cow," said he.

" Would you like a little milk ?" replied she. " It is so warm these early days of May. You are far from the town."

In truth, the sky was a cloudless blue, and glared like a forge. Everything was radiant with youth, the leaves, the air, the girls, the lads ; everything was burning, was green, and smelt like balm. This naïve offer, made without the hope of recompense, though a byzant would not have paid for the special grace of the speech ; and the modesty of the gesture with which the poor girl turned to him gained the heart of the jeweller, who would have liked to be able to put this bondswoman into the skin of a queen, and Paris at her feet.

"Nay, my child, I thirst not for milk, but for you, whom I would have leave to liberate."

"That cannot be, and I shall die the property of the abbey. For years we have lived so, from father to son, from mother to daughter. Like my poor ancestors, I shall pass my days on this land, as will also my children, because the abbot cannot legally let us go."

"What!" said the Tourainian; "has no gallant been tempted by your bright eyes to buy your liberty, as I bought mine from the king?"

"It would cost too dear; thus it is those whom at first sight I please, go as they came."

"And you have never thought of gaining another country in company with a lover on horseback on a fleet courser?"

"Oh yes. But, monsiegneur, if I were caught I should be hanged at least; and my gallant, even were he a lord, would lose more than one domain over it, beside other things. I am not worth so much; besides, the abbey has arms longer than my feet are swift. So I live on in perfect obedience to God, who has placed me in this plight."

"What is your father?"

"He tends the vines in the gardens of the abbey."

"And your mother?"

"She is a washerwoman."

"And what is your name?"

"I have no name, dear sir. My father was baptized Etienne, my mother is Etienne, and I am Tiennette, at your service."

"Sweetheart," said the jeweller, "never has woman pleased me as you please me; and I believe that your heart contains a wealth of goodness. Now, since you offered yourself to my eyes at the moment when I was firmly deliberating upon taking a companion, I believe that I see in you a sign from heaven! and if I am not displeasing to you, I beg you to accept me as your friend."

Immediately the maid lowered her eyes. These words

were uttered in such a way, in so grave a tone, so pene-trating a manner, that the said Tiennette burst into tears.

"No, monseigneur, I should be the cause of a thousand unpleasantnesses, and of your misfortune. For a poor bondsmaid, the conversation has gone far enough."

"Ho!" cried Anseau; "you do not know, my child, the man you are dealing with."

The Tourainian crossed himself, joined his hands, and said—

"I make a vow to Monsieur the Saint Eloi, under whose invocation are the silversmiths, to fashion two images of pure silver, with the best workmanship I am able to perform. One shall be a statue of Madame the Virgin, to this end, to thank her for the liberty of my dear wife; and the other for my said patron, if I am successful in my under-taking to liberate the bondswoman Tiennette here present, and for which I rely upon his assistance. Moreover, I swear by my eternal salvation, to persevere with courage in this affair, to spend therein all I possess, and only to quit it with my life. God has heard me," said he. "And you, little one," he added, turning towards the maid.

"Ha! monseigneur, look! My cow is running about the fields," cried she, sobbing at the good man's knees. "I will love you all my life; but withdraw your vow."

"Let us look after the cow," said the silversmith, raising her, without daring yet to kiss her, although the maid was well disposed to it.

"Yes," said she, "for I shall be beaten."

And behold now the silversmith, scampering after the cursed cow, who gave no heed to their amours; she was taken by the horns, and held in the grip of the Tourainian, who for a trifle could have thrown her in the air, like a straw.

"Adieu, my sweet one! If you go into the town, come to my house, over against Saint Leu's Church. I am called Master Anseau, and am silversmith to the King of France, at the sign of St. Eloi. Make me a promise to be in this field the next Lord's Day; fail not to come, even should it rain halberds."

"Yes, dear sir. For this would I leap the walls, and, in gratitude, would I be yours without mischief, and cause you no sorrow, at the price of my everlasting future. Awaiting the happy moment, I will pray God for you with all my heart."

And then she remained standing like a stone saint, moving not, until she could see the good citizen no longer, and he went away with lagging steps, turning from time to time towards her to gaze upon her. And when he was afar off, and out of her sight, she stayed on, until nightfall, lost in meditation, knowing not if she had dreamed that which had happened to her. Then went she back to the house, where she was beaten for staying out, but felt not the blows. The good silversmith could neither eat nor drink, but closed his workshop, possessed of this girl, thinking of nothing but this girl, seeing everywhere this girl; everything to him being to possess this girl. Now when the morrow was come, went he with great apprehension towards the abbey to speak to the lord abbot. On the road, however, he suddenly thought of putting himself under the protection of one of the king's people, and with this idea returned to the Court, which was then held in the town. Being esteemed by all for his prudence, and loved for his little works and kindnesses, the king's chamberlain—for whom he had once made, for a present to a lady of the Court, a golden casket set with precious stones, and unique of its kind—promised him assistance, had a horse saddled for himself, and a hack for the silversmith, with whom he set out for the abbey, and asked to see the abbot, who was Monseigneur Hugon de Sennecterre, aged ninety-three. Being come into the room with the silversmith, waiting nervously to receive his sentence, the chamberlain begged the abbot to sell him in advance a thing which was easy for him to sell, and which would be pleasant to him.

To which the abbot replied, looking at the chamberlain—

"That the canons inhibited and forbade him thus to engage his word."

" Behold, my dear father," said the chamberlain, " the jeweller of the Court, who has conceived a great love for a

Monseigneur Hugon de Sennecterre, aged Ninety-three

bondswoman belonging to your abbey, and I request you, in consideration of my obliging you in any such desire as you may wish to see accomplished, to emancipate this maid."

"Which is she?" asked the abbot of the citizen.

"Her name is Tiennette," answered the silversmith, timidly.

"Ho! ho!" said the good old Hugon, smiling. "The angler has caught us a good fish! This is a grave business, and I know not how to decide by myself."

"I know, my father, what those words mean," said the chamberlain, knitting his brow.

"Fine sir," said the abbot, "know you what this maid is worth?"

The abbot ordered Tiennette to be fetched, telling his clerk to dress her in her finest clothes, and to make her look as nice as possible.

"Your love is in danger," said the chamberlain to the silversmith, pulling him on one side. "Dismiss this phantasy. You can meet anywhere, even at Court, with women of wealth, young and pretty, who would willingly marry you. For this, if need there be, the king would assist you by giving you some title, which in course of time would enable you to found a good family. Are you sufficiently well furnished with crowns to become the founder of a noble line?"

"I know not, monseigneur," replied Anseau. "I have put money by."

"Then see if you cannot buy the manumission of this maid. I know the monks. With them money does everything."

"Monseigneur," said the silversmith to the abbot, coming towards him, "you have the charge and office of representing here below the goodness of God, who is often clement towards us, and has infinite treasures of mercy for our sorrows. Now, I will remember you each evening and each morning in my prayers, and never forget that I received my happiness at your hands, if you will aid me to gain this maid in lawful wedlock, without keeping in servitude the children born of this union. And for this I will make you a receptacle for the Holy Eucharist, so elaborate, so rich with gold, precious stones, and winged angels, that no other shall be like it in all Christendom. It shall remain unique, it shall dazzle your eyesight, and shall be so far the glory of your altar, that the people of the town and foreign nobles shall rush to see it, so magnificent shall it be."

" My son," replied the abbot, " have you lost your senses ? If you are resolved to have this wench for a legal wife, your goods and your person belong to the Chapter of the abbey."

" Yes, monseigneur, I am passionately in love with this girl, and more touched with her misery and her Christian heart than even with her perfections; but I am," said he, with tears in his eyes, " still more astonished at your harshness, and I say it although I know that my fate is in your hands. Yes, monseigneur, I know the law ; and if my goods fall to your domain, if I become a bondsman, if I lose my house and my citizenship, I will still keep that engine, gained by my labours and my studies, and which lies there," cried he, striking his forehead, " in a place of which no one, save God, can be lord but myself. And your whole abbey could not pay for the special creations which proceed therefrom. You may have my body, my wife, my children, but nothing shall get you my engine ; nay, not even torture, seeing that I am stronger than iron is hard, and more patient than sorrow is great."

So saying, the silversmith, enraged by the calmness of the abbot, who seemed resolved to acquire for the abbey the good man's doubloons, brought down his fist upon an oaken chair, and shivered it into fragments, for it split as under the blow of a mace.

" Behold, monseigneur, what kind of servant you will have, and of an artificer of things divine you will make a mere cart-horse."

" My son," replied the abbot, " you have wrongfully broken my chair, and lightly judged my mind. This wench belongs to the abbey, and not to me. I am the faithful servant of the rights and customs of this glorious monastery ; although

I might grant this woman licence to bear free children, I am responsible for this to God and to the abbey. Now, since there was here an altar, bondsmen and monks, *id est*, from time immemorial, there has never occurred the case of a citizen becoming the property of the abbey by marriage with a bondswoman. Now, therefore, is there need to exercise the right, and to make use of it so that it be not lost, weakened, worn out, or fallen into disuse, which would occasion a thousand difficulties. And this is of a higher advantage to the State and to the abbey than your stones, however beautiful they be, seeing that we have treasure wherewith to buy rare jewels, and that no treasure can establish customs and laws. I call upon the king's chamberlain to bear witness to the infinite pains which his majesty takes every day to fight for the establishment of his orders."

"That is to close my mouth," said the chamberlain.

The silversmith, who was not a great scholar, remained thoughtful. Then came Tiennette, clean as a new pin, her hair raised up, dressed in a robe of white wool with a blue sash, with tiny shoes and white stockings; in fact, so royally beautiful, so noble in her bearing was she, that the silversmith was petrified with ecstasy, and the chamberlain confessed he had never seen so perfect a creature. Thinking there was too much danger in this sight for the poor jeweller, he led him into the town and begged him to think no further of the affair, since the abbey was not likely to liberate so good a bait for the citizens and nobles of the Parisian stream. In fact, the Chapter let the poor lover know that if he married this girl he must resolve to yield up his goods and his house to the abbey, consider himself a bondsman, both he and the children of the aforesaid marriage; although, by a special grace, the abbot would let him his house on the condition of his giving an inventory of his furniture and paying a yearly rent, and coming during eight days to live in a shed adjoining the domain, in order to make it of service. The silversmith, to whom every one spoke of the cupidity of the monks, saw clearly that the abbot would incommutably maintain this order, and his soul was filled with despair. At one time he determined to burn down the monastery ; at another, he proposed co lure the abbot into a place where he could torment him until he had signed a charter for Tiennette's liberation ; in fact, a thousand ideas possessed his brain, and as quickly evaporated. But after much lamentation he determined to carry off the girl, and fly with her into a sure place, from which nothing could draw him, and made his preparations accordingly ; for, once out of the kingdom, his friends or the king could better tackle the monks and bring them to reason. The good man counted, however, without his abbot, for going to the meadows, he found Tiennette no more there, and learned that she was confined in the abbey, and with such rigour, that to get at her it would be necessary to lay siege to the monastery. Then Master Anseau passed his time in tears, complaints, and lamentations ; and all the city, the townspeople, and the housewives, talked of his adventure, the noise of which was so great, that the king sent for the old abbot to court, and demanded of him why he did not yield under the circumstances to the great love of his silver-smith, and why he did not put into practice Christian charity.

"Because, monseigneur," replied the prince, "all rights are knit together like the pieces of a coat of mail, and if one makes default, all fail. If this girl were taken from us against our wish, and if the custom were not observed, your subjects would soon take off your crown, and raise up in various places violence and sedition, in order to abolish the taxes and imposts that weigh upon the populace."

The king's mouth was closed. Every one was eager to know the end of this adventure. So great was the curiosity that certain lords wagered that the Tourainian would desist from his love, and the ladies wagered the contrary. The silversmith having complained to the queen that the monks had hidden his well-beloved from his sight, she found the deed detestable and horrible ; and in consequence of her commands to the lord abbot it was permitted to the Tourainian to go every day into the parlour of the abbey, where came Tiennette, but under the control of an old monk, and she always came attired in great splendour like a lady. The two lovers had no other licence than to see each other, and to speak to each other, without being able to snatch the smallest atom of pleasure, and always grew their love more powerful.

One day Tiennette discoursed thus with her lover— " My dear lord, I have determined to make you a gift of my life, in order to relieve your suffering, and in this wise : in informing myself concerning everything I have found a means to set aside the rights of the abbey, and to give you all the joy you hope for from my fruition.

" The ecclesiastical judge has ruled that as you become a bondsman only by accession, and because you were not born a bondsman, your servitude will cease with the cause that made you a serf. Now, if you love me more than all else, lose your goods to purchase our happiness, and espouse me. Then when you have had your will of me, when you have hugged me and embraced me to your heart's content, before I have offspring will I voluntarily kill myself, and thus you will become free again ; at least, you will have the king on your side, who, it is said, wishes you well. And, without doubt, God will pardon me that I cause my own death, in order to deliver my lord spouse."

" My dear Tiennette," cried the jeweller, "it is finished— I will be a bondsman, and thou wilt live to make my happiness as long as my days. In thy company, the hardest chains will weigh but lightly, and little shall I reck the want of gold, when all my riches are in thy heart, and my only pleasure in thy sweet body. I place myself in the hands of St. Eloi, who will deign in this misery to look upon us with pitying eyes, and guard us from all evils. Now I shall go hence to a scrivener to have the deeds and contracts drawn up. At least, dear flower of my days, thou shalt be gorgeously attired, well housed, and served like a queen during thy lifetime, since the lord abbot leaves me the earnings of my profession."

Tiennette, crying and laughing, tried to put off her good fortune, and wished to die, rather than reduce to slavery a free man ; but the good Anseau whispered such soft words to her, and threatened so firmly to follow her to the tomb, that she agreed to the said marriage, thinking that she could always free herself after having tasted the pleasures of love.

When the submission of the Tourainian became known in the town, and that for his sweetheart he yielded up his wealth and his liberty, every one wished to see him. The ladies of the court encumbered themselves with jewels, in order to speak with him, and there fell upon him as from the clouds, women enough to make up for the time he had been without them ; but if any of them approached Tiennette in beauty, none had her heart. To be brief, when the hour of slavery and love was at hand, Anseau moulded all his gold into a royal crown, in which he fixed all his pearls and diamonds, and went secretly to the queen, and gave it her, saying, " Madame, I know not how to dispose of my fortune, which you here behold. To-morrow everything that is found in my house will be the property of the cursed monks, who have had no pity on me. Then deign, madame, to accept this. It is a slight return for the joy which, through you, I have experienced in seeing her I love ; for no sum of money is worth one of her glances. I do not know what will become of me, but if one day my children are delivered, I rely upon your queenly generosity."

" Well said, good man," cried the king. " The abbey will one day need my aid, and I will not lose the remembrance of this."

There was a vast crowd at the abbey for the nuptials of Tiennette, to whom the queen presented the bridal dress, and to whom the king granted a licence to wear every day golden rings in her ears. When the charming pair came from the abbey to the house of Anseau (now the serf) over against St. Leu, there were torches at the window to see them pass, and a double line in the streets, as though it were a royal entry. The poor husband had made himself a collar of gold, which he wore on his left arm in token of his belonging to the abbey of St. Germain. But in spite of his servitude the people cried out, " Noël ! Noël !" as to a new crowned king. And the good man bowed to them grace-

fully, happy as a lover, and joyful at the homage which
every one rendered to the grace and modesty of Tiennette.
Then the good Tourainian found green boughs and violets
in crowns in his honour ; and the principal inhabitants of
the quarter were all there, who, as a great honour, played
music to him, and cried to him, " You will always be a
noble man in spite of the abbey." You may be sure that the
happy pair indulged in amorous conflict to their heart's content ; that the good man's blows were vigorous ; and that
his sweetheart, like a good country maiden, was of a nature
to return them. Thus they lived together a whole month,
happy as the doves, who in spring-time build their nest
twig by twig. Tiennette was delighted with the beautiful
house and the customers, who came and went away
astonished at her. This month of flowers passed, there
came one day, with great pomp, the good old Abbot Hugon,
their lord and master, who entered the house, which then
belonged not to the jeweller, but to the Chapter, and said to
the two spouses :—" My children, you are released, free and
quit of everything ; and I should tell you that from the first
I was much struck with the love which united you one to
the other. The rights of the abbey once recognised, I
was, so far as I was concerned, determined to restore you
to perfect enjoyment, after having proved your loyalty by
the test of God. And this manumission will cost you
nothing." Having thus said, he gave them each a little tap
with his hand on the cheek. And they fell about his knees
weeping tears of joy for such good reasons. The Tourainian informed the people of the neighbourhood, who picked
up in the streets the largesse, and received the benedictions
of the good Abbot Hugon.

Then with great honour, Master Anseau held the reins of
his mule, as far as the gate of Bussy. During the journey
the jeweller, who had taken a bag of silver, threw the pieces
to the poor and suffering, crying, " Largesse, largesse to
God ! God save and guard the abbot ! Long live the good
Lord Hugon !" And returning to his house he regaled his
friends, and had fresh wedding festivities, which lasted a
fortnight. You can imagine that the abbot was reproached

by the Chapter, for his clemency in opening the door for
such good prey to escape, so that when a year after the
good man Hugon fell ill, his prior told him that it was a
punishment from Heaven, because he had neglected the
sacred interests of the Chapter and of God. " If I have
judged that man aright," said the abbot, " he will not forget
what he owes us."

In fact, this day happening by chance to be the anni-
versary of the marriage, a monk came to announce that the
silversmith supplicated his benefactor to receive him.
Soon he entered the room where the abbot was, and spread
out before him two marvellous shrines, which since that time
no workman has surpassed, in any portion of the Christian
world, and which were named the " *Vow of a Steadfast
Love.*" These two treasures are, as every one knows, placed
on the principal altar of the church, and are esteemed as an
inestimable work, for the silversmith had spent thereon all
his wealth. Nevertheless, this work, far from emptying his
purse, filled it full to overflowing, because so rapidly
increased his fame and his fortune that he was able to buy
a patent of nobility and lands, and he founded the house of
Anseau, which has since been held in great honour in fair
Touraine.

This teaches us to have always recourse to God and the
saints in all the undertakings of life, to be steadfast in all
good things, and, above all, that a great love triumphs over
everything, which is an old sentence ; but the author has re-
written it, because it is a most pleasant one.

CONCERNING A PROVOST WHO DID
NOT RECOGNISE THINGS.

IN the good town of Bourges, at the time when that lord
the king disported himself there, who afterwards abandoned his search after pleasure to conquer the kingdom,
and did indeed conquer it, there lived a provost, entrusted
by him with the maintenance of order, and called the
provost-royal. From which came, under the glorious son of
the said king, the office of provost of the hotel, in which behaved rather harshly my lord Tristan of Méré, of whom
these tales oft make mention, although he was by no
means a merry fellow. I give this information to the friends
who pilfer from old manuscripts to manufacture new ones,
and I show thereby how learned these Tales really are,

without appearing to be so. Very well, then, this provost was named Picot or Picault, of which some made *picottin*, *picoter*, and *picorée;* by some Pitot or Pitaut, from which came *pitance*; by others, in Languedoc, Pichot, from which nothing comes worth knowing, by these Petiot or Petiet; by those Petitot and Petinault, or Petiniaud, which was the masonic appellation; but at Bourges he was called Petit, a name which was eventually adopted by the family, which has multiplied exceedingly, for everywhere you find " des Petits," and so he will be called Petit in this narrative. I have given this etymology in order to throw a light on our language, and show how our citizens have finished by acquiring names. But enough of science. This said provost, who had as many names as there were provinces into which the court went, was in reality a little bit of a man, whose

mother had given him so strange a hide, that when he wanted to laugh he used to stretch his cheeks like a cow making water, and this smile at court was called the provost's smile. One day the king, hearing this proverbial expression used by certain lords, said, jokingly, " You are in error, gentlemen, Petit does not laugh, he's short of skin below the mouth." But with his false laugh, Petit was all the more suited to his occupation of watching and catching evil-doers. In fact, he was worth what he cost. For all malice, he was a bit of a cuckold, for all vice, he went to vespers ; for all wisdom he obeyed God, when it was convenient ; for all joy he had a wife in his house ; and for all change in his joy he looked for a man to hang, and when he was asked to find one he never failed to meet him ; but when he was between the sheets he never troubled himself about thieves. Can you find in all Christendom a more virtuous provost ? No ! All provosts hang too little, or too much, while this one just hanged as much as was necessary to be a provost. This good fellow had for his wife in legitimate marriage, and much to the astonishment of every

one, the prettiest little woman in Bourges. So it was that
often, while on his road to the execution, he would ask God
the same question as several others in the town did—
namely, why he, Petit, he the sheriff, he the provost royal, had

to himself, Petit, provost royal and sheriff, a wife so exquisitely shaped, so dowered with charms, that a donkey
seeing her pass by would bray with delight. To this God
vouchsafed no reply, and doubtless had His reasons. But
the slanderous tongues of the town replied for Him, that the
young lady was by no means a maiden when she became the
wife of Petit. Others said that she did not keep her affections solely for him. The wags answered, that donkeys
often got into fine stables. Every one had taunts ready
which would have made a nice little collection had any one
gathered them together. From them, however, it is necessary to take nearly four-fourths, seeing that Petit's wife was
a virtuous woman, who had a lover for pleasure and a
husband for duty. How many were there in the town as

careful of their hearts and mouths? If you can point out one to me, I'll give you a kick or a halfpenny, whichever you like. You will find some who have neither husband nor lover. Certain females have a lover and no husband. Ugly women have a husband and no lover. But to meet with a woman who, having one husband and one lover, keeps to the deuce without trying for the trey, there is the miracle, you see, you greenhorns, blockheads, and dolts! Now then, put the true character of this virtuous woman on the tablets of your memory, go your ways, and let me go mine. The good Madame Petit was not one of those ladies who are always on the move, running hither and thither, can't keep still a moment, but trot about, worrying, hurrying, chattering, and clattering, and have nothing in them to keep them steady, but are so light that they run after a gastric zephyr as after their quintessence. No; on the contrary, she was a good housewife, always sitting in her chair or sleeping in her bed, ready as a candlestick, waiting for her lover when her

husband went out, receiving the husband when the lover had gone. This dear woman never thought of dressing herself only to annoy and make other wives jealous. Pish! she had found a better use for the merry time of youth, and put life into her joints in order to make the best use of it. Now **you** know the provost and his good wife. The provost's

lieutenant in duties matrimonial, duties which are so heavy
that it takes two men to execute them, was a noble lord, a
landowner, who disliked the king exceedingly. You must
bear this in mind, because it is one of the principal points of
the story. The constable, who was a rough Scotch gentleman, had seen by chance Petit's wife, and wished to have a
little conversation with her comfortably, towards the morning, just the time to tell his beads, which was Christianly
honest, or honestly Christian, in order to argue with her
concerning the things of science or the
science of things. Thinking herself quite
learned enough, Madame Petit, who was,
as has been stated, a virtuous, wise, and
honest wife, refused to listen to the said
constable. After certain arguments, reasonings, tricks, and messages, which
were of no avail, he swore by his great
black *coquedouille* that he would rip up
the gallant although he was a man of mark. But he swore
nothing about the lady. This denotes a good Frenchman,
for in such a dilemma there are certain offended persons
who would upset the whole business of three persons by
killing four. The constable wagered his big, black coquedouille before the king and the lady of Sorel, who were
playing cards before supper; and his majesty was well
pleased, because he would be relieved of this noble, who
displeased him, and that without costing him a *Thank you.*

"And how will you manage the affair?" said Madame
de Sorel to him, with a smile.

"Oh, oh!" replied the constable. "You may be sure,
madame, I do not wish to lose my big black coquedouille."

"What was, then, this great coquedouille?"

"Ha, ha! This point is shrouded in darkness to a
degree that would make you ruin your eyes in ancient
books; but it was certainly something of great importance.
Nevertheless, let us put on our spectacles, and search it
out. *Douille* signifies, in Brittany, a girl, and *coque* means
a cook's frying pan. From this word has come into France

that of *coquin*—a knave who eats, licks, laps, sucks, and fritters his money away, and gets into stews ; is always in hot water, and eats up everything, leads an idle life, and doing this, becomes wicked, becomes poor, and that incites him to steal or to beg. From this it may be concluded by the learned that the great coquedouille was a household utensil in the shape of a kettle, used for cooking things."

" Well," continued the constable, who was the Sieur de Richmond, " I will have the husband ordered to go into the country for a day and a night, to arrest certain peasants suspected of plotting treacherously with the English. Thereupon my two pigeons, believing their man absent, will be as merry as soldiers off duty ; and, if a certain thing takes place, I will let loose the provost, sending him, in the king's name, to search the house where the couple will be, in order that he may slay our friend, who pretends to have this good cordelier* all to himself."

" What does this mean ?" said the Lady of Beauté.

" Equivoque," answered the king, smiling.

" Come to supper," said Madame Agnes. " You are bad men, who with one word insult both the citizens' wives and a holy order."

Now, for a long time, Madame Petit had longed to have a night of liberty, during which she might visit the house of the said noble, where she could make as much noise as she liked without waking the neighbours, because at the provost's house she was afraid of being overheard, and had to content herself well with the pilferings of love, little tastes, and nibbles, daring at the most only to trot, while what she desired was a smart gallop. On the morrow, therefore, the lady's-maid went off about midday to the young lord's house, and told the lover—from whom she received many presents, and therefore in no way disliked him—that he might make his preparations for pleasure, and for supper,

---

* *Cordelier*, a Franciscan friar. The allusion is, of course, to the professional " cord" of the husband. There is not sufficient agreement between the French and English languages to give this passage its full force in the translation.

for that he might rely upon the provost's better half being with him in the evening, both hungry and thirsty.

"Good!" said he. "Tell your mistress I will not stint her in anything she desires."

The pages of the cunning constable, who were watching the house, seeing the gallant prepare for his gallantries, and set out the flagons and the meats, went and informed their master that everything had happened as he wished. Hearing this, the good constable rubbed his hands, thinking how nicely the provost would catch the pair. He instantly sent word to him, that by the king's express commands he was to return to town, in order that he might seize at the said lord's house an English nobleman, with whom he was vehemently suspected to be arranging a plot of diabolical darkness. But before he put this order into into execution, he was to come to the king's hotel, in order that he might understand the courtesy to be exercised in this case. The provost, joyous at the chance of speaking to the king, used such diligence that he was in town just at the time when the two lovers were singing the first note of their evening hymn. The lord of cuckoldom and its surrounding lands, who is a strange lord, managed things so well, that madame was only conversing with her lord lover at the time that her lord spouse was talking to the constable and the king ; at which he was pleased, and so was his wife —a case of concord rare in matrimony.

"I was saying to monseigneur," said the constable to the provost, as he entered the king's apartment, "that every man in the kingdom has a right to kill his wife and her lover if he find them in an act of infidelity. But his majesty, who is clement, argues that he has only a right to kill the man, and not the woman. Now what would you do, Mr. Provost, if by chance you found a gentleman taking a stroll in that fair meadow of which laws, human and divine, enjoin you alone to cultivate the verdure?"

"I would kill everything," said the provost; "I would scrunch the five hundred thousand devils of nature, flower and seed, and send them flying, the pips and the apples, the grass and the meadow, the woman and the man."

"You would be in the wrong," said the king. "That is contrary to the laws of the Church and of the State; of the State, because you might deprive me of a subject; of the Church, because you would be sending an innocent to limbo unshriven."

"Sire, I admire your profound wisdom, and I clearly perceive you to be the centre of all justice."

"We can then only kill the knight—*Amen,*" said the constable, "kill the horseman. Now go quickly to the house of the suspected lord, but without letting yourself be bamboozled, do not forget what is due to his position."

The provost, believing he would certainly be Chancellor of France if he properly acquitted himself of his task, went from the castle into the town, took his men, arrived at the nobleman's residence, arranged his people outside, placed guards at all the doors, opened noiselessly by order of the king, climbs the stairs, asks the servants in which room their master is, puts them under arrest, goes up alone, and knocks at the door of the room where the two lovers are tilting in love's tournament, and says to them—

"Open, in the name of our lord the king!"

The lady recognised her husband's voice, and could not repress a smile, thinking that she had not waited for the king's order to do what she had done. But after laughter came terror. Her lover took his cloak, threw it over him, and came to the door. There, not knowing that his life was in peril, he declared that he belonged to the court and to the king's household.

"Bah!" said the provost. "I have strict orders from the king; and under pain of being treated as a rebel, you are bound instantly to receive me."

Then the lord went out to him, still holding the door.

"What do you want here?"

"An enemy of our lord the king, whom we command you to deliver into our hands, otherwise you must follow me with him to the castle."

This, thought the lover, is a piece of treachery on the part of the constable, whose propositions my dear mistress treated with scorn. We must get out of this scrape in some way. Then turning towards the provost, he went double or quits on the risk, reasoning thus with the cuckold :—

"My friend, you know that I consider you to be as gallant a man as it is possible for a provost to be in the discharge of his duty. Now, can I have confidence in you? I have here with me the fairest lady of the court. As for Englishmen, I have not sufficient of one to make the breakfast of the constable, M. de Richmond, who sends you here. This is (to be candid with you) the result of a bet made between myself and the constable, who shares it with the king. Both have wagered that they know who is the lady of my heart; and I have wagered to the contrary. No one more than myself hates the English, who took my estates in Picardy. Is it not a knavish trick to put justice in motion against me? Ho! ho! my lord constable, a chamberlain is worth two of you, and I will beat you yet. My dear Petit, I give you permission to search by night and by day, every nook and cranny of my house. But come in here alone, search my room, turn the bed over, do what you like. Only allow me to cover with a cloth or a handkerchief this fair lady, who is at present in the costume of an archangel, in order that you may not know to what husband she belongs.

"Willingly," said the provost. "But I am an old bird, not easily caught with chaff, and would like to be sure that it is really a lady of the court, and not an Englishman, for these English have flesh as white and soft as women, and I know it well, because I've hanged so many of them."

"Well, then," said the lord, "seeing of what crime I am suspected, from which I am bound to free myself, I will go and ask my lady-love to consent for a moment to abandon her modesty. She is too fond of me to refuse to save me from reproach. I will beg her to turn herself over and show you a physiognomy, which will in no way compromise her, and will be sufficient to enable you to recognise a noble woman, although she will be in a sense upside down."

"All right," said the provost.

The lady having heard every word, had folded up all her clothes, and put them under the bolster, had taken off her chemise, that her husband should not recognise it, had twisted her head up in a sheet, and had brought to light the carnal convexities which commenced where her spine finished.

"Come in, my friend," said the lord.

The provost looked up the chimney, opened the cupboard, the clothes' chest, felt under the bed, in the sheets, and everywhere. Then he began to study what was on the bed.

"My lord," said he, regarding his legitimate appurtenances, "I have seen young English lads with backs like that. You must forgive me doing my duty, but I must see otherwise."

"What do you call otherwise?" said the lord.

"Well, the other physiognomy, or, if you prefer it, the physiognomy of the other."

"Then you will allow madame to cover herself and arrange only to show you sufficient to convince you," said the lover, knowing that the lady had a mark or two easy to recognise. "Turn your back a moment, so that my dear lady may satisfy propriety."

The wife smiled at her lover, kissed him for his dexterity, arranged herself cunningly; and the husband seeing in full that which the jade had never let him see before, was quite convinced that no English person could be thus fashioned without being a charming Englishwoman.

"Yes, my lord," he whispered in the ear of his lieutenant, "this is certainly a lady of the court, because the towns-women are neither so well formed nor so charming."

Then the house being thoroughly searched, and no Englishman found, the provost returned, as the constable had told him, to the king's residence.

"Is he slain?" said the constable.

"Who?"

"He who grafted horns upon your forehead."

"I only saw a lady in his couch, who seemed to be greatly enjoying herself with him."

"You, with your own eyes, saw this woman, cursed cuckold, and you did not kill your rival?"

"It was not a common woman, but a lady of the court."

" You saw her ?"

" And verified her in both cases."

" What do you mean by those words?" cried the king, who was bursting with laughter.

" I say, with all the respect due to your majesty, that I have verified the over and the under."

" You do not, then, know the physiognomies of your own wife, you old fool without memory! You deserve to be hanged."

"I hold those features of my wife in too great respect to gaze upon them. Besides, she is so modest that she would die rather than expose an atom of her body."

"True," said the king; " it was not made to be shown."

" Old *coquedouille!* that was your wife," said the constable.

" My lord constable, she is asleep, poor girl!"

" Quick, quick, then ! To horse ! Let us be off, and if she be in your house I'll forgive you."

Then the constable, followed by the provost, went to the latter's house in less time than it would have taken a beggar to empty the poor-box. " Hullo ! there, hi !" Hearing the noise made by the men, which threatened to bring the walls about their ears, the maid-servant opened the door, yawning and stretching her arms. The constable and the provost rushed into the room, where, with great difficulty, they succeeded in waking the lady, who pretended to be terrified, and was so soundly asleep that her eyes were full of gum. At this the provost was in great glee, saying to the constable that some one had certainly deceived him, that his wife was a virtuous woman, and was more astonished than any of them at these proceedings. The constable turned on his heel and departed. The good provost began directly to undress to get to bed early, since this adventure had brought his good wife to his memory. When he was unharnessing himself, and was knocking off his nether garments, madame, still astonished, said to him—

"Oh, my dear husband, what is the meaning of all this uproar—this constable and his pages, and why did he come to see if I was asleep? Is it to be henceforward part of a constable's duty to look after our . . . . ."

"I do not know," said the provost, interrupting her, to tell her what had happened to him.

"And you saw without my permission a lady of the court! Ha! ha! heu! heu! hein!" Then she began to moan, to weep, and to cry in such a deplorable manner and so loudly, that her lord was quite aghast.

"What's the matter, my darling? What is it? What do you want?"

"Ah, you wont love me any more after seeing how beautiful court ladies are!"

"Nonsense, my child! They are great ladies. I don't mind telling you in confidence; they are great ladies in every respect."

"Well," said she, "am I nicer?"

"Ah," said he, "in a great measure. Yes!"

"They have, then, great happiness," said she, sighing, "when I have so much with so little beauty."

Thereupon the provost tried a better argument to argue with his good wife, and argued so well that she finished by allowing herself to be convinced that Heaven has ordained that much pleasure may be obtained from small things.

This shows us that nothing here below can prevail against the Church of cuckolds.

ABOUT THE MONK AMADOR,

WHO WAS A GLORIOUS ABBOT OF TURPENAY.

ONE day that it was drizzling with rain—a time when the ladies remain gleefully at home, because they love the damp, and can have at their apronstrings the men who are not disagreeable to them—the queen was in her chamber, at the castle of Amboise, against the window curtains. There, seated in her chair, she was working at a piece of tapestry to amuse herself, but was using her needle heedlessly, watching the rain fall into the Loire, and was lost in thought, where her ladies were following her example. The king was arguing with those of his Court who had accompanied him from the chapel—for it was a question of returning to dominical vespers. His arguments, statements, and reasonings finished, he looked at the queen, saw that she was melancholy, saw that the ladies were melancholy also, and noted the fact that they were all acquainted with the mysteries of matrimony.

"Did I not see the Abbot of Turpenay here just now?" said he.

Hearing these words, there advanced towards the king the monk, who, by his constant petitions, rendered himself so obnoxious to Louis the Eleventh, that that monarch seriously commanded his provost-royal to remove him from his sight; and it has been related in the first volume of these Tales, how the monk was saved through the mistake of Sieur Tristran. The monk was at this time a man whose qualities had grown rapidly, so much so that his wit had communicated a jovial hue to his face. He was a

The Monk Amador, who was a glorious Abbot of Turpenay.

great favourite with the ladies, who crammed him with wine, confectioneries, and dainty dishes at the dinners, suppers, and merry-makings, to which they invited him, because every host likes those cheerful guests of God with nimble jaws, who say as many words as they put away tit-bits. This abbot was a pernicious fellow, who would relate to the ladies many a merry tale, at which they were only offended when they had heard them; since, to judge them, things must be heard.

"My reverend father," said the king, "behold the twilight hour, in which ears feminine may be regaled with certain pleasant stories, for the ladies can laugh without blushing, or blush without laughing, as it suits them best. Give us a good story—a regular monk's story. I shall listen to it, i' faith, with pleasure, because I want to be amused, and so do the ladies."

"We only submit to this, in order to please your lordship," said the queen; "because our good friend the abbot goes a little too far."

"Then," replied the king, turning towards the monk, "read us some Christian admonition, holy father, to amuse madame."

" Sire, my sight is weak, and the day is closing."

" Give us a story, then, that stops at the girdle."

"Ah, sire!" said the monk, smiling, "the one I am thinking of stops there; but it commences at the feet."

The lords present made such gallant remonstrances and supplications to the queen and her ladies, that, like the good Bretonne that she was, she gave the monk a gentle smile, and said—

"As you will, my father; but you must answer to God for our sins."

"Willingly, madame; if it be your good pleasure to take mine, you will be a gainer."

Every one laughed, and so did the queen. The king went and sat by his dear wife, well beloved by him, as every one knows. The courtiers received permission to be seated—the old courtiers, of course, understood; for the young ones stood, by the ladies' permission, beside their chairs, to laugh at the same time as they did. Then the Abbot of Turpenay gracefully delivered himself of the following tale, the risky passages of which he gave in a low, soft, and flute-like voice :—

About a hundred years ago at the least, there occurred great quarrels in Christendom because there were two popes at Rome, each one pretending to be legitimately elected, which caused great annoyance to the monasteries, abbeys, and bishoprics, since, in order to be recognised by as many as possible, each of the two popes granted titles and rights to his adherents, the which made double owners everywhere. Under these circumstances, the monasteries and abbeys that were at war with their neighbours would not recognise both the popes, and found themselves much embarrassed by the others, who always gave the verdict to the enemies of the Chapter. This wicked schism brought about considerable mischief, and proved abundantly that no error is worse in Christianity than the adultery of the Church.

Now at this time, when the devil was making havoc among our possessions, the most illustrious abbey of Turpenay, of which I am at present the unworthy ruler, had a heavy trial on concerning the settlement of certain rights with the redoubtable Sire de Candé, an idolatrous infidel, a relapsed heretic, and most wicked lord. This devil, sent upon earth in the shape of a nobleman, was, to tell the truth, a good soldier, well received at Court, and a friend of the Sieur Bureau de la Rivière, who was a person to whom the king was exceedingly partial—King Charles the Fifth, of glorious memory. Beneath the shelter of the favour of this Sieur de la Rivière, the Lord of Candé did exactly as he pleased in the valley of the Indre, where he used to be master of everything, from Montbazon to Ussé. You may be sure that his neighbours were terribly afraid of him, and to save their skulls let him have his way. They would, however, have preferred him under the ground to above it, and heartily wished him bad luck; but he troubled himself little about that. In the whole valley the noble abbey alone showed fight to this demon, for it has always been a doctrine of the Church to take into her lap the weak and suffering, and use every effort to protect the oppressed, especially those whose rights and privileges are menaced. For this reason this rough warrior hated monks exceedingly, especially those of Turpenay, who would not allow themselves to be robbed of their rights either by force or stratagem. He was well pleased at the ecclesiastical schism, and waited the decision of our abbey, concerning which pope they should choose, to pillage them, being quite ready to recognise the one to whom the Abbot of Turpenay should refuse his obedience. Since his return to his castle, it was his custom to torment and annoy the priests whom he encountered upon his domains in such a manner, that a poor monk, surprised by him on his private road, which was by the water-side, perceived no other method of safety than to throw himself into the river, where, by a special miracle of the Almighty, whom the good man fervently invoked, his gown floated him on the Indre, and he made his way comfortably to the other side, which he attained in full view of the Lord of Candé, who was not ashamed to enjoy the terrors of a servant of God. Now you see of what stuff this horrid man was made. The abbot, to whom, at that time, the care of our glorious abbey was committed, led a most holy life, and prayed to God with devotion; but he would have saved his own soul ten times, of such good quality was his religion, before finding a chance to save the abbey itself from the clutches of this wretch. Although he was very perplexed, and saw the

A poor monk, surprised by him on his private road, which was by the water-side, perceived no other method of safety than to throw himself into the river.

evil hour at hand, he relied upon God for succour, saying
that he would never allow the property of his Church to be
touched, and that He who had raised up the Princess Judith
for the Hebrews, and Queen Lucretia for the Romans,
would keep his most illustrious abbey of Turpenay, and
indulged in other equally sapient remarks. But his monks,
who—to our shame I confess it—were unbelievers, reproached him with his happy-go-lucky way of looking at
things, and declared that, to bring the chariot of Providence
to the rescue in time, all the oxen in the province would
have to be yoked to it ; that the trumpets of Jericho were no
longer made in any portion of the world ; that God was
disgusted with His creation, and would have nothing more
to do with it ; in short, a thousand and one things that were
doubts and contumelies against God. At this desperate
juncture there rose up a monk named Amador. This
name had been given him by way of a joke, since his person
offered a perfect portrait of the false god Ægipan. He
was like him, strong in the stomach ; like him, had crooked
legs ; arms hairy as those of a saddler, a back made to
carry a wallet, a face as red as the phiz of a drunkard,
glistening eyes, a tangled beard, was hairy faced, and so
puffed out with fat and meat that you would have fancied
him in an interesting condition. You may be sure that he
sung his matins on the steps of the wine-cellar, and said his
vespers in the vineyards of the Lord. He was as fond of
his bed as a beggar with sores, and would go about the
valley fuddling, faddling, blessing the bridals, plucking the
grapes, and giving them to the girls to taste, in spite of the
prohibition of the abbot. In fact, he was a pilferer, a
loiterer, and a bad soldier of the ecclesiastical militia, of
whom nobody in the abbey took any notice, but let him do
as he liked from motives of Christian charity, thinking him
mad. Amador, knowing that it was a question of the ruin
of the abbey, in which he was as snug as a bug in a rug,
put up his bristles, took notice of this and of that, went into
each of the cells, listened in the refectory, shivered in his
shoes, and declared that he would attempt to save the
abbey. He took cognisance of the contested points. re-

ceived from the abbot permission to postpone the case, and
was promised by the whole Chapter the vacant office of sub-
prior if he succeeded in putting an end to the litigation.
Then he set off across the country, heedless of the cruelty
and ill treatment of the Sieur de Candé, saying that he had
that within his gown which would subdue them. He went
his way with nothing but this said gown for his viaticum ;
but then in it was enough fat to feed a dwarf. He selected
to go to the château, a day when it rained hard enough to
fill the tubs of all the housewives, and arrived without meeting a soul, in sight of Candé, and looking like a drowned dog,
stepped bravely into the courtyard, and took shelter under
a stye-roof to wait until the fury of the elements had calmed
down, and placed himself boldly in front of the room where
the owner of the château should be. A servant perceiving
him while laying the supper, took pity on him, and told him
to make himself scarce, otherwise his master would give him
a horsewhipping, just to open the conversation, and asked
him what made him so bold as to enter a house where
monks were hated more than a red leper.

"Ah !" said Amador, "I am on my way to Tours, sent
thither by my lord abbot. If the Lord of
Candé were not so bitter against the poor
servants of God, I should not be kept
during such a deluge in the courtyard, but
in the house. I hope that he will find
mercy in his hour of need."

The servant reported these words to his
master, who at first wished to have the
monk thrown into the big trough of the castle among the
other filth. But the lady of Candé, who had great authority
over her spouse, and was respected by him, because through
her he expected a large inheritance, and because she was
a little tyrannical, reprimanded him,
saying, that it was possible this monk
was a Christian ; that in such weather
thieves would succour an officer of
justice ; that, besides, it was necessary to treat him well to find out to

what decision the brethren of Turpenay had come with regard to the schism business, and that her advice was to put an end by kindness and not by force to the difculties arisen between the abbey and the domain of Candé, because no lord since the coming of Christ had ever been stronger than the Church, and that sooner or later the abbey would ruin the castle ; finally, she gave utterance to a thousand wise arguments, such as ladies use in the height of the storms of life, when they have had about enough of them. Amador's face was so piteous, his appearance so wretched and so open to banter, that the lord, saddened by the weather, conceived the idea of enjoying a joke at his expense, tormenting him, playing tricks on him, and of giving him a lively recollection of his reception at the château. Then this gentleman, who had secret relations with his wife's maid, sent this girl, who was called Perrotte, to put an end to his ill-will towards the luckless Amador. As soon as the plot had been arranged between them, the wench, who hated monks, in order to please her master, went to the monk, who was standing under the pigstye, and assuming a courteous demeanour in order the better to please him, said—

" Holy father, the master of this house is ashamed to see a servant of God out in the rain when there is room for him in doors, a good fire in the chimney, and a table spread. I invite you in his name and that of the lady of the house to step in."

" I thank the lady and the lord, not for their hospitality, which is a Christian thing, but for having sent as an ambassador to me, a poor sinner, an angel of such delicate beauty that I fancy I see the Virgin over our altar."

Saying which, Amador raised his nose in the air, and saluted with the two flakes of fire that sparkled in his bright eyes the pretty maidservant, who thought him neither so ugly nor so foul, nor so bestial : when, following Perrotte up the steps, Amador received on the nose, cheeks, and other portions of his face a slash of the whip, which made him see all the lights of the *Magnificat*, so well was the dose administered by the Sieur de Candé, who, busy chastening his greyhounds,

pretended not to see the monk.   He requested Amador to
pardon him this accident, and ran after the dogs who had
caused the mischief to his guest.   The laughing servant, who
knew what was coming, had dexterously kept out of the
way.   Noticing this business, Amador suspected the relations
of Perrotte and the chevalier, concerning whom it is possible
that the lasses of the valley had already whispered something
into his ear.   Of the people who were then in the room
not one made room for the man of God, who remained right
in the draught between the door and the window, where he
stood freezing until the moment when the Sire de Candé,
his wife, and his aged sister, Mademoiselle de Candé, who
had the charge of the young heiress of the house, aged about
sixteen years, came and sat in their chairs at the head of the
table, far from the common people, according to the old
custom usual among the lords of the period, much to their
discredit.   The Sire de Candé, paying no attention to the
monk, let him sit at the extreme end of the table, in a
corner, where two mischievous lads had orders to squeeze
and elbow him.   Indeed, these fellows worried his feet, his
body, and his arms like real torturers, poured white wine
into his goblet for water, in order to fuddle him, and the
better to amuse themselves with him ; but they made him
drink seven large jugfuls without making him belch, break
wind, sweat, or snort, which horrified them exceedingly,
especially as his eye remained as clear as crystal.   En-
couraged, however, by a glance from their lord, they still
kept on throwing, while bowing to him, gravy into his
beard, and wiping it dry in a manner to tear every hair
of it out.   The varlet who served a caudle baptized his head
with it, and took care to let the burning liquor trickle down
poor Amador's backbone.   All this agony he endured with
meekness, because the Spirit of God was in him, and also the
hope of finishing the litigation by holding out in the castle.
Nevertheless, the mischievous lot burst out into such roars
of laughter at the warm baptism given by the cook's lad to
the soaked monk, even the butler making jokes at his expense, that the lady of Candé was compelled to notice what
was going on at the end of the table.   Then she perceived

Amador, who had a look of sublime resignation upon his face, and was endeavouring to get something out of the big beef bones that had been put upon his pewter platter. At this moment the poor monk, who had administered a dexterous blow of the knife to a big ugly bone, took it in his hairy hands, snapped it in two, sucked the warm marrow out of it, and found it good. "Truly," said she to herself, "God has put great strength into this monk !" At the same time she seriously forbade the pages, servants, and others to torment the poor man, to whom out of mockery they had just given some rotten apples and maggoty nuts. He, perceiving that the old lady and her charge, the lady and the servants had seen him manœuvring the bone, pushed back his sleeve, showed the powerful muscles of his arm, placed the nuts near his wrist on the bifurcation of the veins, and crushed them one by one by pressing them with the palm of his hand so vigorouly that they appeared like ripe medlars. He also crunched them between his teeth, white as the teeth of a dog, husk, shell, fruit, and all, of which he made in a second a mash which he swallowed like honey. He crushed them between two fingers, which he used like scissors to cut them in two without a moment's hesitation.

You may be sure that the women were silent, that the men believed the devil to be in the monk ; and had it not been for his wife and the darkness of the night, the Sieur de Candé, having the fear of God before his eyes, would have kicked him out of the house. Every one declared that the monk was a man capable of throwing the castle into the moat. Therefore, as soon as every one had wiped his mouth, my lord took care to imprison this devil, whose strength was terrible to behold, and had him conducted to a wretched little closet where Perrotte had arranged her machine, in order to annoy him during the night. The tom-cats of the neighbourhood had been requested to come and confess to him, invited to tell him their sins in embryo towards the tabbies who attracted their affections, and also the little pigs, for whom fine lumps of tripe had been placed under the bed in order to prevent them becoming monks,

of which they were very desirous, by disgusting them with the style of *libera*, which the monk would sing to them. At every movement of poor Amador, who would find short horsehair in the sheets, he would bring down cold water on to the bed, and a thousand other tricks were arranged, such as are usually practised in castles. Every one went to bed in expectation of the nocturnal revels of the monk, certain that they would not be disappointed, since he had been lodged under the tiles at the top of a little tower, the guard of the door of which was committed to dogs who howled for a bit of him. In order to ascertain in what language the conversation with the cats and pigs would be carried on, the Sire came to stay with his dear Perrotte, who slept in the next room. As soon as he found himself thus treated, Amador drew from his bag a knife, and dexterously extricated himself. Then he began to listen in order to find out the ways of the place, and heard the master of the house laughing with his maid-servant. Suspecting their manœuvres, he waited till the moment when the lady of the house should be alone in bed, and made his way into her room with bare feet, in order that his sandals should not be in his secrets. He appeared to her by the light of the lamp in the manner in which monks generally appear during the night— that is, in a marvellous state, which the laity find it diffi- cult long to sustain ; and the thing is an effect of the frock, which magnifies everything. Then having let her see that he was all a monk, he made the following little speech—

"Know, madame, that I am sent by Jesus and the Virgin Mary to warn you to put an end to the improper perver- sities which are taking place—to the injury of your virtue, which is treacherously deprived of your husband's best attention, which he lavishes upon your maid. What is the use of being a lady if the seigneurial dues are received else- where. According to this, your servant is the lady and you are the servant. Are not all the joys bestowed upon her due to you? You will find them all amassed in our Holy Church, which is the consolation of the affected. Behold in me the messenger, ready to pay these debts if you do not renounce them."

Saying this, the good monk gently loosened his girdle in which he was incommoded, so much did he appear affected by the sight of those beauties which the Sieur de Candé disdained.

"If you speak truly, my father, I will submit to your guidance," said she, springing lightly out of the bed. "You are, for sure, a messenger of God, because you have seen in a single day that which I have not noticed here for a long time."

Then she went, accompanied by Amador, whose holy robe she did not fail to run her hand over, and was so struck when she found it real, that she hoped to find her husband guilty ; and indeed she heard him talking about the monk in her servant's bed. Perceiving this felony, she went into a furious rage, and opened her mouth to resolve it into words—which is the usual method of women—and wished to kick up the devil's delight before handing the

girl over to justice. But Amador told her that it would be
more sensible to avenge herself first, and cry out afterwards.

"Avenge me quickly, then, my father," said she, " that I
may begin to cry out."

Thereupon the monk avenged her most monastically with
a good and ample vengeance, that she indulged in as a
drunkard who puts his lips to the bunghole of a barrel ; for
when a lady avenges herself, she should get drunk with
vengeance, or not taste it at all. And the chatelaine was
revenged to that degree that she could not move ; since
nothing agitates, takes away the breath, and exhausts, like
anger and vengeance. But although she was avenged, and
doubly and trebly avenged, yet would she not forgive, in
order that she might reserve the right of avenging herself
with the monk, now here, now there. Perceiving this love
for vengeance, Amador promised to aid her in it as long
as her ire lasted, for he informed her that he knew, in
his quality of a monk, constrained to meditate long on the
nature of things, an infinite number of modes, methods,
and manners of practising revenge. Then he pointed out
to her canonically what a Christian thing it is to revenge
oneself, because all through the Holy Scriptures God declares Himself, above all things, to be a God of vengeance ;
and, moreover, demonstrates to us, by His establishment in
the infernal regions, how royally divine a thing vengeance
is, since His vengeance is eternal. From which it followed,
that women and monks ought to revenge themselves, under
pain of not being Christians and faithful servants of celestial doctrines. This dogma pleased the lady much, and she
confessed that she had never understood the commandments of the Church, and invited her well-beloved monk
to enlighten her thoroughly concerning them. Then the
chatelaine, whose vital spirits had been excited by the
vengeance which had refreshed them, went into the room
where the jade was amusing herself, and by chance found
her with her hand where she, the chatelaine, often had her
eye — like the merchants have on their most precious
articles, in order to see that they are not stolen. They were

—according to President Lizet, when he was in a merry mood—a couple taken in flagrant delectation, and looked dumfounded, sheepish, and foolish. The sight that met her eyes displeased the lady beyond the power of words to express, as it appeared by her discourse, of which the roughness was similar to that of the water of her big pond when the sluice-gates were opened. It was a sermon in three heads, accompanied with music of a high gamut, varied in the tones, with many sharps among the keys.

"Out upon virtue! my lord; I've had my share of it. You have shown me that religion in conjugal faith is an abuse; this is then the reason that I have no son. How many children have you consigned to this common oven, this poor-box, this bottomless alms-purse, this leper's porringer, the true cemetery of the house of Candé? I will know if I am childless from a constitutional defect, or through your fault. I will have handsome cavaliers, in order that I may have an heir. You can get the bastards, I the legitimate children."

"My dear," said the bewildered lord, "don't shout so."

"But," replied the lady, "I will shout, and shout to make myself heard, heard by the archbishop, heard by the legate, by the king, by my brothers, who will avenge this infamy for me."

"Do not dishonour your husband!"

"This is a dishonour, then? You are right; but, my lord, it is not brought about by you, but by this hussy, whom I will have sewn up in a sack, and thrown into the Indre; thus your dishonour will be washed away. Hi, there!" she called out.

"Silence, madame!" said the sire, as shamefaced as a blind man's dog; because this great warrior, so ready to kill others, was like a child in the hands of his wife, a state of affairs to which soldiers are accustomed, because in them lies the strength and is found all the dull carnality of matter; while, on the contrary, in woman is a subtle spirit and a scintillation of perfumed flame that lights up paradise and dazzles the male. This is the reason that certain women govern their husbands, because mind is the master of matter.

(At this the ladies began to laugh, as did also the king.)

"I will not be silent," said the Lady of Candé (said the abbot, continuing his tale); "I have been too grossly outraged. This, then, is the reward of the wealth I brought you, and of my virtuous conduct! Did I ever refuse to obey you even during Lent, and on fast days? Am I so cold as to freeze the sun? Do you think that I embrace by force, from duty, or pure kindness of heart? Am I too hallowed for you to touch? Am I a holy shrine? Was there need of a papal brief to kiss me? God's truth! have you had so much of me that you are tired? Am I not to your taste? Do charming wenches know more than ladies? Ha! perhaps it is so, since she has let you work in the field without sowing. Teach me the business; I will practise it with those whom I take into my service, for it is settled that I am free. That is as we should be. Your society was wearisome, and the little pleasure I derived from it cost me too dear. Thank God! I am quit of you and your whims, because I intend to retire to a monastery." . . . . . She meant to say a convent, but this avenging monk had perverted her tongue.

"And I shall be more comfortable in this monastery with my daughter, than in this place of abominable wickedness. You can inherit from your wench. Ha! ha! the fine Lady of Candé! Look at her!"

"What is the matter?" said Amador, appearing suddenly upon the scene.

"The matter is, my father," replied she, "that my wrongs cry aloud for vengeance. To begin with, I shall have this trollop thrown into the river, sewn up in a sack, for having diverted the seed of the house of Candé from its proper channel. It will be saving the hangman a job. For the rest I will——"

"Abandon your anger, my daughter," said the monk. "It is commanded us by the Church to forgive those who trespass against us, if we would find favour in the sight of Heaven, because you pardon those who also pardon others.

God avenges Himself eternally on those who have avenged themselves, but keeps in His paradise those who have pardoned. From that comes the jubilee, which is a day of great rejoicing, because all debts and offences are forgiven. Thus is it a source of happiness to pardon. Pardon! pardon! to pardon is a most holy work. Pardon Monseigneur de Candé, who will bless you for your gracious clemency, and will henceforward love you much. This forgiveness will restore to you the flowers of youth; and believe, my dear sweet young lady, that forgiveness is in certain cases the best means of vengeance. Pardon your maid-servant, who will pray heaven for you. Thus God, supplicated by all, will have you in His keeping, and will bless you with male lineage for this pardon."

Thus saying, the monk took the hand of the sire, placed it in that of the lady, and added—

"Go and talk over the pardon."

And then he whispered into the husband's ear this sage advice—

"My lord, use your best argument, and you will silence her with it, because a woman's mouth is only full of words when she is empty elsewhere. Argue continually, and thus you will always have the upper hand of your wife."

"By the body of Jupiter! there's good in this monk after all," said the seigneur, as he went out.

As soon as Amador found himself alone with Perrotte he spoke to her as follows—

"You are to blame, my dear, for having wished to torment a poor servant of God; therefore are you now the object of celestial wrath, which will fall upon you. To whatever place you fly it will always follow you, will seize upon you in every limb, even after your death, and will cook you like a pasty in the oven of hell, where you will simmer eternally, and every day you will receive seven hundred thousand million lashes of the whip, for the one I received through you."

"Ah, holy father," said the wench, casting herself at the monk's feet, "you alone can save me, for in your gown I should be sheltered from the anger of God."

Saying this, she raised the robe to place herself beneath it, and exclaimed—

" By my faith ! monks are better than knights."

" By the sulphur of the devil ! are ·you not acquainted with monks ?"

" No," said Perrotte.

" And you don't know the service that monks sing without saying a word ?"

" No."

Thereupon the monk went through this said service for her, as it is sung on great feast days, with all the grand effects used in monasteries, the psalms well chanted in *fa* major, the flaming tapers, and the choristers, and explained to her the *Introit*, and also the *Ite missa est*, and departed, leaving her so sanctified that the wrath of Heaven would have great difficulty in discovering any portion of the girl that was not thoroughly monasticated.   By his orders, Perrotte conducted him to Mademoiselle de Candé, the lord's sister, to whom he went in order to learn if it was her desire to confess to him, because monks came so rarely to the castle. The lady was delighted, as would any good Christian have been, at such a chance of clearing out her conscience. Amador requested her to show him her conscience, and she having allowed him to see that which he considered the conscience of old maids, he found it in a bad state, and told her that the sins of women were accomplished there ; that to be for the future without sin it was necessary to have the conscience corked up by a monk's indulgence.   The poor ignorant lady having replied that she did not know where these indulgences were to be had, the monk informed her that he had a relic with him which enabled him to grant one, that nothing was more indulgent than this relic, because without saying a word it produced infinite pleasures, which is the true, eternal and primary character of an indulgence.   The poor lady was so pleased with this relic, the virtue of which she tried in various ways, that her brain became muddled, and she had so much faith in it that she indulged as devoutly in indulgences as the Lady of Candé had indulged in vengeances.   This business of confession woke up the younger Demoiselle de Candé, who came to watch the proceedings. You may imagine that the monk had hoped for this occurrence, since his mouth watered at the sight of this fair blossom, whom he also confessed, because the elder lady could not hinder him from bestowing upon the younger one, who wished it, what remained of the indulgences. But, remember, this pleasure was due to him for the trouble he had taken. The morning having dawned, the pigs having eaten their tripe, and the cats having become disenchanted with love, and having watered all the places rubbed with herbs, Amador went to rest himself in his bed, which Perrotte had put straight again. Every one slept, thanks to the monk, so long, that no one in the castle was up before noon, which was the dinner hour. The servants all believed the monk to be a devil who had carried off the cats, the pigs, and also their masters. In spite of these ideas, however, every one was in the room at meal time.

" Come, my father," said the chatelaine, giving her arm to the monk, whom she put at her side in the baron's chair, to the great astonishment of the attendants, because the Sire of Candé said not a word. " Page, give some of this to Father Amador," said madame.

" Father Amador has need of so and so," said the Demoiselle de Candé.

" Fill up Father Amador's goblet," said the sire.

" Father Amador has no bread," said the little lady.

"What do you require, Father Amador ?" said Perrotte.

It was Father Amador here, Father Amador there. He was regaled like a little maiden on her wedding night.

" Eat, father," said madame ; " you made such a bad meal yesterday."

" Drink, father," said the sire. " You are, 'sblood ! the finest monk I ever set eyes on."

" Father Amador is a handsome monk," said Perrotte,

" An indulgent monk," said the demoiselle,

" A beneficent monk," said the little one,

" A great monk," said the lady.

"A monk who well deserves his name," said the clerk of the castle.

Amador muncned and chewed, tried all the dishes, lapped up the hypocras, licked his chaps, sneezed, blew himself out, strutted and stamped about like a bull in a field. The others regarded him with great fear, believing him to be a magician. Dinner over, the Lady of Candé, the demoiselle, and the little one, besought the Sire de Candé with a thousand fine arguments, to terminate the litigation. A great deal was said to him by madame, who pointed out to him how useful a monk was in a castle ; by mademoiselle, who wished for the future to polish up her conscience every day ; by the little one, who pulled her father's beard, and asked that this monk might always be at Candé. If ever the difference were arranged, it would be by the monk : the monk was of a good understanding, gentle and virtuous as a saint ; it was a misfortune to be at enmity with a monastery containing such monks. If all the monks were like him, the abbey would always have everywhere the advantage of the castle, and would ruin it, because this monk was very strong. Finally, they gave utterance to a thousand reasons, which were like a deluge of words, and were so pluvially showered down that the sire yielded, saying, that there would never be a moment's peace in the house until matters were settled to the satisfaction of the women. Then he sent for the clerk, who wrote down for him, and also for the monk. Then Amador surprised them exceedingly by showing them the charters and letters of credit, which would prevent the sire and his clerk delaying this agreement. When the Lady of Candé saw them about to put an end to this old case, she went to the linen chest to get some fine cloth to make a new one for her dear Amador. Every one in the house had noticed how his old gown was worn, and it would have been a great shame to leave such a treasure in such a worn-out case. Every one was eager to work at the gown. Madame cut it, the servant put the hood on, the demoiselle sewed it, and the little demoiselle worked at the sleeves. And all set so heartily to work to adorn the monk, that the robe was ready by supper time, as was also

the charter of agreement prepared and sealed by the Sire
de Candé.

"Ah, my father!" said the lady, " if you love us, you will
refresh yourself after your merry labour by washing yourself
in a bath that I have had heated by Perrotte."

Amador was then bathed in scented water. When he
came out he found a new robe of fine linen and lovely
sandals ready for him, which made him appear the most
glorious monk in the world.

Meanwhile, the monks of Turpenay, fearing for Amador,
had ordered two of their number to spy about the castle.
These spies came round by the moat, just as Perrotte threw
Amador's greasy old gown, with other rubbish, into it.
Seeing which, they thought that it was all over with the poor

madman. They therefore returned, and announced that it was
certain Amador had suffered martyrdom in the service of the
abbey. Hearing which, the abbot ordered them to assemble

in the chapel and pray to God, in order to assist this devoted servant in his torments. The monk having supped, put his charter into his girdle, and wished to return to Turpenay. Then he found at the foot of the steps madame's mare, bridled and saddled, and held ready for him by a groom. The lord had ordered his men-at-arms to accompany the good monk, so that no accident might befall him. Seeing which, Amador pardoned the tricks of the night before, and bestowed his benediction upon every one before taking his departure from this converted place. Madame followed him with her eyes, and proclaimed him a splendid rider. Perrotte declared that for a monk he held himself more upright in the saddle than any of the men-at-arms. Mademoiselle de Candé sighed. The little one wished to have him for her confessor.

" He has sanctified the castle," said they, when they were in the room again.

When Amador and his suite came to the gates of the abbey a scene of terror ensued, since the guardian thought that the Sire de Candé had had his appetite for monks whetted by the blood of poor Amador, and wished to sack the abbey. But Amador shouted with his fine bass voice, and was recognised and admitted into the courtyard ; and when he dismounted from madame's mare there

was uproar enough to make the monks as wild as April moons. They gave vent to shouts of joy in the refectory,

And when he dismounted from madame's mare there was uproar
enough to make the monks as wild as April moons.

and all came to congratulate Amador, who waved the charter over his head. The men-at-arms were regaled with the best wine in the cellars, which was a present made to the monks of Turpenay by those of Marmoutier, to whom belonged the lands at Vouvray. The good abbot having had the document of the Sire de Candé read, went about saying—

"On these divine occasions there always appears the finger of God, to whom we should render thanks."

As the good abbot kept on at this finger of God, when thanking Amador, the monk, annoyed to see the instrument of their delivery thus diminished, said to him—

"Well, say that it was the arm, my father," and drop the subject."

The termination of this trial between the Sieur de Candé and the abbey of Turpenay was followed by a blessing which rendered him devoted to the Church, because nine months after he had a son. Two years afterwards Amador was chosen as abbot by the monks, who reckoned upon a merry government with a mad-cap. But Amador become an abbot, became steady and austere, because he had conquered his evil desires by his labours, and recast his nature

at the female forge, in which is that fire which is the most perfecting, persevering, persistent, perdurable, permanent, perennial, and permeating fire that there ever was in the world. It is a fire to ruin everything, and it ruined so well the evil that was in Amador, that it left only that which it could not eat—that is his wit, which was as clear as a diamond, which is, as every one knows, a residue of the great fire by which our globe was formerly carbonized. Amador was then the instrument chosen by Providence to reform our illustrious abbey, since he put everything right there, watched night and day over his monks, made them all rise at the hours appointed for prayers, counted them in chapel as a shepherd counts his sheep, kept them well in hand, and punished their faults so severely, that he made them most virtuous brethren.

This teaches us to look upon womankind more as the instruments of our salvation than of our pleasure. Besides which, this narrative teaches us that we should never attempt to struggle with the Churchmen.

The king and the queen found this tale in the best taste; the courtiers confessed that they had never heard a better; and the ladies would all willingly have been the heroines of it.

BERTHA THE PENITENT.

I.

HOW BERTHA REMAINED A MAIDEN IN THE MARRIED STATE.

ABOUT the time of the first flight of the Dauphin, which threw our good sire, Charles the Victorious, into a state of great dejection, there happened a great misfortune to a noble house of Touraine, since extinct in every branch; and it is owing to this fact that this most deplorable history may now safely be brought to light. To aid him in this work the author calls to his assistance the holy confessors, martyrs, and other celestial dominations, who, by the commandments of God, were the promoters of good in this affair.

From some defect in his character, the Sire Imbert de

Bastarnay, one of the most landed lords in our land of Touraine, had no confidence in the mind of the female of man, whom he considered much too animated, on account of her numerous vagaries, and it may be he was right. In consequence of this idea he reached his old age without a companion, which was certainly not to his advantage. Always leading a solitary life, this said man had no idea of making himself agreeable to others, having only been mixed up with wars and the orgies of bachelors, with whom he did not put himself out of the way. Thus he remained stale in his garments, sweating in his accoutrements, with dirty hands and an apeish face. In short, he looked the ugliest man in

Christendom. As far as regards his person only though, since so far as his heart, his head, and other secret places were concerned, he had properties which rendered him most praiseworthy. An angel (pray believe this) would have walked a long way without meeting an old warrior firmer at his post, a lord with a more spotless scutcheon, of shorter speech, and more perfect loyalty.

Certain people have stated, they have heard that he gave sound advice, and was a good and profitable man to consult. Was it not a strange freak on the part of God, who plays sometimes jokes on us, to have granted so many perfections to a man so badly apparelled? When he was sixty in appearance, though only fifty in years, he determined to take unto himself a wife, in order to obtain lineage. Then, while foraging about for a place where he might be able to find a lady to his liking, he heard much vaunted, the great merits and perfections of a daughter of the illustrious house of Rohan, which at that time had some property in the province. The young lady in question was called Bertha, that being her pet name. Imbert having been to see her at the castle of Montbazon, was, in consequence of the prettiness and innocent virtue of this said Bertha de Rohan, seized with so great a desire to possess her, that he determined to make her his wife, believing that never could a girl of such lofty descent fail in her duty. This marriage was soon celebrated, because the Sire de Rohan had seven daughters, and hardly knew how to provide for them all, at a time when people were just recovering from the late wars, and patching up their unsettled affairs. Now the good man Bastarnay happily found Bertha really a maiden, which fact bore witness to her proper bringing up and perfect maternal correction. So immediately the night arrived when it should be lawful for him to embrace her, he got her with child so roughly that he had proof of the result two months after marriage, which rendered the Sire Imbert joyful to a degree. In order that we may here finish with this portion of the story, let us at once state that from this legitimate grain was born the Sire de Bastarnay, who was duke by the grace of Louis the Eleventh, his chamberlain, and, more than that, his ambassador in the countries of Europe, and well-beloved of this most redoubtable lord, to whom he was never faithless. His loyalty was an heritage from his father, who from his early youth was much attached to the Dauphin, whose fortunes he followed, even in the rebellions, since he was a man to put Christ on the cross again if he had been required by him to do so, which is the flower of friendship rarely to be found encompassing princes and great people. At first, the fair lady of Bastarnay comported herself so loyally that her society caused those thick vapours and black clouds to vanish, which obscured in the mind of this great man, the brightness of the feminine glory. Now, according to the custom of unbelievers, he passed from suspicion to confidence so thoroughly, that he yielded up the government of his house' to the said Bertha, made her mistress of his deeds and actions, queen of his honour, guardian of his grey hairs, and would have slaughtered without a contest any one who had said an evil word concerning this mirror of virtue, on whom no breath had fallen save the breath issued from his conjugal and marital lips, cold and withered as they were. To speak truly on all points, it should be explained, that to this virtuous behaviour considerably aided the little boy, who during six years occupied day and night the attention of his pretty mother, who first nourished him with her milk, and made of him a lover's lieutenant, yielding to him her sweet breasts, which he gnawed at, hungry, as often as he would, and was, like a lover, always there. This good mother knew no other pleasures than those of his rosy lips, had no other caresses than those of his tiny little hands, which ran about her like the feet of playful mice, read in no other book than his clear baby eyes, in which the blue sky was reflected, and listened to no other music than his cries, which sounded in her ears as angels' whispers. You may be sure that she was always fondling him, had a desire to kiss him at dawn of day, kissed him in the evening, would rise in the night to eat him up with kisses, made herself a child as he was a child, educated him in the perfect religion of maternity; finally, behaved as the best and happiest mother that ever lived, without disparagement to our lady the Virgin, who could have had little trouble in bringing up our Saviour, since he was God. This employment and the little taste which Bertha had for the blisses of matrimony much delighted the old man, since he would have been unable to return the affection of a too amorous wife, and desired to practise economy, to have the wherewithal for a second child. After six years had passed away, the mother was compelled to give her son into the hands of the grooms and other persons to whom Messire de Bastarnay committed the task to mould him properly, in order that his heir should have an heritage of the virtues, qualities, and courage of the house, as well as the domains and the name.

Then did Bertha shed many tears, her happiness being gone. For the great heart of this mother it was nothing to have this well-beloved son after others, and during only certain short fleeting hours. Therefore she became sad and melancholy. Noticing her grief, the good man wished to bestow upon her another child and could not, and the poor lady was displeased thereat, because she declared that the making of a child wearied her much and cost her dear. And this is true, or no doctrine is true, and you must burn the Gospels as a pack of stories if you have not faith in this innocent remark. This, nevertheless, to certain ladies (I do not mention men, since they have a smattering of the science), this will still seem an untruth. The writer has taken care here to give the mute reasons of this strange antipathy; I mean the distaste of Bertha, because I love the ladies above all things, knowing that for want of the pleasure of love, my face would grow old and my heart torment me. Did you ever meet a scribe so complaisant and so fond of the ladies as I am? No ; of course not. Therefore, do I love them devotedly, but not so often as I could wish, since I have oftener in my hands my goosequill than I have the barbs with which one tickles their lips to make them laugh and be merry in all innocence. I understand them, and in this way.

The good man Bastarnay was not a smart young fellow of an amorous nature, and acquainted with the pranks of the thing. He did not trouble himself much about the fashion in which he killed a soldier so long as he killed him ; he would have killed him in all ways without saying a word, in battle, of course, understood. This perfect heedlessness in the matter of death was in accordance with his nonchalance in the matter of life, the birth and manner of begetting a child, and the ceremonies thereto appertaining. The good sire was ignorant of the many litigious, dilatory, interlocutory, and preparatory exploits and the little humourings of the little faggots placed in the oven to heat it ; of the sweet perfumed branches gathered little by little in the forests of love, fondlings, coddlings, huggings, nursing, the bites at the cherry, the cat-licking, and other little tricks and traffic of love which ruffians know, which lovers preserve, and which the ladies love better than their salvation, because there is more of the cat than the woman in them. This shines forth in perfect evidence in their feminine ways. If you think it worth while watching them, examine them attentively while they eat: not one of them (I am speaking of women, noble and well-educated) puts her knife in the eatables and thrusts it into her mouth, as do brutally the males; no, they turn over their food, pick the pieces that please them as they would grey peas in a dovecot; they suck the sauces by mouthfuls; play with their knife and spoon as if they only ate in consequence of a judge's order, so much do they dislike to go straight to the point, and make free use of variations, finesse, and little tricks in everything, which is the especial attribute of these creatures, and the reason that the sons of Adam delight in them, since they do everything differently to themselves, and they do well. You think so too. Good! I love you. Now then, Imbert de Bastarnay, an old soldier, ignorant of the tricks of love, entered into the sweet garden of Venus as he would into a place taken by assault, without giving any heed to the cries of the poor inhabitants in tears, and placed a child as he would an arrow in the dark. Although the gentle Bertha was not used to such treatment (poor child, she was but fifteen), she believed in her virgin faith, that the happiness of becoming a mother demanded this terrible, dreadful bruising and nasty business; so during this painful task she would pray to God to assist her, and recite *Aves* to our Lady, esteeming her lucky, in only having the Holy Ghost to endure. By this means, never having experienced anything but pain in marriage, she never troubled her husband to go through the ceremony again. Now seeing that the old fellow was scarcely equal to it—as has been before stated— she lived in perfect solitude, like a nun. She hated the

society of men, and never suspected that the Author of the
world had put so much joy in that from which she had only
received infinite misery. But she loved all the more her
little one, who had cost her so much before he was born.
Do not be astonished, therefore, that she held aloof from
that gallant tourney in which it is the mare who governs her
cavalier, guides him, fatigues him, and abuses him if he
stumble. This is the true history of certain unhappy
unions, according to the statement of the old men and
women, and the certain reason of the follies committed by
certain women, who too late perceive, I know not how,
that they have been deceived, and attempt to crowd into a
day more time than it will hold, to have their proper share
of life. That is philosophical, my friends. Therefore
study well this page, in order that you may wisely look to
the proper government of your wives, your sweethearts, and
all females generally, and particularly who by chance may
be under your care, from which God preserve you. Thus
a virgin in deed, although a mother, Bertha was in her one-
and-twentieth year a castle flower, the glory of her good
man, and the honour of the province. The said Bastarnay
took great pleasure in beholding this child come, go, and
frisk about like a willow-switch, as lively as an eel, as
innocent as her little one, and still most sensible and of sound
understanding; so much so that he never undertook any
project without consulting her about it, seeing that if the
minds of these angels have not been disturbed in their
purity, they give a sound answer to everything one asks of
them. At this time Bertha lived near the town of Loches,
in the castle of her lord, and there resided, with no desire to
do anything but look after her household duties, after the
old custom of the good housewives, from which the ladies
of France were led away when Queen Catherine and the
Italians came with their balls and merrymakings. To these
practices Francis the First and his successors, whose easy
rays did as much harm to the state of France as the goings
on of the Protestants lent their aid. This, however, has nothing
to do with my story. About this time the lord and lady of
Bastarnay were invited by the king to come to his town of

Loches, where for the present he was with his court, in which
the beauty of the lady of Bastarnay had made a great noise.
Bertha came to Loches, received many kind praises from
the king, was the centre of the homage of all the young
nobles, who feasted their eyes on this apple of love, and of
the old ones, who warmed themselves at this sun. But you
may be sure that all of them, old and young, would have
suffered death a hundred times over to have at their service
this instrument of joy, which dazzled their eyes and muddled
their brains. Bertha was more talked about in Loches than
either God or the Gospels, which enraged a great many ladies
who were not so bountifully endowed with charms, and
would have given all that was left of their honour to
have sent back to her castle this fair gatherer of smiles.
A young lady having early perceived that one of her lovers
was smitten with Bertha, took such a hatred to her that
from it arose all the misfortunes of the lady of Bastarnay;
but also from the same source came her happiness, and her
discovery of the gentle land of love, of which she was
ignorant. This wicked lady had a relation who had confessed to her, directly he saw Bertha, that to be her lover
he would be willing to die after a month's happiness with
her. Bear in mind that this cousin was as handsome as a girl
is beautiful, had no hair on his chin, would have gained his
enemy's forgiveness by asking for it, so melodious was his
young voice, and was scarcely twenty years of age.

"Dear cousin," said she to him, "leave the
room, and go to your house; I will endeavour
to give you this joy. But do not let yourself
be seen by her, nor by that old baboon-face,
by an error of nature on a Christian's body, and
to whom belongs this beauteous fay."

The young gentleman out of the way, the
lady came rubbing her treacherous nose against
Bertha's, and called her "My friend, my treasure, my star of beauty;" trying in every way to
be agreeable to her, to make her vengeance more
certain on the poor child who, all unwittingly,
had caused her lover's heart to be faithless,

which, for women ambitious in love, is the worst of infi-
delities. After a little conversation, the plotting lady suspected that poor Bertha was a maiden in matters of love,
when she saw her eyes full of limpid water, no marks on
the temples, no little black speck on the point of her little
nose, white as snow, where usually the marks of the amusement are visible, no wrinkle on her brow ; in short, no habit
of pleasure apparent on her face—clear as the face of an
innocent maiden. Then this traitress put certain women's
questions to her, and was perfectly assured by the replies of
Bertha, that, if she had had the profit of being a mother,
the pleasures of love had been denied to her. At this she
rejoiced greatly on her cousin's behalf — like the good
woman she was. Then she told her, that in the town of
Loches there lived a young and noble lady, of the family of
Rohan, who at that time had need of the assistance of a
lady of position to be reconciled with the Sire Louis de
Rohan ; that if she had as much goodness as God had
given her beauty, she would take her with her to her castle,
ascertain for herself the sanctity of her life, and bring
about a reconciliation with the Sire de Rohan, who refused
to receive her. To this Bertha consented without hesitation, because the misfortunes of this girl were known to her,
but not the poor young lady herself, whose name was
Sylvia, and whom she had believed to be in a foreign
land.

It is here necessary to state why the king had given this
invitation to the Sire de Bastarnay. He had a suspicion
of the first flight of his son the Dauphin into Burgundy, and
wished to deprive him of so good a councillor as was the said
Bastarnay. But the veteran, faithful to young Louis, had
already, without saying a word, made up his mind. Therefore he took Bertha back to his castle ; but before they set
out she told him she had taken a companion and introduced
her to him. It was the young lord, disguised as a girl, with
the assistance of his cousin, who was jealous of Bertha, and
annoyed at her virtue. Imbert drew back a little when he
learnt that it was Sylvia de Rohan, but was also much
affected at the kindness of Bertha, whom he thanked for

her attempt to bring a little wandering lamb back to the fold. He made much of his wife, when his last night at home came, left men-at-arms about the castle, and then set out with the Dauphin for Burgundy, having a cruel enemy in his bosom without suspecting it. The face of the young lad was unknown to him, because he was a young page come to see the king's court, and who had been brought up by Cardinal Dunois, in whose service he was a knight-bachelor. The old lord, believing that it was a girl, thought him very modest and timid, because the lad, doubting the language of his eyes, kept them always cast down ; and when Bertha kissed him on the mouth, he trembled lest his petticoat might be indiscreet, and would walk away to the window, so fearful was he of being recognised as a man by Bastarnay, and killed before he had made love to the lady. Therefore he was as joyful as any lover would have been in his place, when the portcullis was lowered, and the old lord galloped away across the country. He had been in such suspense that he made a vow to build a pillar at his own expense in the cathedral of Tours, because he had escaped the danger of his mad scheme. He gave, indeed, fifty gold marks to pay God for his delight. But by chance he had to pay for it over again to the devil, as it appears from the following facts, if the tale pleases you well enough to induce you to follow the narrative, which will be succinct, as all good speeches should be.

II.

HOW BERTHA BEHAVED, KNOWING THE BUSINESS OF LOVE.

This bachelor was the young Sire Jehan de Sacchez, cousin of the Sieur de Montmorency, to whom, by the death of the said Jehan, the fiefs of Sacchez and other places would return, according to the deed of tenure. He was twenty years of age, and glowed like burning coal; therefore you may be sure that he had a hard job to get through the first day. While old Imbert was galloping across the fields, the two

cousins perched themselves under the lantern of the portcullis, in order to keep him the longer in view, and waved
him signals of farewell. When the clouds of dust raised by
the heels of the horses were no longer visible upon the
horizon, they came down and went back into the great room
of the castle.

" What shall we do, dear cousin?" said Bertha to the false
Sylvia.   " Do you like music? we will play together.   Let
us sing the lay of some sweet ancient bard.   Eh? what do
you say?   Come to my organ; come along.   As you love
me, sing !"

Then she took Jehan by the hand and led him to the key-
board of the organ, at which the young fellow seated himself prettily, after the manner of women.   " Ah ! sweet coz,"
cried Bertha, as soon as the first notes tried, the lad turned
his head towards her, in order that they might sing together,
" ah ! sweet coz, you have a wonderful glance in your eye;
you move I know not what in my heart."

" Ah, cousin," replied the false Sylvia, that it is which has
been my ruin.   A sweet milord of the land across the sea
told me so often that I had fine eyes, and kissed them so
well, that I yielded, so much pleasure did I feel in letting
them be kissed."

" Cousin, does love, then, commence in the eyes?"

" In them is the forge of Cupid's bolts, my dear Bertha,"
said the lover, casting fire and flame at her.

" Let us go on with our singing."

Then they sang, by Jehan's desire, a lay of Christine de
Pisan, every word of which breathed love.

" Ah, cousin, what a deep and powerful voice you have !
It seems to pierce me."

" Where ?" said the impudent Sylvia.

" There," replied Bertha, touching her little diaphragm,
where the sounds of love are understood better than by the
ears, but the diaphragm lies nearer the heart, and that which
is undoubtedly the first brain, the second heart, and the
third ear of the ladies.   I say this, with all respect and with
all honour, for physical reasons and for no others.

" Let us leave off singing," said Bertha ; " it has too great

Then they sang, by Jehan's desire, a lay of Christine de Pisan,
every word of which breathed love.

an effect upon me. Come to the window; we can do needle-work until the evening."

"Ah, dear cousin of my soul! I don't know how to hold the needle in my fingers, having been accustomed, to my perdition, to do something else with them."

"Eh? what did you do then all day long?"

"Ah, I yielded to the current of love, which makes days seem instants, months seem days, and years months; and if it could last, would gulp down eternity like a strawberry, seeing that it is all youth and fragrance, sweetness and end-less joy."

Then the youth dropped his beautiful eyelids over his eyes, and remained as melancholy as a poor lady who has been abandoned by her lover, who weeps for him, wishes to kiss him, and would pardon his perfidy, if he would but seek once again the sweet path to his once-loved fold.

"Cousin, does love blossom in the married state?"

"Oh no," said Sylvia; "because in the married state everything is duty, but in love everything is done in perfect freedom of heart. This difference communicates an inde-scribable soft balm to those caresses which are the flowers of love."

"Cousin, let us change the conversation; it affects me more than did the music."

She called hastily to a servant to bring her boy to her, who came, and when Sylvia saw him, she exclaimed—

"Ah, the little dear, he is as beautiful as Love!"

Then she kissed him heartily upon the forehead.

"Come, my little one," said the mother, as the child clambered into her lap. "Thou art thy mother's blessing, her unclouded joy, the delight of her every hour, her crown, her jewel, her own pure pearl, her spotless soul, her treasure, her morning and evening star, her only flame, and her heart's darling. Give me thy hands, that I may eat them; give me thine ears, that I may bite them; give me thy head, that I may kiss thy curls. Be happy, sweet flower of my body, that I may be happy too."

"Ah, cousin!" said Sylvia, "you are speaking the lan-guage of love to him."

" Love is a child, then ?"

"Yes, cousin; therefore the heathen always portrayed him as a little boy."

And with many other remarks fertile in the imagery of rove, the two pretty cousins amused themselves until supper time, playing with the child.

" Would you not like to have another ?" whispered Jehan, at an opportune moment, into his cousin's ear, which he touched with his warm lips.

"Ah, Sylvia ! for that I would endure a hundred years of purgatory, if it would only please God to give me that joy. But in spite of the work, labour, and industry of my spouse, which causes me much pain, my waist does not vary in size. Alas ! it is nothing to have but one child. If I hear the sound of a cry in the castle, my heart beats ready to burst. I fear man and beast alike for this innocent darling ; I dread volts, passes, and manual exercises ; in fact, I dread everything. I live not in myself, but in him alone. And, alas ! I like to endure these miseries, because while I fidget and tremble, it is a sign that my offspring is safe and sound. To be brief—for I am never weary of talking on this sub-ject—I believe that my breath is in him, and not in myself."

With these words she hugged him to her breasts, as only mothers know how to hug children, with a spiritual force that is felt only in their hearts. If you doubt this, watch a cat carrying her kittens in her mouth; not one of them gives a single mew. The youthful gallant who had had certain fears about watering this fair, unfertile plain, was reassured by this speech. He thought then that it would only be following the commandments of God to win this saint to love; and he thought rightly. At night Bertha asked her cousin—according to the old custom, to which the ladies of our day object—to keep her company in her big seigneurial bed. To which request Sylvia replied —in order to keep up the rôle of a well-born maiden—that nothing would give her greater pleasure. The curfew rang, and found the two cousins in a chamber richly ornamented with carpeting, fringes, and royal tapestries, and Bertha began gracefully to disarray herself, assisted by her women. You can imagine that her companion modestly declined their services, and told her cousin, with a little blush, that she was accustomed to undress herself ever since she had lost the services of her dearly beloved, who had put her out of conceit with feminine fingers by his gentle ways; that these preparations brought back the pretty speeches he used to make, and his merry pranks while playing the lady's-maid; and that to her injury, the memory of all these things brought the water into her mouth. This discourse considerably astonished the lady Bertha, who let her cousin say her prayers, and make her other preparations for the night beneath the curtains of the bed, into which my lord, inflamed with desire, soon tumbled, happy at being able to catch an occasional glimpse of the wondrous charms of the chatelaine, which were in no way injured. Bertha, believing herself to be with an experienced girl, did not omit any of her usual practices; she washed her feet, not minding whether she raised them little or much, exposed her delicate little shoulders, and did as all the ladies do when they are retiring to rest. At last she came to bed, and settled herself comfortably in it, kissing her cousin on the lips, which she found remarkably warm.

" Are you unwell, Sylvia, that you burn so ?" said she.

" I always burn like that when I go to bed," replied her companion, " because at that time there comes back to my memory the pretty little tricks that he invented to please me, and which made me burn still more."

" Ah, cousin, tell me all about this *he*. Tell all the sweets of love to me, who live beneath the shadow of a hoary head, of which the snows keep me from such warm feelings. Tell me all ; you are cured. It will be a good warning to me, and thus your misfortunes will have been a salutary lesson to two poor weak women."

" I do not know I ought to obey you, sweet cousin," said the youth.

" Tell me why not."

" Ah, deeds are better than words," said the false maiden, heaving a sigh deep as the *ut* of an organ. " But I am afraid that this milord has encumbered me with so much joy that you may get a little of it, which would be enough to give you a daughter, since the power of engendering is weakened in me."

" But," said Bertha, " between us, would it be a sin ?"

" It would be, on the contrary, a joy both here and in heaven ; the angels would shed their fragrance around you, and make sweet music in your ears."

" Tell me quickly, then," said Bertha.

"Well, then, this is how my dear lord made my heart rejoice."

With these words Jehan took Bertha in his arms, and strained her hungering to his heart, for in the soft light of the lamp, and clothed with the spotless linen, she was in this tempting bed, like the pretty petals of a lily at the bottom of the virgin calyx.

" When he held me as I hold thee he said to me, with a voice far sweeter than mine, ' Ah, Bertha, thou art my eternal love, my priceless treasure, my joy by day and my joy by night ; thou art fairer than the day is day ; there is naught so pretty as thou art. I love thee more than God, and would endure a thousand deaths for the happiness I ask of thee ?' Then he would kiss me, not after the manner of husbands, which is rough, but in a peculiar dove-like fashion."

To show her there and then how much better was the method of lovers, he sucked all the honey from Bertha's lips, and taught her how, with her pretty tongue, small and rosy as that of a cat, she could speak to the heart without saying a single word, and becoming exhausted at this game, Jehan spread the fire of his kisses from the mouth to the neck, from the neck to the sweetest forms that ever a woman gave her child to slake its thirst upon. And whoever had been in his place would have thought himself a wicked man not to imitate him.

"Ah !" said Bertha, fast bound in love without knowing it ; " this is better. I must take care to tell Imbert about it."

" Are you in your proper senses, cousin ? Say nothing about it to your old husband. How could he make his hands pleasant like mine ? They are as hard as washer-women's beetles, and his piebald beard would hardly please this centre of bliss, that rose in which lies our wealth, our substance, our loves, and our fortune. Do you know that it is a living flower, which should be fondled thus, and not used like a trombone, or as if it were a catapult of war ? Now this was the gentle way of my beloved Englishman."

Thus saying, the handsome youth comported himself so bravely in the battle that victory crowned his efforts, and poor innocent Bertha exclaimed—

"Ah! cousin, the angels are come ! but so beautiful is their music, that I hear nothing else, and so flaming are their luminous rays, that my eyes are closing."

And, indeed, she fainted under the burden of those joys of love which burst forth in her like the highest notes of the organ, which glistened like the most magnificent aurora, which flowed in her veins like the finest musk, and loosened the liens of her life in giving her a child of love, who made a great deal of confusion in taking up his quarters. Finally, Bertha imagined herself to be in Paradise, so happy did she feel ; and woke from this beautiful dream in the arms of Jehan, exclaiming—

"Ah ! who would not have been married in England !"

"My sweet mistress," said Jehan, whose ecstasy was sooner over, "you are married to me in France, where things are managed still better, for I am a man who would give a thousand lives for you if he had them."

Poor Bertha gave a shriek so sharp that it pierced the walls, and leaped out of the bed like a mountebank of the plains of Egypt would have done. She fell upon her knees before her Prie-Dieu, joined her hands, and wept more pearls than ever Mary Magdalene wore. "Ah, I am dead !" she cried; "I am deceived by a devil who has taken the face of an angel. I am lost ; I am the mother for certain of a beautiful child, without being more guilty than you, Madame the Virgin. Implore the pardon of God for me, if I have not that of men upon earth ; or let me die, so that I may not blush before my lord and master."

Hearing that she said nothing against him, Jehan rose, quite aghast to see Bertha take this charming dance for two so to heart. But the moment she heard her Gabriel moving she sprang quickly to her feet, regarded him with a tearful face, and her eyes illumined with a holy anger, which made her more lovely to look upon, exclaimed, "If you advance a single step towards me, I will make one towards death!"

And she took her stiletto in her hand.

So heartrending was the tragic spectacle of her grief, that Jehan answered her—

"It is not for thee but for me to die, my dear, beautiful mistress, more dearly loved than will ever woman be again upon this earth."

"If you had truly loved me you would not have killed me as you have, for I will die sooner than be reproached by my husband."

"Will you die?" said he.

"Assuredly," said she.

"Now, if I am here pierced with a thousand blows, you will have your husband's pardon, to whom you will say that if your innocence was surprised, you have avenged his honour by killing the man who had deceived you; and it will be the greatest happiness that could ever befal me to die for you, the moment you refuse to live for me."

Hearing this tender discourse spoken with tears, Bertha dropped the dagger; Jehan sprang upon it, and thrust it into his breast, saying— "Such happiness can be paid for but with death."

And fell stiff and stark.

Bertha, terrified, called aloud for her maid. The servant came, and terribly alarmed to see a wounded man in Madame's chamber, and Madame holding him up, crying and saying,

"What have you done, my love?" because she believed he was dead, and remembered her vanished joys, and thought how beautiful Jehan must be, since every one, even Imbert, believed him to be a girl.   In her sorrow she confessed all to her maid, sobbing and crying out, "that it was quite enough to have upon her mind the life of a child without having the death of a man as well."   Hearing this the poor lover tried to open his eyes, and only succeeded in showing a little bit of the white of them.

"Ha! Madame, don't cry out," said the servant, "let us keep our senses together, and save this pretty knight.   I will go and seek La Fallotte, in order not to let any physician or surgeon into this secret, and as she is a sorceress she will, to please Madame, perform the miracle of healing this wound so that not a trace of it shall remain."

"Run!" replied Bertha.   "I will love you, and will pay you well for this assistance."

But before anything else was done the lady and her maid agreed to be silent about this adventure, and hide Jehan from every eye.   Then the servant went out into the night to seek La Fallotte, and was accompanied by her mistress as far as the postern, because the guard could not raise the portcullis without Bertha's special order.   Bertha found on going back that her lover had fainted, for the blood was flowing from the wound.   At this sight she drank a little of his blood, thinking that Jehan had shed it for her.   Affected

by this great love and by the danger, she kissed this pretty varlet of pleasure on the face, bound up his wound, bathing it with her tears, beseeching him not to die, and exclaiming that if he would live she would love him with all her heart.   You can imagine that the chatelaine became still more enamoured while observing what a difference there was between a young knight like Jehan, white, downy, and agreeable, and an old fellow like Imbert, bristly, yellow, and wrinkled. This difference brought back to her memory that which she had found in the pleasure of love. Moved by this souvenir, her kisses became so warm that Jehan came back to his senses, his look improved, and he could see Bertha, from whom in a feeble voice he asked forgiveness. But Bertha forbade him to speak until La Fallotte had arrived. Then both of them consumed the time by loving each other with their eyes, since in those of Bertha there was nothing but compassion, and on these occasions pity is akin to love.

La Fallotte was a hunchback, vehemently suspected of dealings in necromancy, and of riding to nocturnal orgies on a broomstick, according to the custom of witches. Certain persons had seen her putting the harness on her broom in the stable, which, as every one knows, is on the housetops. To tell the truth, she possessed certain medical secrets, and was of such great service to ladies in certain things, and to the nobles, that she lived in perfect tranquillity, without giving up the ghost on a pile of fagots, but on a feather bed, for she made a hatful of money, although the physicians tormented her by declaring that she sold poisons, which was certainly true, as will be shown in the sequel. The servant and La Fallotte came on the same ass, making such haste that they arrived at the castle before the day had fully dawned. The old hunchback exclaimed, as she entered the chamber, " Now, then, my children, what is the matter ?" This was her manner, which was familiar with great people, who appeared very small to her. She put on her spectacles, and carefully examined the wound, saying, " This is fine blood, my dear ; you have tasted it. That's all right, he has bled externally." Then she washed the wound with a fine sponge, under the nose of the lady and the servant, who held their breath. To be brief, Fallotte gave it as her medical opinion, that the youth would not die from this blow, "although," said she, looking at his hand, "he will come to a violent end through this night's deed."

La Fallotte.

La Fallotte was a hunchback, vehemently suspected
of dealings in necromancy.

This decree of chiromancy frightened considerably both Bertha and the maid. Fallotte prescribed certain remedies, and promised to come again the following night. Indeed,

she tended the wound for a whole fortnight, coming secretly at night-time. The people about the castle were told by the servant that their young lady, Sylvia de Rohan, was in danger of death, through a swelling of the stomach, which must remain a mystery for the honour of Madame, who was her cousin. Each one was satisfied with this story, of which his mouth was so full that he told it to his fellows.

The good people believed that it was the malady which was fraught with danger ; but it was not ! it was the convalescence, for the stronger Jehan grew, the weaker Bertha became, and so weak that she allowed herself to drift into that Paradise the gates of which Jehan had opened for her.

To be brief, she loved him more and more. But in the midst of her happiness, always associated by apprehension at the menacing words of Fallotte, and tormented by her great religion, she was in great fear of her husband, Imbert, to whom she was compelled to write that he had given her a child, who would be ready to delight him on his return. Poor Bertha avoided her lover, Jehan, dur-

The servant and La Fallotte came on the same ass.

ing the day on which she wrote the lying letter, over which she soaked her handkerchief with tears. Finding himself avoided (for they had previously left each other no more than fire leaves the wood it has bitten) Jehan believed that she was beginning to hate him, and straightway he cried too. In the evening Bertha, touched by his tears, which had left their mark upon his eyes, although he had well dried them, told him the cause of her sorrow, mingling therewith the confession of her terrors for the future, pointing out to him how much they were both to blame, and discoursing so beautifully to him, gave utterance to such Christian sentences, ornamented with holy tears and contrite prayers, that Jehan was touched to the quick by the sincerity of his mistress. This love innocently united to repentance, this nobility in sin, this mixture of weakness and strength, would, as the old authors say, have changed the nature of a tiger, melting it to pity. You will not be astonished then, that Jehan was compelled to pledge his word as a knight-bachelor, to obey her in whatever she should command him, to save her in this world and in the next. Delighted at this confidence in her, and this goodness of heart, Bertha cast herself at Jehan's feet, and kissing them, exclaimed—

"Oh, my love ! whom I am compelled to love, although it is a mortal sin to do so, thou who art so good, so gentle to thy poor Bertha, if thou wouldst have her always think of thee with pleasure, and stop the torrent of her tears, whose source is so pretty and so pleasant (here, to show him that it was so, she let him steal a kiss)—Jehan, if thou wouldst that the memory of our celestial joys, angel music, and the fragrance of love should be a consolation to me in my loneliness rather than a torment, do that which the Virgin commanded me to order thee in a dream, in which I was beseeching her to direct me in the present case, for I had asked her to come to me, and she had come. Then I told her the horrible anguish I should endure, trembling for this little one, whose movements I already feel, and for the real father, who would be at the mercy of the other, and might expiate his paternity by a violent death, since it is possible that La Fallotte saw clearly into his future life.

This love innocently united to repentance, this nobility in sin, this mixture of weakness and strength, would, as the old authors say, have changed the nature of a tiger, melting it to pity.

Then the beautiful Virgin told me, smiling, that the Church offered its forgiveness for our faults if we followed her commandments ; that it was necessary to save one's self from the pains of hell, by reforming before Heaven became angry. Then with her finger she showed me a Jehan like thee, but dressed as thou shouldst be, and as thou wilt be, if thou dost but love thy Bertha with a love eternal."

Jehan assured her of his perfect obedience, and raised her, seating her on his knee, and kissing her. The unhappy Bertha told him, then that this garment was a monk's frock, and tremblingly besought him—almost fearing a refusal—to enter the Church, and retire to Marmoutier, beyond Tours, pledging him her word that she would grant him a last night, after which she would be neither for him nor for any one else in the world again. And each year, as a reward for this, she would let him come to her one day, in order that he might see his child. Jehan, bound by his oath, promised to obey his mistress, saying that by this means he would be faithful to her, and would experience no joys of love but those tasted in her divine embrace, and would live upon the dear remembrance of them. Hearing these sweet words, Bertha declared to him that, however great might have been her sin, and whatever God reserved for her, this happiness would enable her to support it, since she believed she had not fallen through a man, but through an angel.

Then they returned to the nest which contained their love, but only to bid a final adieu to all their lovely flowers. There can be but little doubt that Seigneur Cupid had something to do with this festival, for no woman ever experienced such joy in any part of the world before, and no man ever took as much. The especial property of true love is a certain harmony, which brings it about that the more one gives, the more the other receives, and vice versâ, as in certain cases in mathematics, where things are multiplied by themselves without end. This problem can only be explained to unscientific people, by asking them to look in their Venetian glasses, in which are to be seen thousands of faces produced by one alone. Thus, in the hearts of two lovers, the roses of pleasure multiply within them in a manner which causes them to be astonished that so much joy can be contained, without anything bursting. Bertha and Jehan would have wished in this night to have finished their days, and thought, from the excessive languor which flowed in their veins, that love had resolved to bear them away on his wings with the kiss of death; but they held out in spite of these numerous multiplications.

On the morrow, as the return of Monsieur Imbert de Bastarnay was close at hand, the lady Sylvia was compelled to depart. The poor girl left her cousin, covering her with tears and with kisses; it was always her last, but the last lasted till evening. Then he was compelled to leave her, and he did leave her, although the blood of his heart congealed, like the fallen wax of a Paschal candle. According to his promise, he wended his way towards Marmoutier, which he entered towards the eleventh hour of the day, and was placed among the novices. Monseigneur de Bastarnay was informed that Sylvia had returned to the Lord, which is the signification of *le Seigneur* in the English language; and therefore in this Bertha did not lie.

The joy of her husband, when he saw Bertha without her waistband—she could not wear it, so much had she increased in size—commenced the martyrdom of this poor woman, who did not know how to deceive, and who, at each false word, went to her Prie-Dieu, wept her blood away from her eyes in tears, burst into prayers, and recommended herself to the graces of Messieurs the Saints in Paradise. It happened that she cried so loudly to God that He heard her, because He hears everything; He hears the stones that roll beneath the waters, the poor who groan, and the flies who wing their way through the air. It is as well that you should know this, otherwise you would not believe in what happened. God commanded the archangel Michael to make for this penitent a hell upon earth, so that she might enter without dispute into Paradise. Then St. Michael descended from the skies as far as the gate of hell, and handed over this triple soul to the devil, telling him that he had permission to torment it during the rest of her days, at the same time indicating to him Bertha, Jehan, and the child.

The devil, who by the will of God is lord of all evil, told the archangel that he would obey the message. During this heavenly arrangement life went on as usual here below. The sweet lady of Bastarnay gave the most beautiful child in the world to the Sire Imbert—a boy all lilies and roses, of great intelligence, like a little Jesus, merry and arch as a pagan love. He became more beautiful day by day, while the elder was turning to an ape, like his father, whom he painfully resembled. The younger boy was as bright as a star, and resembled his father and mother, whose corporeal and spiritual perfections had produced a compound of illustrious graces and marvellous intelligence. Seeing this perpetual miracle of body and mind blended with the essential conditions, Bastarnay declared that for his eternal salvation he would like to make the younger the elder, and that he would do with the king's protection. Bertha did not know what to do, for she adored the child of Jehan, and could only feel a feeble affection for the other, whom, nevertheless, she protected against the evil intentions of the old fellow Bastarnay. Bertha, satisfied with the way things were going, quieted her conscience with falsehood, and thought that all danger was past, since twelve years had elapsed with no other alloy than the doubt which at times embittered her joy. Each year, according to her pledged faith, the monk of Marmoutier, who was unknown to every one except the servant-maid, came to pass a whole day at the Château to see his child, although Bertha had many times besought brother Jehan to yield his right. But Jehan pointed to the child, saying, " You see him every day of the year, and I only once !" And the poor mother could find no word ready to answer this speech with.

A few months before the last rebellion of the Dauphin Louis against his father, the boy was treading closely on the heels of his twelfth year, and appeared likely to become a great savant, so learned was he in all the sciences. Old Bastarnay had never been more delighted at having been a father in his life, and resolved to take his son with him to the Court of Burgundy, where Duke Charles promised to make for this well-beloved son a position, which should be

the envy of princes, for he was not at all averse to clever
people. Seeing matters thus arranged, the devil judged
the time to be ripe for his mischiefs. He took his tail and
flapped it right into the middle of this happiness, so that he
could stir it up in his own peculiar way.

III.

HORRIBLE CHASTISEMENT OF BERTHA AND EXPIA-TION OF THE SAME, WHO DIED PARDONED.

The servant of the lady of Bastarnay, who was then about
five-and-thirty years old, fell in love with one of the master's
men-at-arms, and was silly enough to let him
take loaves out of the oven, until there resulted
therefrom a natural swelling, which certain wags
in these parts call a nine months' dropsy. The
poor woman begged her mistress to intercede
for her with the master, so that he might
compel this wicked man to finish at the altar
that which he had commenced elsewhere. Madame de
Bastarnay had no difficulty in obtaining this favour from
him, and the servant was quite satisfied. But the
old warrior, who was always extremely rough, hastened
into his pretorium, and blew him up sky high, ordering
him, under the pain of the gallows, to marry the girl;
which the soldier preferred to do, thinking more of his
neck than of his peace of mind. Bastarnay sent also for
the female, to whom he imagined, for the honour of his
house, he ought to sing a litany, mixed with epithets and
ornamented with extremely strong expressions, and make
her think, by way of punishment, that she was not going to
be married, but flung into one of the cells in the gaol. The
girl fancied that Madame wanted to get rid of her, in order
to inter the secret of the birth of her beloved son. With
this impression, when the old ape said such outrageous
things to her—namely, that he must have been a fool
to keep a harlot in his house—she replied that he certainly
was a very big fool, seeing that for a long time past his wife

had been playing the harlot, and with a monk too, which was the worst thing that could happen to a warrior. Think of the greatest storm you ever saw in your life, and you will have a weak sketch of the furious rage into which the old man fell, when thus assailed in a portion of his heart where was a triple life. He seized the girl by the throat, and would have killed her there and then, but she, to prove her story, detailed the how, the why, and the when, and said that if he had no faith in her, he could have the evidence of his own ears by hiding himself the day that Father Jehan de Sacchez, the prior of Marmoutier, came. He would then hear the words of the father, who solaced himself for his year's fast, and in one day kissed his son for the rest of the year. Imbert ordered this woman instantly to leave the castle, since, if her accusation were true, he would kill her just as though she had invented a tissue of lies. In an instant he had given her a hundred crowns, besides her man, enjoining them not to sleep in Touraine ; and, for greater security, they were conducted into Burgundy, by De Bastarnay's officers. He informed his wife of their departure, saying, that as her servant was a damaged article he had thought it best to get rid of her, but had given her a hundred crowns, and found employment for the man at the Court of Burgundy. Bertha was astonished to learn that her maid had left the castle without receiving her dismissal from herself, her mistress ; but she said nothing. Soon afterwards she had other fish to fry, for she became a prey to vague apprehensions, because her husband completely changed in his manner, commenced to notice the likeness of his first-born to himself, and could find nothing resembling his nose, or his forehead, his this, or his that, in the youngster he loved so well.

"He is my very image," replied Bertha one day that he was throwing out these hints. "Know you not that in well-regulated households, children are formed from the father and the mother, each in turn, or often from both together, because the mother mingles her qualities with the vital force of the father? Some physicians declare that they have known many children born without any resemblance to either father or mother, and attribute these mysteries to the whim of the Almighty."

"You have become very learned, my dear," replied Bastarnay; "but I, who am an ignoramus, I should fancy that a child who resembled a monk——"

"Had a monk for a father!" said Bertha, looking at him with an unflinching gaze, although ice rather than blood was coursing through her veins.

The old fellow thought he was mistaken, and cursed the servant; but he was none the less determined to make sure of the affair. As the day of Father Jehan's visit was close at hand, Bertha, whose suspicions were aroused by this speech, wrote him that it was her wish that he should not come this year, without, however, telling him her reason; then she went in search of La Fallotte at Loches, who was to give her letter to Jehan, and believed everything was safe for the present. She was all the more pleased at having written to her friend the prior, when Imbert, who, towards the time appointed for the poor monk's annual treat, had always been accustomed to take a journey into the province of Maine, where he had considerable property, remained this time at home, giving as his reason the preparations for rebellion which Monseigneur Louis was then making against his father, who, as every one knows, was so cut up at this revolt that it caused his death. This reason was so good an one that poor Bertha was quite satisfied with it, and did not trouble herself. On the regular day, however, the prior arrived as usual. Bertha seeing him, turned pale, and asked him if he had not received her message.

" What message?" said Jehan.

" Ah! we are lost, then; the child, thou, and I," replied Bertha.

" Why so?" said the prior.

" I know not," said she; " but our last day has come."

She inquired of her dearly beloved son where Bastarnay was. The young man told her that his father had been sent for by special messenger to Loches, and would not be back until evening. Thereupon Jehan wished, in spite of his mistress, to remain with her and his dear son, asserting

that no harm would come of it, after the lapse of twelve
years, since the birth of their boy.   The days when that ad-
venturous night you wot of was celebrated, Bertha stayed in
her room with the poor monk until supper time.   But on
this occasion the lovers—hastened by the apprehensions of
Bertha, which were shared by Jehan directly she had informed him of them—dined immediately, although the prior
of Marmoutier reassured Bertha by pointing out to her the
privileges of the Church, and how Bastarnay, already in bad
odour at Court, would be afraid to attack a dignitary of Marmoutier.   When they were sitting down to table their little
one happened to be playing, and in spite of the reiterated
prayers of his mother, would not stop his games, since he was
galloping about the courtyard on a fine Spanish barb, which
Duke Charles of Burgundy had presented to Bastarnay.
And because young lads like to show off, varlets make
themselves bachelors at arms, and bachelors wish to play
the knight, this boy was delighted at being able to show the
monk what a man he was becoming; he made the horse
jump like a flea in the bedclothes, and sat as steady as a
trooper in the saddle.

"Let him have his way, my darling," said the monk to
Bertha.   "Disobedient children often become great
characters."

Bertha ate sparingly, for her heart was as swollen as a
sponge in water.   At the first mouthful, the monk, who was
a great scholar, felt in his stomach a pain, and on his palate
a bitter taste of poison that caused him to suspect that the
Sire de Bastarnay had given them all their quietus.   Before he
had made this discovery Bertha had eaten.   Suddenly the
monk pulled off the tablecloth and flung everything into the
fireplace, telling Bertha his suspicion.   Bertha thanked the
Virgin that her son had been so taken up with his sport.
Retaining his presence of mind, Jehan, who had not forgotten the lesson he had learned as a page, leaped into the
courtyard, lifted his son from the horse, sprang across it
himself, and flew across the country with such speed that
you would have thought him a shooting-star if you had seen
him digging the spurs into the horse's bleeding flanks and he

The monk stated the case to her in two words.

was at Loches in Fallotte's house in the same space of
time, that only the devil could have done the journey.   He
stated the case to her in two words, for the poison was
already frying his marrow, and requested her to give him an
antidote.

"Alas," said the sorceress, "had I known that it was for
you I was giving this poison, I would have received in my
breast the dagger's point, with which I was threatened, and
would have sacrificed my poor life to save that of a man of
God, and of the sweetest woman that ever blossomed on
this earth ; for, alas ! my dear friend, I have only two drops
of the counter-poison that you see in this phial."

"Is there enough for her ?"

"Yes ; but go at once," said the old hag.

The monk came back more quickly than he went, so that
the horse died under him in the courtyard.   He rushed into
the room where Bertha, believing her last hour to be come,
was kissing her son, and writhing like a lizard in the fire,
uttering no cry for herself, but for the child, left to the
wrath of Bastarnay, forgetting her own agony at the thought
of his cruel future.

"Take this," said the monk ; "my life is saved !"

Jehan had the great courage to say these words with an
unmoved face, although he felt the claws of death seizing
his heart.   Hardly had Bertha drunk when the prior fell
dead, not, however, without kissing his son, and regarding
his dear lady with an eye that changed not even after his
last sigh.   This sight turned her cold as marble, and terrified her so much that she remained rigid before this dead
man, stretched at her feet, pressing the hand of her child,
who wept, although her own eye was as dry as the Red Sea
when the Hebrews crossed it under the leadership of Baron
Moses, for it seemed to her that she had sharp sand rolling
under her eyelids.   Pray for her, ye charitable souls, for
never was woman so agonized, in divining that her lover had
saved her life at the expense of his own.   Aided by her son,
she herself placed the monk in the middle of the bed, and
stood by the side of it, praying with the boy, whom she then
told that the prior was his true father.   In this state she

waited her evil hour, and her evil hour did not take long in coming, for towards the eleventh hour Bastarnay arrived, and was informed at the portcullis that the monk was dead, and not Madame and the child, and he saw his beautiful

Spanish horse lying dead. Thereupon, seized with a furious desire to slay Bertha and the monk's bastard, he sprang up the stairs with one bound; but at the sight of this corpse, for whom his wife and her son repeated incessant litanies, having no ears for his torrents of invective, having no eyes for his writhings and threats, he had no longer the courage to perpetrate this dark deed. After the first fury of his rage had passed, he could not bring himself to it, and quitted the room like a coward and a man taken in crime, stung to the quick by those prayers continuously said for the monk. The night was passed in tears, groans, and prayers. By an express order from Madame, her servant had been to Loches to purchase for her the attire of a young lady of quality, and for her poor child a horse and the arms of an esquire; noticing which, the Sieur de Bastarnay was much astonished. He sent for Madame and the monk's son, but neither mother nor child returned any answer, but quietly put on the clothes purchased by the servant. By Madame's order this servant made up the account of her effects, arranged her clothes, purples, jewels, and diamonds, as the property of a widow is arranged when she renounces her rights. Bertha ordered even her alms-purse to be included, in order that the ceremony might be perfect. The report of these preparations ran through the house, and every one knew then that the mistress was about to leave it, a circumstance that filled every heart with sorrow, even that of a little scullion, who had only been a week in the place, but to whom Madame had already given a kind word. Frightened at these preparations, old Bastarnay came into her chamber, and found her weeping over the body of Jehan, for her tears had come at last; but she dried them directly she perceived her husband. To his numerous questions she replied briefly by the confession of her fault, telling him how she had been duped, how the poor page had been distressed, showing him upon the corpse the mark of the poniard wound; how long he had been getting well; and how, in obedience to her, and from penitence towards God and man, he had entered the Church, abandoning the glorious career of a knight, putting an end to his name, which was certainly worse than death; how she, while avenging her honour, had thought that even God Himself would not have refused the monk one day in the year to see the son for whom he sacrificed everything; how, not wishing to live with a murderer, she was about to quit his house, leaving all her property behind her; because if the honour of the Bastarnays was stained, it was not she who had brought the shame about; because in this calamity she had arranged matters as best she could; finally, she added a vow to go over mountain and valley, she and her son, until all was expiated, for she knew how to expiate all.

Having with noble mien and a pale face uttered these beautiful words, she took her child by the hand and went out in great mourning, more magnificently beautiful than was Mademoiselle Hagar on her departure from the residence of the patriarch Abraham, and so proudly, that all the servants and retainers fell on their knees as she passed along, imploring her with joined hands, like Notre-Dame de la Riche. It was pitiful to see the Sieur de Bastarnay following her, ashamed, weeping, confessing himself to blame, and downcast and despairing, like a man being led to the gallows, there to be turned off.

Bertha turned a deaf ear to everything. The desolation was so great that she found the drawbridge lowered, and hastened to quit the castle, fearing that it might be suddenly raised again; but no one had the right or the heart to do it. She sat down on the kerb of the moat, in view of the whole castle, who begged her, with tears, to stay. The poor sire was standing with his hand upon the chain of the portcullis, as silent as the stone saints carved above the door. He saw Bertha order her son to shake the dust from his shoes at the end of the bridge, in order to have nothing belonging to Bastarnay about him; and she did likewise. Then, indicating the sire to her son with her finger, she spake to him as follows—

"Child, behold the murderer of thy father, who was, as thou art aware, the poor prior; but thou hast taken the name of this man. Give it him back here, even as thou leavest the dust taken by thy shoes from his castle. For the food that thou hast had in the castle, by God's help we will also settle."

Hearing this, Bastarnay would have let his wife receive a whole monastery of monks in order not to be abandoned by her, and by a young squire capable of becoming the honour of his house, and remained with his head sunk down against the chains.

The heart of Bertha was suddenly filled with holy solace, for the banner of the great monastery turned the corner of a road across the fields, and appeared accompanied by the chants of the Church, which burst forth like heavenly music. The monks, informed of the murder perpetrated on their well-beloved prior, came in procession, assisted by the ecclesiastical justice, to claim his body. When he saw this, the Sire de Bastarnay had barely the time to make for the postern with his men, and set out towards Monseigneur Louis, leaving everything in confusion.

Poor Bertha, *en croupe* behind her son, came to Montbazon to bid her father farewell, telling him that this blow

Having with noble mien and a pale face uttered these beautiful words, she took her child by the hand and went out in great mourning, more magnificently beautiful than was Mademoiselle Hagar.

The heart of Bertha was suddenly filled with holy solace, for
the banner of the great monastery turned the corner of a road
across the fields, and appeared accompanied by the chants of
the Church, which burst forth like heavenly music.

would be her death, and was consoled by those of her
family who endeavoured to raise her spirits, but were unable to do so. The old Sire de Rohan presented his grand-
son with a splendid suit of armour, telling him so to acquire
glory and honour that he might turn his mother's faults into
eternal renown. But Madame de Bastarnay had implanted
in the mind of her dear son no other idea than of atoning
for the harm done, in order to save her and Jehan from
eternal damnation. Both then set out for the places then in
a state of rebellion, in order to render such services to Bastarnay that he would receive from them more than life itself.
Now the heat of the sedition was, as every one knows, in the
neighbourhood of Angoulême, and of Bordeaux in Guienne,
and other parts of the kingdom, where great battles and
severe conflicts between the rebels and the royal armies were
likely to take place. The principal one which finished the
war was given between Ruffec and Angoulême, where all
the prisoners taken were tried and hanged. This battle,
commanded by old Bastarnay, took place in the month of
November, seven months after the poisoning of Jehan. Now
the baron knew that his head had been strongly recommended as one to be cut off, he being the right hand of
Monseigneur Louis. Directly his men began to fall back,
the old fellow found himself surrounded by six men determined to seize him. Then he understood that they wished
to take him alive, in order to proceed against his house,
ruin his name, and confiscate his property. The poor sire
preferred rather to die and save his family, and present the
domains to his son. He defended himself, like the brave
old lion that he was. In spite of their number, these said
soldiers, seeing three of their comrades fall, were obliged to
attack Bastarnay at the risk of killing him, and threw themselves together upon him, after having laid low two of his
equerries and a page. In this extreme danger an esquire,
wearing the arms of Rohan, fell upon the assailants like a
thunderbolt, and killed two of them, crying, " God save the
Bastarnays !" The third man-at-arms, who had already
seized old Bastarnay, was so hard pressed by this squire, that
he was obliged to leave the elder and turn against the

younger, to whom he gave a thrust with his dagger through a flaw in his armour. Bastarnay was too good a comrade to fly without assisting the liberator of his house, who was badly wounded. With a blow of his mace he killed

the man-at-arms, seized the squire, lifted him on to his horse, and gained the open, accompanied by a guide, who led him to the castle of Roche-Foucauld, which he entered by night, and found in the great room Bertha de Rohan, who had arranged this retreat for him. But on removing the helmet of his prisoner, he recognised the son of Jehan, who expired upon the table, by a final effort kissing his mother, and saying in a loud voice to her, " Mother, we have paid the debt we owed him !" Hearing these words, the mother clasped the body of her love child to her heart, and separated from him never again, for she died of grief, without hearing or heeding the pardon and repentance of Bastarnay.

This strange calamity hastened the last day of the poor old man, who did not live to see the coronation of King Louis the Eleventh. He founded a daily mass in the church of Roche-Foucauld, where in the same grave he placed mother and son, with a large tombstone, upon which their lives are much honoured in the Latin language.

Then he understood that they wished to take him alive in
order to proceed against his house, ruin his name, and confiscate his property.

The son of Jehan, who expired upon the table, by a final effort
kissing his mother, and saying in a loud voice to her, "Mother,
we have paid the debt we owed him !"

The morals which any one can deduce from this history are most profitable for the conduct of life, since this shows how gentlemen should be courteous with the dearly beloveds of their wives.   Further, it teaches us that all children are blessings sent by God Himself, and over them fathers, whether true or false, have no right of murder, as was formerly the case at Rome, owing to a heathen and abominable law, which ill became that Christianity which makes us all sons of God.

In the same grave he placed mother and son, with a large tombstone, upon which their lives are much honoured in the **Latin** language.

HOW THE

PRETTY MAID OF PORTILLON
CONVINCED HER JUDGE.

THE maid of Portillon, who became, as every one
knows, La Tascherette, was, before she became a
dyer, a laundress at the said place of Portillon, from which
she took her name. If any there be who do not know
Tours, it may be as well to state that Portillon is down the
Loire, on the same side as St. Cyr, about as far from the
bridge which leads to the cathedral of Tours as the said
bridge is distant from Marmoutier, since the bridge is in
the centre of the embankment between Portillon and Marmoutier. Do you thoroughly understand?

Yes? Good! Now the maid had there her washhouse,
from which she ran to the Loire with her washing in a
second, and took the ferry-boat to get to St. Martin, which
was on the other side of the river, for she had to deliver the
greater part of her work in Chateauneuf and other places.
About Midsummer day, seven years before marrying old

This encounter made her so joyful that her mouth
was full of his name.

Taschereau, she had just reached the right age to be loved.
As she was a merry girl she allowed herself to be loved,
without making a choice from any of the lads who pursued her with their attentions.   Although there used to
come to the bench under her window the son of Rabelais,
who had seven boats on the Loir, Jehan's eldest, Marchandeau the tailor, and Peccard the ecclesiastical goldsmith,
she made fun of them all, because she wished to be taken
to church before burthening herself with a man, which
proves that she was an honest woman until she was wheedled
out of her virtue.   She was one of those girls who take great
care not to be contaminated, but who, if by chance they get
deceived, let things take their course, thinking that for one
stain or for fifty a good polishing up is necessary.   These
characters demand our indulgence.

A young noble of the court perceived her one day when
she was crossing the water in the glare of the noonday sun,
which lit up her ample charms, and seeing her, asked who
she was.   An old man, who was working on the banks, told
him she was called the Pretty Maid of Portillon, a laundress,
celebrated for her merry ways and her virtue.   This young
lord, besides ruffles to starch, had many precious linen draperies and things ; he resolved to give the custom of his
house to this girl, whom he stopped on the road.   He was
thanked by her and heartily, because he was the Sire du
Fou, the king's chamberlain.   This encounter made her so
joyful that her mouth was full of his name.   She talked
about it a great deal to the people of St. Martin, and when
she got back to her washhouse was still full of it, and on the
morrow at her work her tongue went nineteen to the dozen,
and all on the same subject, so that as much was said concerning my Lord du Fou in Portillon as of God in a sermon ;
that is, a great deal too much.

" If she works like that in cold water, what will she do
in warm ?" said an old washerwoman.   " She wants du Fou ;
he'll give her du Fou !"

The first time this giddy wench, with her head full of
Monsieur du Fou, had to deliver the linen at his hotel, the
chamberlain wished to see her, and was very profuse in

And seeing her, asked who she was. An old man, who was working on the banks, told him she was called the Pretty Maid of Portillon.

praises and compliments concerning her charms, and wound up by telling her that she was not at all silly to be beautiful,

and therefore he would give her more than she expected. The deed followed the word, for the moment his people were out of the room he began to caress the maid, who thinking he was about to take out the money from his purse, dared not look at the purse, but said, like a girl ashamed to take her wages, " It will be for the first time."

" It will be soon," said he.

Some people say that he had great difficulty in forcing her to accept what he offered her, and hardly forced her at all; others that he forced her badly, because she came out, like an army flagging on the route, crying and groaning, and came to the judge. It happened that the judge was out. La Portillonne awaited his return in his room, weeping and saying to the servant that she had been robbed, because Monseigneur du Fou had given her nothing but his mischief; whilst a canon of the Chapter used to give her large sums for that which M. du Fou wanted for nothing. If she loved a man she would think it wise to do things for him for nothing, because it would be a pleasure to her; but the chamberlain had treated her roughly, and not kindly and gently, as he should have done, and that therefore he owed her the thousand crowns of the canon. The judge came in, saw the wench, and wished to kiss her, but she put herself on guard, and said she had come to make a complaint. The judge replied that certainly she could have the offender hanged if she liked, because he was most anxious to serve her. The injured maiden replied that she did not wish the death of her man, but that he should pay her a thousand gold crowns, because she had been robbed against her will.

" Ha ! ha !" said the judge, " what he took was worth more than that."

" For the thousand crowns I'll cry quits, because I shall be able to live without washing."

" He who has robbed you, is he well off?"

" Oh yes."

" Then he shall pay dearly for it.   Who is it ?"

" Monseigneur du Fou."

" Oh, that alters the case," said the judge.

" But justice ?" said she.

" I said the case, not the justice of it," replied the judge.
" I must know how the affair occurred."

Then the girl related naïvely how she was arranging the
young lord's ruffles in his wardrobe, when he began to play
with her skirts, and she turned round, saying—

" Go on with you !"

" You have no case," said the judge, " for by that speech
he thought that you gave him leave to go on.   Ha ! ha !"

Then she declared that she had defended herself, weeping
and crying out, and that that constitutes an assault.

" A wench's antics to incite him," said the judge.

Finally, La Portillone declared that against her will she
had been taken round the waist and thrown, although she
had kicked and cried and struggled, but that seeing no help
at hand, she had lost courage.

" Good ! good !" said the judge.   " Did you take pleasure
in the affair ?"

" No," said she.   " My anguish can only be paid for with
a thousand crowns."

" My dear," said the judge, " I cannot receive your complaint, because I believe no girl can be thus treated against
her will."

" Hi ! hi ! hi !   Ask your servant," said the little laundress
sobbing, " and hear what she'll tell you."

The servant affirmed that there were pleasant assaults and
unpleasant ones ; that if La Portillone had received neither
amusement nor money, either one or the other was due to
her.   This wise counsel threw the judge into a state of great
perplexity.

" Jacqueline," said he, " before I sup I'll get to the bottom
of this.   Now go and fetch my needle and the red thread
that I sew the law paper bags with."

Jacqueline came back with a big needle, pierced with a
pretty little hole, and a big red thread, such as the judges

use. Then she remained standing to see the question decided, very much disturbed, as was also the complainant at
these mysterious preparations.

"My dear," said the judge, "I am going to hold the
bodkin, of which the eye is sufficiently large, to put this thread
into it without trouble. If you do put it in, I will take up
your case, and will make Monseigneur offer you a compromise."

"What's that?" said she. "I will not allow it."

"It is a word used in justice to signify an agreement."

"A compromise is then agreeable with iustice?" said La
Portillone.

"My dear, this violence has also opened your mind.
Are you ready?"

"Yes," said she.

The waggish judge gave the poor nymph fair play, holding
the eye steady for her; but when she wished to slip in the
thread that she had twisted to make straight, he moved a
little, and the thread went on the other side. She suspected the judge's argument, wetted the thread, stretched it,
and came back again. The judge moved, twisted about,
and wriggled like a bashful maiden; still the cursed thread
would not enter. The girl kept trying at the eye, and the
judge kept fidgeting. The marriage of the thread could
not be consummated, the bodkin remained virgin, and the
servant began to laugh, saying to La Portillone that she
knew better how to endure than to perform. Then the
roguish judge laughed too, and the fair Portillone cried
for her golden crowns.

"If you don't keep still," cried she, losing patience;
"if you keep moving about I shall never be able to put the
thread in."

"Then, my dear, if you had done the same, Monseigneur
would have been unsuccessful too. Think, too, how
easy is the one affair, and how difficult the other."

The pretty wench, who declared she had been forced, remained thoughtful, and sought to find a means to convince
the judge by showing how she had been compelled to yield,

since the honour of all poor girls liable to violence was at stake.

"Monseigneur, in order that the bet may be fair, I must do exactly as the young lord did. If I had only had to move I should be moving still, but he went through other performances."

"Let us hear them," replied the judge.

Then La Portillone straightens the thread, and rubs it in the wax of the candle, to make it firm and straight; then she looks towards the eye of the bodkin, held by the judge, slipping always to the right or to the left. Then she began making endearing little speeches, such as, "Ah, the pretty little bodkin! what a pretty mark to aim at! Never did I see such a little jewel! What a pretty little eye! Let me put this little thread into it! Ah, you will hurt my poor thread, my nice little thread! Keep still! Come, my love of a judge, judge of my love! Wont the thread go nicely into this iron gate, which makes good use of the thread, for it comes out very much out of order?" Then she burst out laughing, for she was better up in this game than the judge, who laughed too, so saucy and comical and arch was she, pushing the thread backwards and forwards. She kept the poor judge with the case in his hand until seven o'clock, keeping on fidgeting and moving about like a schoolboy let loose; but as La Portillone kept on trying to put the thread in, he could not help it. As, however, his joint was burning, and his wrist was tired, he was obliged to rest himself for a minute on the side of the table; then very dexterously the fair maid of Portillon slipped the thread in, saying—

"That's how the thing occurred."

"But my joint was burning."

"So was mine," said she.

The judge, convinced, told La Portillone that he would speak to Monseigneur du Fou, and would himself carry the affair through, since it was certain the young lord had embraced her against her will, but that for valid reasons he would keep the affair dark. On the morrow the judge went to the Court and saw Monseigneur du Fou, to whom he recounted the young woman's complaint, and how she had set forth her case. This complaint lodged in Court, tickled the king immensely. Young du Fou having said that there was some truth in it, the king asked if he had much difficulty, and as he replied, innocently, " No," the king declared the girl was quite worth a hundred gold crowns, and the chamberlain gave them to the judge, in order not to be taxed with stinginess, and said that starch would be a good income to La Portillone. The judge came back to La Portillone, and said, smiling, that he had raised a hundred gold crowns for her. But if she desired the balance of the thousand, there were at that moment in the king's apartment certain lords who, knowing the case, had offered to make up the sum for her, with her consent. The little hussy did not refuse this offer, saying, that in order to do no more washing in the future she did not mind doing a little hard work now. She gratefully acknowledged the trouble the good judge had taken, and gained her thousand crowns in a month. From this came the falsehoods and jokes concerning her, because out of these ten lords jealousy made a hundred, whilst, differently from young men, La Portillone settled down to a virtuous life directly she had her thousand crowns. Even a duke, who would have counted out five hundred crowns,

would have found this girl rebellious, which proves she was niggardly with her property. It is true that the king caused her to be sent for to his retreat of the Rue Quinquangrogne, on the mall of Chardonneret, found her extremely pretty, exceedingly affectionate, enjoyed her society, and forbade the sergeants to interfere with her in any way whatever. Seeing she was so beautiful, Nicole Beaupertuis, the king's mistress, gave her a hundred gold crowns to go

to Orleans, in order to see if the colour of the Loire was
the same there as at Portillon. She went there, and the
more willingly because she did not care very much for the
king. When the good man came who confessed the king
in his last hours, and was afterwards canonized, La Portillone
went to him to polish up her conscience, did penance,
and founded a bed in the leper-house of St. Lazare-les-
Tours. Many ladies whom you know have been assaulted
by more than two lords, and have founded no other beds
than those of their own houses. It is as well to relate this fact,
in order to cleanse the reputation of this honest girl, who
herself once washed dirty things, and who afterwards became famous for her clever tricks and her wit. She gave a
proof of her merit in marrying Taschereau, whom she
cuckolded right merrily, as has been related in the story of
The Reproach. This proves to us most satisfactorily that
with strength and patience justice itself can be violated.

IN WHICH IT IS DEMONSTRATED THAT FORTUNE IS ALWAYS FEMININE.

DURING the time when knights courteously offered to each other both help and assistance in seeking their fortunes, it happened that in Sicily—which, as you are probably aware, is an island situated in the corner of the Mediterranean Sea, and formerly celebrated—one knight met in a wood another knight, who had the appearance of a Frenchman. Presumably, this Frenchman was by some chance stripped of everything, and was so wretchedly attired that but for his princely air he might have been taken for a blackguard. It was possible that his horse had died of hunger or fatigue, on disembarking from the foreign shore from which he came, on the faith of the good luck which happened to the French in Sicily, which was true in every respect. The Sicilian knight, whose name was Pezare, was a Venetian long absent from the Venetian republic, and with no desire to return there, since he had obtained a footing in the Court of the King of Sicily. Being short of funds in Venice, because he was a younger son, he had no fancy for commerce, and was for that reason eventually abandoned by

One knight met in a wood another knight, who had the
appearance of a Frenchman.

his family, a most illustrious one.   He therefore remained at this Court, where he was much liked by the king.   This gentleman was riding a splendid Spanish horse, and thinking to himself how lonely he was in this strange Court, without trusty friends, and how in such cases fortune was harsh to helpless people and became a traitress, when he met the poor French knight, who appeared far worse off than he, who had good weapons, a fine horse, and a mansion where servants were then preparing a sumptuous supper.

" You must have come a long way to have so much dust on your feet," said the Venetian.

" My feet have not as much dust as the road was long," answered the Frenchman.

" If you have travelled so much," continued the Venetian, "you must be a learned man."

"I have learned," replied the Frenchman, " to give no heed to those who do not trouble about me. I have learned that however high a man's head was, his feet were always level with mine ; more than that, I have learned to have no confidence in the warm days of winter, in the sleep of my enemies, or the words of my friends."

"You are, then, richer than I am," said the Venetian, astonished, " since you tell me things of which I never thought."

" Every one must think for himself," said the Frenchman ; " and as you have interrogated me, I can request from you the kindness of pointing to me the road to Palermo or some inn, for the night is closing in."

" Are you, then, acquainted with no French or Sicilian gentleman at Palermo ?"

" No."

" Then you are not certain of being received ?"

" I am disposed to forgive those who reject me.   The road, sir, if you please."

"I am lost like yourself," said the Venetian.   " Let us look for it in company."

" To do that we must go together ; but you are on horse-back, I am on foot."

The Venetian took the French knight on his saddle be hind him, and said—

" Do you know with whom you are ?"

" With a man, apparently."

" Do you think you are in safety ?"

" If you were a robber, you would have to take care of yourself," said the Frenchman, putting the point of his dagger to the Venetian's heart.

" Well, now, my noble Frenchman, you appear to me a man of great learning and sound sense ; know that I am a noble, established at the Court of Sicily, but alone, and I seek a friend. You seem to be in the same plight, and, judging from appearances, you do not seem friendly with your lot, and have, apparently, need of everybody."

" Should I be happier if everybody wanted me ?"

" You are a devil, who turn every one of my words against me. By St. Mark ! my lord knight, can one trust you ?"

" More than yourself, who commenced our federal friendship by deceiving me, since you guide your horse like a man who knows his way, and you said you were lost."

" And did not you deceive me," said the Venetian, " by making a sage of your year's walk, and giving a noble knight the appearance of a vagabond ? Here is my abode; my servants have prepared supper for us."

The Frenchman jumped off the horse, and entered the house with the Venetian cavalier, accepting his supper. They both seated themselves at the table. The Frenchman fought so well with his jaws, he twisted the morsels with so much agility, that he showed himself equally learned in suppers, and showed it again in dexterously draining the wine flasks without his eye becoming dimmed or his understanding affected. Then you may be sure the Venetian thought to himself that he had fallen in with a fine son of Adam, sprung from the right side and the wrong one. While they were drinking together, the Venetian endeavoured to find some joint through which to sound the secret depths of his friend's cogitations. He, however, clearly perceived that he would cast aside his shirt sooner than his prudence, and judged it opportune to gain his esteem by opening his doublet to him. Therefore he told him in what

state was Sicily, where reigned Prince Leufroid and his gentle wife; how gallant was the Court, what courtesy there flourished, that there abounded many lords of Spain, Italy, France, and other countries, lords in high feather and well feathered; many princesses, as rich as noble, and as noble as rich; that this prince had the loftiest aspirations—such as to conquer Morocco, Constantinople, Jerusalem, the lands of Soudan, and other African places. Certain men of vast minds conducted his affairs, bringing together the ban and *arrière* ban of the flower of Christian chivalry, and kept up this splendour with the idea of causing to reign over the Mediterranean this Sicily, so opulent in times gone by, and of ruining Venice, which had not a foot of land. These designs had been planted in the king's mind by him, Pezare ; but although he was high in that prince's favour, he felt himself weak, had no assistance from the courtiers, and desired to make a friend. In this great trouble he had gone for a little ride to turn matters over in his mind, and decide upon the course to pursue. Now, since while in this idea he had met a man of so much sense as the chevalier had proved himself to be, he proposed to fraternize with him, to open his purse to him, and give him his palace to live in. They would journey in company through life in search of honours and pleasure, without concealing one single thought, and would assist each

other on all occasions as the brothers-in-arms did at the
Crusades. Now, as the Frenchman was seeking his fortune,
and required assistance, the Venetian did not for a moment
expect that this offer of mutual consolation would be
refused.

"Although I stand in need of no assistance," said the
Frenchman, "because I rely upon a point which will procure me all that I desire, I should like to acknowledge your
courtesy, dear Chevalier Pezare. You will soon see that
you will yet be the debtor of Gauttier de Montsoreau, a
gentleman of the fair land of Touraine."

"Do you possess any relic with which your fortune is
wound up?" said the Venetian.

"A talisman given me by my dear mother," said the
Tourainian, "with which castles and cities are built and
demolished, a hammer to coin money, a remedy for every
ill, a traveller's staff always ready to be tried, and worth
most when in a state of readiness, a master tool, which
executes wondrous works in all sorst of forges, without
making the slightest noise."

"Eh! by St. Mark you have, then, a mystery concealed
in your hauberk?"

"No," said the French knight; "it is a perfectly natural
thing. Here it is."

And rising suddenly from the table to prepare for bed,
Gauttier showed the Venetian the finest talisman to procure
joy that he had ever seen.

"This," said the Frenchman, as they both got into bed
together, according to the custom of the times, "overcomes
every obstacle, by making itself master of female hearts;
and as the ladies are the queens in this Court, your friend
Gauttier will soon reign there."

The Venetian remained in great astonishment at the sight
of the secret charms of the said Gauttier, who had indeed
been bounteously endowed by his mother, and perhaps also
by his father, and would thus triumph over everything,
since he joined to this corporeal perfection the wit of a
young page, and the wisdom of an old devil. Then they

swore an eternal friendship, regarding as nothing therein a woman's heart, vowing to have one and the same idea,

as if their heads had been in the same helmet ; and they fell asleep on the same pillow enchanted with this fraternity. This was a common occurrence in those days.

On the morrow the Venetian gave a fine horse to his friend Gauttier, also a purse full of money, fine silken hose, a velvet doublet, fringed with gold, and an embroidered mantle, which garments set off his figure so well, and showed up his beauties, that the Venetian was certain he would captivate all the ladies. The servants received orders to obey this Gauttier as they would himself, so that they fancied their master had been fishing, and had caught this Frenchman. Then the two friends made their entry into Palermo at the hour when the princes and princesses were taking the air. Pezare presented his French friend, speaking so highly of his merits, and obtaining such a gracious reception for him, that Leufroid kept him to supper. The knight kept a sharp eye on the Court, and noticed therein various curious little secret practices. If the king was a brave and handsome prince, the princess was a Spanish lady of high temperature, the most beautiful and most noble

woman of his Court, but inclined to melancholy. Looking at her, the Tourainian believed that she was sparingly embraced by the king, for the law of Touraine is that joy in the face comes from joy elsewhere. Pezare pointed out to his friend Gauttier several ladies to whom Leufroid was exceedingly gracious, and who were exceedingly jealous, and fought for him in a tournament of gallantries and wonderful female inventions. From all this Gauttier concluded that the prince went considerably astray with his Court, although he had the prettiest wife in the world, and occupied himself by taxing the ladies of Sicily, in order that he might put his horse in their stables, vary his fodder, and learn the equestrian capabilities of many lands. Perceiving what a life Leufroid was leading, the Sire de Montsoreau, certain that no one in the Court had had the heart to enlighten the queen, determined at one blow to plant his halberd in the field of the fair Spaniard by a master stroke; and this is how. At supper-time, in order to show courtesy to the foreign knight, the king took care to place him near the queen, to whom the gallant Gauttier offered his arm, to take her into the room, and conducted her there hastily, to get ahead of those who were following, in order to whisper, first of all, a word concerning a subject which always pleases the ladies in whatever condition they may be. Imagine what this word was, and how it went straight through the stubble and weeds into the warm thicket of love.

"I know, your majesty, what causes your paleness of face."

"What?" said she.

"You are so loving that the king loves you night and day; thus you abuse your advantage, for he will die of love."

"What should I do to keep him alive?" said the queen.

"Forbid him to repeat at your altar more than three prayers a day."

"You are joking after the French fashion, Sir Knight, seeing that the king's devotion to me does not extend beyond a short prayer a week."

"You are deceived," said Gauttier, seating himself at the table. "I can prove to you that love should go through the whole mass, matins, and vespers, with an *Ave* now and then, for queens as for simple women, and go through the cere-

mony every day, like the monks in their monastery, with fervour; but for you these litanies should never finish."

The queen cast upon the knight a glance which was far from one of displeasure, smiled at him, and shook her head.

"In this," said she, "men are great liars."

"I have with me a great truth which I will show you when you wish it," replied the knight. "I undertake to give you queen's fare, and put you on the high road to joy; by this means you will make up for lost time, the more so as the king is ruined through other women, while I have reserved my advantages for your service."

"And if the king learns our arrangement, he will put your head on a level with your feet."

"Even if this misfortune befel me after the first night, I should believe I had lived a hundred years, from the joy therein received, for never have I seen, after having visited all Courts, a princess fit to hold a candle to your beauty. To be brief, if I die not by the sword, you will still be the cause of my death, for I am resolved to spend my life in our love, if life will depart in the place whence it comes."

Now this queen had never heard such words before, and preferred them to the most sweetly sung mass; her pleasure showed itself in her face, which became purple, for these

words made her blood boil within her veins, so that the strings
of her lute were moved thereat, and struck a sweet note that
rang melodiously in her ears, for this lute fills with its music
the brain and the body of the ladies, by a sweet artifice of
their resonant nature. What a shame to be young, beautiful, Spanish, and queen, and yet neglected. She conceived
an intense disdain for those of her Court who had kept their
lips closed concerning this infidelity, through fear of the
king, and determined to revenge herself with the aid of this
handsome Frenchman, who cared so little for life that in his
first words he had staked it in making a proposition to a
queen, which was worthy of death, if she did her duty. Instead of this, however, she pressed his foot with her own, in
a manner that admitted of no misconception, and said aloud
to him—

"Sir Knight, let us change the subject, for it is very wrong
of you to attack a poor queen in her weak spot. Tell us the
customs of the ladies of the Court of France."

Thus did the knight receive the delicate hint that the
business was arranged. Then he commenced to talk of
merry and pleasant things, which during supper kept the
Court, the king, the queen, and all the courtiers in a good
humour; so much so that when the siege was raised, Leufroid declared that he had never laughed so much in his life.
Then they strolled about the gardens, which were the most
beautiful in the world, and the queen made a pretext of the
chevalier's sayings to walk beneath a grove of blossoming
orange trees, which yielded a delicious fragrance.

"Lovely and noble queen," said Gauttier, immediately,
"I have seen in all countries the perdition of love have its
birth in those first attentions, which we call courtesy; if you
have confidence in me, let us agree, as people of high intelligence, to love each other without standing on so much ceremony; by this means no suspicions will be aroused, our
happiness will be less dangerous and more lasting. In this
fashion should queens conduct their amours, if they would
avoid interference."

"Well said," said she. "But as I am new at this business,
I do not know what arrangements to make."

Then they strolled about the gardens, which were the most beautiful in the world, and the queen made a pretext of the chevalier's sayings to walk beneath a grove of blossoming orange trees, which yielded a delicious fragrance.

" Have you among your women one in whom you have perfect confidence?"

" Yes," said she ; " I have a maid who came from Spain with me, who would put herself on a gridiron for me, like St. Lawrence did for God, but she is always poorly."

" That's good," said her companion, " because you go to see her."

" Yes," said the queen, " and sometimes at night."

" Ah !" exclaimed Gauttier, " I make a vow to St. Rosalie, patroness of Sicily, to build her a golden altar for this fortune."

" O Jesus !" cried the queen. " I am doubly blessed in having a lover so handsome and yet so religious."

" Ah, my dear, I have two sweethearts to-day, because I have a queen to love in heaven above and another one here below, and luckily these loves cannot clash one with the other."

This sweet speech so affected the queen, that for a nothing she would have fled with this cunning Frenchman.

" The Virgin Mary is very powerful in heaven," said the queen. " Love grant that I may be like her !"

" Bah ! they are talking of the Virgin Mary," said the king, who by chance had come to watch them, disturbed by a gleam of jealousy, cast into his heart by a Sicilian courtier, who was furious at the sudden favour which the Frenchman had obtained.

The queen and the chevalier laid their plans, and everything was secretly arranged to furnish the helmet of the king with two invisible ornaments. The knight rejoined the Court, made himself agreeable to every one, and returned to the palace of Pezare, whom he told that their fortunes were made, because on the morrow, at night, he would sleep with the queen. This swift success astonished the Venetian, who, like a good friend, went in search of fine perfumes, linen of Brabant, and precious garments, to which queens are accustomed, with all of which he loaded his friend Gauttier, in order that the case might be worthy the jewel.

" Ah, my friend," said he, " are you sure not to falter,

but to go vigorously to work, to serve the queen bravely, and give her such joys in her castle of Gallardin that she may hold on for ever to this master staff, like a drowning sailor to a plank ?"

"As for that, fear nothing, dear Pezare, because I have the arrears of the journey, and I will deal with her as with a simple servant, instructing her in the ways of the ladies of Touraine, who understand love better than all others, because they make it, remake it, and unmake it to make it again ; and having remade it, still keep on making it ; and having nothing else to do, have to do that which always wants doing.   Now let us settle our plans.   This is how we shall obtain the government of this island.   I shall hold the queen and you the king ; we will play the comedy of being great enemies before the eyes of the courtiers, in order to divide them into two parties under our command, and yet, unknown to all, we will remain friends.   By this means we shall know their plots, and will thwart them, you by listening to my enemies and I to yours.   In the course of a few days we will pretend to quarrel, in order to strive one against the other.   This quarrel will be caused by the favour in which I will manage to place you with the king, through the channel of the queen, and he will give you supreme power, to my injury.

On the morrow Gauttier went to the house of the Spanish lady, whom before the courtiers he recognised as having known in Spain, and he remained there seven whole days. As you can imagine, the Tourainian treated the queen as a fondly loved woman, and showed her so many *terra incognita* in love, French fashions, little tendernesses, &c., that she nearly lost her reason through it, and swore that the French were the only people who thoroughly understood love.   You see how the king was punished, who, to keep her virtuous, had allowed weeds to grow in the grange of love.   Their supernatural festivities touched the queen so strongly that she made a vow of eternal love to Montsoreau, who had awaked her, by revealing to her the joys of the proceeding.   It was arranged that the Spanish lady should take care always to be ill ; and that the only man to whom the lovers would confide their secret should be the court physician, who was much attached to the queen. By chance this physician had in his glottis, chords exactly similar to those of Gauttier, so that by a freak of nature they had the same voice, which much astonished the queen. The physician swore on his life faithfully to serve the pretty couple, for he deplored the sad desertion of this beautiful woman, and was delighted to know she would be served as a queen should be—a rare thing.

A month elapsed and everything was going on to the satisfaction of the two friends, who worked the plans laid by the queen, in order to get the government of Sicily into the hands of Pezare, to the detriment of Montsoreau, whom the king loved for his great wisdom; but the queen would not consent to have him, because he was so ungallant. Leufroid dismissed the Duke of Cataneo, his principal follower, and put the Chevalier Pezare in his place. The Venetian took no notice of his friend the Frenchman. Then Gauttier burst out, declaiming loudly against the treachery and abused friendship of his former comrade, and instantly earned the devotion of Cataneo and his friends, with whom he made a compact to overthrow Pezare. Directly he was in office the Venetian, who was a shrewd man, and well suited to govern states, which was the usual employment of Venetian gentlemen, worked wonders in Sicily, repaired the ports, brought merchants there by the fertility of his inventions and by granting them facilities, put bread into the mouths of hundreds of poor people, drew thither artisans of all trades, because fêtes were always being held, and also the idle and rich from all quarters, even from the East. Thus harvests, the products of the earth, and other commodities, were plentiful ; and galleys and ships came from Asia, the which made the king much envied, and the happiest king in the Christian world, because through these things his Court was the most renowned in the countries of Europe. This fine political aspect was the result of the perfect agreement of two men

who thoroughly understood each other. The one looked
after the pleasures, and was himself the delight of the queen,
whose face was always bright and gay, because she was
served according to the method of Touraine, and because

animated through excessive happiness ; and he also took care to keep
the king amused, finding him every
day new mistresses, and casting him
into a whirl of dissipation. The
king was much astonished at the
good temper of the queen, whom,
since the arrival of the Sire de Montsoreau in the island, he had touched
no more than a Jew touches bacon.
Thus occupied, the king and the
queen abandoned the care of their
kingdom to the other friend, who
conducted the affairs of government,
ruled the establishment, managed the
finances, and looked to the army,
and all exceedingly well, knowing where money was to be
made, enriching the treasury, and preparing all the great
enterprises above mentioned.

This state of things lasted three years, some say four, but
the monks of Saint Benoist have not wormed out the date,
which remains obscure, like the reasons for the quarrel between the two friends. Probably the Venetian had the high
ambition to reign without any control or dispute, and forgot
the services which the Frenchman had rendered him. Thus
do the men who live in Courts behave, for, according to the
statements of Messire Aristotle in his works, that which ages
the most rapidly in this world is a kindness, although extinguished love is sometimes very rancid. Now, relying on the
perfect friendship of Leufroid, who called him his crony, and
would have done anything for him, the Venetian conceived
the idea of getting rid of his friend by revealing to the king
the mystery of his cuckoldom, and showing him the source
of the queen's happiness, not doubting for a moment but
that he would commence by depriving Montsoreau of his

head, according to a practice common in Sicily under similar circumstances. By this means Pezare would have all the money that he and Gauttier had noiselessly conveyed to the house of a Lombard of Genes, which money was their joint property on account of their fraternity. This treasure, increased on one side by the magnificent presents made to Montsoreau by the queen, who had vast estates in Spain, and other, by inheritance in Italy; on the other, by the king's gifts to his prime minister, to whom he also gave certain rights over the merchants, and other indulgences. The treacherous friend, having determined to break his vow, took care to conceal his intention from Gauttier, because the Tourainian was an awkward man to tackle. One night that Pezare knew that the queen was in bed with her

lover, who loved her still as though each night were a wedding one, so skilful was she at the business, the traitor promised the king to let him take evidence in the case, through a hole which he had made in the wardrobe of the Spanish lady, who always pretended to be at death's door. In order to obtain a better view, Pezare waited until the sun had risen. The Spanish lady, who was fleet of foot, had a quick eye and a sharp ear, heard footsteps, peeped out, and perceived the king, followed by the Venetian, through a crossbar in the closet in which she slept the nights that the queen had her lover between two sheets, which is certainly the best way to have a lover. She ran to warn the couple of this betrayal. But the king's eye was already at the cursed hole. Leufroid saw—what? That beautiful and divine lantern which burns so much oil and lights the world —a lantern adorned with the most lovely baubles, flaming brilliantly, which he thought more lovely than all the others, because he had lost sight of it for so long a time that it appeared quite new to him ; but the size of the hole prevented him seeing anything else, except the hand of a man, which modestly covered the lantern, and he heard the voice of Montsoreau saying, "How's the little treasure, this morning?" A playful expression, which lovers use jokingly, because this lantern is in all countries the sun of love, and for this the prettiest possible names are bestowed upon it, while comparing it to the loveliest things in nature, such as my pomegranate, my rose, my little shell, my hedgehog, my gulf of love, my treasure, my master, my little one ; some even dared most heretically to say, my god ! If you don't believe it, ask your friends.

At this moment the lady let them understand by a gesture that the king was there.

"Can he hear?" said the queen.

"Yes."

"Can he see?"

"Yes."

"Who brought him?"

"Pezare."

"Fetch the physician, and get Gauttier into his own room," said the queen.

In less time than it takes a beggar to say "God bless you, sir !" the queen had swathed the lantern in linen and paint,

so that you would have thought it a hideous wound in a state of grievous inflammation. When the king, enraged by what he overheard, burst open the door, he found the queen lying on the bed exactly as he had seen her through the hole, and the physician, examining the lantern swathed in bandages, and saying, "How is the little treasure, this morning?" in exactly

the same voice as the king had heard. A jocular and
cheerful expression, because physicians and surgeons use
cheerful words with ladies and treat this sweet flower
with flowery phrases. This sight made the king look as
foolish as a fox caught in a trap. The queen sprang up,
reddening with shame, and asking what man dared to in-
trude upon her privacy at such a moment, but perceiving
the king, she said to him as follows :—

"Ah ! my lord, you have discovered that which I have
endeavoured to conceal from you ; that I am so badly treated
by you that I am afflicted with a burning ailment, of which
my dignity would not allow me to complain, but which
needs secret dressing in order to assuage the influence of
the vital forces. To save my honour and your own, I am
compelled to come to my good Lady Miraflor, who consoles
me in my troubles."

Then the physician commenced to treat Leufroid to an
oration, interlarded with Latin quotations and precious
grains from Hippocrates, Galen, the school of Salerno, and
others, in which he showed him how necessary to woman
was the proper cultivation of the field of Venus, and that
there was great danger of death to queens of Spanish temperament, whose blood was excessively amorous. He delivered himself of his arguments with great solemnity of
feature, voice, and manner, in order to give the Sire de
Montsoreau time to get to bed. Then the queen took the
same text to preach the king a sermon as long as his arm,
and requested the loan of that limb, that the king might
conduct her to her apartment instead of the poor invalid,
who usually did so in order to avoid calumny. When they
were in the gallery where the Sire de Montsoreau resided,
the queen said, jokingly, "You should play a good trick
on this Frenchman, who I would wager is with some lady,
and not in his own room. All the ladies of Court are in
love with him, and there will be mischief some day through
him. If you had taken my advice he would not be in
Sicily now."

Leufroid went suddenly into Gauttier's room, whom he
found in a deep sleep, and snoring like a monk in church.

The queen returned with the king, whom she took to her
apartments, and whispered to one of the guards to send to
her the lord whose place Pezare occupied. Then, while she
fondled the king, taking breakfast with him, she took the
lord directly he came, into an adjoining room.

"Erect a gallows on the bastion," said she, "then seize
the knight Pezare, and manage so that he is hanged instantly, without giving time to write or say a single word on

any subject whatsoever. Such is our good pleasure and
supreme command."

Cataneo made no remark. While Pezare was thinking to
himself that his friend Gauttier would soon be minus his
head, the Duke Cataneo came to seize and lead him on to
the bastion, from which he could see at the queen's window
the Sire de Montsoreau in company with the king, the
queen, and the courtiers, and came to the conclusion that
he who looked after the queen had a better chance in
everything than he who looked after the king.

"My dear," said the queen to her spouse, leading him to
the window, "behold a traitor, who was endeavouring to
deprive you of that which you hold dearest in the world,

and I will give you the proofs when you have the leisure to study them."

Montsoreau, seeing the preparations for the final cere-mony, threw himself at the king's feet, to obtain the pardon of him who was his mortal enemy, at which the king was much moved.

"Sire de Montsoreau," said the queen, turning towards him with an angry look, "are you so bold as to oppose our will and pleasure?"

"You are a noble knight," said the king, "but you do not know how bitter this Venetian was against you."

Pezare was delicately strangled between the head and the shoulders, for the queen revealed his treacheries to the king, proving to him, by the declaration of a Lombard of the town, the enormous sums which Pezare had in the Bank of Genes, the whole of which were given up to Montsoreau.

This noble and lovely queen died, as related in the his-tory of Sicily, that is, in consequence of a heavy labour, during which she gave birth to a son, who was a man as great in himself as he was unfortunate in his undertakings. The king believed the physician's statement, that the sad ter-mination of this accouchement was caused by the too chaste life the queen had led, and believing himself responsible for it, he founded the Church of the Madonna, which is one of the finest in the town of Palermo. The Sire de Mont-soreau, who was a witness of the king's remorse, told him that when a king got his wife from Spain, he ought to know that this queen would require more attention than any other, because the Spanish ladies were so lively that they equalled ten ordinary women, and that if he wished a wife for show only, he should get her from the north of Ger-many, where the women are cold as ice. The good knight came back to Touraine laden with wealth, and lived there many years, but never mentioned his adventures in Sicily. He returned there to aid the king's son in his principal attempt against Naples, and left Italy when this sweet prince was wounded, as is related in the Chronicle.

Besides the high moralities contained in the title of this

tale, where it is said that fortune, being female, is always on the side of the ladies, and that men are quite right to serve them well, it shows us that silence is the better part of wisdom.   Nevertheless, the monkish author of this narrative seems to draw this other no less learned moral therefrom, that interest which makes so many friendships, breaks them also.   But from these three versions you can choose the one that best accords with your judgment and your momentary requirement.

CONCERNING A POOR MAN WHO WAS CALLED LE VIEUX PAR-CHEMINS.

THE old chronicler who furnished the hemp to weave the present story, is said to have lived at the time when the affair occurred in the city of Rouen. In the environs of this fair town, where at that time dwelt Duke Richard, an old man used to beg, whose name was Tryballot, but to whom was given the nickname of *Le Vieux par-Chemins*, or Old Man of the Roads; not because he was yellow and dry as vellum, but because he was always in the high-ways and the by-ways—up hill and down dale— slept with the sky for his counterpane, and went about in rags and tatters. Notwithstanding this, he was very popular in the duchy, where every one had grown used to him, so much so that if the month went by without any one seeing his cup held towards them, people would say, "Where is the old man?" and the usual answer was, "On the roads."

This said man had had for a father a Tryballot, who was in his lifetime a skilled artisan, so economical and careful, that he left considerable wealth to his son. But the young lad soon frittered it away, for he was the very opposite of the old fellow, who, returning from the fields to his house,

Le Vieux par-Chemins.

picked up, now here, now there, many a little stick of wood
left right and left, saying, conscientiously, that one should
never come home empty handed. Thus he warmed himself in winter at the expense of the careless ; and he did
well. Every one recognised what a good example this was
for the country, since a year before his death no one left a
morsel of wood on the road ; he had compelled the most
dissipated to be thrifty and orderly. But his son made
ducks and drakes of everything, and did not follow his wise
examples. The father had predicted the thing. From the

boy's earliest youth, when the good Tryballot set him to
watch the birds who came to eat the peas, the beans, and
the grain, and to drive the thieves away, above all, the jays,
who spoiled everything, he would study their habits, and
took delight in watching with what grace they came and
went, flew off loaded, and returned, watching with a quick
eye the snares and nets ; and he would laugh heartily at
their cleverness in avoiding them. Tryballot senior went
into a passion when he found his grain considerably less in
measure. But although he pulled his son's ears whenever
he caught him idling and trifling under a nut tree, the little
rascal did not alter his conduct, but continued to study the

habits of the blackbirds, sparrows, and other intelligent marauders. One day his father told him that he would be wise to model himself after them, for that if he continued this kind of life, he would be compelled in his old age, like them, to pilfer, and, like them, would be pursued by justice. This came true; for, as has before been stated, he dissipated in a few days the crowns which his careful father had acquired in a lifetime. He dealt with men as he did with the sparrows, letting every one put a hand in his pocket, and contemplating the grace and polite demeanour of those who assisted to empty it. The end of his wealth was thus soon reached. When the devil had the empty money bag to himself, Tryballot did not appear at all cut up, saying, that he " did not wish to damn himself for this world's goods, and that he had studied philosophy in the school of the birds."

After having thoroughly enjoyed himself, of all his goods, there only remained to him a goblet bought at Landict, and three dice, quite sufficient furniture for drinking and gambling, so that he went about without being encumbered, as are the great, with chariots, carpets, dripping-pans, and an infinite number of varlets. Tryballot wished to see his good friends, but they no longer knew him, which fact gave him leave no longer to recognise any one. Seeing this, he determined to choose a profession in which there was nothing to do and plenty to gain. Thinking this over, he remembered the indulgences of the blackbirds and the sparrows. Then the good Tryballot selected for his profession that of begging money at people's houses, and pilfering. From the first day, charitable people gave him something, and Tryballot was content, finding the business good, without advance money or bad debts; on the contrary, full of accommodation. He went about it so heartily, that he was liked everywhere, and received a thousand consolations refused to rich people. The good man watched the peasants planting, sowing, reaping, and making harvest, and said to himself, that they worked a little for him as well. He who had a pig in his larder owed him a bit of it, without suspecting it. The man who baked a loaf in his oven often cooked it for Tryballot without knowing it. He took nothing by force; on the contrary, people said to him kindly, while making him a present, "Here, Vieux par-Chemins, cheer up, old fellow. How are you? Come, take this; the cat began it, you can finish it."

Vieux par-Chemins was at all the weddings, baptisms, and funerals, because he went everywhere where there was, openly or secretly, merriment and feasting. He religiously kept the statutes and canons of his order—namely, to do nothing, because if he had been able to do the smallest amount of work no one would ever give him anything again. After having refreshed himself, this wise man would lay at full length in a ditch, or against a church wall, and think over public affairs; and then he would philosophise, like his pretty tutors, the blackbirds, jays, and sparrows, and thought a good deal while mumping; for, because his apparel was poor, was that a reason his understanding should not be rich? His philosophy amused his clients, to whom he would repeat, by way of thanks, the finest aphorisms of his science. According to him, suppers produced gout in the rich; he boasted that he had nimble feet, because his shoemaker gave him boots that did not pinch his corns. There were aching heads beneath diadems, but his never ached, because it was touched neither by luxury nor any other chaplet. And again, that jewelled rings hindered the circulation of the blood. Although he covered himself with sores, after the manner of cadgers, you may be sure he was as sound as a child at the baptismal font. The good man disported himself with other rogues, playing with his three dice, which he kept to remind him to spend his coppers, in order that he might always be poor. In spite of his vow, he was, like all the order of mendicants, so wealthy that one day at the Paschal feast, another beggar wishing to rent his profit from him, Vieux par-Chemins refused ten crowns for it; in fact, the same evening he spent fourteen crowns in drinking the healths of the alms-givers, because it is in the statutes of beggary that one should show one's gratitude to donors. Although he carefully got rid of that which had been a source of anxiety to others, who having too much

This wise man would lay at full length in a ditch or against
a church wall, and think over public affairs.

The good man disported himself with other rogues,
playing with his three dice.

wealth went in search of poverty, he was happier with nothing in the world than when he had his father's money. And seeing what are the conditions of nobility, he was always on the high road to it, because he did nothing except according to his fancy, and lived nobly without labour. Thirty crowns would not have got him out of a bed when he was once in it. The morrow always dawned for him as it did for others, while leading this happy life ; which, according to the statement of Plato, whose authority has more than once been invoked in these narratives, certain ancient sages had led before him. At last Vieux par-Chemins reached the age of eighty-two years, having never been a single day without picking up money, and possessed the healthiest colour and complexion imaginable. He believed that if he had persevered in the race for wealth he would have been spoiled and buried years before. It is possible he was right.

In his early youth Vieux par-Chemins had the illustrious virtue of being very partial to the ladies ; and his abundance of love was, it is said, the result of his studies among the sparrows. Thus it was that he was always ready to give the ladies his assistance in counting the joists, and this gene-rosity finds its physical cause in the fact that, having nothing to do, he was always ready to do something. His secret virtues brought about, it is said, that popularity which he enjoyed in the provinces. Certain people say that the lady of Caumont had him in her castle, to learn the truth about these qualities, and kept him there for a week, to prevent him begging. But the good man jumped over the hedges and fled in great terror of being rich. Ad-vancing in age, this great quintessencer found himself disdained, although his notable faculties of loving were in no way impaired. This unjust turning away on the part of the female tribe caused the first trouble of Vieux par-Chemins, and the celebrated trial of Rouen, to which it is time I came.

In this eighty-second year of his age he was compelled to

remain continent for about seven months, during which time he met no woman kindly disposed towards him; and he declared before the judge that that caused the greatest astonishment of his long and honourable life. In this most pitiable state he saw in the fields during the merry month of May a girl, who by chance was a maiden, and minding cows. The heat was so excessive that this cowherdess had stretched herself beneath the shadow of a beech tree, her face to the ground, after the custom of people who labour in the fields, in order to get a little nap while her animals were grazing. She was awakened by the deed of the old man, who had stolen from her that which a poor girl can only lose once. Finding herself ruined without receiving from the process either knowledge or pleasure, she cried out so loudly that the people working in the fields ran to her, and were called upon by her as witnesses, at the time when that destruction was visible in her which is appropriate only to a bridal night. She cried and groaned, saying that the old ape might just as well have played his tricks on her mother, who would have said nothing.

He made answer to the peasants, who had already raised their hoes to kill him, that he had been compelled to enjoy himself. These people objected that a man can enjoy himself very well without enjoying a maiden—a case for the provost, which would bring him straight to the gallows; and he was taken with a great clamour to the gaol at Rouen.

The girl, interrogated by the provost, declared that she was sleeping in order to do something, and that she thought she was dreaming of her lover, with whom she was then at loggerheads, because before marriage he wished to take certain liberties; and, jokingly, in this dream she let him reconnoitre to a certain extent, in order to avoid any dispute afterwards, and that in spite of her prohibition he went further than she had given him leave to go, and finding more pain than pleasure in the affair, she had been awaked by Vieux par-Chemins, who had attacked her as a grey-friar would a ham at the end of Lent.

This trial caused so great a commotion in the town of Rouen that the provost was sent for by the duke, who had an

intense desire to know if the thing were true. Upon the affirmation of the provost, he ordered Vieux par-Chemins to be
brought to his palace, in order that he might hear what defence
he had to make.   The poor old fellow appeared before the
prince, and informed him naïvely of the misfortune which his
impulsive nature had brought upon him, declaring that he was
like a young fellow impelled by imperious desires; that up to
the present year he had sweethearts of his own, but for the last
eight months he had been a total abstainer; that he was too
poor to find favour with girls of the town; that honest
women, who once were charitable to him, had taken a dislike to his hair, which had feloniously turned white, in spite
of the green youth of his love, and that he felt compelled to
avail himself of the chance when he saw this maiden, who,
stretched at full length under the beech tree, left visible the
lining of her dress and two hemispheres white as snow,
which had deprived him of reason; that the fault was the
girl's and not his, because young maidens should be forbidden to entice passers-by by showing them that which
caused Venus to be named *Callipyge;* finally, the prince
ought to be aware what trouble a man has to control himself at the hour of noon, because that was the time of day
at which King David was smitten with the wife of the Sieur
Uriah; that where a Hebrew king, beloved of God, had
succumbed, a poor man, deprived of all joy, and reduced to
begging his bread, could not expect to escape; that for the
matter of that, he was quite willing to sing psalms for the
remainder of his days, and play upon the lute by way of
penance, in imitation of the said king, who had had the
misfortune to slay a husband, while he had only done a
trifling injury to a peasant girl.   The duke listened to the
arguments of Vieux par-Chemins, and said that he was a
man of good parts.   Then he made this memorable decree,
that if, as this beggar declared, he had need of such gratifi-
cations at his age he gave him permission to prove it at the
foot of the ladder which he would have to mount to be
hanged, according to the sentence already passed on him
by the provost; that if then, the rope being round his neck,

between the priest and the hangman, a like desire seized
him he should have a free pardon.

This decree becoming known, there was a tremendous
crowd to see the old fellow led to the gallows. There was
a line drawn up as if for a ducal entry,
and in it a many more bonnets than
hats. Vieux par-Chemins was saved
by a lady curious to see how this precious violator would finish his career.
She told the duke that religion demanded that he should have a fair
chance. And she dressed herself out
as if for a ball; she brought inten-
tionally into evidence two hillocks of
such snowy whiteness that the whitest
linen neckerchief would have paled
before them; indeed, these fruits of
love stood out, without a wrinkle, over
her corset, like two beautiful apples,
and made one's mouth water, so exquisite were they. This noble lady,
who was one of those who rouse one's
manhood, had a smile ready on her
lips for the old fellow. Vieux par-
Chemins, dressed in garments of coarse
cloth, more certain of being in the desired state after hanging than before

it, came along between the officers of justice with a sad
countenance, glancing now here and there, and seeing
nothing but head-dresses; and he would, he declared, have
given a hundred crowns for a girl tucked up as was the cowherdess, whose charms, though they had been his ruin, he
still remembered, and they might still have saved him; but,
as he was old, the remembrance was not sufficiently recent.
But when, at the foot of the ladder, he saw the twin charms
of the lady, and the pretty delta that their confluent rotun-
dities produced, the sight so much excited him that his
emotion was patent to the spectators.

"Make haste and see that the required conditions are fulfilled," said he to the officers. "I have gained my pardon, but I cannot answer for my saviour."

The lady was well pleased with this homage, which, she said, was greater than his offence. The guards, whose business it was to proceed to a verification, believed the culprit to be the devil, because never in their writs had they seen an I so perpendicular as was the old man. He was marched in triumph through the town to the palace of the duke, to whom the guards and others stated the facts. In that period of ignorance, this affair was thought so much of that the town voted the erection of a column on the spot where the old fellow gained his pardon, and he was portrayed thereon in stone in the attitude he assumed at the sight of that honest and virtuous lady. The statue was still to be seen when Rouen was taken by the English, and the writers of the period have included this history among the notable events of the reign.

As the town offered to supply the old man with all he required, and see to his sustenance, clothing, and amusements, the good duke arranged matters by giving the injured maiden a thousand crowns and marrying her to her seducer, who then lost his name of Vieux par-Chemins. He was named by the duke the Sieur de Bonne-C——. This wife was confined nine months afterwards of a perfectly formed male child, alive and kicking, and born with two teeth. From this marriage came the house of Bonne-C——, who, from motives modest but wrong, besought our well-beloved king Louis Eleventh to grant them letters patent to change their name into that of Bonne-Chose. The king pointed out to the Sieur de Bonne-C—— that there was in the State of Venice an illustrious family named *Coglioni*, who wore three "C—— au naturel" on their coat of arms. The gentlemen of the House of Bonne-C—— stated to the king that their wives were ashamed to be thus called in public assemblies; the king answered that they would lose a good deal, because there is a good deal in a name. Nevertheless, he granted the letters. After that this race was known by this name, and founded families in many provinces. The first Sieur de Bonne-C—— lived another twenty-seven years, and had another son and two daughters. But he grieved much at becoming rich, and no longer being able to pick up a living in the streets.

From this you can obtain finer lessons and higher morals than from any story you will read all your life long—of course, excepting these hundred glorious Droll Tales— namely, that never could adventure of this sort have happened to the impaired and ruined constitutions of court rascals, rich people, and others who dig their graves with their teeth by over-eating and drinking many wines that impair the implements of happiness; which said over-fed people were lolling luxuriously in costly draperies and on feather beds, while the Sieur de Bonne-Chose was roughing it. In a similar situation, if they had eaten cabbage, it would have given them the diarrhœa. This may incite many of those who read this story to change their mode of life, in order to imitate Vieux par-Chemins in his old age.

ODD SAYINGS OF THREE
PILGRIMS.

WHEN the pope left his good town of Avignon to take up his residence in Rome, certain pilgrims were thrown out who had set out for this county, and would have to pass the high Alps, in order to gain this said town of Rome, where they were going to seek the *remittimus* of various sins. Then were to be seen on the roads, and in the hostelries, those who wore the collar of the order of Cain, otherwise the flower of the penitents, all wicked fellows, burthened with leprous souls, which thirsted to bathe in the papal piscina, and all carrying with them gold or precious things to purchase absolution, pay for their beds, and present to the saints. You may be sure that those who drank water going, on their return, if the landlords gave them water, wished it to be the holy water of the cellar. At this time three pilgrims came to this said town of Avignon to their injury, seeing that it was widowed of the pope. While they were passing the Rhodane, to reach the Mediterranean coast, one of the three pilgrims, who had with him a son about ten years of age, parted company with the others, and near the town of Milan suddenly appeared again, but without the boy. Now in the evening, at supper, they had a hearty feast in order to celebrate the return of the pilgrim, who they thought had become disgusted with penitence through the pope not being in Avignon. Of these three roamers towards Rome, one had come from the city of Paris, the other from Germany, and the third, who doubtless wished to instruct his son on the journey, had his home in the duchy of Burgundy, in which he had certain fiefs, and was a younger son of the house of Villers-la-Faye (*Villa in Fago*), and was named La Vaugrenand. The German baron had met the citizen of Paris just past Lyons, and both had accosted the Sire de la Vaugrenand in sight of Avignon.

Now, in this hostelry the three pilgrims loosened their tongues, and agreed to journey to Rome together, in order the better to resist the footpads, night-birds, and other malefactors, who made it their business to ease pilgrims of that which weighed upon their bodies before the pope eased them of that which weighed upon their consciences. After drinking, the three companions commenced to talk together, for the bottle is the key of conversation, and each made this confession—that the cause of his pilgrimage was a woman. The servant who watched them drinking, told them that of a hundred pilgrims who stopped in the locality, ninety-nine were travelling from the same thing. These three wise men then began to consider how pernicious is woman to man. The baron showed the heavy gold chain that he had in his hauberk to present to Saint Peter, and said his crime was such that he would not get rid of with the value of two such chains. The Parisian took off his glove, and exposed a ring set with a white diamond, saying that he had a hundred like it for the pope. The Burgundian took off his hat, and exhibited two wonderful pearls, that were beautiful ear pendents for Notre-Dame-de-Lorette, and candidly confessed that he would rather have left them round his wife's neck.

Thereupon the servant exclaimed that their sins must have been as great as those of Visconti.

Then the pilgrims replied that they were such that **they** had each made a solemn vow in their minds never to go astray again during the remainder of their days, however beautiful the woman might be, and this in addition to the penance which the pope might impose upon them.

Then the servant expressed her astonishment that all had made the same vow. The Burgundian added, that this vow had been the cause of his lagging behind, because he had been in extreme fear that his son, in spite of his age, might go astray, and that he had made a vow to prevent people and beasts alike gratifying their passions in his house, or upon his estates. The baron having inquired the particulars of the adventure, the sire narrated the affair as follows :—

"You know that the good Countess Jeanne d'Avignon made formerly a law for the harlots, whom she compelled to live in the outskirts of the town in houses with window-shutters painted red and closed. Now passing in your company through this vile neighbourhood, my lad remarked these houses with closed window-shutters, painted red, and his curiosity being aroused—for these ten-year old little devils have eyes for everything—he pulled me by the sleeve, and kept on pulling me until he had learned from me what these houses were. Then, to obtain peace, I told him that young lads had nothing to do with such places, and could only enter them at peril of their lives, because it was a place where men and women were manufactured, and the danger was such for any one unacquainted with the business that if a novice entered, flying chancres and other wild beasts would seize upon his face. Fear seized the lad, who then followed me to the hostelry in a state of agitation, and not daring to cast his eyes upon these said bordels. While I was in the stable, seeing to the putting up of the horses, my son went off like a robber, and the servant was unable to tell me what had become of him. Then I was in great fear of the wenches, but had confidence in the laws, which forbade them to admit such children. At supper time the rascal came back to me looking no more ashamed of himself than did our divine Saviour in the temple among the doctors. 'Whence come you?' said I to him. 'From the houses with the red shutters,' he replied. 'Little blackguard,' said I, 'I'll give you a taste of the whip.' Then he began to moan and to cry. I told him that if he would confess all that had happened to him I would let him off the beating. 'Ha,' said he, 'I took good care not to go in, because of the flying chancres and other wild beast. I only looked through the chinks of the windows, in order to see how men were manufactured.' 'And what did you see?' I asked. 'I saw,' said he, 'a fine woman just being finished, because she only wanted one peg, which a young workman was fitting in with energy. Directly she was finished she turned round, spoke to, and kissed her manufacturer.'

" ' Have your supper,' said I ; and the same night I returned into Burgundy, and left him with his mother, being sorely afraid that at the first town he might want to fit a peg into some girl."

"These children often make these sort of answers," said the Parisian. "One of my neighbour's children revealed the cuckoldom of his father by a reply. One day I asked, to see if he were well instructed at school in religious matters, 'What is hope?' 'One of the king's big archers, who comes here when father goes out,' said he. Indeed, the sergeant of the archers was named Hope. My friend was dumbfounded at this, and, although to keep his countenance he looked in the mirror, he could not see his horns there."

The baron observed that the boy's remark was good in this way : that Hope is a person who comes to bed with us when the realities of life are out of the way.

"Is a cuckold made in the image of God?" asked the Burgundian.

"No," said the Parisian, "because God was wise in this respect, that he took no wife ; therefore is He happy through all eternity."

"But," said the maid-servant, "cuckolds are made in the image of God before they are horned."

Then the three pilgrims began to curse the women, saying that they were the cause of all the evil in the world.

"Their heads are as empty as helmets," said the Burgundian.

"Their hearts as straight as bill-hooks," said the Parisian.

"Why are there so many men pilgrims and so few women pilgrims?" said the German baron.

"Their cursed member never sins," replied the Parisian; "it knows neither father nor mother, the commandments of God, nor those of the Church, neither laws divine nor human: their member knows no doctrine, understands no heresies, and cannot be blamed; it is innocent of all, and always on the laugh; its understanding is *nil;* and for this reason do I hold it in utter detestation."

"I also," said the Burgundian, "and I begin to under-stand the different reading by a learned man of the verses of the Bible, in which the account of the Creation is given. In this Commentary, which in my country we call a *Noël,* lies the reason of imperfection of this feature of women, of which, different to that of other females, no man can slake the thirst, such diabolical heat existing there. In this Noël it is stated that the Lord God, having turned His head to look at a donkey, who had brayed for the first time in his Paradise, while he was manufacturing Eve, the devil seized this moment to put his finger into this too divine creature, and made a warm wound, which the Lord took care to close with a stitch, from which comes the maid. By means of this frenum, the woman should remain closed, and children be made in the same manner in which God made the angels, by a pleasure far above carnal pleasure as the heaven is above the earth. Observing this closing, the devil, wild at being done, pinched the Sieur Adam, who was asleep, by the skin, and stretched a portion of it out in imitation of his diabolical tail; but as the father of man was on his back this appendage came out in front. Thus these two produc-tions of the devil had a desire to reunite themselves, follow-ing the law of similarities which God had laid down for the conduct of the world. From this came the first sin and the sorrows of the human race, because God, noticing the devil's work, determined to see what would come of it."

The servant declared that they were quite correct in their statements, for that woman was a bad animal, and that she herself knew some who were better under the ground than on it. The pilgrims, noticing then how pretty the girl was, were afraid of breaking their vows, and went straight to bed. The girl went and told her mistress that she was harbouring infidels, and told her what they had said about women.

"Ah!" said the landlady, "what matters it to me the thoughts my customers have in their brains, so long as their purses are well filled."

And when the servant had told of the jewels, she exclaimed—

"Ah, these are questions which concern all women. Let us go and reason with them. I'll take the nobles, you can have the citizen."

The landlady, who was the most shameless inhabitant of the duchy of Milan, went into the chamber where the Sire de la Vaugrenand and the German baron were sleeping, and congratulated them upon their vows, saying that the women would not lose much by them; but to accomplish these said vows it was necessary they should endeavour to withstand the strongest temptation. Then she offered to lay down beside them, so anxious was she to see if she would be left unmolested, a thing which had never happened to her yet in the company of a man.

On the morrow, at breakfast, the servant had the ring on her finger, her mistress had the gold chain and the pearl earrings. The three pilgrims stayed in the town about a month, spending there all the money they had in their purses, and agreed that if they had spoken so severely of women it was because they had not known those of Milan.

On his return to Germany the baron made this observa-tion: that he was only guilty of one sin, that of being in his castle. The citizen of Paris came back full of stories for his wife, and found her full of Hope. The Burgundian saw Madame de la Vaugrenand so troubled that he nearly died of the consolations he administered to her, in spite of his former opinions. This teaches us to hold our tongues in hostelries.

INNOCENCE.

B Y the double red crest of my fowl, and by the rose
lining of my sweetheart's slipper! By all the horns
of well-beloved cuckolds, and by the virtue of their blessed
wives! the finest work of man is neither poetry, nor painted
pictures, nor music, nor castles, nor statues, be they carved
never so well, nor rowing, nor sailing galleys, but children.
Understand me, children up to the age of ten years, for
after that they become men or women, and cutting their
wisdom teeth, are not worth what they cost: the worst are
the best. Watch them playing, prettily and innocently,
with slippers; above all, cancellated ones, with the household utensils, leaving that which displeases them, crying
after that which pleases them, munching the sweets and
confectionery in the house, nibbling at the stores, and
always laughing as soon as their teeth are cut, and you will
agree with me that they are in every way lovable; besides
which they are flower and fruit—the fruit of love, the flower
of life. Before their minds have been unsettled by the
disturbances of life, there is nothing in this world more
blessed or more pleasant than their sayings, which are naïve
beyond description. This is as true as the double chewing
machine of a cow. Do not expect a man to be innocent

after the manner of children, because there is an, I know
not what, ingredient of reason in the naïveté of a man,
while the naïveté of children is candid, immaculate, and
has all the finesse of the mother, which is plainly proved
in this tale.

Queen Catherine was at that time Dauphine, and to make
herself welcome to the king, her father-in-law, who at that
time was very ill indeed, presented him, from time to time,
with Italian pictures, knowing that he liked them much,
being a friend of the Sieur Raphaël d'Urbin and of the
Sieurs Primatice and Leonardo da Vinci, to whom he sent
large sums of money. She obtained from her family—who
had the pick of these works, because at that time the Duke
of Medicis governed Tuscany—a precious picture, painted
by a Venetian named Titian (artist to the Emperor Charles,
and in very high favour), in which there were portraits of
Adam and Eve at the moment when God left them to
wander about the terrestrial Paradise, and were painted
their full height, in the costume of the period, in which it is
difficult to make a mistake, because they were attired in
their ignorance, and caparisoned with the divine grace
which enveloped them—a difficult thing to execute on account of the colour, but one in which the said Sieur Titian
excelled. The picture was put into the room of the poor
king, who was then ill with the disease of which he eventually died. It had a great success at the Court of France,
where every one wished to see it; but no one was able to
until after the king's death, since at his desire it was allowed
to remain in his room as long as he lived.

One day Madame Catherine took with her to the king's
room her son Francis and little Margot, who began to talk
at random, as children will. Now here, now there, these
children had heard this picture of Adam and Eve spoken
about, and had tormented their mother to take them there.
Since the two little ones at times amused the old king,
Madame the Dauphine consented to their request.

" You wished to see Adam and Eve, who were our first
parents; there they are," said she.

Then she left them in great astonishment before Titian's

picture, and seated herself by the bedside of the king, who delighted to watch the children.

"Which of the two is Adam?" said Francis, nudging his sister Margaret's elbow.

"You silly!" replied she, "to know that, they would have to be dressed!"

This reply, which delighted the poor king and the mother, was mentioned in a letter written in Florence by Queen Catherine.

No writer having brought it to light, it will remain, like a sweet flower, in a corner of these Tales, although it is in no way droll, and there is no other moral to be drawn from it except that to hear these pretty speeches of infancy one must beget the children.

THE FAIR IMPERIA MARRIED.

I.

HOW MADAME IMPERIA WAS CAUGHT IN THE VERY NET SHE WAS ACCUSTOMED TO SPREAD FOR HER LOVE-BIRDS.

THE lovely lady Imperia, who gloriously opens these tales, because she was the glory of her time, was compelled to come into the town of Rome, after the holding of the council, for the Cardinal of Ragusa loved her more than his cardinal's hat, and wished to have her near him. This rascal was so magnificent, that he presented her with the beautiful palace that she had in the Papal capital. About this time she had the misfortune to find herself in an interesting condition by this cardinal. As every one knows, this pregnancy finished with a fine little daughter, concerning whom the Pope said jokingly that she should be named Theodora, as if to say *The Gift of God*. The girl was thus named, and was exquisitely lovely. The cardinal left his inheritance to this Theodora, whom the fair Imperia established in her hotel, for she was flying from Rome as from a pernicious place, where children were begotten, and where

She should be named Theodora, as if to say *The Gift of God*.

she had nearly spoilt her beautiful figure, her celebrated perfections, lines of the body, curves of the back, delicious breasts, and serpentine charms, which placed her as much above the other women of Christendom as the Holy Father was above all other Christians. But all her lovers knew that with the assistance of eleven doctors of Padua, seven master surgeons of Pavia, and five surgeons come from all parts, who assisted at her confinement, she was preserved from all injury. Some go so far as to say that she gained therein superfineness and whiteness of skin. A famous man, of the school of Salerno, wrote a book on the subject, to show the value of a confinement for the freshness, health, preservation, and beauty of women. In this very learned book it was clearly proved to readers that that which was beautiful to see in Imperia, was that which it was permissible for lovers alone to behold; a rare case then, for she did not disarrange her attire for the petty German princes whom she called her margraves, burgraves, electors, and dukes, just as a captain ranks his soldiers.

Every one knows that when she was eighteen years of age, the lovely Theodora, to atone for her mother's gay life, wished to retire into the bosom of the Church. With this idea she placed herself in the hands of a cardinal, in order that he might instruct her in the duties of the devout. This wicked shepherd found the lamb so magnificently beautiful that he attempted to debauch her. Theodora instantly stabbed herself with a stiletto, in order not to be contaminated by the evil-minded priest. This adventure, which was consigned to the history of the period, made a great commotion in Rome, and was deplored by every one, so much was the daughter of Imperia beloved.

Then this noble courtesan, much afflicted, returned to Rome, there to weep for her poor daughter. She set out in the thirty-ninth year of her age, which was, according to some authors, the summer of her magnificent beauty, because then she had attained the acme of her perfection, like ripe fruit. Sorrow made her haughty and hard with those who spoke to her of love, in order to dry her tears. The pope himself visited her in her palace, and gave her certain words of admonition. But she refused to be comforted, saying that she would henceforward devote herself to God, because she had never yet been satisfied by any man, although she had ardently desired it ; and all of them, even a little priest, whom she had adored like a saint's shrine, had deceived her. God, she was sure, would not do so. This resolution disconcerted many, for she was the joy of a vast number of lords. So that people ran about the streets of Rome crying out, "Where is Madame Imperia? Is she going to deprive the world of love?" Some of the ambassadors wrote to their masters on the subject. The Emperor of the Romans was much cut up about it, because he loved her

to distraction for eleven weeks ; had left her only to go to the wars, and loved her still as much as his most precious member, which, according to his own statement, was his eye, for that alone embraced the whole of his dear Imperia. In this extremity the Pope sent for a Spanish physician, and

The principal men of the town of Rome came and
crowded the rooms.

conducted him to the beautiful creature, to whom he proved, by various arguments, adorned with Latin and Greek quotations, that beauty is impaired by tears and tribulation, and that through sorrow's door wrinkles step in.   This proposition, confirmed by the doctors of the Holy College in controversy, had the effect of opening the doors of the palace that same evening.   The young cardinals, the foreign envoys, the wealthy inhabitants, and the principal men of the town of Rome came, crowded the rooms, and held a joyous festival ; the common people made grand illnminations, and thus the whole population celebrated the return of the Queen of Pleasure to her occupation, for she was at that time the presiding deity of Love.   The experts in all the arts loved her much, because she spent considerable sums of money in improving the church in Rome which contained poor Theodora's tomb, the which was destroyed during that pillage of Rome in which perished the traitorous constable of Bourbon, for this holy maiden was placed therein in a massive coffin of gold and silver, which the cursed soldiers were anxious to obtain.   This basilic cost, it is said, more than the pyramid erected by the Lady Rhodepa, an Egyptian courtesan, eighteen hundred years before the coming of our divine Saviour, which proves the antiquity of this pleasant occupation, the extravagant prices which the wise Egyptians paid for their pleasures, and how things deteriorate, seeing that now for a trifle you can have a chemise full of female loveliness in the Rue du Petit-Heulen, at Paris.   Is it not an abomination ?

Never had Madame Imperia appeared so lovely as at this first gala after her mourning.   All the princes, cardinals, and others declared that she was worthy the homage of the whole world, which was there represented by a noble from every known land, and thus was it amply demonstrated that beauty was in every place queen of everything.   The envoy of the King of France, who was a cadet of the house of l'Ile Adam, arrived late, although he had never yet seen Imperia, and was most anxious to do so.   He was a handsome young knight, much in favour with his sovereign, in whose court he had a mistress, whom he loved with infinite tenderness, and who was the daughter of Monsieur de Montmorency,

Directly this gentleman joined her circle and her eyes had
rested upon him, Madame Imperia felt herself bitten by a
strong desire.

a lord whose domains bordered upon those of the house of
l'Ile Adam. To this penniless cadet the king had given
certain missions to the duchy of Milan, of which he had
acquitted himself so well that he was sent to Rome to
advance the negotiations concerning which historians have
written so much in their books. Now if he had nothing of
his own, poor little l'Ile Adam relied upon so good a beginning. He was slightly built, but upright as a column,
dark, with black, glistening eyes, and a man not easily taken
in; but concealing his finesse, he had the air of an innocent
child, which made him gentle and amiable as a laughing
maiden. Directly this gentleman joined her circle, and her
eyes had rested upon him, Madame Imperia felt herself
bitten by a strong desire, which stretched the harp strings
of her nature, and produced therefrom a sound she had not
heard for many a day. She was seized with such a vertigo
of true love at the sight of this freshness of youth, that but
for her imperial dignity she would have kissed the good
cheeks which shone like little apples. Now take note of
this; that so called modest women, and ladies whose skirts
bear their armorial bearings, are thoroughly ignorant of the
nature of a man, because they keep to one alone, like that
queen of France who believed all men had ulcers in the
nose because the king had; but a great courtesan, like
Madame Imperia, knew man to his core, because she had
handled a great many. In her retreat every one came out
in his true colours, and concealed nothing, thinking to himself that he would not be long with her. Having often deplored this subjection, sometimes she would remark that
she suffered from pleasure more than she suffered from pain.
There was the dark shadow of her life. You may be sure
that a lover was often compelled to part with a nice little
heap of crowns in order to pass the night with her, and
was reduced to desperation by a refusal. Now for her it
was a joyful thing to feel a youthful desire, like that she had
for the little priest, whose story commences this collection;
but because she was older than in those merry days, love
was more firmly established in her, and she soon perceived
that it was of a fiery nature when it began to make itself felt;

indeed, she suffered in her skin like a cat that is being scorched, and so much so that she had an intense longing to spring on to this gentleman, and bear him in triumph to her nest, as a kite does its prey, but with great difficulty she restrained herself. When he came and bowed to her, she threw back her head, and assumed a most dignified attitude, as do those who have a love infatuation in their hearts. The gravity of her demeanour to the young ambassador caused many to think that she had work in store for him ; equivocating on the word, after the custom of the time. L'Ile Adam, knowing himself to be dearly loved by his mistress, troubled himself but little about Madame Imperia, grave or gay, and frisked about like a goat let loose. The courtesan, terribly annoyed at this, changed her tone, from being sulky became gay and lively, came to him, softened her voice, sharpened her glance, gracefully inclined her head, rubbed against him with her sleeve, and called him Monseigneur, embraced him with loving words, trifled with his hand, and finished by smiling at him most affably. He, not imagining that so unprofitable a lover would suit her, for he was as poor as a church mouse, and did not know that his beauty was equal in her eyes to all the treasures of the world, was not taken in her trap, but continued to ride the high horse with his hands on his hips. This disdain of her passion irritated Madame to the heart, which by this spark was set in flame. If you doubt this, it is because you know nothing of the profession of Madame Imperia, who by reason of it might be compared to a chimney, in which a great number of fires had been lighted, which had filled it with soot ;′ in this state a match was sufficient to burn everything there, where a hundred faggots had smoked comfortably. She burned within herself from top to toe in a horrible manner, and could not be extinguished save with the water of love. The cadet of l'Ile Adam left the room without noticing this ardour. Madame, disconsolate at his departure, lost her senses from her head to her feet, and so thoroughly that she sent a messenger to him in the galleries, begging him to pass the night with her. On no other occasion of her life had she had this cowardice, either for king, pope, or

When he came and bowed to her, she threw back her head
and assumed a most dignified attitude, as do those who have a
love infatuation in their hearts.

emperor, since the high price of her favours came from the
bondage in which she held her admirers, whom the more
she humbled the more she raised herself. The disdainful
hero of this history was informed by the head chamber-
woman, who was a clever jade, that in all probability a great
treat awaited him, for most certainly Madame would regale
him with her most delicate inventions of love. L'Ile Adam
returned to the salons, delighted at this lucky chance.
Directly the envoy of France reappeared, as every one had
seen Imperia turn pale at his departure, the general joy
knew no bounds, because every one was delighted to see
her return to her old life of love. An English cardinal, who
had drained more than one big-bellied flagon, and wished to
taste Imperia, went to l'Ile Adam and whispered to him,
" Hold her fast, so that she shall never again escape us."
The story of this night was told to the pope at his levée,
and caused him to remark, *Lætamini, gentes, quoniam
surrexit Dominus*. A quotation which the old cardinals
abominated as a profanation of sacred texts. Seeing which,
the pope reprimanded them severely, and took occasion to
lecture them, telling them that if they were good Christians
they were bad politicians. Indeed, he relied upon the fair
Imperia to reclaim the emperor, and with this idea syringed
her well with flattery.

The lights of the palace being extinguished, the golden
flagons on the floor, and the servants drunk and stretched
about on the carpets, Madame entered her bed-chamber,
leading by the hand her dear lover-elect ; and she was well
pleased, and has since confessed that so strongly was she
bitten with love, she could hardly restrain herself from rolling
at his feet like a beast of the field, begging him to crush her
beneath him if he could. L'Ile Adam slipped off his
garments, and tumbled into bed as if he were in his own
house. Seeing which, Madame hastened her preparations,
and sprang into her lover's arms with a frenzy that
astonished her women, who knew her to be ordinarily one
of the most modest of women on these occasions. This
astonishment became general throughout the country, for
the pair remained in bed for nine days, eating, drinking, and

embracing in a marvellous and most masterly manner.
Madame told her women that at last she had put her hand
upon a phœnix of love, since he revived from every attack.
Nothing was talked of in Rome and Italy but the victory
that had been gained over Imperia, who had boasted that
she would yield to no man, and spat upon all of them, even
the dukes. As to the aforesaid margraves and burgraves,
she gave them the tail of her dress to hold, and said that if
she did not tread them under foot, they would trample upon
her. Madame confessed to her servants that, differently to
all the other men she had had to put up with, the more she
fondled this child of love, the more she desired to do so,
and that she would never be able to part with him; nor his
splendid eyes, which blinded her; nor his branch of coral,
that she always hungered after. She further declared that if
such were his desire, she would let him suck her blood, and
eat her breasts—which were the most lovely in the world—and
cut her tresses, of which she had only given a single one to
the Emperor of the Romans, who kept it in his breast, like
a precious relic; finally, she confessed that on that night
only had life begun for her, because the embrace of Villiers
de l'Ile Adam sent the blood to her in three bounds and
in a brace of shakes. These expressions becoming known,
made every one very miserable. Directly she went out,
Imperia told the ladies of Rome that she should die if she
were deserted by this gentleman, and would cause herself,
like Queen Cleopatra, to be bitten by an asp. She declared
openly that she had bidden an eternal adieu to her former
gay life, and would show the whole world what virtue was
by abandoning her empire for this Villiers de l'Ile Adam,
whose servant she would rather be than reign over
Christendom. The English cardinal remonstrated with the
pope that this love for one, in the heart of a woman who was
the joy of all, was an infamous depravity, and that he
ought with a brief *in partibus*, to annul this marriage, which
robbed the fashionable world of its principal attraction.
But the love of this poor woman, who had confessed the
miseries of her life, was so sweet a thing, and so moved the
most dissipated heart, that she silenced all clamour, and

every one forgave her her happiness. One day during
Lent, Imperia made her people fast, and ordered them to go
and confess, and return to God. She herself went and fell
at the pope's feet, and there showed such penitence, that she
obtained from him remission of all her sins, believing that
the absolution of the pope would communicate to her soul
that virginity which she was grieved at being unable to offer
to her lover. It is impossible to help thinking that there
was some virtue in the ecclesiastical piscina, for the poor
cadet was so smothered with love that he fancied himself
in Paradise, and left the negotiations of the King of France,
left his love for Mademoiselle de Montmorency — in
fact, left everything to marry Madame Imperia, in order
that he might live and die with her. Such was the effect
of the learned ways of this great lady of pleasure directly
she turned her science to the profit of a virtuous love.
Imperia bade adieu to her admirers at a royal feast, given in
honour of her wedding, which was a wonderful ceremony,
at which all the Italian princes were present. She had, it is
said, a million gold crowns ; in spite of the vastness of this
sum, every one, far from blaming l'Ile Adam, paid him
many compliments, because it was evident that neither
Madame Imperia nor her young husband thought of anything but one. The pope blessed their marriage, and said
that it was a fine thing to see the foolish virgin returning to
God by the road of marriage.

But during that last night in which it would be permissible for all to behold the Queen of Beauty, who was about
to become a simple chatelaine of the kingdom of France,
there were a great number of men who mourned for the
merry nights, the suppers, the masked balls, the joyous
games, and the melting hours, when each one emptied his
heart to her. Every one regretted the ease and freedom
which had always been found in the residence of this lovely
creature, who now appeared more tempting than she had
ever done in her life, for the fervid heat of her great love
made her glisten like a summer sun. Much did they
lament the fact that she had had the sad phantasy to become
a respectable woman. To these Madame de l'Ile Adam

answered jestingly, that after twenty-four years passed in the service of the public, she had a right to retire. Others said to her, that however distant the sun was, people could warm themselves in it, while she would show herself no more. To these she replied that she would still have smiles to bestow upon those lords who would come and see how she played the rôle of a virtuous woman. To this the English envoy answered, he believed her capable of pushing virtue to its extreme point. She gave a present to each of her friends, and large sums to the poor and suffering of Rome; besides this, she left to the convent where her daughter was to have been, and to the church she had built, the wealth she had inherited from Theodora, which came from the Cardinal of Ragusa.

When the two spouses set out they were accompanied a long way by knights in mourning, and even by the common people, who wished them every happiness, because Madame Imperia had been hard on the rich only, and had always been kind and gentle with the poor. This lovely queen of love was hailed with acclamations throughout the journey in all the towns of Italy where the report of her conversion had spread, and where every one was curious to see pass, a case so rare as two such spouses. Several princes received this handsome couple at their courts, saying that it was but right to show honour to this woman who had the courage to renounce her empire over the world of fashion, to become a virtuous woman. But there was an evil-minded fellow, one my lord Duke of Ferrara, who said to l'Ile Adam that his great fortune had not cost him much. At this first offence Madame Imperia showed what a good heart she had, for she gave up all the money she had received from her lovers to ornament the dome of St. Maria del Fiore, in the town of Florence, which turned the laugh against the Sire d'Este, who boasted that he had built a church in spite of the empty condition of his purse. You may be sure he was reprimanded for this joke by his brother the cardinal. The fair Imperia only kept her own wealth and that which the Emperor had bestowed upon her out of pure friendship since his departure, the amount of which was, however, considerable. The cadet of l'Ile Adam had a duel with the duke, in which he wounded him. Thus neither Madame de l'Ile Adam nor her husband could be in any way re-

proached. This piece of chivalry caused her to be gloriously received in all places she passed through, especially in Piedmont, where the fêtes were splendid. Verses, which the poet then composed, such as sonnets, epithalamias, and odes, have been given in certain collections; but all poetry was weak in comparison with her, who was, according to an expression of Monsieur Boccacio, poetry itself.

The prize in this tourney of fêtes and gallantry must be

awarded to the good Emperor of the Romans, who, knowing of the misbehaviour of the Duke of Ferrara, despatched an envoy to his old flame, charged with Latin manuscripts, in which he told her that he loved her so much for herself, that he was delighted to know she was happy, but grieved that all her happiness was not derived from him; that he had lost the right to make her presents, but that, if the king of France received her coldly, he would think it an honour to acquire a Villiers to the holy empire, and would give him such principalities as he might choose from his domains. The fair Imperia replied that she was extremely obliged to the Emperor, but that had she to suffer contumely upon contumely in France, she still intended there to finish her days.

II.

HOW THIS MARRIAGE ENDED.

Not knowing if she would be received or not, the lady
of l'Ile Adam would not go to Court, but lived in the
country, where her husband made a fine establishment,
purchasing the manor of Beaumont-le-Vicomte, which gave
rise to the equivoke upon this name, made by our well-
beloved Rabelais, in his most magnificent book.   He
acquired also the domain of Nointel, the forest of Carenelle,
St. Martin, and other places in the neighbourhood of l'Ile
Adam, where his brother Villiers resided.   These said
acquisitions made him the most powerful lord in the Ile de
France and county of Paris.   He built a wonderful castle
near Beaumont, which was afterwards ruined by the English,
and adorned it with the furniture, foreign tapestries, chests,
pictures, statues, and curiosities of his wife, who was a great
connoisseur, which made this place equal to the most
magnificent castles known.   The happy pair led a life so
envied by all, that nothing was talked about in Paris and
at Court but this marriage, the good fortune of the Sire
de Beaumont. and, above all, of the perfect, loyal, gracious,

The lady of l'Ile Adam would not go to Court, but
lived in the country.

The wonderful castle of the cadet of l'Ile Adam.

and religious life of his wife, who from habit many still called *Madame Imperia;* who was no longer proud and sharp as steel, but had the virtues and qualities of a respectable woman, and was an example in many things to a queen. She was much beloved by the Church on account of her great religion, for she had never once forgotten God, having, as she once said, spent much of her time with churchmen, abbots, bishops, and cardinals, who had sprinkled her well with holy water, and under the curtains worked her eternal salvation. The praises sung in honour of this lady had such an effect, that the king came to Beauvoisis to gaze upon this wonder, and did the sire the honour to sleep at Beaumont, remained there three days, and had a royal hunt there with the queen and the whole Court. You may be sure that he was surprised, as were also the queen, the ladies, and the Court, at the manners of this superb creature, who was proclaimed lady of courtesy and beauty. The king first, then the queen, and afterwards every individual member of the company, complimented l'Ile Adam on having chosen such a wife. The modesty of the chatelaine did more than pride would have accomplished ; for she was invited to Court, and everywhere, so imperious was her great heart, so tyrannic her violent love for her husband. You may be sure that her charms, hidden under the garments of virtue, were none the less exquisite. The king gave the vacant post of lieutenant of the Ile de France and provost of Paris to his ancient ambassador, giving him the title of Viscount of Beaumont, which established him as governor of the whole province, and put him on an excellent footing at Court. But this was the cause of a great wound in Madame's heart, because a wretch, jealous of this unclouded happiness, asked her, playfully, if Beaumont had ever spoken to her of his first love, Mademoiselle de Montmorency, who at that time was twenty-two years of age, as she was sixteen at the time the marriage took place in Rome—the which young lady loved l'Ile Adam so much that she remained a maiden, would listen to no proposals of marriage, and was dying of a broken heart, unable to banish her perfidious lover from her remembrance, and was desirous

The happy pair led a life so envied by all, that nothing was
talked about in Paris and at Court but this marriage.

of entering the convent of Chelles. Madame Imperia, during the six years of her marriage, had never heard this name, and was sure from this fact that she was indeed beloved. You can imagine that this time had been passed as a single day, that both believed they had only been married the evening before, and that each night was as a wedding night, and that if business took the knight out of doors, he was quite melancholy, being unwilling ever to have her out of his sight, and she was the same with him. The king, who was very partial to the viscount, also made a remark to him which stung him to the quick, when he said, "You have no children?" To which Beaumont replied, with the face of a man whose raw place you have touched with your finger, "Monseigneur, my brother has; thus our line is safe."

Now it happened that his brother's two children died suddenly—one from a fall from his horse at a tournament and the other from illness. Monsieur l'Ile Adam the elder was so stricken with grief at these two deaths that he expired soon after, so much did he love his two sons. By this means the manor of Beaumont, the property at Carenelle, St. Martin, Nointel, and the surrounding domains, were re-united to the manor of l'Ile Adam, and the neighbouring forests, and the cadet became the head of the house. At this time Madame was forty-five, and was still fit to bear children; but, alas! she conceived not. As soon as she saw the lineage of l'Ile Adam destroyed, she was anxious to obtain offspring. Now, as during the seven years which had elapsed she had never once had the slightest symptom of pregnancy, she believed, according to the statement of a clever physician whom she sent for from Paris, that this barrenness proceeded from the fact, that both she and her husband, always more lovers than spouses, allowed pleasure to interfere with business, and by this means engendering was prevented. Then she endeavoured to restrain her impetuosity, and to take things coolly, because the physician had explained to her that in a state of nature animals never failed to breed, because the females employed none of those artifices, tricks, and hanky-pankies with which women accommodate the olives of Poissy, and for this reason they thoroughly de-

You can imagine that this time had been passed
as a single day.

served the title of *beasts*. She promised him no longer to
play with such a serious affair, and to forget all the ingenious
devices in which she had been so fertile. But, alas!
although she kept as quiet as that German woman who lay
so still that her husband embraced her to death, and then
went, poor baron, to obtain absolution from the pope, who
delivered his celebrated brief, in which he requested the
ladies of Franconia to be a little more lively, and prevent a
repetition of such a crime. Madame de l'Ile Adam did not
conceive, and fell into a state of great melancholy. Then she
began to notice how thoughtful had become her husband,
l'Ile Adam, whom she watched when he thought she was
not looking, and who wept that he had no fruit of his great
love. Soon this pair mingled their tears, for everything was
common to the two in this fine household, and as they
never left each other, the thought of the one was necessarily
the thought of the other. When Madame beheld a poor
person's child she nearly died of grief, and it took her
a whole day to recover. Seeing this great sorrow, l'Ile Adam
ordered all children to be kept out of his wife's sight, and
said soothing things to her, such as that children often
turned out badly ; to which she replied, that a child made
by those who loved so passionately would be the finest child
in the world. He told her that their sons might perish, like
those of his poor brother ; to which she replied, that she
would not let them stir further from her petticoats than a
hen allows her chickens. In fact, she had an answer for
everything. Madame caused a woman to be sent for who
dealt in magic, and who was supposed to be learned in these
mysteries, who told her that she had often seen women
unable to conceive in spite of every effort, but yet they had
succeeded by studying the manners and customs of animals.
Madame took the beasts of the field for her preceptors, but
she did not increase her size ; her flesh still remained firm
and white as marble. She returned to the physical science
of the master doctors of Paris, and sent for a celebrated
Arabian physician, who had just arrived in France with a
new science.   Then this *savant*, brought up in the school of
one Sieur Averroes, entered into certain medical details, and

declared that the loose life she had formerly led had for
ever ruined her chance of obtaining offspring. The physical
reasons which he assigned were so contrary to the teaching
of the holy books which establish the majesty of man, made
in the image of his Creator, and were so contrary to the
system upheld by sound sense and good doctrine, that the
doctors of Paris laughed them to scorn. The Arabian
physician left the school where his master, the Sieur Averroes,
was unknown. The doctors told Madame, who had come
to Paris, that she was to keep on as usual, since she had had
during her gay life the lovely Theodora, by the cardinal of
Ragusa, and that the right of having children remained with
women as long as their blood circulated, and that all she
had to do was to multiply the chances of conception.
This advice appeared to her so good that she multiplied her
victories, but it was only multiplying her defeats, since she
obtained the flowers of love without its fruits. The poor
afflicted woman wrote then to the pope, who loved her
much, and told him of her sorrows. The good pope replied
to her with a gracious homily, written with his own hand, in
which he told her that when human science and things terrestrial failed, we should turn to Heaven, and implore the
grace of God. Then she determined to go with naked feet,
accompanied by her husband, to Notre Dame de Liesse,
celebrated for her intervention in similar cases, and made a
vow to build a magnificent cathedral in gratitude for the
child. But she bruised and injured her pretty feet, and
conceived nothing but a violent grief, which was so great
that some of her lovely tresses fell off and some turned
white. At last the faculty of making children was taken
from her, which brought on the vapours consequent upon
hypochondria, and caused her skin to turn yellow. She was
then forty-nine years of age, and lived in her castle of l'Ile
Adam, where she grew as thin as a leper in a lazar-house.
The poor creature was all the more wretched because l'Ile
Adam was still amorous, and as good as gold to her, who
failed in her duty because she had formerly been too free
with the men, and was now, according to her own disdainful
remark, only a cauldron to cook chitterlings. "Ha!" said

When Madame beheld a poor person's child she nearly died
of grief, and it took her a whole day to recover.

she, one evening when these thoughts were tormenting her. " In spite of the Church, in spite of the king, in spite of everything, Madame de l'Ile Adam is still the wicked Imperia !" She fell into a violent passion when she saw this handsome gentleman have everything man can desire, great wealth, royal favour, unequalled love, matchless wife, pleasure such as none other could procure, and yet fail in that which is dearest to the head of a house—namely, lineage. With this idea in her head, she wished to die, thinking how good and noble he had been to her, and how much she failed in her duty in not giving him children, and in being henceforward unable to do so. She hid her sorrow in the secret recesses of her heart, and conceived a devotion worthy her great love. To put into practice this heroic design she became still more amorous, took extreme care of her charms, and made use of learned precepts to maintain her bodily perfections, which threw out an incredible lustre.

About this time the Sieur de Montmorency conquered the repulsion his daughter entertained for marriage, and her alliance with one Sieur de Chatillon was much talked about. Madame Imperia, who lived only three leagues distant from Montmorency, one day sent her husband out hunting in the forest, and set out towards the castle where the young lady lived. Arrived in the grounds she walked about there, telling a servant to inform his mistress that a lady had a most important communication to make to her, and that she had come to request an audience. Much interested by the account which she received of the beauty, courtesy, and manners of the unknown lady, Mademoiselle de Montmorency went in great haste into the gardens, and there met her rival, whom she did not know.

" My dear," said the poor woman, weeping to find the young maiden as beautiful as herself, " I know that they are trying to force you into a marriage with Monsieur de Chatillon, although you still love Monsieur de l'Ile Adam. Have confidence in the prophecy that I here make you, that he whom you have loved, and who only was false to you through a snare into which an angel might have fallen, will be free from the burden of his old wife before the leaves fall.

Thus the constancy of your love will have its crown **of**
flowers.   Now have the courage to refuse this marriage they
are arranging for you, and you may yet clasp your first and
only love.   Pledge me your word to love and cherish l'Ile

Adam, who is the kindest of men; never to cause him a
moment's anguish, and tell him to reveal to you all the
secrets of love invented by Madame Imperia, because, in
practising them, being young, you will be easily able to
obliterate the remembrance of her from his mind."

Mademoiselle de Montmorency was so astonished that she
could make no answer, and let this queen of beauty depart,
and believed her to be a fairy, until a workman told her that
the fairy was Madame de l'Ile Adam.   Although the adventure was inexplicable, she told her father that she would not
give her consent to the proposed marriage until after the
autumn, so much is it in the nature of Love to ally itself with

Hope, in spite of the bitter pills which this deceitful and gracious companion gives her to swallow like bulls' eyes. During the months when the grapes are gathered, Imperia would not let l'Ile Adam leave her, and was so amorous that one would have imagined she wished to kill him, since l'Ile Adam felt as though he had a fresh bride in his arms every night.   The next morning the good woman requested him to keep the remembrance of these joys in his heart. Then, to know what her lover's real thoughts on the subject were, she said to him, " Poor l'Ile Adam, we were very silly to marry—a lad like you, with your twenty-three years, and an old woman close on forty."   He answered her, that his happiness was such that he was the envy of every one, that at

her age her equal did not exist among the younger women, and that if ever she grew old he would love her wrinkles, believing that even in the tomb she would be lovely, and her skeleton lovable.

To these answers, which brought the tears into her eyes, she one morning answered maliciously, that Mademoiselle Montmorency was very lovely and very faithful. This speech forced l'Ile Adam to tell her that she pained him by telling him of the only wrong he had ever committed in his life— the breaking of the troth pledged to his first sweetheart, all love for whom he had since effaced from his heart. This candid speech made her seize him and clasp him to her heart, affected at the loyalty of his discourse on a subject from which many would have shrunk.

"My dear love," said she, "for a long time past I have been suffering from a retraction of the heart, which has always since my youth been dangerous to my life, and in this opinion the Arabian physician coincides. If I die, I wish you to make the most binding oath a knight can make, to wed Mademoiselle Montmorency. I am so certain of dying, that I leave my property to you only on condition that this marriage takes place."

Hearing this, l'Ile Adam turned pale, and felt faint at the mere thought of an eternal separation from his good wife.

"Yes, dear treasure of love," continued she. "I am punished by God there where my sins were committed, for the great joys that I feel dilate my heart, and have, according to the Arabian doctor, weakened the vessels which in a moment of excitement will burst; but I have always implored God to take my life at the age in which I now am, because I would not see my charms marred by the ravages of time."

This great and noble woman saw then how well she was beloved. This is how she obtained the greatest sacrifice of love that ever was made upon this earth. She alone knew what a charm existed in the embraces, fondlings, and raptures of the conjugal bed, which were such that poor l'Ile Adam would rather have died than allow himself to be deprived of the amorous delicacies she knew so well how to prepare. At this confession made by her that, in the excitement of love, her heart would burst, the chevalier cast himself at her knees, and declared that to preserve *her* life he would never ask her for love, but would live contented to see her only at his side, happy at being able to touch but the hem of her garment.

She replied, bursting into tears, " that she would rather die than lose one iota of his love ; that she would die as she had lived, since luckily she could make a man embrace her when such was her desire without having to put her request into words."

Here it must be stated that the cardinal of Ragusa had given her as a present an article, which this holy joker called *in articulo mortis*. It was a tiny glass bottle, no bigger than a bean, made at Venice, and containing a poison so subtle that by breaking it between the teeth death came instantly and painlessly. He had received it from the Signora Tophana, the celebrated maker of poisons of the town of Rome.

Now this tiny bottle was under the bezel of a ring, preserved from all objects that could break it by certain plates of gold. Poor Imperia put it into her mouth several times without being able to make up her mind to bite it, so much pleasure did she take in the moment she believed to be her last. Then she would pass before her in mental review all her methods of enjoyment before breaking the glass, and determined that when she felt the most perfect of all joys she would bite the bottle.

The poor creature departed this life on the night of the first day of October. Then was there heard a great clamour in the forests and in the clouds, as if the loves had cried aloud, " The great Noc is dead !" in imitation of the pagan gods who, at the coming of the Saviour of men, fled into the skies, saying, " The great Pan is slain !" A cry which was heard by some persons navigating the Eubean Sea, and preserved by a father of the Church.

Madame Imperia died without being spoiled in shape, so much had God made her the irreproachable model of a woman. She had, it was said, a magnificent tint upon her flesh, caused by the proximity of the flaming wings of Pleasure, who cried and groaned over her corpse. Her husband mourned for her most bitterly, never suspecting that she had died to deliver him from a childless wife, for the doctor who embalmed her said not a word concerning the cause of her death. This great sacrifice was discovered six years after the marriage of l'Ile Adam with Mademoiselle de Montmorency, because she told him all about the visit of Madame Imperia. The poor gentleman immediately fell into a state of great melancholy, and finished by dying, being unable to banish the remembrance of those joys of love which it was beyond the power of a novice to restore to him; thereby did he prove the truth of that which was said at the time, that this woman would never die in a heart where she had once reigned.

This teaches us that virtue is well understood but by those who have practised vice; for among the most modest women few would thus have sacrificed life, in whatever high state of religion you look for them.

AH! mad little one, thou whose business it is to make the house merry, again hast thou been wallowing, in spite of a thousand prohibitions, in that slough of melancholy, whence thou hast already fished out Bertha, and come back with thy tresses dishevelled, like a girl who has been ill-treated by a regiment of soldiers! Where are thy golden aiglets and bells, thy filagree flowers of fantastic design? Where hast thou left thy crimson head-dress, ornamented with precious gewgaws that cost a minot of pearls? Why spoil with pernicious tears thy black eyes, so pleasant when therein sparkles the wit of a tale, that popes pardon thee thy sayings for the sake of thy merry laughter, feel their souls caught between the ivory of thy teeth, have their hearts drawn by the rose point of thy sweet tongue, and would barter the holy slipper for a hundred of the smiles that hover round thy vermilion lips? Laughing lassie, if thou wouldst remain always fresh and young, weep no more; think of riding the bridleless fleas, of bridling with the golden clouds thy chameleon chimeras, of metamorphosing the realities of life into figures clothed with the rainbow, caparisoned with roseate dreams, and mantled with wings blue as the eyes of the partridge. By the Body and the Blood, by the Censer and the Seal, by the Book and the Sword, by the Rag and the Gold, by the Sound and

the Colour, if thou dost but return once into that hovel of
elegies where eunuchs find ugly women for imbecile
sultans, I'll curse thee; I'll rave at thee; I'll make thee
fast from roguery and love; I'll——

Phist! Here she is astride a sunbeam, with a volume
that is ready to burst with merry meteors! She plays in
their prisms, tearing about so madly, so wildly, so boldly,
so contrary to good sense, so contrary to good manners, so
contrary to everything, that one has to touch her with
long feathers, to follow her siren's tail in the golden facets
which trifle among the artifices of these new peals of
laughter. Ye gods! but she is sporting herself in them
like a hundred schoolboys in a hedge full of blackberries,
after vespers. To the devil the magister! The volume is
finished! Out upon work! What ho! my jovial friends;
this way!

The Author of " The Human Comedy."